SAM WOOD

Floods of Ungodly Men

BY

HENRY E. PEAVLER

"I do not feel obliged to believe that the same God who has endowed us with sense, reason, and intellect has intended us to forgo their use." **Galileo Galilei**

This is a work of fiction. These events happened over 175 years ago. I wasn't there. Many of the characters existed in 'real life' but I didn't know them, so I created conversations, personalities and actions to fit my needs, not theirs. If you want a textbook description of the events in Bleeding Kansas and the actual people caricatured in this book, look elsewhere. I condensed dates and arranged events in an order that helped the narrative. This is a work of fiction.

Paperback ISBN: 978-1-7344593-1-9
eBook ISBN: 978-1-7344593-2-6

Library of Congress Control Number: TBD

WWW.LivingSpringsPublishers.com

Cover design by John McNees/ NOW Illustration & Design
nowillustration@gmail.com

All quotes and verses are in the public domain.

Dedicated to the best friends ever, my brothers and sisters: Bill, Dan, Debbie, Veryle and Allen.

Author's Note

Historical fiction has often been criticized, and rightly so, for failing to accurately portray the culture of the time depicted. I admit that this narrative falls woefully short of accurately describing life in the 1850s, but that was not my intention. Historical Fantasy would better describe 'Sam Wood'. He was a real person bravely fighting the forces of evil in the battle to end slavery and a textbook style description of his life could be written based on the mundane historical records to be found in the Ohio and Kansas state archives. I've taken liberty with Sam's life and imbued him with certain powers that seem mythical. The few anecdotes I know about him leads me to believe that he had some kind of divine protection, or the luck of the Irish, because he lived life on the edge of danger. He challenged the Border Ruffians and the slave hunters face to face, and came out victorious every time, and without giving away the ending, he did so until the day of his death.

I've chosen to make Sam larger than life; where there is myth and there is reality, I selected the myth. In no way is this meant to demean the subject matter, slavery, the aftermath of which continues to haunt America to this day. There were many brave abolitionists, both black and white, who chose to go to Kansas and fight the slaveholders on their own ground, outnumbered and outgunned, yet, I have to believe that slavery would have ended eventually anyway, ground down by the weight of its own depravity. The black abolitionists mentioned herein have each been the subject of books, movies and plays. Frederick Douglass, Harriet Tubman, Sojourner Truth and lesser known activists were the instigators of the entire abolitionist crusade, letting the whites know the true story of molestation, cruelty, wickedness and complicity by the churches and the slaveholders.

Sam's fictional friend, Sally Thompson, writes a book about lesser known black insurgents such as Gabriel Prosser, Denmark Vessy, Anthony Burns and Harriet Jacobs. The people she writes about are real and there are hundreds, if not thousands, of examples of enslaved people who risked, and, in most cases, gave their lives in pursuit of freedom. These incredibly brave people were the catalysts for the abolitionist movement and the ultimate realization that slavery was the 'greatest sin ever invented'.

Outspoken men and women of that time are still influential and well known even today, over 180 years after the passage of the Fugitive Slave Act. Politicians like Salmon Chase, who is the namesake of Chase National Bank and Chase County, Kansas, named in his honor by his good friend, Sam Wood. The abolitionists like John Brown, who generated tremendous controversy in the 1850's, and his contribution to the end of slavery is debated still. He is best known for an ill-fated, ill-timed raid on the U.S. Armory in Harper's Ferry, Maryland, but he also fought alongside Sam in Kansas. Female activists of the day, such as Susan B. Anthony and Elizabet Cady Stanton, were driven to action on behalf of the enslaved and insisted on equality for all. The right to vote for all men and women regardless of color or property ownership was their battle cry. Fascinating and brave people, all of them, both black and white, who fought the good fight against the foulest of institutions, slavery.

I have wrestled with the terminology used in this narrative, knowing that the words commonly used to describe the enslaved in the 1850's, were degrading then and even more so today. I chose to use these demeaning words because that is what the enslaved were called at that time and to better convey the horrid conditions of those days. In addition, I have tried to standardize the capitalization of terms such as black, white, Negroes etc.

Where the word is used as a reference to race it is capitalized. Where it is an adjective describing color, I have used the lower case. We, my editor and I, have attempted to be consistent in that regard. It is a sensitive issue and I hope that we have been evenhanded in dealing with a most unfortunate subject.

Sam Wood was a natural born leader, influential in changing the course of our nation, yet he failed in the court of public opinion since he would not compromise. History is better for it, because without him and others like him, the aggressors would conquer those who constantly turn the other cheek. Men who preached that slavery was ordained in Christ's name—the ultimate blasphemy in Sam's mind—were the evilest of men and he could not fathom how they corrupted the word of God to fit their unholy needs. As long as he lived, Sam vowed to fight against those evil powers, with words if possible and with force if need be.

The Mosher and Wood families were Quakers. They fled England, chased by the ignorance of fellow Christians, who viewed them as heretics. They sought relief from persecution on the distant shores of America only to find the same ignorance in a different coat. They fought back using the weapons of their faith, perseverance and determination, because their religion forbade striking out or taking weapons. But there were some, who, when the ugly aberration of slavery was too much to bear, refused to turn the other cheek because appeasement was fruitless and negotiations futile.

Sam Wood refused to compromise on any point when it came to equality—free the enslaved, give women the right to vote or go to war. He interpreted these words from the Declaration of Independence literally: 'We hold these truths to be self-evident, that all men are created equal….', and he was ready and willing to die for the cause.

Henry E. Peavler July 1, 2020

Acknowledgements

I want to thank Living Springs Publishers and especially the Managing Partner, J.V. Peavler, without whom this book would never have become reality. In addition, those early readers of the Sam Wood story who helped with context, grammar, and sequence: R. T. Kilgore; JJ Wooldridge; Candace Kearns Read; and Gayle Bowring. Your kind words and astute guidance made my job much easier.

Contents

"I therefore hate the corrupt, slaveholding, women-whipping, cradle-plundering, partial and hypocritical Christianity of the land... I look upon it as the climax of all misnomers, the boldest of all frauds, and the grossest of all libels. Never was there a clearer case of 'stealing the livery of the court of heaven to serve the devil in.' I am filled with unutterable loathing when I contemplate the religious pomp and show, together with the horrible inconsistencies, which everywhere surround me. We have men-stealers for ministers, women-whippers for missionaries, and cradle-plunderers for church members. The man who wields the blood-clotted cowskin during the week fills the pulpit on Sunday, and claims to be a minister of the meek and lowly Jesus. . . . The slave auctioneer's bell and the church-going bell chime in with each other, and the bitter cries of the heart-broken slave are drowned in the religious shouts of his pious master. Revivals of religion and revivals in the slave-trade go hand in hand together. The slave prison and the church stand near each other. The clanking of fetters and the rattling of chains in the prison, and the pious psalm and solemn prayer in the church, may be heard at the same time. The dealers in the bodies of men erect their stand in the presence of the pulpit, and they mutually help each other. The dealer gives his blood-stained gold to support the pulpit, and the pulpit, in return, covers his infernal business with the garb of Christianity. Here we have religion and robbery the allies of each other—devils dressed in angels' robes, and hell presenting the semblance of paradise." **Frederick Douglass**

PART ONE
FLOODS OF UNGODLY MEN

"Quakers almost as good as colored. They call themselves friends and you can trust them every time." **Harriet Tubman**

1848
Free State of Ohio

"Papa....Papa, they're coming. I hear them down by the gate."

"Go tell Sam to light the lamp," David Wood said, calmly, from his desk in the study.

Sarah had been up for two hours waiting for the conductor and passengers on the Underground Railroad and was beside herself with excitement although she had been a part of the scene for twelve years. The sun was near rising and the air moist with cool, pre-dawn Ohio mist floating up from the river. Sarah's dress and petticoat rustled as she ran to the barn. The darkness didn't frighten her like it did when she was little. Sarah Wood, at 13, was a gangly, loose limbed girl, all knees and elbows, almost as tall as her brother Sam who, at 23, was short in stature but brutally strong; a baby-face worked to his advantage when others underestimated him. He looked a contemporary of his brother, Stephan, who was five years younger, but Sam was thickset with massive thighs, large forearms and hands that could crush a skull. His eyes were blue but seemed black when the light was low, or his temper flared.

"Sam, Stephan, are you in there?"

"Yes, we're getting everything ready. Stephan is filling the water cask. Are they here?"

"They're coming up the drive now, Papa said to light the yard lamp, I'll go meet them."

The light cast her shadow dashing ahead until she was out of the rays and well down the lane, her senses alert for any changes in the familiar buzz of the Ohio night. She stopped as the sound of baying hounds drifted up on the wispy fog.

"Hurry," she urged.

"Who dah?" asked a deep baritone, a man's voice.

"It's me, Sarah Wood."

A woman answered, "Sarah, run tu yo mammy and tell her we be in da barn."

Sarah's words caught in her throat at the sound of the woman's voice, "Is that you, Mrs. Tubman?"

"Yes chile. Hurry long now, we doan got much time. It be light soon."

Sarah tore back to the house. She found her mother, Esther, in the kitchen. "Mama, Mrs. Tubman is with them."

"Really! What in the world is Harriet doing in Ohio? I'll meet them in the barn."

Sarah hurried to the barn as the fugitive's arrived, led by Harriet Tubman, the whip-thin former slave who escaped from her oppressive master to become a leader on the Underground Railroad. She was accompanied by John Thompson, a tall muscular man of ebony skin, born free, a conductor on the Ohio and Illinois lines; he was leading two men, a woman with a baby and a young girl about Sarah's age. Stephan urged them to hurry to the ladder leading to the hidden room under the horse stalls, but they were interrupted when the girl entered the light and the lamp revealed a bloody mess. Sarah gasped, "Your back is bleeding. Did you fall?"

"No, she didn't fall, Massa Wilson, he whup her good. She's in pain," John Thompson said. "We need water to clean her. We ain't had the time."

Esther Wood was not squeamish, but she was aghast at the sight of the brutalized girl. She set her children to action, "Sarah, run get your old grey shift. Sam, there's boiling water on the stove, bring the basin. Stephan, get some of those old rags from the bin on the mud porch, the clean ones, mind you. Come child, take that dress off."

Esther raised the ragged shift from the girl who clenched her eyes in pain. Sarah gasped when she saw the naked child, the blood and welts crossed her back in grotesque images of the cross like a sign mocking the Christian master who did it. The girl lay on a blanket with Mrs. Wood tending to her. The welts and blood didn't stop on her back but extended down her buttocks and legs. The sound of the dogs baying and the light from the lamp lent an eerie pall to the scene in the Wood's barn as the exhausted slaves slumped on bales of hay and the floor while Esther Wood cleansed the wounds.

Mrs. Tubman said, "We got bout 20 minutes fore them dogs be on us, Ms. Wood, best hurry."

She nodded at Harriet and said, "Stephan, get the alcohol and bring the salve from the pantry. Sam, put the basin here. What's your name, Honey?"

"Jinny"

"Does it hurt, Jinny?" Sarah asked. "Why did he whip you? What did you do?" she pestered the girl without giving her a chance to answer.

"She run off," Thompson answered quickly.

"Don't you lie tu dese folk, John," Mrs. Tubman scolded him. "Run off, my laws, you think you protectin' dey honor or sumpin'? I tell you why dey done it. Cause dis chile, right here, bit dat ole man when he stick his bidness in her mouf. Might near chewed it off and I wisht she did. Filthy ole man. Not fit tu call hisself a human person. Not a Christian for damn sure," Harriet snarled.

Sarah turned to her mama in horror.

"Oh, Jinny!" Esther cried, "I'm sorry you had to suffer such a thing, but we'll fix you up real good. Dear Lord, give me strength," she prayed as she washed the blood from the child's body. Esther was tall with dark hair that was turning grey. She had the ruddy glow of a farm wife who had borne ten children and nursed them through the maladies inherent in life, and did it with a smile, but she could not believe the inhuman cruelty of the slaveholders. David came into the barn in time to hear Harriet's denunciation and gave orders with the bearing of one accustomed to taking charge.

"Sam, you and Stephan go meet the trackers. Tell them that the runaways went on past our place and down to Bray's crick. They won't believe you but buy us a little time to cover the scent from the dogs. It should be light by the time they get here so you won't need a lamp. Take a pick and shovel to work on the fence post and scatter some of the ground onion up our lane. John, who are they tracking?"

"I reckon Abraham here. They got some o' his clothes from Massa Wilson."

"Which Wilson?"

"Dat sinful old Jonas Wilson over in Clarksburg…., Deacon o' de Methodist Church, laws, he a Deacon o' de Devil. Dat what he is," Harriet shook her head. "Dey doan come no more evil dan dat man."

"Yes, I know him," David Wood said shaking his head in disgust. "John, you and Abraham run back to the road and then take the path to the crick. Leave a good trail, then back here as fast as you can. Sam, take the dogs just in case there's trouble. What's your name?" he asked the other man.

"Carl, suh"

"Carl, if you would help the ladies down the ladder."

Esther finished her treatments, "That's all I can do for you, Jinny. You'll have to sleep on your stomach or side, but I have some laudanum and that'll help. Now, down the ladder. You can keep the lamp on but…."

"We'll be all right, Ms. Wood, we most grateful fo' yore kindness,"

"I know, Harriet, I'm just worried about those bounty hunters. Sarah, go with Jinny and help her get settled on the bunk. Cover her with one of the blankets, only to her waist, we'll take the bandages off this afternoon and let the air get to her wounds."

Mrs. Wood turned to the mother with her baby. "What's your name, Missus?"

"I Charlotte n' dis my babe, Homer. His daddy be Abraham," she said rapidly although the baby, about 18 months, appeared to be a mulatto. "We couldn't stay der no more, Ma'am. Massa Wilson, he gonna' sell me an' de baby down de river. Miss Tubman save us and Mr. Thompson takin, us tu de British up nort'. Dey doan llow' no slavery."

"Yes, dear, you'll be safe there. Harriet, come to the kitchen, please. You can stay in the house; David won't let them search the house even if they do come up here. Charlotte, you best go on down the ladder, your husband and Mr. Thompson will be back soon."

"Here, Charlotte, let me hold de babe, while'st you climb down," Carl said.

"I be long soon as Jinny settled," Harriet answered. She was a free woman, but her name was well known among the slave traders who knew that she was inciting the slaves to escape to the north. She had a price on her head.

Sarah helped Jinny ease down on the wooden bunk protected with a straw filled mattress. She lay on her side staring at Sarah, with large glistening eyes, black as the raised hand of tyranny and vacant with the despair of lost hope. Sarah comforted the girl by swabbing her forehead with a wet cloth. She had the same beliefs as her mother and father, but certain ideas and thoughts were confusing to her, the slippery inconsistencies of the adult world. Mysteries why certain things were true to some but not to others, why some people believed one thing and others believed the opposite.

"What did he do when he came to you, Jinny?" Sarah asked. Her curiosity getting the best of her manners.

"He tole me wut he were gwin tu do. He say when de Missus gone tu bed he were gwin tu come fer me…., I cried! Den I bite him but it weren't him whut whup me it war de missus, she call dat man, Ike, who work fer her. I feared I uz gwin die. De Missus say it my fault he came tu me like a husband. She say I tempt him, but don't matter, cain't be no Christian now," Jinny's eyes filled with tears.

Sarah took her hand, "Yes you are a Christian. You didn't do nothing wrong; I promise you. Ain't that right Mrs. Tubman?"

"Yes, yo right, Sarah, but you best git back up de ladder, chile, yo mama be worried for yu."

"Yes, ma'am, soon as Mr. John gets back, I will. I want to help Jinny if I can. Maybe she needs some water or to use the chamber pot, I can help her if she does. Mama says I'm a good nurse. I helped Aunt Ruth when she was laid up with her new baby last month."

"I spek' you a fine nurse, missy. But Jinny fas' asleep," Mrs. Tubman indicated the drugged child.

Sarah twisted the hem of her skirt and rubbed at some dirt on her wrist with the wet cloth. Mrs. Tubman watched the girl's discomfort. "What on yo mind, Sarah? You about tu squirm out'n yo clothes. What you want tu ax me?"

"Did you see the way Jinny looked at me, Mrs. Tubman? Like she was the saddest person who ever lived."

"Dat de look of a slave, chile. She been whupped so many times and call horrible things and been use bad by de massa til she got nufin' lef', even at sich a young age. Ya see, de body can take a lot a pain cause' it heal, but de soul…., when dat gone, ain't nufin' lef' inside. Dat de look you see on Jinny's face. De look of a human person dat done loss all hope."

"My friend, Lilly Anne Beauregard…., she's from Georgia…."

Mrs. Tubman nodded. "What do Lilly Anne Beauregard say dat got you so bother'."

"She says the bible condones slavery," Sarah said.

Harriet leaned back in the cane bottomed chair and scoffed a sneer of derision, "She use dat word, did she? Condone? Dat a heavy word…., fill dis little room it so big. Look roun you, Sarah Wood, at dis prison we in down here, look at dem dirt walls, dirt floor and dat chile layin' dar wit' her back stripped o' de flesh God put der'. Do dis look like a place for a human person tu crawl down inta like a snake on its belly? I don't believe dat God condone no such a thing. Dat idea o' condonin' come from de New Testament and dat de word o' man not de word o' God."

'The sorrows of death compassed me, and the floods of ungodly men made me afraid.

He delivereth me from mine enemies: yea, thou liftest me up above those that rise up against me: thou hast delivered me from the violent man….'

"Dat from the Psalm of David—de Ole Testament--God don't condone no slavery, man do. You ax yo daddy and yo brother, Sam. Dey good people, tell you whats right an you best believe it when dey do. You put yo mind on deliverance and leave de condonin' tu de heathens."

###

"Why, der language down dar in de far South is jus' as different from ours in Maryland, as you can think. Dey laughed when dey heard me talk, an' I could not understand 'dem, no how." **Harriet Tubman**

"Which way de path, John?"

"Follow me, Abe, but we got to hurry. Is your foot holdin' steady? I hate to make you run but we about out a time."

"I be fine. De thought o' dem white folk hepin' us got me all frazzle down. I doan unnerstan' it."

"They Friends, Abe."

"How you come to be friend of a white man? I never thought no such thing possible. Is dat why you talks like a white man?"

"No, I mean that's their religion. They call themselves Friends, or Quakers, I ain't exactly sure, but they believe that all men and women should be free. They believe that each man, black or white, is equal to each other and women too. Hell, they want to get the vote for Negroes and women."

Abe stopped short; he could not begin to comprehend such an idea. He had no formal education, couldn't read nor write, and believed everything he had been told about life. His place as a slave had been pre-ordained and although his family could be traced through five generations in America, he considered himself to be stateless, not a citizen but a piece of property. His Master refused to educate him, in fact, it was against the law to educate a slave in Virginia. Abe was incredulous, "De hell you talkin bout', get de vote for Negroes? Dat ain't possible."

John laughed, but urged Abe on, "Come on man we got to hurry. You need to pee? Do it right there on that patch o' grass. I'll do it over here, lead the dogs down here. You gonna' see some things and learn some ideas like you never heard before, Abe. The world ain't all like that hell you been livin' down in Virginia. There are good people of every color and even some like Mrs. Tubman and the Wood family trying to change the world. I know it sound crazy but it's true."

###

"Think how long we clung to the institution of human slavery, how long lashes upon the naked back were a legal tender for labor

performed. Think of it." **Robert G. Ingersoll, The Liberty Of Man, Woman And Child 1833-1899**

Stephan rocked the fence post back upright and Sam held the plumb bob steady. They both watched the road as the hounds came closer.

"Let me do the talking, Sam. You always get us in trouble. Let me handle it, ok?"

"Sure, as long as you're making the point clear, little brother."

"You know Dad doesn't want any trouble…., if we can avoid it."

"Course not, Stevey, you know I always avoid trouble."

Stephan scoffed, "You NEVER avoid trouble…."

The dawn streaked in and the sun emblazoned the horses and the men with their track dogs. The Wood dogs, Bull Terriers named John and Adams, stood up, their ears and tails twitching with excitement. Stephan cautioned them, "Sit!" and they did, waiting for a command, ears pricked and their bodies tense. The boys stopped working and watched the men approach on horseback.

"Good morning to you. I'm Captain Johnson from Meridian, Mississippi. Would you be so kind as to tell us where our slaves are?" he asked. He was a stately man, upright with good carriage and relatively clean buckskins. He appeared to be a man of some distinction.

"Who?" Stephan asked.

"The four runaway slaves that we're tracking. You know very well whom I mean. I believe them to be at your house, yonder. You are some of David Wood's boys, aren't you?"

"How would we know where they are? Sam and I've been up at the barn milking. I imagine if they came by here, they're clean to Columbus by now."

"You won't mind if'n we have a look for ourselves do ya? It

wouldn't be hard to hide four Niggers in that barn," the filthy tracker said, his beard full of debris, his mouth full of tobacco and his dogs pulling at their leashes.

"Four Niggers?" Sam spat indignantly. "Hell, we've got a dozen up there. But you gentlemen can't have em', cause' they are free now. This is Ohio and every man, woman and child in this great state is free as a bird in the air."

"They are the property of Jonas Wilson and I have a warrant to bring them back to their owner and you are obliged to comply with the law."

"I, sir, am obliged to comply with the laws of the Lord God Almighty. We must obey God, not men--that is from the book of Acts, Mr. Johnson, I advise you to read it."

"I can quote the bible with you, if you please, Mr. Wood, Slaves, submit yourselves to your masters with all respect, not only to the good and gentle but also to the cruel, First Peter 2:18," the Captain countered.

"Whoever steals a man and sells him, and anyone found in possession of him, shall be put to death; Exodus 21:16," Sam fired back.

"Okay, now, stop it," Stephan pulled his brother back from the road where he was advancing with impunity.

"Stop? I will not. And if these gentlemen take one step onto this property, we will set the dogs on them and I'll bet Father is not far away with a rifle to defend our land."

"Well, I'll be damned," sputtered the dumbstruck dog handler. "This one smart-mouthed Quaker we got here, Captain."

"Captain?" Sam spat. "Captain of what? The ignorant army of the South."

"You best watch that smart-ass mouth, you Nigger-lovin' pup," the dog handler dribbled tobacco juice down his beard in frustration.

"Don't insult Mr. Sam Wood, Ike, he's a well-respected representative of the Liberty Party, aren't you Mr. Wood? A friend of Salmon Chase and delegate to the democratic convention."

"Sal is our cousin," Stephan interjected.

Sam ignored the banter and said to the ugly tracker, "Do you consider calling me a Nigger-lover an insult you dirt-covered bastion of ignorance?"

"What?"

"He's callin' you stupid, Ike," the other rider snarled.

"No, he gives stupid a bad name," Sam said.

. "What?…., what the hell you talkin' bout?" Ike pulled his grimy slouch hat from his head and peered at Sam.

Stephan interrupted, "Captain Johnson, go on down the road to Bray's Crick and see if you can find their scent. But don't come on our property or there will be trouble. We don't know where your slaves are."

Johnson ordered the others on and reined his horse by Sam. "Yes, Mr. Wood, I know who you are. I understand that you are a friend of influential people, but I caution you not to push me too far. I fear that mouth of yours is going to cause you a great deal of pain in the future."

###

"When Virginian John Randolph's 518 slaves were emancipated (in 1833 by his will) and a plan was hatched to settle them in southern Ohio, the population rose up in indignation. An Ohio congressman warned that if the attempt were made, 'the banks of the Ohio…would be lined with men with muskets on their shoulders to keep off the emancipated slaves.'" **Appendix to the "Congressional Glove," 30 Cong. 1 Sess., p. 727**

Esther and her daughters bustled about the kitchen and dining table preparing for the morning meal. Estelle stared at her father for the longest time until he said, "What is it Pumpkin, why are you staring at me?"

"Do you feel all right, Daddy?"

His sons and John Thompson trooped in from their chores and heard Estelle. Sam said, "You do look tired, Dad."

"I feel fine, I had some indigestion this morning but I'm fine now. Let's enjoy our meal. Sarah, would you please offer the blessing?"

Sarah puffed up with pride at this great honor from her father, "Bless, O Father, Thy gifts to our use and us to Thy service; for Christ's sake. Amen." Everyone chorused 'Amen', and Sarah glanced around expecting praise, but they turned their attention to the meal. She enjoyed public speaking but was sorely hurt if it wasn't acknowledged. She pouted, her dark eyes clouding with anger when she saw her sister, Estelle, smirking at her.

The family, Harriet Tubman and John Thompson gathered around the large table in the dining room to a breakfast of eggs, ham, fried potatoes, buttermilk, coffee and pan biscuits. As freemen, John and Harriet could move about as they pleased, but had to be careful because the slavers were known to grab freemen and haul them to the Deep South, where no one asked questions. Many a freed slave found himself in chains if he wasn't careful, especially if suspected of aiding runaway slaves.

"Stephan, are the dogs out?"

"Yes, Daddy, we'll have plenty of warning if anyone comes around."

"They won't come back during the day, but they'll be back tonight when they think the passengers will move on to the north," Sam added.

"Mr. Wood, Abe was asking me about your religion, and I couldn't answer all of his questions. Are you called Friends or Quakers?"

"Both, John. Society of Friends is a reflection of a term used in the New Testament. As for the term Quakers, somewhere back when our sect began, back in England, one of our people was brought up before a magistrate for religious blasphemy. Our form of Christianity was not viewed favorably by the Church of England. He told the magistrate that he bade him to tremble at the word of the Lord. The judge said he was a quaking in his boots and that the defendant was a Quaker. He meant it in ridicule, but I guess some of the members liked it, so the term stuck. Our beliefs are simple, John. Every man, regardless of color, is equal to every other man. Just like it says in the Bible...."

"and the Constitution," Sam interjected.

David continued, "We believe that the light of God is in each of us and we should wear that belief proudly and shout it to the world. But in a peaceful way."

Harriet pointed at Sam, "Well der sit one dat doan unnerstan' no peaceful way. He a fightin' Quaker."

David Wood laughed with a glow of pride he couldn't conceal. "That comes from his Grandfather Mosher," David said, with a sidelong glance at Esther. "Sam can take care of himself and I hope the good Lord forgives him for his methods."

Esther added, "I believe his Grandfather Mosher meant for him to exercise a little caution. I don't always approve of the means. Sam doesn't often pick his fights very well."

"Well, you shore is a friend tu us. Dat why I come here today. I needs tu know wut you think we can do bout' dis new Fugitive Slave Law dey tryin' tu pass," Mrs. Tubman said.

"I doubt I know any more than you do, Harriet. Ephraim Cutler and I have opposed it in Columbus and I've even traveled to Washington to talk with as many members of Congress as I can. I fear that it will pass."

"Yassir, I feels de same way. A good many folk in Pennsylvania and Vermont say dey goin' tu jus' ignore it. But I fraid' dat might not be so easy tu do. James Polk and specially

Stephen Douglas think dis de onliest way tu keep de peace. Might keep de peace, but gonna' kill a whole passle o' Negroes. And, Esther, I know you means well when you out tryin' tu git de vote for de Negroes, but I fear dat fus we needs tu get our freedom."

Esther Wood poured coffee as Sarah and Estelle cleared the table. "I understand that, Harriet and I know that it adds flame to the fire of rhetoric by the slaveholders, but I want all adults to have the vote. Negro men are allowed to vote in some elections in Pennsylvania. As for the new law, Reverend Simpson says that nothing will change, they just make the penalties for harboring a slave more punitive."

"It's not just that, Mother," Sam said. "The law will prohibit a slave from having a trial or representation of any kind. He has no recourse, no rights under the law whatsoever. He can't even testify on his own behalf. Even in the northern states, the Whites don't want the Blacks in their neighborhood. Equality isn't even a consideration, the northern papers cry for freeing the slaves...., 'but don't let them settle next to me'. They want them to stay in the south or go to Canada. It's a travesty of moral behavior."

Harriet interjected, "We got no rights now, Sam. Nufin' be differen'. At leas' in de northern states dey don't beat us."

John closed his eyes and tried to smile. He raised his coffee cup but sat it down again. "I'm a free man, been so since birth, and should be able to travel anywhere in any state. But under this new law if a slaver slaps me in iron and hauls me south, I would have a devil of a time convincing anyone that I am a free man. Ohio no different than anyplace else. The white folk here, present company excluded, are just as prejudiced as in the south. They won't let us go to the schools, they ran most of the colored folk out of Cincinnati, most 2,000 of them. It's a long uphill battle everyone has to face. I'm just trying to save one at a time, but we going to have to go to Canada, we can't stay in the north just because they don't allow slavery."

"There'll be bounty hunters all over this country ignoring property rights, and I don't mean Negroes as property, I mean our property rights. They'll come right up the lane and claim the law warrants their actions," Sam added.

"John and Sam right," Harriet continued. "Der gonna' be a plague o' unrighteous men arter dat bounty money. Dey woan let nufin' stan' in de way."

Sarah pulled a chair up beside Harriet and waited until the adults were finished and had moved on to other chores. "Mrs. Tubman, why do the white people in the south hate the Negro so much? Lilly Ann Beauregard says that the Negroes are just like animals," Sarah said.

Harriet laughed, "Oh, chile, dat de question ain't it. I doubt we got nough' time till you growed tu answer dat question. But de truf' is most folk down der doan owns no slaves nohow. Most o' dem jus' plain folk but dey hate us de wors' just cause dey can."

David added, "The slave owners have convinced the small landowners that the bottom will drop out of the economy if we abolish slavery. The poor white farmers like the fact that they have a poorer class to look down on."

John finished his coffee and rose from the table, slowly, "Man, these old bones gettin' mighty cranky. Best go down and get some sleep before we move on. Are you goin' on with us Moses?" he asked Harriet, using her nickname from the Underground Railroad.

"No, John, I bes' get on back tu Maryland. Dis as far west as I gwin. I needs tu talk to a few mo o' de station masters and sum o' de reverends in Pittsburgh. Wit dis new law I reckon we be takin' de passengers' futher north tu Ontario mo' and mo'. Need tu git de line ready for de changes."

Sam walked with John to the door. "John, with those bounty hunters sneaking around I want to move you all to the next station this afternoon. They won't be expecting us, they figure you'll travel at night."

"I agree with you, Sam. What time do you want to leave?"

"About noon. I'll rig the farm wagon and you can lay in the back and I'll cover it with the tarp like I'm taking a load of feed somewhere. What's the next station...., if you're free to say?"

"The Lyon's place over in Harris County."

"We know Bill and Elizabeth. They're members of our church. That's only about 15 miles. We can make that in three hours if we push it a little and I can be back by dark."

"That'll make it a lot easier on the women if we don't have to walk."

Sarah and Mrs. Tubman sat at the table while the others went about their household business. The Wood family was large with ten children, six at home. Sam, 23, was the oldest of the family still on the farm, but he didn't farm full time since he was employed as a schoolteacher by the local citizens. The Wood children were all imbued with the beliefs of their religion, foremost being the abolishment of slavery and women's suffrage. The children were well acquainted with the glorious history of Quaker authorship of the Bill of Rights.

"Mrs. Tubman, weren't you born a slave?"

"Laws, yes I was, chile. I still a slave if de truf' be know'd. I jus' up and lef' one spring morn when de Missus took de switch tu me fur de las time. I was watchin' de babe in de nursery and he commence tu cry an' his mama took a switch tu me like always when de babe fuss, so I jus' lit out soons she turn her haid. I been goin' back tu bring out other slaves ever since. I got my parents out fust."

"Why can't slaves pronounce English right, like the word master? Mr. John speaks good English but he's not a slave."

"Chile, I tell you why de Negro talk dat way, caus' most Negroes got no education like John do and dey language in Africa was different so dey jus' learn English from listenin' to dey massa. But a good many colored folk talks jus' as clear as any white man, in fact, some even better. You ought tu hear Frederick Douglass speak, oh my, he got a voice sweet as molasses and speak de King's English like a Senator."

"I want to hear him and meet him. Will you introduce me, Mrs. Tubman?"

"Just as sure as daybreak, next time you come tu New York. As fo' Massa', dat word doan mean master, it mean burden. It a Hebrew word and dat de language o' many o' de firs' slaves. So we doan mean dey our master. We mean dey our burden tu bear.

"I member de fus time I step intu Pennsylvania a free woman. When I foun' I had cross de line, I look at my hands tu see if I war de same person. Der was sich a glory over everythin'; de sun came like gold trou' de trees, and over de fields and I felt like I was in heaven."

Esther bustled back through the kitchen taking laundry to the porch where Estelle, was washing clothes, in disgust since Sarah was not doing her share. "Harriet, if you're tired don't sit there and answer that child's questions. She'll keep you up all day...., the most inquisitive child I have ever seen. I've got a bed made for you in that back room by the stairs. You go on and get some sleep whenever you need to."

Harriet laughed; her dark eyes sparkled with delight. "Why, Esther, answerin' dis chile's questions de mos' important task I got in my life. Tu bring low de falsehood o' dis slavery, tu teach ever chile in dis land de truf'. I won't sleep till dat job done."

"What did Mr. Wilson do to Jinny," Sarah whispered. "Isn't he married? Why would he go to a little girl like that when he's married?"

Harriet took Sarah's face in her hands, held her softly, looking into the child's upturned innocent eyes. "Sarah, der turible evil in de soul o' some men. I cain't even begins tu describe it tu ya. You take dat girl Charlotte, dat babe o' hers is no more

Abraham's dan I am. I'll wager it de babe o' ole man Wilson hisself. Dat why he gonna' sell em down de river cause his Misses won't abide dat chile raisin' up and mindin' her o' whut her husband did. But doan think dat Jonas Wilson de onliest one. Der many evil men in dis worl' but...., ders good'uns to. You got tu make certain dat you knows how tu tell de difference."

###

"My marser's name was Isaac Hunter. Him an' de missus bofe hellcats . . . Marser daid now an' I ain' plannin' on meetin' him in heaven neither." **Armaci Adams, age 93, Huntersville, Virginia**

Sam fed and watered the dogs while Efren went to get the draft horses. Stephan rode off to see if Captain Johnson and the bounty hunters were still lurking about.

"Dad, I'm going to take them on to Bill Lyon's place in the wagon."

"They won't expect you on the road during the day. See if Bill has any news about the Fugitive Slave Law or at least anything we don't know."

"I will. I think Sarah wants to go. You have any problems with that?"

"Not at all. She wants to help that girl Jinny and she likes to play with Caroline Lyon. She'll enjoy the trip. Do you need some help getting things together?"

"Not really. Stephan and Efren are helping. What are you going to do?"

"I'm going to take the buggy and drive Harriet to Wheeling. She can take the steamboat on to Pittsburgh. I'll take Stephan with me. Do we need anything from Toby's, other than the blinders?"

"Some of those feed sacks...., that's all I can think of, Father. Hey, are you not feeling well?"

"Why do you ask, Son?"

"You just look a little under the weather, maybe a little pale."

"No, I'm fine," he said and started for the house. David reached the front porch, stumbled on the first step and sat down breathing heavily. Sam ran to his side, shouting, "Mother, Mother, come quick." Esther was already coming out of the kitchen having heard him fall. David was up and brushing off his britches as Sam arrived and took him by the arm.

"I'm fine, all of you, go on about your business. I just stumbled," and he hurried inside. Sam looked at his mother, questioningly. She shrugged and followed her husband into the house.

Sam worked as quietly as he could in the tack room pulling out the harnesses. He knew that a pair of blinders needed replacing so he finished the repair, as best he could, before dragging out the collars and straps. Probably two horses were all that was needed but to fool the bounty hunters he decided to hitch all four. By the time he had the traces and lines to the wagon Efren was back with the horses and Stephan was riding up the lane.

"I rode all the way to the crossroads and no sign of them," he announced. His horse was unsaddled, and Efren took him to the corral.

"They're around somewhere, I imagine," Sam said.

"Maybe you'll make it all the way to the Lyon place without seeing them."

"I'm not worried one way or the other," Sam grinned.

For a spring afternoon the sun was hotter than usual which did not bode well for those riding in the bed of the wagon covered by the heavy tarp, but there were no other options. Sarah and Efren opened the trap door into the safe room and called down for the travelers, "Mr. Thompson, are you up? The wagon is hitched."

"Is it noon already? I feel like I just got to sleep. You awake Abe? Carl? Charlotte? Best get your baby ready to go. We'll be up shortly," John shouted up the ladder.

Sam backed the wagon into the barn so the loading would be private although there was no sign of the bounty hunters. Esther packed some food, and fresh water was loaded into the wagon for the trip.

"Say goodbye to Mrs. Tubman for me, will you Mama?" Sarah said. "I'll see her when we go to New York this summer, won't I?"

"I'm sure we will, Sarah, I'll tell her. You give this apple pie to Elizabeth. Enjoy your visit with Caroline. I'll see you this evening, honey. I love you."

"I love you too, Mama."

Goodbyes were said all around and the wagon rolled down the drive, onto Bray's Road with Sam driving and Sarah next to him. At the crossroads, the road north to the Lyons was not as well maintained.

"Damn, Sam, it's hotter than hades back here and we're rattling all over the place. We should have put more straw to cushion the ride," John said.

"Sorry, but nothing I can do about the rough road. At least the dust isn't bad. We'll have to do something to keep the baby quiet if someone comes. I don't want any sound from back there, but we'll have time, Sarah and I can see for a long way in both directions."

Five miles from Bill and Elizabeth's house, Sarah spotted movement on the horizon. Riders coming over a hill about a mile distance.

"Someone's coming," she shouted. "You've got to keep the baby quiet, Charlotte. Can't you do something?"

The riders were coming on quickly. Sam stopped the wagon trying to think. He could still hear the muffled sound of the baby as Charlotte put her hand over its mouth.

"John, pull the tarp back...., up here by the seat. Hand the baby to Sarah. Wrap it up so they can't see his face. Sarah you pretend the baby's yours. Ok, here we go. Be quiet back there."

Sam could see four riders as they closed on the wagon. It was the same men from the morning encounter, only no sign of the dogs.

"Whoa," Sam pulled on the reins as the men arrived.

"Mr. Wood, we meet again."

"Hello, Captain Johnson. My sister, Sarah," Sam introduced. "Did you find your slaves?"

The Captain tipped his hat but declined to answer.

"What you got in that wagon," Ike asked?

Sam looked back nonchalantly and said, "Oh, this is a wagonload of runaway Niggers."

Sarah held her breath as Ike pulled up short and stared at the tarp expecting it to rise up with runaway slaves scattering. The Captain shook his head and laughed.

"I don't want to be impolite, Ike, but I've got to deliver them to Wileyville and get back for another load before dark. We've got runaway slaves stacked up in the barn so high that we can't get the cows in to milk, so if you don't mind, get your ugly carcass out of the way so we can be off."

Ike stared open mouthed and finally said, "You the damndest fool I ever met, maybe I'll far a shot through that'air tarp and test ye out. See if yer bluffin'."

"Go ahead, Ike, but before you do, give me five...., no, seven dollars so I can buy a new one when I get back to Wheeling. You can run as many holes in it as you want soon as you give me the money," and Sam held his hand out to the bounty hunter.

"Hell, no cover made cost that kind o' money."

"Some of it's for the trouble of going to get it," Sam said continuing to hold his hand out to the angry slaver.

"Let's go, Ike. Goodbye Miss Wood…., Sam," the Captain said.

"One day, I'm gonna' git you alone, ya little shit-ass and when I do, I'll whup you good," Ike said in parting.

"If I were you, I'd leave him alone, Ike. He's like a rattlesnake," The Captain warned as they rode away,

Brother and sister watched the riders fade in the distance. Sam was worried that the Captain would figure the deception and come back, but he put up a cheerful front for his passengers.

"I pulled the wool over their eyes, didn't I John?"

"We bout melted through the floor when you said that. Damn man, you got some balls about you to pull that off."

"I couldn't think of nothing else to say. It just come out, but they're gone so it worked."

The sound of sobs was coming from the bed of the wagon. Sarah asked, "What's wrong, Jinny? Oh, I bet I know what it is. That mean man, Ike, he's the one that whipped you, isn't he?"

"Yass'm he de one," she moaned.

A look of hatred came across Sam's face. A look that his sister recognized and knew meant not to press him.

"I'm glad I didn't know that before. Don't know if I could have kept from killing that man. I sure hope I don't run into him again," Sam whispered to Sarah as she handed the baby back to Charlotte.

He glanced back and was satisfied they weren't being followed then reached down to make certain his customized ax handle with the weighted end was in its scabbard. Sam didn't carry a gun, he wasn't afraid of any man, but he didn't want his mother to find out about the club. He was afraid of her. They pulled into the Lyon's yard about three-fifteen having made good time. The dogs barked their greeting and Sarah jumped down before the wagon was fully stopped.

"Why are you here, Sarah?" Carolyn said twirling her friend

around.

"We brought Mr. Thompson and the passengers from the Underground Railroad."

"We didn't expect them till tomorrow morning. Isn't it thrilling to be a part of it?"

Sarah told Caroline about the excitement of the trip and how Sam had fooled the bounty hunters. Suddenly she remembered Jinny and urged her friend to help look after the injured girl. She was already whispering the ugly details of what had happened to her.

"Oh, dear," Caroline said. "We've got to go get Beulah. She'll know what to do."

Sam was rolling the tarp back when Beulah, a large ebony woman about 40, came rushing up, took one look and began giving orders. John and the others were just getting out of the wagon, their joints stiff from the confinement.

"My Lord, would you look at this pack o' Africans. Y'all look like you slept in the pig sty and, God forgive us, you smell like it too. Get over to the wash house John Thompson, you know where it is. Silas, help get they clothes off and get cleaned up. Ain't no way they goin to the Promised Land smellin' like that, not long as Mama Beulah got somthin' to say bout' it."

She followed them to the wash house, babbling all the way.

"Get out them clothes and put em in this tub, you all ain't going nowhere with clothes smell like that...., the bounty hunters sniff you out from Atlanta. You can help me wash em, Misses, soon's you get washed yo self," she announced to Charlotte.

"Damn, Beulah, we ain't got no clothes to put on if we give you these," John complained.

"Get to it man. You too good to parade around the way God made you? I won't stand for it. Get them clothes off...., I can't abide the smell no more. Oh, my God, chile what happened to you? John, who done this little girl that way?"

"She owned by Jonas Wilson over in Clarksburg, Virginia."

"Well, we got some work to do, honey. It look like Mrs. Wood fix you up pretty good but Ole Mama Beulah gonna' make it even better. You come with me. The rest of you get to washing. Silas, come on, I'll give you some old sheets for them to cover up since they so uppity can't be seen in God's glory. Damn sure ain't got nothin' I haven't seen or want to either...., fools, get to it."

"Who de hell is dat, John?" Carl asked when she was out of hearing range. "Dese folk got Niggers act like dey own de damn place."

"She's not a slave, Carl, and don't you let her hear you say that. She works for the Lyons and she do run the place, but she is a fine person and will help anybody, black or white, that comes here needing something," John answered.

Abraham shook his head and said, "Laws, I never thought I'd see nuthin' like that."

###

"God knows I detest slavery but it is an existing evil, and we must endure it and give it such protection as is guaranteed by the Constitution." **Millard Fillmore, President of the United States, 1850-1853**

Sam sat at the dining room table while Bill Lyon was giving orders to his son, Richard, to have the team fed and rested. Mrs. Lyon was making sandwiches for the travelers. A door slammed, the sound of footsteps echoed in the upstairs hallway and down rushed a beautiful light-haired girl wearing only under-drawers with leggings to her knees and a chemise, her large breasts swaying heavily as she skipped down the stairs...., until she spotted Sam.

"Mama, where's my white muslin...., Oh, Lord," she shouted and ran back up the stairs her arms wrapped over her breasts.

Sam sat wide-eyed, his mouth open. Mrs. Lyon stood at the kitchen door with her hand to her face. Sam couldn't tell if it was a look of horror or if she was laughing at him. Mr. Lyon walked in, "The horses are in the corral and Rich is feeding them. Should be well rested and...., What's wrong, Sam? You look like you've seen a ghost."

"Who in God's name was that?" Sam pointed up the stairs.

"What's he talking about, Liz?"

"Oh, for heaven's sakes, Sam Wood. It's Margaret."

"Margaret who?"

"Our daughter, Peggy."

"Peggy? Peggy Lyon is a little girl about as wide as my finger, kicked me in the shin when she was running after my brother Stephan at the church social."

Elizabeth laughed, "That was five years ago. She's 18 now and came back last week from school. You should call her Margaret if you want to be friends."

They sat at the table in silence, Mr. Lyon waiting for Sam to start the conversation. Finally, he said, "Well, Sam, when will you start the classes back up? I know Rich and Caroline can't wait to get back to school. They say you make class fun."

Sam didn't acknowledge the remark and Bill wasn't sure he had heard, Sam jumped up, "I need a glass of water, Bill. I'll be right back." He darted into the kitchen.

"Elizabeth, do you think she's going to come back down any time soon?"

"I just don't know, Sam. Why?"

"Well, I ought to say hello in a proper way, let her know that I'm sorry for...."

"For what? You didn't do anything wrong."

"I know...., I know, but I ought to say something."

"Do you want me to go get her?"

"I think that would be the proper thing, yes, definitely that would be the correct way to approach this matter, don't you think? I'm afraid that I, well, you know, didn't react in an honorable…., in the proper, yes…., proper way." Sam sputtered and stalled, much to Mrs. Lyon's delight.

She handed Sam a tray with a pitcher of lemonade and four glasses. She went upstairs with a wink at Mr. Lyon.

"What did you want to ask me, Sam?"

Sam watched Mrs. Lyon disappear up the stairs before he sat the lemonade on the table and realized that Mr. Lyon was waiting for him, "Father wanted to know if you've heard any more about the Fugitive Slave Act. Harriet Tubman was at our house, asking about it. She thinks the escaped slaves are all going to have to go to Canada instead of just staying north of the river. The bounty makes it too dangerous to risk, even in Pennsylvania or Vermont. They're going to charge a fine of one thousand dollars to anyone harboring a runaway. Can you imagine that?"

"I'm going to Washington in a couple of months. You want to go with me? We can find out what's going on. Your Liberty Party is trying to lobby against it, aren't they? We should be able to get in to see Henry Clay…., but those boys from Kentucky are getting mighty unreasonable toward us. You know Stephen Douglas, you were at the convention last year, with Chase, weren't you?"

"Yes, why?"

"Well, Douglas can tell us what's going to happen. He's working with Clay on the compromise. All Polk cares about is adding more territory.

"I don't consider it a compromise, Bill, I think they're giving away everything we've worked for. There's no compromise on freedom. Either we do away with slavery, or we go to war."

Margaret and Elizabeth appeared on the stairs. Sam jumped up and approached the young beauty who was almost as tall as he, "Margaret, I'm so glad to see you again. You've changed."

"Well, you got to see more than I wanted you to. You've changed too, Sam. I've been following your career in the papers."

"Margaret is as avid an abolitionist as you, Sam. Plus she's working with your mother on setting up the women's suffrage meeting in Mt. Goliad."

"I didn't know that. Mother didn't tell me that you're involved." Sam felt awkward and clumsy around this girl, someone he had grown up with, but never thought of as a female. He was overwhelmed and at a loss for words, very unusual for Sam Wood. Sarah and Caroline dashed into the house chattering about Beulah doctoring Jinny and the others sitting in bedsheets behind the washhouse looking like Roman senators in a Shakespeare play.

"Why is she doctoring Jinny," Margaret asked?

"Oh, Mrs. Lyon, you should see her back," Sarah answered.

"Jonas Wilson, over in Clarksburg," Sam said as explanation.

"Do you know him, Bill?" Elizabeth asked her husband.

"I know of him, Liz. He's one of the worst slaveowners, as far as reputation. Even his fellow owners have tried to reason with him. Cruel and heartless."

"He tried to rape her, Mother," Caroline said.

"We'd better go see if we can help Beulah," Margaret said, as she, her mother and the girls left.

Sam drifted to the door and watched them walk away.

"She grew up, didn't she Sam?"

"I don't even know what to say. She takes my breath away."

###

"....violence is an evil thing, but when the guns are all in the hands of the men without respect for human rights, then men are really in trouble." **Louis L'Amour, The Daybreakers**

Sam drove away as Margaret, Sarah and Caroline waved goodbye. They decided that Sarah would spend the night and Sam would ride back the next day, leading Sarah's horse, Buttercup, and they would ride home together. His strategy had been humorously transparent, he wanted to see Margaret again. Elizabeth and Bill Lyon had no qualms about their daughter and Sam Wood. He was a well-respected member of the community and the church, in addition to being a schoolteacher and one of the youngest political representatives in the four-state region.

Sam tried to get his mind off the pretty college student, but he couldn't get past the pleasant image, startled on the stairway, eyes wide with surprise and the lithe body vaulting back up the stairs. Sensations that he had never felt flooded his body, reddening his face and causing his heart to beat so loud that he was sure the horses could hear it. Sam was in love.

The sun was low in the west, behind the grove of trees across from the Wood driveway as he arrived back at the farm. He spotted the two men from a distance sitting on tree stumps across from the gate. Ike and his tracker friend watched him pull the wagon to a halt.

"What can I do for you fellows?"

"We waitin' for them Niggers," Ike said.

"Where's Captain Johnson?"

"He's gone on back. Told us to stay here and wait for em' to come out."

"I told you they aren't here."

"Say, where's that pretty little gal was with you? Looked about 14 had a baby with her."

"That was my sister."

"Even better, ain't it, Clem?"

"I guess tis if yo're from Arkansas like you and them cousins you always talking about."

"Hell, if'n their old enough to pee they're old enough for

me," Ike guffawed then sneered at Sam.

Sam's voice caught in his throat as anger surged through his body replacing the glow of new love, "You pile of pig dung, get out of here and don't come back. You make me sick to my stomach, you bucket of spit. Get on your horses and get out of here before I do something unpleasant."

The men stood looking at him, "You don't even have a gun," Clem said.

"I don't need one for worthless garbage like you."

"I'm gonna' jerk you off'n that wagon and kick your ass from here to Clarksburg," Ike said moving to attack. Sam swung the weighted axe handle and smashed him on the left side of his head. Ike fell to his knees, poleaxed, put his head down and threw up in the road. Sam stepped down, watching Clem. He went to Ike's horse, took his rifle, and said, "Put your rifle on the ground."

Clem didn't say a word, just obeyed.

"Now walk over to the other side of the road."

Ike had a cowhide whip attached to his saddle. Sam untied it.

"Is this what Ike whipped the girl with?"

Clem nodded yes. Sam unfurled the evil instrument. It consisted of a hard leather handle with a length of rolled and hardened cowhide and a knot at the end; about three feet long it was destructive in the hands of an overseer who could beat a man or woman bloody after two or three lashes.

"I don't know how to do this. What's the secret, Clem?"

"You gonna' whip him?" Clem asked incredulously. "Wail, ye've gotter sorta throw that chord out ahine ye and then hump it inta him on his back." Sam reached back as if he were going to throw the end of the lash away and smashed it over Ike's back, ripping his shirt.

"Ahhhh," he wailed and rolled over. Sam cracked him again

on his legs and Ike tried to crawl under the wagon, but Sam caught him and pulled him back then tied his hands to the wagon wheel and lashed him four more times causing serious cuts on his back.

Sam was breathing hard and threw the whip down in disgust, "Maybe those marks will make him think twice before he whips another little girl. You, Clem, help me get him on his horse, before I change my mind and kill him, which is what he deserves."

Ike was disoriented and couldn't walk straight. He was moaning in pain. They hoisted him onto his horse, but it was obvious he wouldn't be able to hold on, so Sam and Clem tied his hands around the horse's neck with Ike lying flat and his feet jammed in the stirrups.

"Take him back to Virginia. Tell Jonas Wilson that Sam Wood did this and will do the same to him if I see him. Tell him that this is justice for what he did to the girl. You got that?"

"Mister, you're crazy," Clem said reining around as David and Stephan pulled up in the buggy from delivering Harriett to Wheeling. They watched the two men ride off with Clem leading Ike's horse."

"What's that all about, Son? What did you do?" David asked.

"Long story, Papa, but I'm exhausted. Let's get up to the house and I'll explain it there. Maybe Mother has something for supper."

###

Beulah finished washing the clothes as Margaret and her mother walked into the wash house. Sarah and Caroline helped by hanging the clothes on the line to dry.

"Beulah, is there anything I can do?" Margaret asked.

"Help me pour out this water. Those sad folks don't have much more than rags, but I found some old shirts for the men and a couple of dresses that you girls don't wear no more. We'll send em off lookin' decent. I got that girl bandaged up but she gonna' have some God-awful scars."

"The girls were just telling me about it," Elizabeth said.

"Her owner must be a bad, bad man, and John tell me that baby probably his too. God give thanks that we live in the North."

"I know it, Beulah, but the time will come that these evil things will end. They have to," Elizabeth answered.

"Guess what, Beulah," Margaret couldn't contain herself any longer.

"What now?"

"I think Sam Wood took a liking to me. I came running down the stairs in my underwear and the look on his face...., like he'd seen the Virgin herself in the buff."

"I had to cover my mouth to keep from laughing," Elizabeth giggled.

"Took a liking to you," Beulah laughed. "After seeing you naked I guess he took more than that. It don't surprise me none, that Sam Wood is a fine young man, from a good family. No, it don't surprise me a'tall."

"What doesn't surprise you?" Caroline asked, coming in to hear the last of the conversation.

"Sarah's brother done took a shine to Margaret. Maybe we gonna' have a wedding next fall."

Sarah and Caroline danced around the embarrassed Margaret who finally joined them in premature celebration.

###

"The compact which exists between the North and the South is a covenant with death and an agreement with hell." **William Lloyd Garrison**

David, his sons and their hired hand, Silas, finished

unhitching the wagon and buggy. They rubbed down the horses, cleaned and put away the tack then trudged, tired into the house where Esther had a meal of chicken soup ready. Estelle joined them with the youngest Wood sibling, seven-year-old Carl.

"I saw what happened on the road, Sam. I was hiding behind the buggy shed when you pulled up. Mama told me to sneak down and see what those men were doing," Estelle reported.

"Sam, I am certain that I do not condone you whipping that man," Esther Wood said, almost crying.

"I'm sorry, Mother. It was not necessary. I'm afraid that it was arrogance on my part. I apologize to you and Estelle."

"What led you to that, Sam? I've never known you to be cruel."

"That man is the one who whipped the slave girl, Jinny," Estelle interrupted. "I heard him tell Sam that he was proud of doing it."

"I guess I just lost control when I found out what he had done. I wanted to punish him for it. I doubt it does any good and I'm truly sorry that you saw it, Pumpkin," Sam said kissing his sister's forehead.

"We'll have to be on the alert if he decides to come back for revenge," David said. "We'll rely on the dogs to warn us if they come sneaking around, but I doubt they do, that fellow was high-tailin' it for the river last I saw of him."

"How was your trip to the Lyon's, Sam? I take it Sarah is going to stay with them until Sunday and we'll fetch her at church."

"No, Mama. I'm going to ride back over there tomorrow and get her," Sam said. "By the way, why didn't you tell me that Margaret Lyon is back from school and she's going to work with you on the suffragette meeting in Mt. Gilead?"

"We've been pre-occupied with all of the excitement here for the past few days. Of course, if you'd have been at church last

Sunday, you'd know for yourself that she's back. I take it you saw her today?"

"Saw her? Oh Mother, she was like a vision floating down from heaven. She took my breath away."

Stephan and Efren looked at each other and burst out laughing.

"Boys!" David warned his sons with a glare.

"If you'd have seen her you would say the same, Stephan. Anyway, I know you were sweet on her once," Sam said.

"Well, so what if I was, she went away and looked different when she came back."

"Margaret is a brilliant young lady. She's passionate about getting the vote for women and abolition of slavery. I want her involved. We need more young people. Susan Anthony is going to be there and we're trying to get Olympia Brown and Elizabeth Cady Stanton. Margaret met her in Philadelphia last year, and of course Lucretia Mott will be there," Esther said, her eyes gleaming with excitement.

"I'm proud of you, Mother," David said to his wife. "President of the Ohio Women's Rights Convention."

"We're all proud, Mama," Estelle said.

Esther had been involved in women's suffrage all of her life. She was imbued with a fiery glow of radicalism from her father, Asa Mosher, a leader of the Hicksites, the most progressive of the Quakers. Esther would not rest until women, black and white, were given the vote and her passion had been passed on to the children. In Sam's case, Grandfather Mosher had created a fighter with no qualms about taking up arms in God's name, much to the vexation of his mother, who couldn't fathom the need to take up arms in any cause, believing that reason and morality would rule the day.

Sam was a realist.

###

"We are not for Names, nor Men, nor Titles of Government, nor are we for this Party, nor against the other, because of its Name and Pretense, but we are for Justice and Mercy, and Truth and Peace, and true Freedom, that these may be exalted in our Nation."

Edward Burrough, Quaker Elder, 1634-1663

Sunday was a special day, a brilliant spring morning that made Sarah forget her complaints about the harsh Ohio winter. Black Oaks along the north side of the house and the Sugar Maple's on the south were budding. Seth Miller was busy getting the wagon ready, he was invited to the festivities but declined. Seth was a failed Methodist and looked forward to Sundays when he had the day to himself. He was as religious as the next man but wanted to worship in his own way. Seth had been set free by his owner in Kentucky after 25 years of being a slave. He found his way to Ohio and hadn't left the employee of the Wood family since.

Sarah put on her Sunday dress, and hurried the rest of the family. Sam and Stephan were riding horses. Sarah, Efren, Estelle and Carl rode in the wagon with their mother and father. It took an hour to get to the church in Wileyville. They spent the morning packing a picnic lunch for the afternoon church social, Sarah was beside herself with excitement.

"Don't think you're fooling me Sarah," Estelle whispered. "You act like you can't wait to see Caroline, but I know that you can't wait to see Jimmy Kendrick. You're sweet on him and I'll tell mama if you sneak off in the woods like you did last Sunday."

"Estelle, all we did was talk, just mind your own business. I'll tell mama myself, anyway, Jimmy is the sweetest boy and you know he wants to be a preacher. You have a dirty mind sometimes for a little girl."

"I'm only a year younger than you."

"Yeah, but you're a child and I'm a woman."

"Oh, fiddlesticks, you cried for two days and made such a fuss even Mama said to quit."

"Oh, just mind your own business, sometimes you make me so mad, Estelle."

"Let's go girls. Put the food in the wagon. Estelle, carry the tea. Sarah get the blankets in case it's cool tonight on the way home." The girls forgot their argument and scrambled to finish the chores. Esther sat in the driver's seat with Carl between her and David. Sarah, Estelle and Efren sat in the back on straw with the two dogs, John and Adams. Sam and Stephan led the way.

"Is someone going to talk at service today or are we just going to sit there?" Efren asked.

"You're in for a treat today, Ef. We actually have a guest speaker."

"Who?" Estelle said.

Sam had dropped back alongside the wagon. "His name is Hartman Bache and he's a grandson of Benjamin Franklin," Esther answered.

"Actually, he's a great-grandson," Sam corrected. "A career Army man, Major, I believe, but he's not going to talk about Ben Franklin. He's taken up the cause of Benjamin Lay."

"Who's that?" Carl asked.

"Ah, ha, this will be fun children," Esther laughed. "Benjamin is a legend in the Quaker church. You've actually seen his picture but didn't know it was him. In Grandfather Mosher's den the picture of the little man in front of the cave. That's Benjamin Lay, The Quaker Comet."

"I thought that he was crazy in the head," Sarah said.

"Not a bit of it. That's what his critics wanted people to think. He was just ahead of his time, plus he was a strange looking little fellow. Didn't measure up to what folks thought of as a man of prominence."

"Someone's coming on fast," Stephan announced

David pulled the wagon over as far as he could. The riders rode on without acknowledging the Wood family. Clem, the tracker was with them. He looked back as they passed but didn't say anything.

"Did you see who that was, Sam?" Estelle gestured excitedly. "It's that man, Clem."

"That guy in front was Elijah Wilson, brother of Jonas. Whatever they're up to it's not good, I can assure you," David said.

###

"If the comparison be admissible, he appeared rather like a comet, which threatens, in its irregular course, the destruction of the worlds near which it passes, than as one of those tranquil orbs which hold their accustomed place, and dispense their light, in the harmonious order of heaven." **Robert Vaux, Benjamin Lay Biographer, 1815**

They intercepted the Lyons two miles from the church. Sarah jumped down and ran to join Caroline and her family, while Sam rode alongside chatting with Margaret and her parents. It was three whirlwind weeks since the momentous meeting and he spent a good deal of time traveling back and forth, courting the beautiful woman.

The meeting house was packed with more than 80 men, women and older children. The young children were supervised in the house of the minister while services were in progress. The children in the meeting were of various ages, welcomed as long as they could sit still. Most Sundays the service consisted of members sitting quietly for up to two hours waiting for someone to speak. The brethren believed that the Lord would inspire a member at the appropriate time. But this Sunday there was a buzz in the room while waiting for their guest. The bare wood walls and austere wooden benches ringed the rectangular building. The speaker would stand in the center of the hall. Finally, Reverend Simpson entered with a tall, bearded man, regal in bearing, sporting a full military uniform, something not normally seen in a Quaker service.

"Ladies and Gentlemen, it gives me great pleasure to introduce Major Hartman Bache, who is the great-grandson of the legendary Benjamin Franklin. He is a Major in the Corp of Engineers and has been instrumental in the construction of bridges and canals throughout…., the world, as a matter of fact, as he is just back from South America. His main focus has been on lighthouses and he has designed and built many of the most famous structures on the East Coast, but he is here for a much different purpose. Major Bache will share with us his intimate knowledge of one of my favorite historical figures, a man so far ahead of his time in the early part of the 1700's, over a hundred years ago, that he was considered a lunatic and even dangerous. Benjamin Lay became a close friend of Hartman Bache's great-grandfather Ben Franklin. I could go on and on, but we are here to benefit from, and I will add, we are in great debt to, Major Hartman Bache."

As the congregation shuffled and muttered, Esther rolled her eyes at Elizabeth Lyon. Reverend Simpson was known to be long-winded.

"Thank you. Fred. We go way back, Fred and I, just outside of Philadelphia, fifty years ago, we were born a few days apart and inseparable for the early years of our lives, but I must admit to you, I am not a Quaker. Please don't hold that against me because I embrace many of the same esteemed values as you do, which is why Benjamin Lay has become a passion of mine.

"Of course, in our family, Benjamin is somewhat of a legend. Ben Franklin, who we always referred to as Papa, had a hand in promoting Benjamin because Papa was the only person in the world who would print his book, 'All Slave-Keepers That Keep the Innocent in Bondage, Apostates'. What an incredible story...., both the book and the printing. I hold in my hand an original copy of this priceless volume, hot off Great-Grandfathers press, well, 112 years ago in 1737…."

Sam had heard the presentation in Philadelphia the year prior and had been instrumental in bringing Bache to Wileyville for the exhibition. His eyes drifted to Margaret Lyon sitting with her parents across the room. He tried to get her attention, but she purposefully avoided him, sometimes smiling and pretending to look at someone nearby. Sam was enthralled by the beautiful, gifted young woman who shared the same passions he held so dear.

Bache continued, "But who was Benjamin Lay? What did he look like? What made him unique? Fortunately, we have a portrait painted by the famous William Williams, who also painted George Washington. Again, Papa was instrumental in bringing Lay and William Williams together. Fred, if you will, please."

Reverend Simpson paraded around the room with a copy of the painting.

"As you can see," Bache said, "Benjamin Lay was a unique individual physically. He was no more than 4 feet 5 inches tall with spindly legs that didn't seem to be capable of supporting his upper body. That would make him about as tall as this young man right here," and Bache indicated Efren Wood, standing next to the Major who towered over him by more than a foot and a half.

"He had a hunched back and a protruding chest that made him appear barrel chested, with arms that reached below his knees. His head was overly large for his body, with bug eyes and wide grey beard that lay flat on his chest, almost to his belly. He was a common site on the streets of Philadelphia in the mid seventeen hundreds. Every citizen recognized Ben Lay."

Margaret Lyon finally deemed Sam worthy of her glance and a demure smile. He nodded politely, then discretely threw her a silent kiss, which greatly embarrassed the young lady because her mother witnessed the gesture and nudged Margaret with her elbow, while frowning at Sam. He laughed but found his own mother glaring at him, so he turned his attention to Major Bache.

Bache wiped his brow as he paused, seemingly spent from the emotion of his narrative. The audience sat motionless, enthralled at the passion churning within this man so much a part of the history of the nation. Sarah and Estelle could scarcely breathe from the exertion of following the ardent anti-slavery advocate.

Reverend Simpson stepped forward and said, "Brothers and Sisters let us pause here and prepare for our afternoon meal. I believe that Major Bache could use some time to recover and we have a wonderful program planned for later. Those of you whom I spoke to before the meeting, please adjourn to my house. The rest should begin preparing the meal."

###

"I've heard 'Uncle Tom's Cabin read, and I tell you Mrs. Stowe's pen hasn't begun to paint what slavery is as I have seen it at de far South. I've seen de real thing, and I don't want to see it on no stage or in no theater." **Harriet Tubman**

Sarah and Jimmy walked briskly to Reverend Simpson's home. They were greeted by a mob of small children streaming out of the house to join their parents under the shade of the elm trees where tables had been set to accommodate the afternoon meal. Sarah and Jimmy were excited to be a part of the planned evening program and couldn't wait to meet with Major Bache to learn their parts.

Sam and Margaret were busy helping with preparations for the meal. "What do you suppose they're up to, Sam?"

"I already know what it is, Margaret. You forget that I was at Major Bache's program in Philadelphia last fall. I think you'll enjoy it; I know I did. Sarah is the perfect choice for the part she'll play. She can be quite dramatic."

"I know and Caroline is red with jealousy. She's moping about over by the well."

"I'll go see if I can cheer her up," Sam said. "She should be in the play; I know they have a part for her."

Esther Wood had been up early frying chicken, preparing for the picnic. Beulah brought her famous apple and berry pies, not to be outdone by Elizabeth Lyons biscuits, fresh fruits, steamed and fried beans. Each family contributed food or drink to the festivities with lemonade and tea in abundance. The men helped to some extent but mainly discussed politics or farming.

"Bill, I understand that Sam is going to accompany you to Washington next month."

"We plan to learn as much as we can about the new slave law. By the way, David, have you read the newspaper accounts of Frederick Douglass? He spoke in Columbus and I hear that he makes a powerful speaker. His descriptions of the brutality are almost beyond belief."

"There are those who accuse him of being a fraud and believe those eloquent words are spoon fed to him by William Lloyd Garrison," David said.

"Exactly the stuff that Major Bache points out. The slaveholders promote this lie that Africans are ignorant and incapable of independent thought and actions. An intelligent, free-thinking slave doesn't fit the story the South needs to maintain their grip on the slaves. Yet we know Douglass' tale is true because all of his accusations can be verified. Sam and I will be able to attend one of his lectures in Washington."

"I believe that Sam is going to propose to Margaret. Has he discussed it with you?"

"I'm not sure 'discussed' is the right word. What he said is, 'I'm going to marry your daughter, Mr. Lyon. I hope that you will come to accept me as part of your family.' But Elizabeth and I couldn't be happier. He's a fine young man. I'm sure we'll discuss it further on the trip to Washington."

After their meal, Sam and Margaret strolled, arm in arm around the church grounds, out to the road, then down by the stream that flowed to the river. Their conversation always seemed to revolve around their shared passions of freeing the slaves and getting the vote for women.

"I'm tired of being dismissed as too young or inexperienced to be a legitimate political candidate. Margaret, did you hear what Beebee said about me?"

"No Dear, I haven't heard that story. I can't believe there's one I missed during the past three wonderful weeks," She playfully tweaked his ear.

"I only talk about my favorite subject, which is you and me. Anyway, he said that he wouldn't debate such weighty issues with me because I'm only a nonprofessional farmer and he's a lawyer. Can you believe that?"

"Well, at least he didn't say anything about your age, dear."

"Margaret, it isn't funny."

"What are you going to do?"

"As soon as we're married, I'm going to study the law and get admitted to the bar. I'll set the record for the fastest law student in history, because I'll have you by my side making me the happiest man in history," he kissed her hand while she blushed.

The decision to marry was forgone, at least in Sam's mind, but he planned a formal proposal when he returned from

Washington. His love for the beautiful young woman was evident in his every glance and caress. He could scarce keep his hand from her arm or around her waist. Sam Wood had never felt such passion for another human and it seemed to him that Margaret felt the same.

The dogs began barking and raced to the lane where a group of riders approached but stopped before entering the church grounds. Reverend Simpson and Major Bache stepped out of the parsonage to check the commotion.

David Wood yelled, "Stephan, call off the dogs."

Stephan ran to John and Adams, "Sit!" he commanded. Stephan knelt down to scratch their ears while he watched the men confront each other in the drive.

"Gentlemen," Bache greeted them, "What is your business on this fine spring day?"

"Niggers is our business and I see a bunch of em' yonder in them trees. We'll be checkin' for they passes or papers."

Reverend Simpson bristled at the impunity. "You'll do no such thing. Get off this land and I mean now. This is church ground and I won't have you desecrate it with your blasphemy."

David and Sam joined the Reverend as did most of the other men. They outnumbered the Slavers' by a large margin.

"My name is Elijha Wilson and…."

"We know who you are," Sam interrupted him. "You heard the Reverend, now do as he says. We don't want any trouble."

"That's him, Mr. Wilson. That's the one whupped Ike," Clem pointed.

"You got to be shittin' me, that little runt done fer Ike that way. Why, I've a mind to take the bullwhip to him right now, by God. You Goddamned Quakers, we used to burn your kind in Pennsylvania. Nigger-luvin' bastards, yer gonna' ruin this country, hell, if it was up to you we'd be takin orders from the Niggers and lettin' women run the gov'ment."

Sam walked slowly to Wilson, looked up at him and said, "We don't have your slaves, don't know where they are either. Those people you see are all free men and women, most of them born right here in Ohio. Now, I know you're mad, but this is not the way to deal with the matter. I'm going to Washington in six weeks and to be fair I will give my word to come to Clarksburg and meet you anywhere you would like."

"Why you little turd, you won't come to Clarksburg in a month of Sundays."

"Clem, I'm a man of my word, am I not? Didn't I do exactly what I said I would after I warned Ike of the consequences?"

Clem didn't answer, just shrugged at Elijah Wilson who had turned to look at him. Wilson seemed to weigh the odds of his three men arrayed against the dozens of able-bodied men now forming around him. He leaned down and said to Sam, "If I don't see you within two months, I'm coming back here for you, understand?"

Sam reached out his hand in a gesture of agreement, but Wilson reigned his horse around and rode off without a backward glance.

"Sam, you really going to Clarksburg to meet that man?" Stephan asked.

"Mainly I was giving him a way to save face. Don't know what I'm gonna' do about that promise but I expect I'll keep it, Stevie. Man's reputations' only as good as his word.

###

"Enslaved men, Plow, sow, thresh, and winnow, split Rails, cut Wood, clear Land, make Ditches and Fences, fodder Cattle, run and fetch up the Horses. Enslaved women face all the Drudgery in Dairy and Kitchen, within doors and without. These grinding labors are contrasted with the idleness of the slave owners—the growling, empty bellies of the enslaved and the lazy Ungodly bellies of their masters. Worse, slave

keepers perpetuate this inequality by leaving these workers as property to proud, Dainty, Lazy, Scornful, Tyrannical and often beggarly Children for them to Domineer." **A quote from Benjamin Lay in his pamphlet, All Slave-Keepers That Keep the Innocent in Bondage, Apostates.**

Picnic over and the dogs resettled, everyone returned to the Meeting House for the main event. A play! Something so unusual that even the young children were allowed to attend. Pre-printed play bills were passed among the church members who waited for the performance to begin. The prospects of a dramatic reenactment created a buzz of excitement. Major Bache hurried about making final preparations for the production that he had written and directed. Because of the short time for rehearsal, each part was written on scripts that the actors could read, if need be. The actors themselves were as nervous as new mothers.

The play utilized church members to portray the characters from the 1750's. Ben Lay was one of the first to use social protest to draw attention to the hypocrisy of Quaker Elders owning slaves. Benjamin, as portrayed by Efran Wood, stood outside the large meeting hall with his bare leg stuck in a snow drift to symbolize the poorly clad slaves working in the fields, while their masters enjoyed the warmth of the Church.

At the end of the first act, seven-year-old Carl Wood stood between his mother and father and shouted to Efren, as he exited the meeting room, "Efren, you said some bad words, you said damn."

"Mother, please control your son," Efren begged, as he blushed under his Benjamin Lay disguise.

Esther turned to her husband with a look of consternation, not knowing whether to chastise Carl or Efren. David said, "Well, it is a good play, but a bit intense, my dear. Carl, best not bother your brother while he's performing. I think he's doing a good job on such short notice, don't you?"

"I think Efren may be getting stage-struck. He needs to mind his manners, not to mention watch his language," Esther countered.

David avoided the issue by turning his attention to narrator Bache who was returning for the next act.

###

"In every man's mind the good seeds of liberty are planted, and he who brings his fellow down so low, as to make him contented with a condition of slavery, commits the highest crime against God and man."
Henry Highland Garnett, Former Slave

"Benjamin Lay was a brave man wasn't he Sam?" Stephan said.

"Beyond brave, Stephan. He was fearless. He had firsthand knowledge of the atrocities being committed against the slaves. Slaveholders make it seem the slaves are content and happy while they assault the women, brutalize the men and live off the labors of both. What a travesty. I'm appalled that it still goes on today over a hundred years later."

"We saw that for ourselves, didn't we Sam, with that slave girl, Jinny? I wonder what happened to her."

"I haven't heard anything. If they'd been captured, we would hear about it. I believe they made it to Canada."

"I hope they made it....," Stephan rattled on about something, but Sam's gaze had strayed across the room and he scarce heard the words let alone contemplated the meaning. Margaret seemed to have a glow about her, emanating from a radiant smile and brilliant blue eyes, a white bonnet framed her face like a painting. Sam felt a fever of desire that was almost a burden, but one that he couldn't wrap up and stow in his room, where it could be ignored until he had need for it. It wasn't that simple, this first love, so different from the attractions of adolescence. Sam was not a child but a full-grown man with the passions of his sex and to realize suddenly that he was at the beginning of a great adventure shared with another human gave him a warm glow to match the warmth from Margaret. He glanced around the room at his family and friends, content in who he was and where he was going.

Nana Mosher, his maternal grandmother, was watching him closely, he nodded and smiled. Nana was his favorite grandparent because he spent a great deal of time with her and Papa Asa Mosher in their home near Ripley, which was also a stop on the Underground Railroad. His mind drifted to an afternoon in the late winter of 1838, Sam was thirteen, Stephan was eight, and Sarah six, when Esther took them to Nana and Papa's home where they found a black woman and her small daughter, about two years old.

A group of local activists sat in Nana's living room with the large, dark skinned, buxomous lady, who shared her harrowing story with them. Her master was going to separate them, the mother destined for Georgia, and the daughter…, well there was no describing the mother's anguish. She recalled dashing through the Kentucky night, freezing cold, with the little girl in her arms, fleeing from the slave catchers hired by her owner. She expected to find the Ohio River frozen, only to discover the river broken and ice chunks banging and clunking against each other. Rather than let the slave hunters catch her, she dashed into the river leaping from ice flow to ice flow. She fell into the icy water, emerged choking and gasping for air, and pushed the baby onto a chunk of ice. Somehow, she pulled herself up and bounded, dangerously, to the other side.

No one would have believed it had she not been observed by a local farmer, Mose Robinson, who was astonished at what he witnessed, and bundled her off to John Rankin's house where he knew she would be sheltered. Reverend Rankin was in Grandma Mosher's house that day and verified the events as described. It was he who brought the woman and child to the Mosher's because the bounty hunters were on his doorstep even at that moment. There were others present, including Professor Calvin Stowe and his wife, Harriet Beecher Stow, Sam's cousin, Salmon Chase, Sam's parents, and several other anti-slavery activists. Sam was profoundly moved by this narrative and vowed at that moment to do what he could to end slavery.

Efren, in his Benjamin Lay costume, was standing in the door waiting for the next act. Sam's thoughts turned to the brave little man, who over a hundred years ago stood up for what he knew to be right. Little had changed, and just across the river, at that very moment, slaves were being flogged beyond endurance by their white masters. Sam felt that he would burst with anger as he ground his teeth and gripped the bench with both hands saying aloud, "By God, I'll end it, or I'll die trying."

"What Sam, what do you mean?" Stephan was shaking his brother trying to understand. "What are you talking about? You're scaring mother."

Sam regained his senses to see Esther watching him in horror. "Die trying what?" she exclaimed.

###

And, dear sisters, in a country where women are degraded and brutalized, and where their exposed persons bleed under the lash-- where they are sold in the shambles of "negro brokers"-- robbed of their hard earnings-- torn from their husbands, and forcibly plundered of their virtue and their offspring; surely in such a country, it is very natural that women should wish to know "the reason why"-- especially when these outrages of blood and nameless horror are practiced in violation of the principles of our Constitution. We do not, then, and cannot concede the position, that because this is a political subject woman ought to fold their hands in idleness and close their eyes and ears to the "horrible things" that are practiced in our land. **Lucretia Mott**

August 15, 1848
Washington, D. C.

My Dearest Margaret:

I just received your letter dated the sixth. I treasure the knowledge that you held it in your hands not more than ten days ago. Just thinking of you gives me the second greatest pleasure I have ever known—the first is, of course, being with you, even if just holding your hand and sharing the pleasure of your touch. You write that your love grows stronger in our absence and that gives me great comfort as I feel the same. I can scarcely breathe when I think of the times that I held you in my arms, and I shudder at the thought that it can't be again in the next moment. The only thing that keeps me from rushing home is the knowledge that what we do here will have an impact on our world for as long as our Republic exists.

We're staying at the Frenchman's Hotel on fourth and F Street, just off Pennsylvania Avenue. Not the best accommodations, but not bad. There is a House of Prostitution behind us, but the patrons of that establishment do not come through this property.

Margaret, I wish you could be here because this must be the most exciting time in all of history. Construction is underway on almost every building including the Capitol, the Smithsonian Institution, the Patent Office and the new monument for General Washington. The town is full of abolitionists; Frederick Douglass, Harriet Tubman, Sojourner Truth, William Lloyd Garrison, Susan B. Anthony, James and Lucretia Mott, (be sure to tell mother they send their love and look forward to seeing you all in October). Professor and Harriet Stowe were here yesterday but they left to return to Brunswick this morning. She is writing a book about slavery and reminded me of a meeting she and I shared in 1838 with a slave woman who ran across the frozen Ohio

River with her child. She's going to include that adventure in the book.

We visited Stephen Douglas and then Henry Clay yesterday. Their Compromise Act will be passed next year and slave trading will be outlawed in the District (but not slavery itself). We have a chance of defeating it if James Polk can maintain his hold on the government, but I have my doubts. I believe that Zachary Taylor will be elected in '49', and that will help. We have no leadership at the top level of Government so the Fugitive Slave Act will be strengthened and that is the worst part of the entire matter. Slave hunters will be paid a bounty for every slave that they return, and it will be a crime, even in Ohio, for aiding a runaway slave. We will have to act with great care in what we do but I for one will not be cowed by this new law and I know that you agree with me, my love.

It breaks my heart, the atrocities I witnessed traveling here. The nearby communities are full of slaves and they toil ceaselessly in the fields under the supervision of the cruelest class of men I have ever met. They are called overseers. The man that I struck with my ax handle, Ike, is a specimen of this category.

Today a program of lectures from the abolitionists and then dinner tonight with the Mott's. We are meeting them at the City Tavern on Wisconsin at M Street. Your father is leaving tomorrow so I send this letter with him. I will be home in a week or ten days as classes will begin and my students will be waiting anxiously for me (I am being facetious, of course.) I glory in the thought that we will be married and then together for the rest of our lives. My heart leaps at the thought and I can't wait to begin our new adventure as Mr. and Mrs. Samuel Wood.

I remain always, faithfully yours, Sam.

He sealed the envelope and passed it to his future father-in-law who promised to see that it reached its destination safely. Bill had purchased a new horse and was riding back to Ohio, leaving the next day. Mr. Lyon was under the impression that Sam would be returning home within that time, but Sam had other plans, specifically, to detour through Clarksville and fulfill his promise to the Wilsons. He relished the opportunity of venturing into the enemy camp and dealing with the slave owners on their own turf.

That evening, Sam and Bill walked to the City Tavern for dinner with the Mott's. The air was humid and still quite warm. The streets of Washington were rapidly improving and there were new board sidewalks down F Street and brick sidewalks on Pennsylvania Avenue. Lucretia Mott was a best friend to Esther Wood, having known each other since childhood. In October, Lucretia was attending the Ohio Women's Rights Convention in Mt. Gilead, as keynote speaker.

The evening was pleasant enough and the tavern full as a result of all of the activity in the city. They discussed the events of the day and especially the speech by Frederick Douglass who was fast becoming the most popular anti-slavery speaker on the circuit. That meant, of course, that he was a curse to the pro-slavery group and had a target on his back. He kept his location a secret while south of the free states. Lucretia had spoken just after him, so she had a full house for her very well received lecture.

Suddenly the four guests were interrupted by a drunk who addressed himself to Lucretia from an adjoining table. He did so by waving a bible and saying to his dining companions loudly enough so that Mrs. Mott and her friends could hear, "Women who speak in public are harlots, I tell you. It is against the Lord's will and I cannot keep my peace about it when I am forced to sit in the very presence of such a promiscuous woman." Sam and Bill were slow to recognize that the man was speaking about Lucretia. He continued by reading from the bible, loudly, to the entire room, which had grown quiet, "I quote from First Timothy, 'a woman should learn in quietness and full submission. I do not permit a woman to teach or to assume authority over a man, she must be quiet. For Adam was formed first, then Eve. And Adam was not the one deceived.' How can it be any clearer, Lucretia Mott...."

Bill Lyon sat open mouthed as Lucretia closed her eyes and bowed her head. But Sam, when he realized what was happening, stood up, reached out and snatched the bible from the dumbstruck man, and said, "One more word from you and I will drag you out of this room, you drunken lout."

"Sir that is Reverend Martin Woodbine of the Congregational Church. You cannot...."

"ONE MORE word out of any of you and I will drag you all by the scruff of your necks, one at a time, if no one will help me."

"I'll help, by God," Bill Lyon stood up.

"As will I," James Mott announced. "And I," said a stranger, and then another, as more and more gentlemen stood.

The Reverend's wife took the bible from Sam, grabbed her husband's hand and dragged him and their friends from the room which was quiet except for the footfalls of their exit. Then, as if nothing had happened, everyone sat and continued with their meal.

"Thank you, gentlemen," Lucretia nodded to each. "It happens more often than one would think, but less and less as time goes on. I long for the day when men and women will be equal, in reality, not just in the eyes of God." They resumed their conversation with a feeling of excitement from the encounter. In fact, the entire dining room seemed charged with electricity. Sam was glad to see so many come to the aid of the famous abolitionist; he felt that the movement was gaining momentum and would eventually carry the day.

Bill Lyon said, "I fear that this new law will create a stronger Southern resolve even though they want to admit California as a free state, it's so far away and so difficult to reach that it's of no help to us. The new state of Texas will be free to decide if they are a slave state or not.

"I agree with you Bill," James Mott answered, "My guess is that Utah and New Mexico will vote to be free states because there aren't any large plantations and the soil is not conducive to agriculture to the extent they need the slaves."

Mr. Lyon continued, "But it's the unorganized territories in the Missouri Compromise that worry me. If Kansas and Nebraska become slave states all will be lost, and, believe me, those Ruffians from Missouri will do everything in their power to see that they are slave states. Mark my words, in a few years there will be bloodshed…."

"Excuse me gentlemen and Mrs. Mott," a tall man with flowing locks of dark brown hair and penetrating blue eyes addressed them. He was broad of shoulder and had a commanding presence that made Sam think he had met him somewhere. Then he realized who it was and before the man could continue, Sam rose and greeted him enthusiastically, "Mr. Dana, what a pleasure, sir."

"No, the pleasure is mine. I very much enjoyed your conversation with the Right Reverend Woodbine, who is becoming a thorn in the side of all true thinking men…., and women," with a bow and acknowledgement of Lucretia. "I wanted to find out the name of the gentleman who handled the situation so deftly."

"Sam Wood, sir, from Mt. Gilead, Ohio, and a great admirer of your writing and your social activism. May I present my future father-in-law, Mr. Bill Lyon. Bill, this is Richard Henry Dana, attorney and originator of the Free-Soil Party AND author of "Two Years Before the Mast", one of my favorite novels."

"Oh, my, Mr. Dana, what a pleasure," Bill said rising to his feet. "I have most certainly read your wonderful book."

"My pleasure, Mr. Lyon and I already know Mr. and Mrs. Mott. So good to see you again, James. I very much enjoyed your speech today, Lucretia. Mr. Wood, I believe that I recently heard tell of another of your adventures several weeks ago. I was talking to Harriet Tubman and she recounted a story about a wagon load of slaves fleeing in broad daylight under the very noses of the bounty hunters. Wasn't your name mentioned in that exquisite tale?"

"If it was, then most certainly the details were exaggerated beyond my small role," Sam laughed.

"Well, it's fortunate that we meet because I want to enlist your aide in representing the Free-Soil Party in Ohio. I know that you've been a Liberty Party spokesman and we need your support in the elections in 52'."

"And you shall have it, Mr. Dana."

"Please, call me Richard and stop by my hotel tomorrow. I'm at the Freemont on Jersey. We can discuss it further."

###

"I was the conductor of the Underground Railroad for eight years, and I can say what most conductors can't say — I never ran my train off the track and I never lost a passenger." **Harriet Tubman at a suffrage convention, NY, 1896.**

The next morning Sam accompanied Bill to the livery where his new horse was being boarded prior to the trip back to Ohio. The rough, plain building was north of the hotel and comprised a large enough lot for several corrals in addition to the stalls in the livery itself.

"Where are you planning to stay tonight?" Sam asked.

"Probably at the hotel in Leesburg. I want to get to the ferry early or I won't be home Saturday."

"This has been a wonderful trip, Bill. I look forward to seeing you back home in a short time. Give my love to Margaret and the rest of the family and when you see Father, fill him in on our visits with Senators Clay and Douglas. I plan on visiting Richard

Dana after you leave. I know that he'll be a tremendous help to us in Ohio."

The goodbyes over, Bill Lyon rode down F Street toward Jersey Avenue. Sam turned to the stable hand and said, "I need to get to Clarksburg, Virginia. Is there a stage heading west?"

"I don't know about that, but I do know Burton's freight wagons are going that way later today. You can probably ride with them."

"Where's their office?"

"Right behind us, those are some of their animals over there," he indicated six large mules in a corral.

Sam hurried around the building and found the entrance to the freight office on G Street. A large sign over the door announced: Burton's Freight Line. A beefy, red faced lady wearing dirty coveralls and heavy boots sat behind the counter arguing with a local merchant.

"Now, Arnie, I told you, we wouldn't be responsible for packing those dishes. Your man in Baltimore packed them, we just hauled them from the train station. Not our fault that some of them got cracked."

"Cracked, hell," the merchant yelled. "They're all broken to pieces. Can't use a damn single plate or saucer of em."

"I ain't arguin' with ya, Arnie. Read the damn contract, it says right there that we ain't responsible for the packing."

"Highway robbery, by God. I'm getting my attorney and we're gonna' shut you down, by God. This is an outrage, by God," he stammered and stormed out past Sam.

"What can I help you with, stranger?" she asked, as cheerful as if she just came from a picnic.

"He seems to be on close terms with God," Sam laughed.

"Oh, Arnie screams and hollers, but he knows I'm right. Hell, he's family. He's married to Burton's sister."

"I take it Burton is the owner?"

"Yep!"

"And are you Mrs. Burton?"

She laughed raucously, slapping the counter with the flat of her hand, not once but twice, "Oh Lordy, that's one for the books. Nope, I'm one of the teamsters. Burton, he owns the business here and he's married to a rough old gal from Georgia. But he's taken with her, so don't let im' hear ya say nuthin' crude bout' her. Now, what can I do ya for?"

Sam couldn't imagine any woman rougher than the one he was looking at, but he felt it best to move on, "I'm interested in getting to Clarksburg and I understand you're taking a load of freight that way. Could I purchase passage with you?"

"Well, you're in luck and it might not cost you a nickel. Burton needs someone to deliver a brougham to a buyer in Wellington and that ain't far from Clarksburg. You could probably get them to take you on into town. Here comes Burton, let's see what he says."

A mostly bald man entered, with bushy red beard and a smile with gaps in the teeth, but a smile easily given with no pretense. He walked straight to Sam and put his hand out in greeting, while the counter lady told him what Sam wanted. Grinning widely, he welcomed him with gusto, declaring that it was Sam doing him the favor. When he discovered Sam's full name, he declared that Sam would have the use of one of his riding horses.

"Why didn't you say that you're a brother of Tobias Wood? He's one of my best customers over in Wheeling," he said, still shaking Sam's hand. "You drive the new brougham to the Smithson farm and trail a saddle horse, then when you're done with the horse take it to Toby's and we'll pick it up when we deliver his dry goods."

"Done, and I'm much obliged to you, Mr. Burton."

"Now, Sam…., Burton's my first name, and since we're

almost kin you call me Burton, and don't be shy bout' askin' for nothin'. We'll get you to Clarksburg and you remember my name to all your friends and neighbors. That's called word-o-mouth, Sam. Good for bidness, you understand."

"I do understand, Burton and consider it done. Now, when do we leave?"

"Well, I reckon you can leave soons' I get the buggy ready and you gather you some provisions for the trip. It'll take you three days and you'll need to stay at the Inn in Jonestown and then Marion. They set a right nice table and the beds'r fairly clean. Sally'll take care o' the horses. Do you know the canal and rail systems twixt here and there?"

"I do know my way around, Burton. We won't have any trouble. Trouble is one thing I always avoid. Let me get my satchel and a few items from the market and I'm ready to go. Who am I delivering the brougham to?"

"Not to worry, Sam, I'm gonna' send Sally with you and she'll ride the draft horse back. She's a good Nigger gal, knows the animals well, and won't cause you no problem. The Niggers along the way will put her up so's ya don't hafta worry bout' her none and she knows where she's a goin, plus she's got all her papers."

After meeting Mr. Dana, Sam left from the freight shippers office about 12 a.m. with Sally riding in the back seat of the shiny new brougham. The fancy conveyance had all the newest comforts, black with mahogany trim, and a black canvas cover. They followed F Street to Massachusetts, then north to follow the Leesburg Pike northwest and veer due west instead of going to the Cumberland Road. They crossed the Potomac at Long's Bridge and made good time dodging the occasional rider and some foot traffic.

The extravagant buggy didn't rate a second glance in the fast-growing city, full of landed gentry as well as common laborers. Washington, D.C. was quickly replacing Philadelphia as the seat of government and beginning to rival Baltimore and Boston as an important business port. Farm wagons loaded with fresh produce made their way to the market at Jersey and F Streets. The noise of teamsters shouting, horses and mules laboring, workers of all description hammering, yelling and going about the business of shaping the nation's capital. It was a bustling city that Sam and Sally departed. They met many riders, walkers and wagons, of all description, as they reached the turnpike. When they left the hustle and bustle behind, Sam tried to engage Sally in conversation, but found that she was reluctant to share much with him.

"My name is Sam Wood. I'm pleased to be traveling with you."

"Yas' suh." She answered.

He glanced back and couldn't tell much because she was huddled in the corner, but she did appear young.

"Burton must trust you completely with his horses. How old are you, Sally?"

"Don't rightly know, suh."

"Didn't your mother tell you how old you are?"

"Never really knew her, suh."

"Haven't you ever wondered how old you are," Sam persisted?

"I studied on it, one'st," she said then fell silent again.

"Well, what did you decide?"

"I's maybe 16 or 17, maybe 15."

"How did you arrive at those numbers, you can count, can't you?"

"I kin count tolerable well but I cain't read. My friend, George, he members dat he were five when I was born and he's 21 or 22 now, so I reasoned it out, dat a way, but George's a bit slow so I ain't fer sure."

"Where's your mother?"

"De Missus make Massa Clay sell her down de river tu Georgia. She mos' likely daid now cause field Niggers doan last long in Georgia."

"You mean that your owner is Henry Clay the Senator?"

"Yas'suh,"

Sam decided to stop, rest the horses, and take some lunch when they reached the bridge at Difficult Run. Sally leapt from the buggy and expertly unhitched the draft horse calling, it by name, Bear, and staking him in the meadow where he could reach the stream. Sally then tended to the saddle horse, named Felix. There was enough grass in the meadow to let the horses graze while Sam refreshed himself, taking off his shirt and washing his face in the cool river. Sally sat under a Mahogany Tree enjoying the shade. Sam finished his ablutions and took a box of provisions to the tree and sat next to Sally. She watched him warily.

"Apple, Sally?" he offered.

She hesitated but then accepted his offer, "Thank you, suh."

"You sure are an expert in caring for horses, Sally."

"Yas' suh, I likes horses and de mules and de oxen. Dey mo' friendlier dan de people."

Sam laughed, "And a lot less trouble, I expect. Sally, I'm curious, if you are owned by Senator Clay, why do you work for Burton?"

"Cause' Massa Clay hire me out cause' there ain't nough' work for me at his house in Washington."

"I see, and how much do you earn working for Burton?"

"Two dollar a week," she said proudly.

"What do you do with all that money?"

"Why, I gives it to Massa Clay, suh, ever nickel of it, I swear."

Sam could tell she was concerned that he was accusing her of something, but he was confused by her answer.

"Why do you give it to Clay?"

Sally hesitated, mixed up, in turn, by Sam's question. "Cause' he own me," she said in a manner more question than answer.

"So, if your master hires you out to someone, you give the money you earn to him and don't keep it yourself. Is that the way it works for all slaves?"

"I spect' so! Don't rightly know for sure, only know dat de way it work for Massa' Clay," she said with finality.

"Doesn't it bother you that you do the work but the money goes to him?"

Again, she was confused, "No, suh it doan bother me, cause' he my Massa'."

Sam handed Sally some dried beef and biscuits which she took without comment. They filled their water bags and re-hitched the horses, at least Sally did. She wouldn't think of Sam helping. The horses were her responsibility and she held the office in high regard. Sam was intrigued with the pretty young slave. There was a story here, he felt certain. One that could be exploited to the advantage of the abolitionist cause, to the detriment of the slaveholders who were marketing their actions as being beneficial to the Africans, the economy and the country.

"Sally," he began hesitatingly, "I suppose that you've always been a slave. Is that correct?"

"Yas, suh, I's born to it."

This encouraged Sam somewhat, being more than a two-syllable response seemed to him to be progress in their social intercourse. "Have you ever thought of what it might be like to not be a slave?"

"No, suh, why would I think of such a thing as dat, when I already is a slave?" She said this with such a philosophical finality that Sam had to rethink his tactics.

"Well, do you know who Harriet Tubman is?"

"No, suh."

"How about Sojourner Truth or William Lloyd Garrison?"

"No, Suh, I don't know none o' dem. Is dey slaves too?"

"No, Harriet and Sojourner were slaves, but they aren't now. Today they are free. Have you heard of Frederick Douglass?"

At the mention of Douglass' name Sally went silent. They rode for a few miles in this manner until Sam looked back to see if she had fallen asleep, but she was eyeing him nervously.

"What is it Sally, do you know him?"

"I heard o' him, Mr. Sam. Is you tryin' to git me into trouble? I doan' want no trouble, suh."

"Not at all, Sally. I was just curious about your situation. I want to see all the slaves freed. I work with those people I mentioned because I am an abolitionist. In fact, I met with Richard Henry Dana just this morning to discuss expanding the Free-Soil Party in Ohio and even further West. We want to ensure that slavery is abolished forever in these United States."

He turned to see if she was listening and found her cowering in the corner.

"I doan' want no trouble, Mr. Sam."

"Haven't you ever thought of being free? Don't you want to escape to the north and live free like humans are supposed to live?"

"No, Suh," she sobbed. What bout George? Who look arter him? He jus' a simple boy and need someone tu help him. What bout Bear n' Felix an' de other animals? Who take care o' dem? I doan' know nothin' bout no nort' and don't know nobody. You shouldn't say things like dat tu me, Mr. Sam. Massa' Burton and Clay, dey be mighty upset if dey hear bout dis bidness' you preachin'."

Sam smiled to himself at this outburst and could tell that she had indeed thought of the matter and the mention of Frederick Douglass had touched a nerve. He vowed to help her in some way, but he wasn't certain what that might be, "Well then, my friend Sally, we shall say nothing more of this matter."

"I waren't sayin' nufin' ta'll bout de matter no how," she announced firmly, crossing her arms and glaring at Sam.

###

"The matter came up for judicial investigation, but as might have been expected, the white people concluded it was unnecessary to wait the result of the investigation—that it was preferable to hang the accused first and try him afterward." **Ida B Wells, 1862-1931**

There was little conversation the remainder of the trip to the Inn at Jonestown, a small community on a crossroads that was destined to be forever not much more than what it was at that point in time, due to its location bereft of rail or navigable waterway. But the Inn was comfortable and there was a sizeable community of slaves owned by various small farmers and businessmen. The Negroes seemed to know Sally and she disappeared with the horses and buggy before Sam knew what was happening, but he didn't worry since Burton had given those very instructions.

He entered the hotel through the dining room where a group of local citizens was eating and three rough looking men at the bar drinking. They eyed Sam, who carried his satchel and his ax handle which he used as a cane. He had begun going everywhere with it and enjoyed the feeling of security and the glances from coarse fellows such as these. He engaged a room for the evening, took his satchel up and retired to the bar for a lemonade. The men were gone by the time he returned.

"What's the main crop grown around here?" Sam asked the bartender, just for the pleasure of something to say.

"Don't know much about it. Only what I hear from the farm hands that come in. I think they grow a lot of produce that they haul east. Like apples and lettuce and such."

"That makes sense. I haven't seen many large farms. Most of them look pretty small."

Before they could continue their conversation, a racket of crying voices and screams was heard from outside. Sam ran to find the cause of the ruckus, as did the bartender. Across from the Inn was a vacant field with a stand of maple and mulberry trees. The three men from the bar were gathered around a Negro man preparing to hang him from a branch of a sugar maple tree.

"Hey, what's going on here?" Sam yelled.

A group of slaves had gathered around Sally on the ground, her dress torn, and her breasts exposed, her mouth bloody. He turned to the men and said, "What are you doing?"

"What do it look like? We fixin' tu hang this Nigger."

"Why?"

The men looked at each other, then looked at Sally. The largest man, a gruff, bearded man with dirty hands said, "Cause he's a' uppity Nigger. Got a' attitude. He interfered with our bidness'."

"No, suh, I was jus' tryin' to hep Sally," the old man said.

"Shut yo' mouth, Nigger," the man with the rope hit him in the stomach with his fist.

"Ok, I've seen enough. There won't be any hanging and I believe that you men were molesting this young girl. Now let that man go."

The bounty hunters all stared at Sam while he leaned against his cane looking every bit like a northern dandy, with his broad brimmed hat and fancy boots, something these men did not respect. They laughed at him.

"Now, Mister, you just wait till we're done here then you can have your turn with the Nigger gal, sorta' sloppy seconds," one of them said.

"More like sloppy fourths," another joked, and they laughed again.

"Gentlemen, I won't repeat myself a third time. Let him go and leave town right now or I will be forced to take action and believe me you won't like it. Leave while you can."

"You startin' to piss me off you Nigger-lovin' bastard. They's somethin' funny about you anyway. Now bugger off fore I cut you up," the man closest to Sam said, as he pulled a large knife from a sheath in his pants. Sam swung the ax handle and smashed the man across his nose, breaking it and several teeth in the process. He fell unconscious to the ground.

Startled though he was, the second man reached for his rifle which was propped against another tree. Sam took two strides and broke his arm with a mighty swing of the cane. He then smashed the right knee before he even knew his arm was broken. He fell, screaming in pain. The third ruffian stood gap-mouthed still holding the old man, finally he said, "You kilt' Herman."

Sam looked at the unconscious man and said, "Maybe not. I think he's still breathing, but you should get him to a doctor. Where's your sheriff?"

"Right here." It was one of the men who had been eating in the hotel when Sam arrived.

"Why didn't you do something, sheriff? You saw what those men were about to do."

"There were three of them."

"Do you know this man?" Sam indicated the old man who was about to be hanged.

"Yes, I do. Known him all my life."

"Is he a troublemaker or criminal?"

"No. Lawrence is a fine person."

"Yet you just stood there while this crime was being committed. Shame on you. Now then," Sam said turning back to the third man. "Where are you from?"

"Leesburg."

"Why are you here?"

"Lookin' for runaway slaves. We collect the bounty."

"Get your horses right now."

While the man went to get the horses, Sam knelt down to Sally and helped her to her feet. A grandmotherly type stepped up and said, "I'll take her and get her cleaned up."

Sam leaned down to the unconscious man and felt in his pockets. He found a silver dollar, which he gave to the woman, and told her to buy Sally a new dress. Sam looked at the sheriff who shrugged as if to say, 'none of my business.'

"Help me tie this man to his horse," Sam instructed the sheriff when the horses were produced. He ordered the able-bodied man to help the invalid with the broken bones onto his saddle. Amidst much moaning and carrying on, Sam reflected that tying men to horses was becoming a common thing in his life.

"I am Sam Wood. You tell these men my name, you got that?" he instructed. "You tell them, and if I hear of you mistreating another slave, I will find you and by all that is Holy I will bring down the wrath of the Lord upon your heads. Do you understand?"

The man nodded affirmatively.

"Do you believe me?"

"I surely do, mister. I hope I never see you again, but if I do, I will have a gun in my hand." He rode off into the night, leading the other horses, searching for a doctor.

Sam prepared to check on Sally, but they all disappeared, except for the sheriff. He and Sam returned to the hotel where Sam sat at a table, still shaken by the encounter. His mind wandered to Margaret and his brothers and sisters. Trouble was brewing and he appeared to be causing a good deal of it, yet he felt vindicated by his actions, knowing that they were justified. Still he couldn't help worrying that his loved ones might suffer on his account. It was vanity that he tell the criminals his name and insist that they acknowledge him. Sam was worried, not for his actions but for what might result from them.

"I don't like this much," the sheriff said. "Those men might come back and take out their revenge on us and you'll be gone."

"You should have stood up to them, sheriff. We can't allow these ruffians to run rough shod over us."

"Well, they are just Niggers. That wench probably offered herself for a dime or a quarter. It ain't like they got any feelings. I don't understand why you made such a big deal of the whole thing."

Sam tried to control his anger. He breathed deeply and closed his eyes trying to conjure up an image of his beloved Margaret, but all he could see was the crying, cowering Sally, bloody on the ground, and the sneering men who would have violated her if it wouldn't have been for his actions.

Sam snarled, "Did it look to you like Sally had no feelings when she was laying on the ground, bleeding and crying? Did it look to you like that old man was ready to die? He had more guts in his little finger than you've got in your entire body. Get away from me."

The Sheriff turned and walked away without a word. Sam followed him to the door. The bartender was behind the bar, and a couple of local farmhands were having a whiskey. Sam could see the old black man standing in the lamplight from the window and he beckoned him over.

"Come inside, I'd like to talk to you," Sam said. The man entered and one of the hands at the bar said, "Hey, we don't allow Niggers' in here."

Sam turned to begin his attack, stopped short, and said under his breath, 'Sam, pick your fights.'

"Beg pardon, Mr. Sam, I didn't catch that," the man said.

"Nothing let's sit outside. I like the air better out here anyway. What is your name, sir?"

"Lawrence."

"Lawrence, I'm sorry you had to experience such a thing."

"I knew they was trouble when they first came to town, yesterday. When I tried to tell them that young Sally belonged to Senator Clay, they took exception. That's when the trouble started."

"You seem like an educated man, Lawrence."

"Yassir, I learned to read and write from Mister Jones. He own the mill on the crick and he needed me to keep track of the accounts. I been doing that for 30 some years."

"Are you a freeman?"

"Well, sir, I think I might be. Mister Jones, he told me that he set me free some years ago. Even gave me a paper says so, but I just kept on workin'. I wouldn't know where to go if I was to leave. Nobody wants an old man like me."

"How old are you, Lawrence?"

"I'm not sure, probably 70 or 75. I was born a slave in Georgia but was sold to Mister Jones when he war' a young man. He's 80 now so I must be five or ten year younger. I appreciate Mister Jones cause if I'da stayed in Georgia I'd be dead today."

"Is he good to you?"

"Yassir, he just fine. I know what you're getting at, but I never was mistreated like some o' the folk. Some of the slaves here get whipped by their Massa's but I never did, not by Mister Jones, but I did back in Georgia and it is a bad memory. It is true that probably not a good idea to educate the colored if you want em' to work as a slave. I know that when I started readin' I began to see things different. Wondered what it'd be like to be free, by then I had a wife and children and we got to stay together. Mister Jones never did try to separate us. If he would have, I might have done things different."

"How well do you know Sally?"

"She come through regular with Mister Burton or that gal

what works for him, Miss Annie. They usually stay here and rest and feed their livestock. Sally stays with me and the Missus. That was her that took Sally off for repairs."

"She doesn't know her parents."

"Oh hell, Mr. Sam. Her daddy is Senator Clay's overseer, everybody knows that. Mister Clay sent Sally's mammy off down the river cause' she didn't want her causing more trouble. You see the overseer is married to Mister Clay's sister."

"Seems to me that the overseer is the one that caused the trouble."

"Well, when it come to colored and white folk, the Nigger is always wrong...., it don't matter the circumstances. Mr. Sam, the reason I come was to thank you for what you done."

"I hope that those men don't come back. I won't be here to help you, and the sheriff is worthless in these matters."

"He a good man, but he won't step in tween' white and colored."

"Lawrence, it's been a pleasure talking with you. My goal in life is to put a stop to this ungodly slavery and I hope our paths cross again."

"You have set yourself a pretty lofty goal there, Mr. Sam. I wish you the best of luck. But I don't think I'll see it in my lifetime."

"There will be a war," Sam said. "I don't know when, but it is coming."

"You really think so?"

"I do. But not tonight. I best get to bed. Would you tell Sally that we are leaving at the crack of dawn?"

"Yassir, I will. It's been a pleasure, Mr. Sam," Lawrence extended his hand. Sam shook it gladly and watched him walk off into the night then went to bed, bypassing the saloon.

###

"The South! The poor South! God knows what will become of her." **John C. Calhoun American Politician and strong proponent of slavery, on his deathbed in 1850.**

The next morning, Sam smelled coffee as he left his room and went searching, he found it in the kitchen and helped himself. As he finished pouring, the lady who'd checked him in the night before said, "Help yourself, Mr. Wood. I was out in the hen house. Can I interest you in some ham and eggs?"

"You sure can. I didn't expect a good breakfast this morning, but I'll eat it. I'm going to go check on my horses and the buggy, make sure they're ready to go. I'll be back in just a few minutes."

"I'll bet Sally has them hitched and ready by now. She knows what to do."

As he stood on the front porch of the hotel, Sam took in the cool morning air of the awakening day. He sipped the coffee and marveled at the fine clean appearance of this village where so much ugliness had taken place just a few hours earlier.

"Hello, Mr. Sam," Sally shouted from the end of the street where she was leading Bear, already hitched to the brougham with Felix trailing. Horses and handler were ready to go.

"Good morning, Sally, how are you this morning? You're up bright and early. It looks like a good day for traveling."

"It do look like a good day and I feels fine, thank ya kindly fer askin'."

"I'm about to have some breakfast. Would you like to join me?"

"Oh, no suh, I had me a fine breakfast with Granny Johnson and she pack me some food fur de road. You take your time. I be right here."

Breakfast finished and the bills paid, Sam and Sally drove off bound for the Smithson farm. They passed the sheriff's office as he was unlocking the door. They waved in a friendly kind of way and the sheriff stared at them for a couple of beats before he finally raised his hand in a tentative goodbye. Sam and Sally had a good laugh over that.

"I don't reckon he think too highly o' you, Mr. Sam."

"I believe you're right, but that isn't anything new to me. You know, I'm getting married soon. I wish that you would come and work for me and my wife. You would be very welcome, and I know that you'll like her. We'll need someone to help when we have children. I wish you would think about it."

"I might think on it. But I doan' think Massa Clay take kindly to me jus' leavin'."

"Maybe we can work something out. Do you mind if I try?"

Sally studied it for a while before answering, "No suh, I doan mind if'n ya try. You done us all a good turn yestiday evnin' and Mr. Johnson he thinks de worl' o' you so maybe I will think on it some."

Sam watched the young girl who was riding on the driver's seat with him and he felt that she had already been thinking about it. Margaret and Sam had discussed asking Beulah to come work for them, but Mr. and Mrs. Lyon needed her, and she didn't really want to leave the farm. This might be a good solution. Sam planned to write a letter to Senator Clay that night; and he penned a short note to Margaret about the day's events.

By flat bottomed boat, a short ride on the railroad, but mostly on the Northwestern Turnpike; the travelers finally reached the Smithson farm near Grafton, Virginia. As they pulled into the yard, children, both black and white, came running to see the new conveyance. Mr. Smithson soon appeared with his wife and several slaves; they oohed and awed over the new buggy and invited Sam to stay for the night before traveling to Clarksburg, a distance of about 25 miles. He readily agreed. Sally decided to start back immediately, riding Bear straight through to the Cheat River where she was to meet Burton and the wagons. Sam had some misgivings about the young girl riding off on her own, but she seemed surprised that he was concerned. She assured him she traveled the road often and knew many people along the way, plus she had all the proper paperwork.

"I promise that you will hear from me, Sally. I mean what I said about you coming to live with us."

"I hope so Mr. Sam. I enjoyed the trip with ya. Bye now." And she was gone, with the farm dogs barking at her heels and the children running alongside; she turned at the gate and waved.

###

"What man or woman of common sense now doubts the intellectual capacity of colored people? Who does not know, that with all our efforts as a nation to crush and annihilate the mind of this portion of our race, we have never yet been able to do it?" **Angelina Grimke 1805-1879**

Sam road into Clarksburg about noon the next day. It was a dusty little town, with three saloons and five churches; a rundown hotel and a large milling operation on the river. He discovered Felix to be an excellent horse with fine stamina and a steady gait. After placing Felix in the care of the livery, he found the nearest saloon and asked for a lemonade. The bartender produced the drink, Sam turned to the seven or eight men in the room and said, "Gentlemen, I don't drink alcohol; but I would like to buy a lemonade for anyone who will join me in drinking to the end of slavery in this country, and denouncing Jonas Wilson as a slave-monger and defiler of young women."

He stood watching the men, a glass of lemonade in his left hand and the cane in his right. The room was quiet until a gentleman of average height with a thick brown beard and dark eyes, wearing a fashionable hat on his disheveled hair, stood and said, "I'll join you friend, a lemonade sounds good to me, but I don't know anything about a Jonas Wilson, we're just passing through."

A couple of men slipped out the front door while a second man joined Sam and his new friend. "I'm Sam Wood from Mt. Gilead, Ohio, and who do I have the honor of drinking a toast with."

"I am Allan Pinkerton of Chicago, Illinois and this is my partner Ed Ruker. We're on our way back from Washington. Been on a business trip and took the opportunity to see Fred Douglass' speech at the convention. I sure didn't expect to find an abolitionist in Clarksburg, Virginia. I'm proud to drink a toast and say that Ed and I are activists, ourselves, but I'm not sure why you would want to come into a saloon like this and make such a statement."

"It's a long story Mr. Pinkerton and I have a feeling it will all become clear soon enough, since those men who slipped out a few minutes ago are probably reporting to Wilson about my arrival. This is a wonderful coincidence, the very reason I was in Washington was to participate in the convention. In fact, I was at the Douglass speech and had dinner with Lucretia and James Mott that night."

"Wait a minute...., Sam Wood, we almost met you the next day. We had a meeting with Rich Dana at seven before we hit the road and you were meeting him later in the morning. He wanted us to wait, but we needed to get going because we had a business meeting we couldn't miss. We heard about your run in with the Reverend at dinner that night, but I want to know if that story about the wagonload of runaways is true? Did you really fool a whole posse of bounty hunters and their dogs, in broad daylight, by telling them you had a load of runaway slaves?"

Sam shook his head and laughed. "It wasn't nearly that dramatic Allan, in fact, these men, about to show up, were involved in that little incident." As he spoke, the door burst open and Elijah Wilson stormed in followed by Clem and the two men who left to report Sam's presence.

Wilson had a look of pure hatred on his face and said, "Well I'll be Goddamned. I never would have believed you'd come down here you irresponsible fool. What do you think you're gonna' prove pulling this kind of stupid stunt?"

"Just that I'm a man of my word, Mr. Wilson."

"You should a' stayed away, but since you're here I'm gonna' teach you a lesson. You damned Nigger-lovers are gonna' learn one way or the other, stay outta' our business or we will destroy you."

The barkeeper shouted, "Now Elijah, I ain't gonna' let you tear up my business. You take this outside."

"No, no, there isn't going to be any trouble," Sam said calmly. "I'm just here to ask these gentlemen to look at the issue with some reason and give up their slaves to the cause of righteousness. Slaveholding is the greatest sin in the world and putting our brothers and sisters in chains has to stop or there will be bloodshed. It cannot continue. I'm asking you in the spirit of justice and in God's name…., to free your slaves."

There was a good bit of shuffling of feet and clearing of throat, but no one said anything. Wilson stood, mouth open, unable to believe his ears.

"I don't think that's too much to ask, gentlemen. What do you say?" Sam added, holding his lemonade high.

Allan and Ed looked at each other and wondered if their new friend might be insane. Rich Dana had not mentioned any such fact, but now they were beginning to wonder. Both men were dumbstruck that anyone would have the gall to say such a thing in a slave-holding state in the middle of a bar full of slaveholders.

"Well I'll be Goddamned," Wilson said again, not being able to think of anything else more appropriate.

"I've had my say, and if that's all you have to add, Wilson, then I'll be on my way. I need to get back to Ohio because I plan to be married soon, don't want to keep the little lady waiting," Sam smiled, then added, "I surely do appreciate you giving some thought to what I'm saying."

Wilson said again, "I'll be Goddamned," then added, "This fella's only got one oar in the water, boys, he's crazier than an outhouse rat."

The crowd had a good laugh at Wilson's joke. Sam put a dime on the bar and walked to the door followed by Pinkerton and Ruker. He tipped his hat to Wilson then said, "Hello Clem, how's your friend Ike? I hope no lasting effects from his beating."

"Well, he still ain't quite right, Mr. Wood, but Doc says he'll recover."

"Oh, shut the hell up, Clem," Wilson shouted and stormed out the door and down the street. Sam and his friends watched them leave.

"Well, that was a close one. I guess I better get out of town while the getting is good. Would you gentlemen like to ride along with me? We're going in the same direction, I believe. And you're invited to our house, I want you to meet my mother and father and my lovely bride Margaret Lyon, although I haven't formally asked her yet."

Pinkerton laughed and said, "Sam, I wouldn't miss riding along with you for anything. You have a way of making a situation lively, just the kind of man we need in our business."

Pinkerton and Ruker rode in a new buggy with a canvas boot that contained their luggage and business materials. They had two horses, which they alternated every twenty miles or so. Sam rode alongside and they visited when they could, but because of a summer rainstorm they stopped at an Inn along the Turnpike to wait out the squall.

"What business are you fellows in?" Sam asked.

"I'm a cooper by trade but got into the detective business,

pretty much by accident. Ed and I are starting a detective and protection business, call it the North-Western Police Agency."

"Then I guess you were good ones to have around in a scrape like I got myself into back there. How did you get into the abolitionist movement?"

"I'm from Glasgow, Scotland and my parents taught me that all people are equal. My wife and I open our house to any person who's being persecuted. We put up the fugitive slaves heading to Canada. I hear that your house is also a stop on the railway."

"Yes, it is but I agree with Fred Douglass on that issue, the locations are getting way too much publicity, why John Rankin's house over in Ripley is so well known that the bounty hunters have set up a permanent watch for runaways. Actually, our farm west of Wheeling is on the line, and the main house in Mt. Gilead. I'm going to catch a steamboat in Parkersburg and go north to Wheeling. Where are you fellows going? If I could entice you to go with me, I'd like you to meet my family."

"That is a tempting offer, Sam, but we plan to go the other way to Cincinnati and then up to Indianapolis, then home. We stop at banks and businesses along the way that might be in need of our services," Ed Rucker said.

"Then we'll part ways in Parkersburg, but not before exchanging addresses. I have a strong feeling that our paths will cross again," Pinkerton added.

"I agree with you Allan. There are going to be difficult times ahead. I fully expect war within a few years."

###

"[Slavery] was established by decree of Almighty God ... it is sanctioned in the Bible, in both Testaments, from Genesis to Revelation ... it has existed in all ages, has been found among the people of the highest civilization, and in nations of the highest proficiency in the arts." **Jefferson Davis, 1808-1889, Mississippi Senator and President, Confederate States of America**

Sam booked passage on board the steamship America bound for Wheeling, where he wanted to work at the mercantile for a few days and leave Felix for Burton to pick up later. Sam thought of the girl Sally and wondered if his letter had reached Henry Clay and what the response would be. He thought of Margaret and trusted that Tobias had procured the gold bands he ordered. He wanted to make a formal proposal, to Margaret, probably on Sunday after the church meeting. He needed to travel to Columbus and make arrangements with the law firm of Stinchcomb & Brumbaugh to study law with them and read for the bar by the summer of 1853. So many things to do and so little time.

Sam stood at the rail and watched the scenery drift by. The farms and fields along the east side of the river, full of Negroes working in the sun. After the rainstorm the day before, the heat had pulled up the humidity and Sam was glad for the slight breeze caused by the progress of the boat. At a bend in the river, where they came close to the slave-state side, Sam could hear the sound of singing from the field, and the Negroes on the lower deck picked up the song. The words had a profound effect on Sam who had never thought of the Negro spirituals as anything more than entertainment:

Go down, Moses
'Way down in Egypt land,
Tell ole Pharaoh,
To let my people go.

When Israel was in Egypt's land;
Let my people go,
Oppressed so hard they could not stand,
Let my people go.

But each song had a special meaning. Sam was intrigued

because he had never actually heard the song in the fields. He wondered if there were runaway slaves in the field finding their way north.

"Sam Wood…., Sam is that you."

He was interrupted in his deliberations by an unknown voice. He found himself looking at a short man wearing a Calvary uniform and a fancy plumed hat. It was Captain Johnson.

"Captain Johnson, this is a surprise. I met some of your friends just a few days ago."

"And who would that be?"

"Why Elijah Wilson, Clem, and several other men, but I didn't catch their names. I made a hasty exit."

Johnson laughed and shaking his head said, "I can't believe you went to Clarksburg. And by the way, those men aren't friends of mine, they are undignified ruffians and not worth wasting your good time."

"Why do you work for them?"

"It is a long ugly story, Sam, maybe someday I'll share it with you. The bottom line is that I'm a contractor. I work for whoever pays me. In fact, I'm off into Ohio in search of a runaway that escaped from Georgia. I have it on good authority that he is in Antioch. I'll be getting off in Sistersville and proceeding north from there. I take it you're going on to Wheeling?"

"Yes, I am Captain. But I'm very confused, you're an educated man, yet you work with the slaveholders and keep our brothers and sisters in chains. I don't understand, not a bit."

Johnson leaned against the railing, watched the Negroes work and listened to the song. "I'm not a philosopher, Sam. I don't engage in debates about right and wrong or good and bad. The laws of this great land are what I live by. If you want to change the system you have to change the laws and when you do…., I will live by that set of laws."

"It won't come by changing laws. There will be a war,

Captain."

"My God, I hope not. If there is, the bloodshed will be beyond belief. The destruction will be absolute. Cities will be destroyed."

"Which side will you fight on?"

"I know that you have brothers, Sam. Do they all feel the same way you do?"

"Absolutely!"

"I'm from Mississippi. Two of my brothers will fight for secession, another brother and I will fight to preserve the Union. None of us have slaves, so my father and mother will see their sons die for reasons that they don't even understand. Do you see where this is heading, Sam? Brother against brother, families divided for many years to come. It's not a matter to be taken lightly. The ramifications go way beyond freeing the slaves. The aftermath may be worse than what we have now."

The boat had traveled far enough that the sounds of the song died away along with the sight of slaves. They entered a wooded area heavily treed, blocking any view past the shore but a lone voice from the deck below was clear in the bright sunlight, a sorrowful voice:

Oh, bye an' bye, bye an' bye
I'm goin' to lay down my heavy load...
I'm troubled, I'm troubled,
I'm troubled in mind
If Jesus don't help me
I surely will die. . .

"I don't dispute what you say, Captain Johnson, but I can't let the fact that we have a system that will cause havoc when it's dismantled keep me from doing what's right. Any government that allows the enslavement of a portion of its people is a wrongful government and must be changed. People will look back on us and say, 'how could you do this to human beings?'

Slaves are treated worse than animals. I've seen, in Tennessee, horses with blankets and warm stalls in the winter while their grooms and stable boys wear rags and sleep on dirt floors in unheated shacks. I cannot abide that, and will not stand for it, regardless of the hardships that it creates for the South when the system is destroyed. History will not be kind to us."

"I thought that you are a Quaker, Sam."

"I am, what's that got to do with it?"

"Well, Quakers are peace lovers. They don't fight."

Sam laughed, "We prefer not to fight, but my Grandfather Mosher fought in the Revolutionary War and when I asked him why, he said that God was real busy with all that was going wrong in the world and he needed some help right then. So, Papa Mosher was doing God's work, and that's what I'm doing, Captain Johnson, God's work and if it requires protecting myself or someone else, I will do so with whatever means required."

They drifted along in silence both contemplating the river.

"Tell me, Sam, what is a man? I think he's nothing more than what he was born to. You and your kind were born to the Quaker religion and the traditions that you have; the Wilson brothers were born to slaveholding with two hundred and fifty years of that tradition embedded in their souls. I was born, in Mississippi, to farming and slaves all around me. The only way I escaped was by education. That is the key, Sam, education, but it won't happen. You start educating the Africans and there will be rebellion, and what about jobs? Where are the jobs they'll demand?"

"Why you are a philosopher, Captain, and I do agree with you about education, but I'm an optimist and believe that the jobs will follow. The colored race will help build this great land."

"You believe in the intermingling of the races?" Johnson said incredulously.

"I do not, but where do you think the mulattos are coming

from? Not by choice of the colored people. Those are the result of your slaveholders and their sons raping and molesting the women."

"Now hold on there, Wood, that is a misstatement of the facts."

"Tell me then, set me straight on the matter. How else do you interpret what's happening?"

"Well, those Africans are owned by…., well that is to say that the owner wants to produce more workers…., you see, Sam, it's not that simple a matter, and there are other factors that must be considered. Many of the slaves are treated well."

"If any slave is treated well, which I doubt, then it is for the purpose of enhancing his value to be sold as part of the slave trade; which is more repulsive than slavery itself. But it doesn't matter how he's treated, the owning of another person is outrageous. The slave is property, denied any feelings or emotions, no rights to education or marriage, no status above the horse or pig. It's against all that is righteous and Holy not only in this world but in Gods' heaven. Captain Johnson, there are no other considerations. Slavery is an abomination of the worst kind and not justifiable under any circumstances." Sam banged his cane on the rail to make the point.

Again, they rode along in silence until Johnson said, "That's why I don't argue and debate. I always lose."

Sam shook his head, laughed, and asked, "By the way, how did you get to be a Captain?"

"Mexican-American War, I served with General Kearny in 47, Army of the West, stationed at Ft. Leavenworth, Kansas Territory. We were posted to New Mexico Territory but Kearny and most of the army left for California and he put Colonel Price in charge of the rest of us…., hell, I ended up fighting the Indians more than the Mexicans. The Indians didn't want us in their territory any more than the Mexicans did. Anyway, Colonel Price made me a Captain. He said, 'Johnson, you're the onliest sonofabitch left that can string three words together without tripping on your tongue. You're a Captain, now go get your men together.' We were in the Battle of Red River Canyon on the Canadian River. I never did get into Mexico. It was a hell of a war, that's all I can say. But that's how I got to be a Captain. I was mustered out six months later because the war was over, and I was not needed. I've been chasing slaves ever since."

"Well it's an unfortunate time for all of us. I wish you would have chosen a different occupation. I'm a schoolteacher and a farmer. My family has a mercantile in Wheeling that my brother Tobias runs and it's pretty successful with all the riverboat traffic; that, and our farming operations keep us busy. But I plan on studying law as soon as I'm married. I will see this slavery matter to an end, or it'll be the death of me, I can't seem to keep myself out of trouble."

"That is a fact, Sam. You will talk yourself into a fix you can't get out of. But if it's any consolation, I will do what I can to help if that does occur. By the way, I strongly suspect that those slaves were in that wagon we passed these several months ago, weren't they?"

"My goodness, Captain I wouldn't tell a lie," Sam chuckled and changed the subject, "Well sir, I'd best go check on my horse. It's been a pleasure and I'm glad to hear that we'll be fighting on the same side when that day comes. Regardless, I'm sure our paths will cross again." Sam extended his hand and Johnson shook it enthusiastically.

###

"Our village (Wheeling, West Virginia) was built on the Ohio River, and was a halting place on this great national road, then the only avenue of traffic between the South and the North." **Rebecca H. Davis**

1831-1910 Author, Newspaper Reporter

The docks in Wheeling were busy, three downstream boats and two upstream, all docked at the same time. Slaves and free Blacks, white laborers, farmers, merchants, all bustled about taking care of their business. Sam departed the boat with his satchel and cane to wait for Felix to be brought up to the wharf.

"Uncle Sam," he turned to find his nephew, Billy Wood, son of Tobias and Stacey waving at him through the crowd.

"Billy, good to see you, son. Why are you here?"

"We have a consignment of goods on the Andrew Jackson up from St. Louis; buffalo hides and books and some cloth. I'm in charge of getting it onto the wagons and back to the warehouse," he said proudly. At 15, Billy was a strapping boy with dark hair and eyes from his mother and a ruddy complexion and large shoulders from his father.

"Can I help with anything Billy?"

"No sir, I've got Richard with me and he and the dock hands can manage it."

A large black man, an employee of the mercantile for many years, could be seen backing a wagon down to the docks. Sam waved at Richard who yelled, "Welcome back, Mr. Sam, we expected you two days ago."

"Yeah, Uncle Sam, where've you been? We heard all about you throwing that drunk out of the City Tavern in Washington."

"What did you hear?"

"That you picked up some drunk who was yelling at Mrs. Mott and threw him out the door."

Sam laughed so hard that he dropped his cane. "Lord Almighty, the truth fades as the time passes. I'll tell you about it later, Bill, but that is an exaggeration worthy of Benedict Arnold."

"You go on to the house, Uncle Sam. Mother is there with a surprise."

Sam walked the three blocks to the mercantile leading Felix. Tobias' home was just behind the store building on Market Street, providing easy access to the docks and well located for foot and wagon traffic. In addition to the mercantile, the business included a stable and a restaurant, but, of course, no saloon, because of the owners' Quaker beliefs. Sam left Felix with the stable boy and proceeded inside the store where Tobias met him with gusto.

"Samuel, where have you been? We expected you two days ago."

"I had some unfinished business but that's all taken care of."

"We heard about your run in with the troublemaker in Washington."

"I still don't know how that news traveled so fast, plus the story grew considerable by the time it got here. I know that version didn't come from Bill Lyon," Sam said, laughing.

"Lucretia's brother came through on a steamship bound for St. Louis. He was in Baltimore when someone told him about it. It only takes two days to get here on the railway and canals from Baltimore. You just missed him. He left yesterday," Toby said.

"I'll tell you the real story at supper. I'll take my satchel up to the house. I'm only staying tonight," Sam said.

"You haven't been to the house yet?"

"No, I borrowed a horse from your friend, Burton, and they're going to pick it up here in a few days. I left it with Ray in the stable."

"Well, you'd better get to the house. Stacey has a surprise for you."

Sam went through the store, dodging the ladies examining dresses, blouses, and cloth; around the food stuffs, and barrels of beans and peas, past the hardware, shovels, and small tools; through the back door; down the loading docks, across the boardwalk into the backyard of the large house, occupied by Tobias and Stacey Wood. It was more boarding house than private residence.

Before he reached the step to the back porch, the door flew open and he was overwhelmed with pretty girls and a cacophony of greetings. Sarah, Caroline Lyon, Estelle, his mother, and finally Margaret, who hugged and kissed him generously, not even giving him a chance to breath.

Sam held Margaret and wouldn't let her go. He whispered, "I hoped you would be here. I missed you so much."

"I wasn't going to leave until you got back. We've been waiting two days."

"Come on you two," Stacey Wood called from the door. We have a lot of work to do before the others get here." Meaning David Wood, Stephan, and Efren who were coming into town from the farm. Supper was going to be a major event with most of the Wood children present, and Margaret and her sister, Caroline. Sam excused himself to wash up and stash his satchel before the evening began. What they didn't realize was that Bill and Elizabeth Lyon were on their way with sons, Rich and Fred.

Then Stacey's parents, Harold and Maude Lemming, heard about the party. Tobias had Richard and some of the other clerks bring extra tables and chairs. The ladies fried more chicken and boiled more potatoes and beans. The evening was turning out to be an event to be remembered in the family folklore.

The children, including Sarah and her cousin Billy, much to their dismay, were assigned smaller tables on the porch. The adults were crowded into two larger tables in the dining room. Guests shouted back and forth to each other across the room. Stacey motioned to Tobias and made him meet her in the foyer where she said, not altogether in a pleasant way, "Where am I expected to put all of these people?"

"Calm down, Honey, we can put the older kids in the storeroom in the shop. Your parents can take the Lyons family home with them. We'll be fine."

Stacey took a deep breath, glared at her husband and went to tell her mother of the new arrangements. Tobias knew there would be hell to pay later, but the order of the moment was to endure.

Supper over, the ladies cleared while the men moved tables, arranged chairs, and prepared for the evening conversation. The lamps were lit, and arrangements made for the children to play in the yard. The weather was cooperating, so Estelle Wood and Rich Lyon planned to lead an excursion to the river to watch the steamboats arrive. Apple cider, lemonade, and sweet tea were made available. David Wood called for attention, gave a short prayer of thanks and then said, "By way of beginning, I would like a report from Bill and Sam on their trip to Washington." This was met with a chorus of agreement.

Bill Lyon spoke up, "I can tell you that the excitement in Washington is thick. So much going on. New construction everywhere…."

Sam chimed in, "You should see the castle they're building for the new Smithsonian history displays. It's magnificent."

"They finally started the monument for President Washington, but I doubt they can finish it before they run out of money. The waste in Washington is beyond belief. Why they're paying carpenters 45 dollars a month on those government jobs. They're paying unskilled laborers 26; half the time they stand around doing nothing," Bill continued.

"You can't find a place to live. Tent cities are springing up, and the filth is everywhere. There will be outbreaks, I promise you," Sam said.

"What about the Senate and House? Did you see the President?"

"No, Polk was in Philadelphia," Bill said.

"As long as Taylor can keep control, we have a chance of derailing the compromise; but Filmore and Henry Clay are pushing hard for it," Sam continued.

"Sam, what is this about you assaulting some preacher and throwing him out of a meeting?" Esther Wood asked.

"What? When did you do that?" Bill asked looking at Sam.

"They're talking about the dinner with Lucretia. I believe the story has gotten a bit twisted out of shape, Bill. Maybe you should explain it because I'm beginning to come off as the villain as the story travels west," Sam laughed.

Later, Sam walked arm in arm with Margaret to the Lemming home where she was to spend the night.

"Sam, Mother Wood and I have been so busy planning the suffrage meeting that I completely forgot to tell your students about school beginning next week. I hope you aren't mad at me."

"No, Margaret, we can tell most of them at the meeting on Sunday. The rest will hear about it through word of mouth. I expect about fifteen students to show up. I hope not many more, because I don't have enough benches."

They stood on the boardwalk in front of the telegraph office. Other citizens strolled by, and Sarah said, sneaking up behind them, "Oh, why don't you just kiss her, Sam," and ran past giggling with Caroline. Sam smiled and did just that.

###

"Who talks most about freedom and equality? Is it not those who hold a Bill of Rights in one hand and a whip for affrighted slaves in the other?" **Alexander Hamilton 1755-1804 Founding Father**

Wheeling, Virginia

The next morning, Richard and his crew were unloading wagons in the back of the store; while farmers, shop keepers, ranchers, longshoremen, and housewives from the village, were bargain hunting in the crowded rooms of the market. Toby's, as everyone called it, also served as a post office and meeting place for the local citizens. Sam stopped to help Richard unload sacks of flour, sugar and beans before he went inside to find Tobias. The walls were cluttered floor to ceiling with shelves crammed with canned goods, thread, needles, cloth, utensils, dungarees, hats, dresses, tools, and candy.

"Hey, Billy," Sam called out to his nephew, who was helping a woman carry merchandise to her buggy. The street was macadamized so the dust was not a problem, plus there was a sprinkle of rain during the night. The traffic was brisk going to and coming from the wharfs serving the Ohio River steamboats and barges.

"Uncle Sam, there's a letter for you. It came in yesterday," Billy said.

Sam found Sarah sorting a pouch of mail which had arrived on an early morning packet ship from Pittsburgh. She studied each envelope carefully, her lips puckered in concentration, double checked it and then slid it into the proper cubby hole in the postal boxes. The postmaster was a local citizen who never bothered to show up at the post office, leaving the day to day operations to Stacey Wood for the sum of twenty dollars a month. The citizen in question was also a well-known drunk who received his postal commission from James Polk because he was married to a first cousin. The man was sure to be replaced and everyone in town had championed Stacey for the job.

"Stacey told me to organize the mail, Sam," Sarah said defensively. "You know they're going to replace the Franklin five-cent stamp next year? There's going to be more than two stamps and more than two prices."

"She must really trust you Sarah. That's a big responsibility. Maybe you'll go into the postal service yourself."

She dropped a handful of letters and bumped her head on the counter trying to retrieve them. Sam suppressed a laugh as the awkward teenager struggled to maintain dignity while recovering the fallen letters. The family consensus was that Sarah would grow into a beautiful woman, but the between years were a tussle for her.

"You have two letters, one from Washington and one from Cincinnati. This one from Washington is from Senator Clay. Do you want me to open it?" Sarah asked excitedly.

"Sure, go ahead. It must be the answer to my letter about the slave girl, Sally. See what he says. I'll open the other one. Who's it from?"

"Ummmm...., somebody named Pinkerton. Who's that?"

"He's a fellow I met in Clarksburg. I wonder what he wants."

"What who wants," Stephan asked yawning and rubbing his eyes?

"Did you just get up," Sam asked?

Stephan's hair was rumpled, and his coveralls wet to the knees. "No, me and Efren and Rich went fishin' already this morning. We caught a bunch and took them to Stacey to cook em' up. She's in the house making breakfast right now. I love fish and eggs. So, who's the letter from?"

"From Allan Pinkerton, a fellow I met in Clarksburg. Says that he'll be in Wheeling tomorrow or the next day. Well, I guess I'll have to wait for him. You guys go on back to the farm without me and I'll catch up after I see what he wants."

"What who wants?" Margaret asked coming in late.

"Good morning, beautiful. Allan Pinkerton, the fellow I told you about that I met in Clarksburg."

"Is he coming today? I hope not because I want to go on a picnic. What do you say, Sam?"

"Oh, can Caroline and I go, please?" Sarah asked.

"We'll all go, and Margaret and I'll sneak off and find a quiet spot all to ourselves," Sam kidded.

###

"Love cannot be found where it doesn't exist, nor can it be hidden where it truly does." **William Shakespeare**

"I'll bet they kiss soon," Estelle whispered to Caroline and Sarah as they spied on the young lovers from a copse of choke cherry bushes. The Virginia air was sweet with the sounds of the stream tumbling and the fragrance of the lush carpet of alluvial soil.

"No, they're talking," Sarah replied. "I'll bet he's telling her that her eyes are more beautiful than morning glories and her breasts like gifts from God."

"Oh, my goodness, Sarah, where did you hear such things?" Caroline said.

"Don't be so childish, you two, I think it's all so romantic."

Sam and Margaret sat on a rock overlooking Wheeling Creek, some three miles east of town, far enough to be away from the bustle of workers at the nail manufacturing plants, cattle yards, shipyards and other businesses in the growing port city. A new suspension bridge to Wheeling Island had opened the area to commerce, and the Cumberland Road passed through town so the feeling was that the area would grow rapidly, and the Wood family would prosper in the Ohio Valley.

The sun glistened off the pristine stream. The young couple could hear their brothers and sisters playing some fifty yards away. Sam's hand rested lightly on Margaret's knee as they conversed in quiet tones next to the sound of the flowing water. The subject of their conversation was less passionate than Sarah's conjecture.

"Read it again, Sam and we'll examine every detail. Maybe we can make sense of what to do."

"He dates it August 25 from Washington D.C., *Dear Sam, I truly enjoyed the visit with you and Bill Lyon, when you were in*

Washington, and was delighted to receive your letter. While we do not see eye to eye on the slavery question, I think we do agree that the issue must be resolved in a peaceful manner and will require compromise by all parties....

Margaret interrupted to ask, "What kind of a person is he Sam?"

"Well, he's getting old, and shakes a bit, but he's extremely intelligent. He's been involved in all of the important events in Washington for the past 50 years."

"Is it true that he represented Aaron Burr in his trial for treason?"

"Yes, and when Clay found out that Burr really was guilty, he was beside himself with anger, then he fought a duel with someone else about forty years ago and they actually shot each other, but I guess their wounds weren't severe. He's a slaveholder and that says it all. Shall I read on?"

"Yes, dear but first I think you should tell the girls to go and play, or else give me a kiss to satisfy their curiosity."

"I will do both and repeat the second task at regular intervals," he laughed, while taking her in his arms. He turned to where the girls were hidden and said, "Now move on you busybodies and leave us to ourselves."

The girls ran to find their brothers and report the intimacy of Sam and Margaret.

Sam continued...., *As for the girl Sally, I would gladly let you 'take her off my hands' as you put it and the charge would be nothing as she has been a thorn in my side for many years due to reasons that I need not express here. However, she has disappeared. Upon her return from the delivery, that she attended with you, Annie Robertson and she departed on another business trip and Sally disappeared somewhere in the vicinity of Hagerstown, Maryland. Annie searched for her but to no avail. She either escaped into Pennsylvania or was captured by bounty hunters and removed to the Deep South or some worse fate that I cannot imagine. I wish I had better news for you, but I do not. If further details come available, I will let you know….,* "He urges me to visit again the next time I'm in Washington, and signs Senator Henry Clay."

"What do you suppose has happened to her?"

"My guess is that she finally made the decision to escape. Hagerstown is only a few miles from the Pennsylvania State line. Maybe she'll show up here…., but I don't feel good about it. She seemed determined to let Clay and Burton know her plans, and to make the transition to freedom in the correct manner. I wish I knew the truth."

"Maybe you should go look for her, Sam."

"Do you mean it, Margaret? I have so much to do. I promised Tobias to finish the accounting today, I'm at least three weeks behind in the books, my classes are scheduled to start. But mainly I'm concerned about our plans. I don't want you to think for a moment that you are anything but first in my heart and mind."

Margaret reached her hand out to Sam and they walked together along the stream, upriver from the others. Sam could see that she had something on her mind, and he was mortally afraid that she was having second thoughts about him, and their commitment to each other. But he wasn't sure how to ask.

Finally, she said, "Sam, do you have much experience with women?"

His eyes widened and he stopped, speechless, at this intimate question. His mind and his heart raced as he tried to fathom the meaning behind her words. The truth was that he did not have much experience outside his family and the church. He took a deep breath, "I'm not certain of your meaning, but if you mean beyond my relationship with family and friends, I would have to say that my experience…., is limited."

Margaret stifled a laugh and quickly recovered when she saw the look of hurt on Sam's face. "Sam, I don't mean to embarrass you, but if we are to be married, we must be completely open and honest with each other in all regards, don't you think?

"Oh, yes, Margaret," he enthused happily, relieved to have her speak of marriage, "I agree wholeheartedly but haven't we been honest with each other?"

"As far as it goes, we have. Let's sit down here and talk about ourselves."

Sam stared at her not knowing what to expect, he was almost in a sweat trying to anticipate where the conversation would lead and what her intentions might be. If she broke off their engagement, she did say 'IF we are to be married', he would go away and not come back until he had made a tremendous success of himself….

Margaret broke into his reverie, "Elizabeth Cady Stanton spoke to a group of us when I was in Pennsylvania last summer. She spoke about being a woman."

"About being a woman?" He was obviously confused.

"Yes, about what it means in these modern times."

"Being a woman in modern times?"

"Yes!" she said, then gathered her thoughts, taking his hand resting it in her lap, "A woman has the same needs and desires as a man. For years we've been forced to hide our feelings, and men have come to expect us to be subservient and docile."

"Docile?" Sam repeated, even more confused.

"But the fact is women…., I, Sam, meaning me…., have the same needs and desires as you do…., the same physical cravings, so to speak."

"Physical cravings," Sam said slowly.

"Sam, quit repeating what I say. It's very distracting."

"You're going to break our engagement, aren't you?" he said, putting his hand on hers as if to prevent her from running away.

"What? Sam, how could you say such a thing?"

"Oh Margaret, I love you with all my heart. I'll do anything to make you happy. Just tell me what you want."

"What I want is to be with you forever, for better or for worse, and that we shall conquer the world together. But I also want you to understand that I am a passionate woman that won't break if you make love to me."

Sam gazed into her eyes in shock at this speech, "I wish we wouldn't have brought the children."

She laughed and put her hands to his face, holding him, "Oh Sam, I don't mean now, because I don't want it to be contrived, but soon, and because we will be together as man and wife we can't be afraid to talk to each other about these things, or any matter that concern us. I know that you will be off on adventures to save damsels in distress and rescue the oppressed. I want you to know that I will be your partner every step of the way. We really shall be as one."

"I don't know what to say Margaret," they stood as he held her close. "I have physical cravings all the time, but I didn't want to offend you."

"I know dear, that's why I bring it up," she took his hand and pressed it to her breast.

They kissed while the stream flowed behind them, and the troubled thoughts vanished from Sam's mind as he pressed his cheek to hers.

###

"I have said a hundred times, and I have no inclination to take it back, that I believe there is no right, and ought to be no inclination in the people of the free States to enter into the slave States, and to interfere with the question of slavery at all. I have said that always." **Abraham Lincoln**

The picnickers reached home with designated tasks for each. The girls took the basket full of dishes for washing, the boys took the horse and wagon to the stable, Margaret and Sam retired to the office above the store where she helped him with the accounting. It was a major job with the success of the mercantile and the constant delivery of goods from the steamboats and freight wagons. Two windows provided plenty of light, and because of the pleasant day both were open to allow the breeze from the river. They heard a voice from below asking, "I'm looking for Sam Wood. Could you tell me where to find him?"

Sam couldn't see who was speaking because of the wooden awning extending over the front doors. He leaned out the window and shouted, "Hello, Sam Wood here. Who's there?"

A head with plumed hat poked out and Sam was looking into the face of his new friend. "Captain Johnson, what a surprise, I'll be right down. What brings you to Wheeling," Sam asked, as they settled on the front porch of the house?

"Strange set of circumstances, Sam. After I left you, I ended up in Cincinnati looking for that runaway and I met some friends of yours, Pinkerton and Rucker. They offered me a job, they got a letter from one of the big banks in Philadelphia with a job offer and they asked me to be the supervisor. So, I guess I'll do like you said and get out of the runaway slave business."

"That's wonderful news Captain. Say, what is your first name anyway?"

"Ellis."

Margaret, Stacey Wood and Sam's older sister, Mary, entered with Sam making the introductions. Johnson seemed particularly taken with Mary Wood who was about the Captain's age.

"Have we met somewhere, Miss Wood?" Captain Johnson asked Mary.

"Not that I recall, Captain Johnson, but I have heard of you from my brother Stephan and what I heard was not flattering in your favor. My entire family is stanchly anti-slavery."

"You will be happy to hear that I'm no longer in that business," he replied.

"How long have you been out of the business?"

"Since I met you," he smiled and bowed.

Mary rolled her eyes. Sam and Margaret laughed.

"Captain, I didn't take you to be a lady's man," Margaret said.

"Only when there is a lady that I deem worthy," he said kissing Mary's hand.

"Ellis, did you know that Pinkerton is coming to Wheeling? I received a letter from him this morning," Sam said.

"Yes, I know about it because we planned to rendezvous here; Allan is going on to Philadelphia with me and Ed is going back to Chicago. I think they want to offer you a job. It might be a good opportunity, Sam."

"Do you know anything about them?"

"A little. I served in the army with one of Allan's cousins. Pinkerton was Chief of Police up in Chicago, at the time. Now he's started a new Detective Agency named Pinkerton's North-Western Police Agency. I know he has a good reputation. It might be a ground floor opportunity."

"Sam, are you seriously considering it?" Margaret asked.

"We'll discuss it later, but as of now I am sticking with the plans we discussed this morning."

"Which is what?" Mary asked.

"Well," Sam began, "Margaret is going back to Wileyville to take over my classes until I finish some business in Virginia. There's a slave girl named Sally that I need to find."

"What do you mean, Sam?" Captain Johnson asked.

By this time, most of the Wood family had gathered on the porch. Sam explained the details of how he came to know Sally.

Margaret read the Clay letter to everyone.

"Sam, that's right up my alley. I'll find her for you before I go on to Philadelphia to start the new job."

"Do you think you can, Ellis? I'll go with you and we'll find her together."

"Done," Captain Johnson smiled. "And I'll do it for free to prove to Miss Wood my good intentions. I have an excellent contact in Hagerstown, a most unsavory character, a blight on humanity, just the sort of fellow we'll need for this job."

###

"Vice may triumph for a time, crime may flaunt its victories in the face of honest toilers, but in the end the law will follow the wrong-doer to a bitter fate, and dishonor and punishment will be the portion of those who sin." **Allan Pinkerton**

Allan Pinkerton was tired. He'd been meeting with bankers and government officials on behalf of his business; abolitionists and Underground Railroad activists as part of his passion. His stomach rumbled and cramped from a bout of dysentery. He could barely keep his eyes open as he rode the ferry into Wheeling, but he felt a sense of excitement. If he could convince Sam Wood to join his burgeoning company, it would be a boost to the business and one more asset in his battle against slavery.

If he could just keep things together at home then all would be well, but the last letter he received from his wife was not pleasant. She was ready for him to return to Chicago to help with the demands of raising a family--but the demands of expanding his business were more important to him right now. He would write a detailed letter begging her to hold on just a few more weeks.

Wheeling was a dirty, noisy city along the river docks, warehouses belching smoke from forge fires molding nails for the advancement of the western frontier. Men, both black and white, were bustling about tending to the business of their employers and masters. Wheeling was predominately anti-slavery having been settled by progressive Germans and isolated as it was between Ohio and Pennsylvania, closer to the Free State ideal than the slaveholding south.

Allan called out to a man leading a horse, "Excuse me, which way to Toby's general store?"

"Second street ta de leff, suh. Ya cain't miss it."

Allan tipped his hat in thanks and drove on as directed. Toby's was bustling with several buggies and farm wagons parked in front. A young boy was carrying boxes to one of the wagons.

"Son, I'm looking for Sam Wood."

"He's my uncle," Billy said.

"Is he around somewhere that I could speak with him?"

"No, but my dad and grandpa are inside, and they know where to find him."

Allan climbed down from his buggy and tied the horse to the rail. He stretched and groaned from the pain in his back and the ache in his stomach. Maybe they would have something inside to provide some relief. He almost bumped into a man backing out of the store carrying one end of a large box. Allan leaned in and held the door while the men struggled with the awkward container.

"Thank you, sir," Richard said. "It's a new double plow blade," as if that said it all.

"It looks heavy. Where can I find Mr. Wood?"

"Mr. Wood is upstairs in the office. You go on up, I think the door is open."

Allan found the stairs at the back of the building, and climbed to the second floor, where a hallway led to the front, and an open door to an office, with two men sitting at a table going over ledger books. Allan knocked and announced himself, "Hello, Mr. Wood. I'm Allan Pinkerton looking for Sam and another fellow by the name of Johnson."

Toby and David stood and shook hands with the detective and directed him to a third chair at the table. "We've been expecting you, Mr. Pinkerton, actually, we thought you'd be here a couple of days ago."

"I've been tied up on business and this was the earliest I could get away. Is Sam around somewhere? One of my men is also supposed to be here, Captain Johnson."

"They were here," David Wood said, "but they left two days ago to tend to some business in Virginia. I think they plan on meeting you in Philadelphia. Here's a letter to explain the situation."

Pinkerton read the letter which directed him to the Girard Hotel on Chestnut Street, in Philadelphia, within a week to ten days. He sat quietly contemplating his options. It would take him two days by riverboat, stage, and canals to get to Philadelphia.

"Mr. Wood," he began….

"David," Sam's father replied at the same time that Toby announced his name. They all laughed while Pinkerton continued, "Gentlemen, I am exhausted from my trip and need a place to rest for a few days before I start for Philadelphia. Is there a good hotel nearby?"

"No sir," Tobias began, "I mean yes, there is a good hotel, but you'll stay at the house with us. It's practically deserted with my family all going back home…., to Ohio," he added when he saw the questioning look on Pinkerton's face.

"That's a generous offer, Toby, but I don't want to put you out."

"Nonsense, it isn't any bother at all. Let's go right now and I'll show you to your room and get someone to draw a bath. You can get cleaned up and then relax all you want. Dinner will be at seven and you won't want to miss it, Stacey is a wonderful cook."

"Thank you, Toby. I'll take you up on that offer."

"I'll say goodbye here, Allan, because my wife and kids will be going back to Mt. Gilead shortly."

"I've heard a great deal about you, David. I'm also an abolitionist and hope to work with you and your family to resolve this slavery matter as soon as possible, hopefully without a war, as Sam seems to think is coming."

"I hope he's wrong, Allan, but I'm afraid that if the Fugitive Slave Act is passed then the writing will be on the wall. There will be no stopping hostilities, and I'm certain the Act will be voted into law next year." David coughed and clutched his throat.

"Dad," Toby helped him sit down.

"Just a little indigestion," he said breathing heavily, "I'll see Doctor Toft when I get back to Mt. Gilead. Go ahead and take Allan to his room, I'm fine...., Allan, I'll look forward to seeing you on your next trip down."

Toby escorted Pinkerton to his room and ordered a bath to be drawn. The house seemed quiet after the commotion of the past few days. He hurried back to the office to finish his accounting and to put Sam's new wedding rings into the safe. They had arrived on a boat from Pittsburgh soon after he left with Ellis Johnson to search for Sally.

###

"You may choose to look the other way but you can never say again that you did not know." **William Wilberforce, British leader of anti-slavery movement, 1759-1833**

Captain Johnson and Sam Wood were sitting in a public house eating a supper of steak and fried potatoes; a fire pit offered warmth and a congenial atmosphere. The new, well-constructed, brick building was located near the Cumberland

Road not far from Hagerstown, Maryland. The men had been traveling all day and discovered the inn and restaurant just as they were preparing to bed down alongside the road. Ellis Johnson drank a dark German beer brewed by the innkeeper, and Sam drank water while they carried on a conversation begun in the landau.

"I met her when I attended Mississippi College in Clinton. She was the daughter of the President of the school, but she was also a student. We fell in love right away and spent all of our time together, studying and talking. She wasn't like any of the girls I knew at home, they were all farm girls with no education and no ambition other than to get married and raise a family. She was different. It might surprise you to know that she was anti-slavery. Very much so. She influenced me considerably in that matter."

"No, Ellis, that doesn't surprise me. There are abolitionists in every state and a good many in the southern states. What happened to your romance?"

"I decided to join the army and even thought about making it a career. She was opposed to it, but we couldn't get married yet because her father insisted that she wait until she was eighteen, so I enlisted, and that's when I got sent west. She promised to wait for me though." Captain Johnson sat, melancholy, and despondent at the memory.

"What happened to her?" Sam asked.

"She married someone else while I was down fighting the Indians and Mexicans. I found out about it in a letter from my mother." He sipped his beer and watched the small fire warding off the cool of the fall evening, before adding, "She married my brother, Fred."

Sam waited patiently for further information recognizing that Captain Johnson was struggling with a difficult memory, one that he had suppressed with a great deal of conscious effort. Finally, Sam said, "That is most unfortunate."

Johnson chuckled and said, "That's one way to put it, Sam, but I was devastated. They met when I brought Lily home to meet my parents. I had no idea that they...." And he drifted again into meditations of his own, finally adding, "Mother's letter begged me not to take action, she couldn't bear to see her sons at odds. But the more I thought about it the angrier I became. I had thoughts of killing him. We were never that close, he was two years older and an ignorant bully as far as I was concerned, but he was against slavery as much as I was. My oldest and youngest brothers are pro-slavery. He sat quietly for a few moments then added, "My intention had been to become a career officer especially after making Captain, but they were scaling back the Army, so I was tossed aside by my country and my girl. You can imagine that I was pretty low. I left to go back to Mississippi, but by the time I got there, Fred and Lily had moved to Georgia."

"What did you do?"

"Went to work tracking runaway slaves. I guess I was trying to get even with her and chose the profession that would upset her the most. My oldest brother, Rod worked for Stephen Duncan as an overseer on one of his plantations and he hired me on."

"The same Stephen Duncan who bought the land for the Wilberforce Colony?"

"Yes, he wanted to get the free Blacks out of the country because they were stirring up the slaves by urging rebellion; at the same time, he was the largest slave owner in Mississippi. Anyway, Rod knew I needed to work, and I saw it as a way to get back at Fred and Lily. That kind of sums it up, Sam. I haven't thought about them for over a year and don't even know if they know what I've been doing. When I met your sister, Mary, that was the first I'd felt anything for a woman in a long time. She is something special."

"Did you tell her this story?"

"Yes, and she was very supportive. I asked her to come to

Philadelphia once I get settled there."

"I hope she does, Ellis, she's had some heartbreak in the romance department herself."

"So she told me. I have high hopes for the future, yet I can't help but worry that Mary will find someone else before we can be together. Don't you feel that way about Margaret?"

Sam reflected back to the embrace that he shared with Margaret on the stream in Wheeling, and the pledge they made to each other, before answering, "At one time I brooded over it, Ellis, but I don't today. I feel we're destined for each other…., both in love and our desire to end slavery. But it wasn't long ago that I went to sleep every night worried something would happen to cause her to lose her feelings for me, so I guess I know what you're saying."

"Well, affairs of the heart are always a challenge, Sam. Once we finish this business we'll get on with our life and our loves and I pray that someday I'll be a part of your family."

"Wouldn't that be ironic given the circumstances of our first meeting and by the way, Captain Johnson, those slaves were in the back of my wagon and the baby belonged to the slave woman. How about that?"

Johnson laughed and raised his beer to Sam, "I hate to be the butt of a joke, but I salute you for having the nerve to pull it off."

###

"These are the woes of Slaves;
They glare from the abyss;
They cry, from unknown graves,
"We are the Witnesses!"

Henry Wadsworth Longfellow, Poems on Slavery.

Friday, at noon, as they drove along the Potomac River, a convoy of several freight wagons approached going west, the lead wagon driven by Annie the clerk from Burton's freight office. Burton's Freight Service was emblazoned in bold letters on the sideboards.

"Miss Annie," Sam shouted, "It's me, Sam Wood from Ohio."

"I remember ya from takin Sally tu the Smithson place with that new buggy they bought. Sally run'ed oft you know, damn shame too cause' she's the onliest one could make these stubborn mules behave." Annie wore rough dungarees and a coarse flannel shirt with a wide-brimmed hat covering her hair. She was a harsh looking woman, one that any man would give a wide berth in case of trouble.

"I know about it. That's why I'm here, we're going to find her. This is Captain Johnson and he's a detective going to help us find out what happened."

"Pull up and chatter fer a spell," she called out. "Get them Goddamned pickaninnies off there," she shouted at one of the teamsters who had let some slave children climb on the wagon while they were stopped.

"Good God in Heaven, I've never, in all my days, seen a woman such as this," Captain Johnson whispered to Sam.

"Evidently her boss's wife is even worse," Sam replied.

"How's Burton doing?" Sam asked as she stood next to the buggy. Annie leaned over and spit a stream of tobacco juice next to the wagon wheel. "Oh Lord, he's just sick over losing Sally like that. We can't believe she up and left without a how-do-ya-do."

"I don't believe she did run off, Annie. I think she was captured by bounty hunters. She's just an innocent child."

"Yessir, I believe yore right bout' that. But who took her? I looked all over and there warn't no bounty hunters round there. We deliver dry goods to Hager's mercantile, he's old man Hager's son ya see, and he knows everything that happens in that town."

Captain Johnson tipped his hat and said, "Beggin' pardon Miss Annie but I been chasing runaway slaves for a long time and if she escaped, I'll find her. Do you really believe that she crossed the river?"

"Damn, you a fine lookin' hunk of a man. I've a mind to stay right here and show you what a real woman's made for. I'm damned tired of these skinny-assed excuses of men I got to work with." Sam and Ellis looked at the men teamsters and not a one of them weighed less than 250 pounds so she must have been referring to some other men. When she saw that Johnson wasn't taking the bait, she continued, "Shy, huh? Wail that's alright we got to be gittin' anyways. The truth is I don't think that little gal run off and I hope ya find er', but I hate tu think whut some o' them men would do to that little thing if'n they got aholt of her. Let's move you worthless slugs," she shouted and climbed into her wagon. "If'n ya get yer nerve up come and see me sometime, Captain."

Johnson and Sam watched the wagons rumble by, "Well, if it doesn't work out with Mary, you've got a fallback position ready-made, Ellis."

"That isn't funny, Sam."

Hagerstown is located north of the Potomac between Conococheague Creek on the west and Antetieum Creek on the east, only five miles from the Pennsylvania State Line. Both men had been through Hagerstown several times and decided to stop at the courthouse to see if the sheriff might have any information about Sally. They could see the Little Heiskell weathervane from two blocks away. The image, of a Hessian Soldier made in 1769 by a German tinsmith, had become a symbol of Hagerstown and signaled the end of their journey from Wheeling.

"I wish I had one of those new Sharp's Rifles," Captain Johnson said.

"Why, Ellis?"

"I'll bet you a penny to a lemonade that I could hit that tin soldier from here and put a hole right through it."

"That would be a heck of a shot. I'd probably take that bet."

The men climbed down and left their horses and buggy in the care of a stable assistant stationed on Main Street, as a valet. The Sheriff's office was located on the first floor of the beautiful limestone building.

"Can I help you gentlemen?"

Sam explained why they were there. Sheriff Anderson shook his head, "I told Annie before and again last night that I don't know nothing about what happened to her. I've got my suspicions, but I can't prove nothing."

"What do you think happened?"

"I think the Pritkin clan got her and if they did, she's gone now."

"Who are they?"

"Pig farmers south of town, old man and his idiot boy. The meanest, nastiest sumbitches you'll ever meet. Plus, they got two old Niggers that work for em' are just as bad. Bunch of slave women disappeared into that mess."

"Why don't you go out there and question them?" Johnson asked.

"Last sheriff did that we ain't seen hide ner' hair of since. They got a pack o' mean dogs that'll kill ya as look at ya. You can't get near the house and if you do, they'll shoot ya without warning."

"Don't they ever come to town?"

"Yeah."

"Well, why don't you question them then?"

"I did."

Sam was getting frustrated with this conversation, "What happened?"

"The old man just looked at me and that retard boy of his

said, "Ya want I should kill'im', Pa? Then they rode out of town and didn't look back. I've got nothing to arrest em' for, but if you want to come with me, I know where we can get a look at their place without them seeing us. Do you have field glasses or a telescope?"

The three men rode south, on a rough track, for about two miles, with heavy woods on each side, until they came to a bend where the trail curved back to the west. "See that opening down there on the right-hand side? That's where their property starts. If we went down there, they'd hear us, but we'll backtrack about 200 yards and get these horses out of sight, then we'll climb this hill behind us."

They followed the sheriff through the trees and brush as he wound up a slope that led to a steep drop off and a panoramic view of the valley. In the distance was a rough shack with smoke curling from a chimney and pens full of hogs and small plots of tobacco and corn. They could see people working in the fields and moving about around the house. Captain Johnson searched the scene through his field glasses and said, "I see several women working down there, Sam. One of them might be Sally." He passed the glasses over. Sam watched for a few minutes and finally said with mounting excitement, "That's her walking from the other side of the house carrying those buckets. Let's get our horses and ride in there and get her," he started back down the slope.

"Ain't you heard anything I've said," the sheriff asked, grabbing Sam. You won't get within 200 yards of that house."

"We can't just sit and wait, we have to do something," Sam argued.

"There's a team and wagon leaving with two men in it," Johnson said looking through his field glasses.

"It's the old man and his son. They must be taking some hogs into Reinhardt's Butcher Shop. If we hurry, we can get ahead of em' and I'll get a warrant from Judge Harkness to arrest em'. He's been wanting to get em' behind bars for a long time, but he's scared to death of em', and so am I. I'll need you to help me," Sheriff Anderson said.

They hurried back to their horses and galloped into town. The sheriff left to find the judge. Sam and Ellis waited inside the courthouse, watching the Pritkin wagon go by and turn down an alley next to the butcher shop. They circled around to a vantage point behind the stable and watched as the men climbed down from the wagon. The younger man walked to the back of the wagon and hoisted a pig carcass to his shoulder and carried it effortlessly inside the shop. Johnson said, "That's the biggest human being I've ever seen. He must be six feet six inches."

"And weighs 350 pounds."

"More like 400 and the old man isn't much smaller. What are we going to do?"

"Let's wait and see if Anderson shows up," Sam added. "But if there's any trouble, let them go. I don't want an innocent bystander to get hurt. You do have your pistols loaded, don't you Ellis?"

"I'm more worried about you and me getting hurt. They don't look any too friendly."

The men returned to the wagon and climbed back up. They were dressed in dirty coveralls over ragged cotton shirts, their hair long and matted. While the younger man was clean shaven the old man had a grey beard that grew wide and hung to his chest. Sam and Ellis followed them to the Mercantile where they began loading supplies for the return trip. Still no sign of the sheriff by the time the pig farmers were ready to leave.

"Ellis, we can't let them go before the sheriff gets back. What do you propose we do?"

"You're a good talker, Sam. Go over there and tell them who we are, and we want to buy the girl back, you know what to say, smooth talk them. I'll step over in front of the horses and keep them from leaving. Hurry, before they start moving."

Sam moved quickly to the middle of the street, dodging an oncoming buggy and looking both ways for other traffic. "Mr. Pritkin, a word, if you please," Sam said, walking up to about five feet of the large smelly man. "Allow me to introduce myself, I'm Sam Wood, from Mt. Gilead, Ohio, and that is my friend, Captain Ellis Johnson, from the State of Mississippi," indicating Johnson who had taken a position next to the horse on the street side of the team. "We would like to discuss a…., certain matter with you in a business-like way…."

"What you want, pigs, goat? We got backy' and corn. That's bout' it."

"No sir, you misunderstand my meaning. I don't need any meat or produce. I'm looking to buy back a certain young Negro girl you've stolen. She belongs to Senator Henry Clay and that man, Captain Johnson, is a detective hired to find her. We know she's out at your place and rather than cause trouble we propose to purchase her from you…., to save time and the trouble of beating you to death, which is what you truly deserve, you fat bucket of pig guts…."

"Way to smooth things over, Sam," Johnson said with his hands on his pistols."

The sheriff came rushing up with a deputy and the judge in tow. "Clem Pritkin, you're under arrest for slave-stealing. Now both of you get down off'n that wagon and come with me. Don't cause no trouble, Clem," the sheriff added, indicating the deputy who held a heavy Colt-Walker pistol at the ready.

"And you neither, Clarence," the deputy said to the large boy.

Clarence turned to his father, "What you want me tu do, Pa? Kill em'?"

"Nah, jus' sit still, Big-un, whilst I think on it a spell," the old man said scratching his beard.

Clem Pritkin looked from Sam to Ellis and back again trying to decide what to do. His slack-jawed boy sat patiently holding the reins. Sam stepped closer, as the old man stood, reached down behind the seat and came up with a gun; as he turned toward the deputy, Sam hit him on the forearm with his cane, smashing his arm, causing him to drop the gun, and fall out of the wagon screeching in pain. Clarence squealed an ungodly pig noise and bolted out of his seat straight for Sam. "Shoot him," Ellis yelled, but the deputy fired over the head of the enraged giant. Captain Johnson pulled his pistol but hesitated for fear of hitting Sam. The crazed son came on fast, but Sam was able to take a full swing, like chopping wood, striking Clarence in the forehead, killing him instantly, knocking Sam backward, stumbling, but keeping his feet.

Meanwhile, the old man regained his senses and when he saw his boy bludgeoned to the ground, pulled a knife from his waist with his left hand, his right dangling useless at his side. He charged forward swinging the knife within inches of Sam's face. Sam staggered back, as a shot rang out, and the old man fell dead at his feet, the back of his head blown open. Ellis was ready to fire another shot if needed. The judge, Sheriff Anderson and deputy all stood, open-mouthed, at what they had witnessed.

"Did you see that, Judge? Blew his head clean apart."

"You saved my bacon, Ellis," Sam said picking up his hat and dusting his britches.

"Looks like we saved you the cost of a trial, Judge," Johnson said.

"It was self-defense, I was a witness to the whole thing," Judge Harkness said, wiping his brow. "I've never seen nuthin' like that. What you got in that club?" he asked.

"We've got to get Sally," Sam said. That's what we came for. You want to go, Sheriff, to see what they've got hidden out there?"

"I guess me and Skinny Bob mights' well tag along," the sheriff said, indicating his deputy. "You eliminated all the crime we got in Hagerstown anyway. Nothing for us to do here, and I want to see how many bodies they have out there. We got to be careful of them old Niggers, Toothless Joe and Bean, they're just as bad as these two."

The four men rode back to the Pritkin place hurried along by Sam's impatience. Captain Johnson rode alongside the deputy and asked him, "Why do they call you Skinny Bob? You ain't all that skinny."

"Cause' I got a cousin here in town also name of Bob, but he's a lot bigger than me, so he's always been Fat Bob, to tell us apart."

The men could hear the dogs coming as soon as they entered the trail to the cabin.

Ellis said, "Sam, I'm going to ride ahead and make sure those men don't try to do something unkind. You take care of the dogs."

Sam, Skinny Bob and the sheriff rode full tilt into the pack of dogs, Sam swinging his club and the deputy shooting the lead dog in the hip. It went down and then tried to limp away. The others hesitated a second, while Ellis rode on, but then they charged at Sam who clubbed one in the head as his horse danced and kicked at one nipping at his forelocks. The sheriff shot one with his pistol before Sam got control of his horse and hit two more dogs who ran off yelping in pain. They heard a shot from the farmhouse.

"Sounds like Captain Johnson had to shoot one," Sam yelled.

"That sounded more like a rifle," Skinny Bob answered and spurred his horse. They rode hard the two hundred yards to the house where they found Ellis lying on the ground with Sally and another black woman tending to him. Sally ran to Sam when she saw him, "Old Toothless Joe shot your friend. He in a bad way…., Mr. Sam, is dat you?"

"Where's the man who shot him?" Sam asked.

"He in de house wid' Bean, dey loadin' der rifles. You best watch out."

Infuriated, Sam grabbed Ellis' still loaded pistols and ran to the door breaking it in with a smash from his foot and firing at the first thing that moved, killing a man trying to get out of a back window. The other man rushed by Sam and was shot by the deputy as he reached the front stoop. Sam turned back to where Johnson lay. Sally looked up at him, tears in her eyes, "He daid, Mr. Sam."

###

"'Tis the star-spangled banner;
O long may it wave
O'er the land of the free,
and the home of the brave!"

Francis Scott Key 1779-1843 Lawyer, Slaveholder and Poet

Allan Pinkerton left his wagon and horses with Tobias at the Wood Stables in Wheeling and boarded the steamboat, Intrepid, bound for Pittsburgh. He was in high spirits, well rested and fed, as he made his way to Philadelphia and the new contract job for Stephan Girard's Bank. He had a good man, in Captain Johnson, set to take over the management of the contract for payroll security at the oldest Bank in America. But primarily, Pinkerton was pleased with the letter he had received from his wife, Joan, who expressed sorrow at being so negative. She and the children had been sick, and she missed him. He wrote back telling her of his success with the new contract and promising to be home within the month.

Billy helped Pinkerton carry his valise and a satchel full of papers down to the boat. As the Intrepid pulled away, he waved at Allan from the dock, and shouted, "I'll take good care of your horses and buggy."

He kept himself busy, not requiring his father to tell him what to do. Billy was as familiar with the operation of Toby's as was the proprietor himself, with the exception of Richard, who knew every aspect of the business even better than the boss. Richard controlled the labor force, mostly free Blacks and Irish immigrants.

Billy made his way back to the store. A scream from the house frightened the boy who dashed through the store, ignoring the questions of shoppers about the problem. He didn't know either. As he exited the back door, his mother shouted for him to run get Doctor Lisco. Billy didn't wait to ask what had happened, he ran, as fast as he could. When they returned, Billy's grandfather was stretched out on the front porch of the house; Esther and the children sobbing over him. The doctor pronounced him dead at the scene. Heart failure had claimed the great abolitionist, David Wood.

###

"It should be held as an eternal truth, that what is morally wrong can never be politically right." **Hannah More 1745-1833, British Writer, Philanthropist, Abolitionist**

Allan settled into a chair on the Boiler Deck and lit a cigar. The day was overcast, and rain threatened, but the temperature was comfortable. The captain blew the ship's horn startling Pinkerton who was deep in thought about the events of the past week. He was well aware of the recent series of boiler explosions on the river, with many lives lost. The powerful expulsion of steam reminded him of the dangers. Congress was debating ways to pass legislation requiring new standards for boiler construction and licensing for those who operated them. He felt secure knowing that the Intrepid was well designed and built with the newest and safest boilers in existence.

Toby Wood had proven to be a wonderful host and they spent the evenings writing abolitionist letters and attending meetings with other likeminded citizens in the Wood home. They had scheduled several Underground Railroad deliveries and participated in helping an entire family reach Canada.

Shouting from the stairwell interrupted his musing and caused him to turn his attention to an argument between two officers of the deck and a large black man clothed in a fine suit, cut in the European style, wearing a fashionable bowler. The Negro was smiling politely but insistent upon being granted admittance to the first-class level.

"The darkies are required to ride below, I don't give a goddamned flip who you are," the first mate shouted. "This deck is for whites only."

In a pronounced British accent, the man calmly said, "Quite right, your honor, however, when I purchased my ticket, I paid for a first-class berth and the agent could see quite clearly the color of my skin. Now I insist that I be given my cabin."

The mate appeared flustered and angry, "I'm sick and tired of this, you uppity son-of-a-bitch. I don't care if you're from England or Africa or goddamned Hell, I don't care. I don't give a good goddamn if you own a circus or this boat, which you don't. Now, listen to me you black bastard, I will have my crew remove you below and toss you overboard if I have to."

"I traveled first class from England aboard the American Flyer and then first class to this point on the Empress. I fail to see why your boat should be any different."

Pinkerton strolled slowly to the altercation where he stepped between the officers and introduced himself, "Hello Mr. Darby, my name is Allan Pinkerton. I recognize you from an illustration in the Chicago Tribune. How's your American visit going?"

"Very pleased, I'm sure, Mr. Pinkerton. I'm afraid this type of behavior has become all too familiar. My wife, Elizabeth, and I are traveling to Philadelphia for discussions about a possible American tour but because of incidents like this, I am predisposed to believe that such an undertaking would be futile."

Allan looked up and tipped his hat to the captain who was listening intently from the hurricane deck. "Captain, this is Mr. William Darby, who's also known as Pablo Fanque. He is a well-known businessman and circus owner from England. Now I would like to invite him and his wife to my cabin for a chat and don't want any interference in doing so. That is a reasonable request, isn't it Captain?"

"His wife's white, Captain Johannson," one of the officers shouted.

The captain addressed the two officers, "Mr. Smith, Mr. Pollard, come to the hurricane deck at once."

"Now Captain?" The first-mate asked"

"NOW, Mr. Smith!" The captain commanded and the two men ran to the stairs leading up to the Pilot House. The captain tipped his hat to Allan and Mr. Darby.

"William, please fetch your wife and meet me in my suite, number 210," Allan said.

Mr. Darby hurried back down the stairs to find Elizabeth. They rendezvoused in Pinkerton's room, where they spent the rest of the morning discussing Darby's visit. He and Elizabeth operated the most successful equestrian and performance circus in England, Scotland and Ireland, very lucrative and the Darby's were among the wealthiest people of color in Europe. William thought that an American tour might be a good idea, but after witnessing, first-hand, the treatment of the slaves and the animosity toward people of color he changed his mind. He planned to travel back to the East Coast and depart for England at the earliest opportunity.

"Do you suppose those officers will give us any more trouble, Mr. Pinkerton?" Mrs. Darby asked.

"I know Captain Johannson quite well. He's a Scotsman who is anti-slavery. He won't allow them to harass you anymore, but to be safe I want you to stay here tonight, you can have the main bedroom behind that door, and I'll sleep right here on the couch."

The Darby's accompanied Allan all the way to Philadelphia where they parted company. Pinkerton promised to come and visit them when he and his family traveled to England. Allan thought that Joan would like the idea of visiting the home of her ancestors in London. He resolved to write her from the hotel that very afternoon.

Before checking in, Allen decided to stop by the Girard Bank on South Third Street and let Harold Lloyd, the President, know that he was in town. He and Lloyd stepped over to the Philadelphian, a fine restaurant, and had a late lunch while they discussed some of the details of what would be a rather large contract requiring three or four men, in addition to Captain Johnson. Pinkerton was cautiously hopeful that he could convince Sam Wood to join his company as a supervisor. The room was still bustling with activity as various businessmen stopped by and spoke with the banker and detective.

Glowing with a feeling of euphoria at the turn of fortune his life had taken, Allan began composing a letter, in his mind to Ed Rucker, outlining some new business ideas, including concentrating on their detective business rather than the protection and bodyguard divisions. He arrived at the Girard Hotel at five p.m. expecting to find Sam Wood and Ellis Johnson. Instead he was handed a letter by the desk clerk.

Hagerstown, Maryland

September 15, 1848
Dear Allan,

It is with heavy heart that I write these words. Our good friend and companion, Captain Ellis Johnson, was murdered, in a rescue operation on Friday last, under terrible circumstances. Captain Johnson had become a good friend and I find that I must notify not only you, his employer, but my sister Mary, who had become his close confidant. Neither of you can shed more tears than I, searching my soul for clues as to what I could have done differently, yet I know that this is the will of God. I will discover what it is that I must do to vindicate the death of a gallant warrior because that is what I consider his death to be, a casualty of war, the war between the forces of good and evil. His death will be avenged.

I am returning to Ohio after having sent Ellis' body on to his parents in Mississippi. Please stop in Ohio on your return from Philadelphia so that I may tell you of the details.

Yours Truly,
Samuel N. Wood

###

"A teacher who is attempting to teach without inspiring the pupil with a desire to learn is hammering on cold iron." **Horace Mann 1796-1859, Politician and Educational Reformer**

The clang of the school bell startled Sarah as she and Jimmie Kendrick sat side by side on a swing in the church yard, which also served as a schoolhouse during the week. Margaret stopped ringing the bell and said, "Hurry now children, we have a great deal to get done today before we dismiss."

"I wish Sam would get back," Caroline Lyon whispered, "My sister is a slave driver and Sam lets us have longer for recess."

"I know," Efren Wood said, "She made me write my letters

twenty times yesterday. My hand hurt when I got done. She must think we don't have anything else to do with our time. I have to help Papa milk the cows when I get home."

"I have to help Beulah with the laundry and cooking and cleaning, Efren, you don't have it any worse than the girls do."

"I didn't say I did...."

"Quiet everyone! Open your bibles to Psalms 127 and start with verse three, let me see...., Freddie, will you please read and the rest of you follow along."

Freddie groaned, but turned to the passage and began reading in a struggling voice, as if he were sneezing the words rather than reading them, "*Children are a heritage from the LORD, offspring a reward from him. Like ARROWS in the hands of a warrior are children BORN in one's youth....*"

Suddenly the door burst open and Sam charged into the room catching his future bride in a sweeping embrace. He waved to the class as they cheered. The flustered and surprised Margaret could only repeat, "Oh, Sam," several times while she tried to kiss him and chastise him at the same time. When order had been restored Sam announced that class would be over until Monday, which ignited another cheer, quickly extinguished by news that they had to read several pages of the Gospel of Matthew. Sam sent his brothers and sisters home and had Rich and Caroline ride ahead to the Lyon home while Sam and Margaret followed in Sam's buggy so that he could tell her the news in private. They rode silently for a mile or so before Margaret said, "I sense something's wrong Sam, are you going to tell me what it is?"

He turned to face her, "I don't know how you can tell; I've been putting on my best face, Margaret. I've dreaded the thought of telling you for fear that it would cause you more worry, but here it is, the good Lord has seen fit to call Captain Johnson home. He was murdered in Hagerstown during the rescue of young Sally."

She clasped her hand to her mouth as tears sprang to her eyes. "Oh, Sam, please stop and let me off for a moment, I need to walk; I can't breathe." She walked to the side of the road and gazed over the Ohio countryside as Sam held his arms around her waist until she was composed.

"Poor Mary," she finally said. "She was taken with him."

Sam nodded with his face in Margaret's hair, "I know! She did not react well to the news. Stacey had to comfort her all night last night. I was sick with worry about telling her."

"Sam, you need to understand how I feel," she said turning to face him. "I know men and women are going to die in this struggle, but I believe that you are an instrument of God just like your Grandfather Mosher. You aren't going to die on the battlefield, but in my arms and of old age, after we've accomplished all that we desire, the end of slavery, equality for women, the future of our unborn children and, best of all, the love that we will share for the rest of our lives. I'm sorry about the loss of your friend but I'm certain that he was doing God's work under your guidance...., did you really rescue Sally?"

"Yes, we did, Margaret. She's at the farm helping Silas and Miriam. I want her to come live with us when we're married, she can be our living testament to the ungodliness of slavery and what the Africans can become. Let's get you home, I want to talk to your mother and father about our wedding plans, and I'll fill you in on all the details.

"By the way, hold out your hand." He slipped a ring on her finger. "Will you marry me?"

PART TWO
EVIL OF COLOSSAL MAGNITUDE

"Remember them that are in bonds, as bound with them; and them which suffer adversity, as being yourselves also in the body." **Hebrews 13:3**

"I have observed this in my experience of slavery, - that whenever my condition was improved, instead of its increasing my contentment, it only increased my desire to be free, and set me to thinking of plans to gain my freedom. I have found that, to make a contented slave, it is necessary to make a thoughtless one. It is necessary to darken his moral and mental vision, and, as far as possible, to annihilate the power of reason. He must be able to detect no inconsistencies in slavery; he must be made to feel that slavery is right; and he can be brought to that only when he ceased to be a man." **Frederick Douglass, Narrative of the Life of Frederick Douglass**

February 1854
Columbus, Ohio

The law offices of Stinchcomb and Brumbaugh occupied a prime spot along Broad Street, leading from the Scioto River and the Franklinton Bridge, east into the burgeoning business district. The new train depot was four blocks north in what was becoming the commercial district. Columbus, Ohio was beginning to show signs of its newfound political and economic powers with a State House being constructed at Third and Broad Street just down from the office. Sam's efforts on behalf of his last client, a Negro slave family, had garnered nationwide attention, not all of it favorable, certainly not in the slave states, but the abolitionists had found a new champion in the feisty schoolteacher turned attorney.

Robert Brumbaugh, Sam's mentor, looked the part of a kindly grandfather, but he was also a successful attorney, who shared the same beliefs as the Wood family. Brumbaugh was bald with a fringe of curly white hair, his crown burned red from hours spent tending the vegetable garden at his home along the Scioto. He was anti-slavery, but he was also getting older and yearned for a less stressful career.

"Sam, I'm begging you to be reasonable. Forget the fact that I've invested over three years in teaching you the law; forget about throwing away your brilliant future in politics; but you can't ignore the danger to your family. You have two small children. How can you even consider dragging them off to the wilderness? For heaven sakes man, there are still Indians out there, and what about the Border Ruffians? I've heard they're worse than the Indians. Sam, at least talk to Salmon about this, or Pinkerton."

"I've already discussed it with them. My friends and my family are well aware of my intentions. I gave my word, Bob. Maybe I shouldn't have been so rash, but I said, 'if they pass the Kansas-Nebraska Act, I'm going to Kansas'"

"What about Margaret? Have you truly discussed this matter with her, or did you just tell her 'we're going' and that was the end of it?"

"I begged her to wait here until I send for her, but she won't have it. She swore to stick with me through thick and thin, and that's what she's going to do, Bob. If you want to tell her, have at it, but make sure I'm out of the line of fire when you do."

"What about your work with Lincoln? You've just now got the Republican Party on its feet and you're going to traipse off to the territories? KANSAS, for God's sake, man, what in the hell are you thinking? You promised Abe that you'd campaign with him in Illinois, and what about working with Pinkerton and Fred Douglass on the John Brown business? You're just now establishing a reputation as a top-notch lawyer. Are you going to throw that away? Here come's Margaret, I want to hear what she has to say about this."

Margaret Wood strolled across the dirt street from the mercantile. A black buggy pulled up next to her and stopped in the road, forcing horses, wagons and pedestrians to go around, but no one seemed put out by the inconvenience. Margaret was radiant in motherhood, with a few pounds added, but all in proper proportion; she exuded confidence, bare-headed in the glow of the Ohio Spring morning, her head thrown back in laughter and the sun framing her face like a sunbeam-filled meadow.

Sam went to the window and watched Margaret visiting with Reverend James Preston Poindexter, Preacher of the Second Baptist Church, the first Negro church in Columbus. Poindexter, a passionate abolitionist, was a friend and confidant of the Wood family.

Sam was consumed with love for his bride of five years, more so than when they wed. Love was unconditional, and forever in Sam's mind, and the decision to go to Kansas was a joint one, as inflexible as his affection for Margaret, who was of an independent mind and as strong, in her own way, as Sam. He was proud of her and what she had accomplished in fighting for the rights of women, working alongside Sam's mother, Esther, and other women like Lucretia Mott and Susan B. Anthony.

He turned back to the discussion, "Abe Lincoln is not an abolitionist, Bob. He may be anti-slavery, but he doesn't believe that African's are truly equal to Whites. The only reason he's against slavery is because he believes that it's bad for the advancement of the white race, not the detriment of the Blacks.

His only concern is keeping the Union from being torn apart."

"But you're working together on the Republican platform. When I was in Springfield last month, he told me that he's counting on you to help with the campaign."

"You really think that'll come off?"

"Abe thinks so and that's all that matters right now. He needs you, Sam."

"Abe's still a Whig," Sam said in disgust. "He's blowing whichever way the winds of politics push him. He's got the gift of gab, I'll grant you that, but he rubs some people the wrong way."

"Oh," Brumbaugh laughed, "And you don't? The problem with you is that you don't give a damn who gets the credit. You do all the work and the others get the benefit. That's not the mark of a good politician, Sam."

"I only care about the end result and I do think I could lead the cause, but I won't get the support from the Whigs or the Republicans. I'm a realist. I'll do better keeping Kansas a free state than I would tilting at these partisan windmills."

He walked back to the window to see what was keeping Margaret. She continued to chat with Poindexter, but Sam wasn't watching Margaret anymore, his attention was riveted on a man across the street.

"Robert, come here, quick."

"What is it?"

"Look there across the street outside the saloon."

"Oh my, that's trouble," Brumbaugh said. "Don't go out there Sam, I'll run get Sheriff Hunt."

Robert hurried out the front door as the man walked across the street in front of the buggy. Margaret saw him and it frightened her into looking at Sam's office, where she spotted him in the window; he motioned for her to get in the buggy. Poindexter understood immediately and moved on at a trot.

"Wood, you Nigger lovin' son-of-a-bitch, get out here," the staggering lout shouted, stopping all traffic, and causing citizens to scurry into the shops and houses lining Broad Street. He was drunk enough to ramp up his courage but not drunk enough to impair his actions, a dangerous combination in an angry man. Sam calmly glanced to see if Sheriff Hunt was coming.

Merle Caldwell pulled a pistol from his coat, holding it at his side, not aimed at anyone, but more the menacing for it, "Wood, I hate your guts and I'm gonna' kill you today. You ruined me, now I'm gonna' ruin you. I know you're in there you goddamned coward," he sobbed and brandished the gun toward the office, finally focusing enough to see Sam standing at the window.

Caldwell was a ruddy man of average height with thick black hair and an overbite like a hungry rat. He was cruel and heartless, even depraved, to his slaves, but a reputable family man with three children and many friends throughout the south. He stood alone in the sunlight a stark and ugly counterpoint to the beauty of a few moments earlier.

Caldwell's wife suddenly appeared and attempted to calm him. His oldest son was also begging Merle to put the gun down. Sheriff Hunt was still missing but Robert hurried back toward the office. Sam was relieved that Margaret pulled away in the buggy without being seen by Caldwell. Mrs. Caldwell's presence seemed to be calming the situation, which surprised Sam, because the last time he had seen her she had threatened to kill Merle Caldwell.

"Sheriff's on his way. Let's just stay in here and wait for Hunt to handle this," Robert said. Sam glanced back to the street as Merle pulled the gun away from his son and fired through the window, the bullet created a neat round hole just above and to the left of Sam's head.

"Ok, by all that's Holy, enough is enough," Sam said, and grabbed his cane. Another shot rang out. Sam jerked the door open and watched as Merle's son sank to the ground cradled in his father's arms. Caldwell screamed in anguish and disbelief. Mrs. Caldwell wailed in anger and fell to the ground by her son. Sheriff Hunt rushed up, took one look and pushed Sam down the street. "Get out of here, Sam. I'll handle this."

Merle Caldwell glanced up in tormented agony, saw Sam and crawled over his son, scrambling for the gun, his face contorted in a mask of hatred and loathing. Sam turned to face him. He'd never, in his life, run from a fight and he wasn't about to begin now.

###

"The slave girl is reared in an atmosphere of licentiousness and fear."

Harriet Ann Jacobs 1813-1897 Incidents in the Life of a Slave Girl

Merle Caldwell's case aroused intense emotions among those observers in the courtroom, and people throughout the nation following the case in the newspapers. The abolitionists celebrated Sam's every courtroom victory and suffered with the setbacks, which were many. The pro-slavery press vilified the name of Sam Wood and cheered as the judge handed down ruling after ruling, all going against Sam and his clients, Mary Fedder, and her husband, Tom. The trial was known throughout the south as the Sam Wood Show. He was happy to expose the hypocrite Caldwell for the kind of brutal, perverted man he was, overcoming the prejudices of the white neighbors, and the unsuspecting Mrs. Caldwell, but also distraught at the pitiless degeneration of the white race when it came to slavery. Captain Johnson's words, as they cruised up the Ohio River some five years earlier, came back to Sam; what could he have done differently and how many lives were affected by his actions? Was the resulting freedom of the slaves worse than the problem of slavery, as Johnson predicted? Not in Sam's mind, Caldwell created this situation and now it was time to pay the piper.

Merle Caldwell was born in Ohio, but moved to Georgia with his parents, when he was a young boy. When Caldwell's grandfather died leaving a farm near the Ohio River to the grandchildren, Merle Caldwell returned to manage the family holdings. He brought several slaves with him including a family: mother, father, two strapping boys, and a young girl about thirteen, a mulatto. Caldwell made them live on the Kentucky side, and ferried them across the river in chains to work on his farm in Ohio.

One cold November afternoon, six months earlier, Sam and Margaret received a visit from the slave family, who showed up on their front porch unannounced. Sam did not know them, nor did he know Caldwell. The father, Tom, no last name, and the mother, Mary Fedder, stood in the warmth of the Wood living room dressed in their best clothes, which were rags to most folk. The children remained standing as Margaret urged the parents to sit in the straight back chairs at the dining table where Sam waited patiently for the story. They were visibly distraught, rigid, while the children stared wide-eyed like frightened animals who've stumbled into a hunter's glare. The two boys sheltered their younger sister. When the silence grew unbearable Tom said, quietly, "I'z a free man, Mister Wood."

"Everyone in Ohio is free, Tom. Why do you feel a need to tell me that you are a free man?"

"Because Massa Caldwell holdin' me n' ma fambly cross de river in Kentucky. Has been fo' dese many year. I been lookin' for a chance to run. Dat's why we here today. You a fair man, we know from de udder Negro folk here bout'. Dey tole me, come see Mr. Sam Wood, he know what tu do."

"So, you want passage to Canada, is that it?"

Tom fidgeted, looked to his wife who put her hand on his arm and nodded for him to continue, "No suh, I wants tu take him tu court and prove I'm a free man. I don't want tu run nowhere."

"You want to take him to court?" Sam said incredulously, "Why in the world would you want to do such a thing? I doubt that you can even get a trial, a slave has no legal rights. We can get you to Canada and save years of heartache and possibly worse. I don't know this Caldwell, but he and his slaveholding friends will bring down the full force of their laws on you and your family. Not to mention other…., disgusting methods they will employ, they'll make your life miserable."

Mary Fedder spoke for the first time. She was a tall, beautiful, dark skinned woman with a wonderful smile, kept hidden, but all the more powerful when employed; lines were etched in her face from years of slavery. A distinctive scar marred one eyebrow. It became obvious to the Woods, from her first utterance, that she was not an ordinary slave woman.

"Mr. and Mrs. Wood, we are both freeborn, captured into slavery 13 years ago. We shouldn't be forced to run anywhere. We have done nothing wrong except be born black. We want justice for our children," she said.

"Does this Caldwell know where you are?" Margaret asked gently.

"No Ma'am," Tom exclaimed emphatically. "We cain't go back der now. He kill us if'n we do. Look what he done to my boy cause he tried to skip out with Cecily here. Take off your shirt, Joseph."

The older boy pulled the coarse shirt over his head and showed the scars across his back.

"Massa beat him cause' we sent him nort' with de girl," he indicated his daughter, "tu save her from what de Massa doin' tu her. Dey caught Joseph, but Cecily run off to Reverend Rankin's place. Caldwell kill her if he find her."

"Why?" Sam asked.

"Cause he her daddy and doan' want us tu tell de Missus Caldwell, she think de father ole Massa Caldwell, Merle's daddy. But ain't so, Merle Caldwell de daddy, now he after her jus' like he done my wife. I'll mos' likely kill him if he come roun', Mr. Wood. We cain't carry on dis way no mo'."

Sam rose, went to the fireplace and added kindling. He gazed into the flames and then paced the floor, finally stopping to look at Margaret.

"Sally and John will let them stay at their house," Margaret said. Sam merely nodded.

"Do you have papers that show you're free?"

"We did Mr. Wood, but when de bounty hunters come on us dey took the papers and gave em' tu Massa Caldwell in Georgia. We was visitin' my parents in Virginia when dey dun' it. We was travlin' from Maryland, I war' workin' in de ship yards dar'."

"Can anyone in Maryland vouch for you being a free man?"

"Yessir, Frederick Douglass, hisself, can. He a cousin o' Mary."

"Why didn't Fred come and get you in Georgia?"

"Well, suh, firs' off he didn't know where we wuz, and when he foun' out, he couldn't go into de slave states, or dey would'a captured him after de Bloodhound Law was passed."

"All too common a story," Sam said more to himself than anyone else in the room.

"Beg pardon, Mr. Wood, I didn't catch that."

"Tom, Mary...., I beg you to go to Canada. I can guarantee you free passage and you'll be safe. You can raise your children in peace...., but if you pursue this matter, I can't begin to tell you how terrible the consequences will be. I doubt, very much, we can even get a hearing and the burden of proof will be on you. Your word against his, and I don't think I need to spell out who will be believed."

They sat quietly, David age five, and Lloyd three, crept up next to their mother and watched the black children with the same wide-eyed look of wonder. Lloyd waved at the girl who tentatively waved back. Sam looked at Margaret, almost pleading with her to back his attempt to sway them from the dangerous path they wanted to follow.

Margaret said, "Sam, we can't turn our backs on them just because we're afraid of the consequences. We have to do something."

"You're sure your minds are made up about this?"

"Yas'sir!"

Sam took a deep breath and said, "I'll do everything I can to get you a trial. But if I fail, then you have to promise me that you'll run to Canada with utmost speed."

Tom looked at his wife and they both nodded yes to Sam.

He looked at Margaret and said, "We may have to go with them."

###

"Negro Slavery is an evil of colossal magnitude and I am utterly averse to the admission of Slavery into the Missouri Territories." **John Adams, Familiar Letters of John Adams**

March 1854

The trial was held in Cincinnati. The proceedings were conducted against all odds, after months of wrangling over the venue, whether Kentucky or Ohio; even Virginia was mentioned as a possibility. Sam fought successfully against any slave state location. Another month was required to fill the jury, with each side recusing anyone even remotely antagonistic to their point of view. The Federal Government took an interest because of the

Fugitive Slave Law and sent a participating attorney to sit with Caldwell's private attorney and a third attorney from the State of Kentucky. The trial generated a sensation throughout the nation and citizens both pro and anti-slavery filled the seats in the courthouse.

Judge Thaddeus Wilcox presided. He was an honest man, appointed a State of Ohio Court Judge by Governor Reuben Wood in 1846. Wood was a democrat who happened to be a distant cousin of Sam's. Governor Wood made it clear that his loyalty was with Sam, as did Salmon Chase who would be Governor of Ohio following Reuben Wood. The influence of these men swayed the decision to have the trial in Ohio rather than Kentucky, which the Federal Government Representative preferred.

Duncan Trimble, the State Attorney from Kentucky had the floor questioning the respondent Merle Caldwell, "Mr. Caldwell, you have produced a Bill of Sale for the Negro man Tom and his wife, Mary Fedder, is that correct?"

"Yeah, you got it right there in your hand."

"Your Honor, I submit this document as evidence that these are legal slaves owned by Mr. Caldwell and as such, are not entitled to a trial by jury or to testify in court on their behalf."

"I object, your Honor," Sam said. "These folks aren't on trial, Mr. Caldwell is."

"A slave can't sue a white man," The Federal attorney, Richard Morgan said from his seat at the defendants table. "African slaves are not accorded any rights under the constitution because they are not citizens of the United States. Mr. Wood knows this perfectly well."

"Not citizens," Sam shouted jumping to his feet. "Are you a citizen, Mr. Morgan?"

"Of course I am," he replied indignantly.

"What makes you a citizen?"

"Why I was born here. Your Honor, what has this got to do with the matter at hand?"

"I'll explain it to you, Richard, and I'll go real slow cause' I know you're from Washington." Sam waited until the laughter from the packed house slowed, during which time the judge pounded his gavel and glared at Sam. "They were born here just like you. And you know what? Their parents and their grandparents, before them. I checked it out, Richard, because I knew that you would bring it up. I happen to know that your parents were born in Ireland and immigrated here. Why, these people are more citizens of the United States than Mr. Morgan ever thought of being."

Morgan stood and pounded the table, red-faced, with spittle shooting from his angry lips, "This is an outrage your honor, this man is maligning me, a representative of the United States Government and taking the side of a naked savage, an African slave who is ignorant of any sense of civilized…."

"Now just a minute there, Richard," Sam interrupted him and turned to Tom, "You ever been to Africa, Tom?"

"No suh, I'm not rightly sure where it is."

"Sit down, both of you," Judge Wilcox ordered, pounding his gavel as deputies stepped forward to keep order. "Gentlemen, this is not a debate or, worse, a minstrel show, this is a trial, and I warn you that I won't put up with this bickering between the attorneys. Now continue with your questioning of the witness, Mr. Trimble, and you, Sam Wood, are on a short leash."

Morgan sat back visibly trembling in anger, while Trimble continued, "Thank you, Your Honor, I just get all riled up inside when we allow ignorant slaves to make a comment in a court of law. They have no standing either legally or morally, and we have in the witness box an American citizen, a man following the laws of our land, drug into court by slaves…., property, Your Honor, not citizens, but chattel just like his cotton or his cattle, owned legally by him. Merle Caldwell is honest and an upstanding father, a neighbor and fine gentleman of southern raising, who…."

Sam jumped up, "Objection, Your Honor…."

"What now, Sam? Let me guess, where is the question in all of this, right?"

"No, Your Honor, it's just that there isn't any evidence that Merle is honest or upstanding."

The spectators howled with laughter while the judge, banged his gavel.

The argument raged for days. Sam introduced the Commonwealth of Massachusetts v. Aves case which held that a slave transported by his master into a free state was entitled to freedom because of the laws of the state. The attorney from the Federal Government, Morgan, argued that Sam couldn't have it both ways that he couldn't argue that Tom and Mary were free then argue that they were slaves transported to a free state who should be set free under those circumstances. The case looked bad for Sam until Caldwell's attorneys made the mistake of saying that the slaves had no right to run off because they were treated, 'as well as my own children.'

Sam stood with his cane in hand and strolled to the jury box banging the famous club on the floor as he went, then stood with his back to the jury and tapped the weapon against the railing of the witness stand.

"Your Honor, Mr. Wood is attempting to intimidate my client with this ostentatious display of aggression and hostility."

"Sam, put that club down," Judge Wilcox ordered.

"Oh, I'm sorry, Judge, just my way of thinking of how to best address this new evidence. I apologize to the court, I certainly meant no disrespect and definitely no malice toward Mr. Caldwell, a paragon of virtue and southern morals. But, Your Honor, because the declaration has been made, that Merle treats his slaves like his own children, I feel it obligatory to examine the issue." Sam turned to face the jury, twelve men equally divided between pro and anti-slavery sentiments. "Now, Merle, you state that you treat your slaves as well as you treat your own children. Let's have a look. Your family is here in the gallery above us are they not?"

"Yeah, they're up there."

"Please stand, Mrs. Caldwell and children. Ah, there they are and a fine-looking family, I grant you that. In fact, those two boys don't look like they've missed many meals have they, Merle."

Caldwell looked up proudly and said, "I provide for my own."

"So you've declared," Sam glared at the man. "Please remain standing, boys. Now, let's compare them with Tom and Mary's children, please stand Joseph, Michael, and Cecily."

The black children rose to a murmur of unrest from the audience, the children conspicuous in their raggedy clothes and reed-thin bodies, their hang-dog look from years of being told not to look a white man in the face.

"Raise your shirt, Joseph and turn around so the jury can see your back."

Cries from the ladies in the gallery caused Judge Wilcox to pound his gavel as the ugly scars from the overseer's whip stood out in a grotesque portrait of barbarity. The raised welts looked like giant black centipedes clawing across his back.

"Your Honor, I beg you to stop this disgrace," Attorney Trimble cried as both the other attorneys' shouted in anger.

"Sit down, boy" the judge ordered. "Sam, this type of demonstration is best conducted in private. There are ladies present."

"Yes, there are, Judge, and they need to see what's going on down there in the South. They're ignorant of it or they turn a blind eye. Now, I want to see the back of those Caldwell boys standing up there to see if they have the same markings. That will prove if Mr. Caldwell is truthful or not."

"Your Honor, please don't allow this travesty," Trimble shouted.

"This is an outrage, Judge, the Federal Government insists that you stop this mockery, immediately."

"All of you sit down…., everyone sit down and let me think. This is most unusual, and I want to make certain that we proceed according to the law not emotion." Judge Wilcox ordered. "I need a break. We'll resume after lunch, One o'clock. Sam Wood, I want you in my chambers at 12:45."

Margaret rushed into the courtroom followed by Sally with David and Lloyd and her son, Caleb. "Stephan will be here today," Margaret told Sam, who grabbed her in a hug.

"When did you get here, darling?" He embraced the boys and squeezed Sally's arm. "How are they, Sal?"

"Just fine, Sam. They healthy as horses."

"We came down last night but stayed at Aunt Ruth's house. We wanted to surprise you with the news about Stephan."

"When did you find out?"

"Efren got to Columbus Tuesday with word that Stephan had one more trip to Philadelphia to get whatever he was looking for and would leave immediately for Cincinnati. He should be here today unless something happened to slow him down."

At 12:30, Sam, Robert Brumbaugh, and the three attorneys for Caldwell were in the judge's chambers discussing the procedure for the afternoon. Trimble began, "Your Honor, this request to have white children disrobe in the courtroom is beyond belief…."

"Oh," Sam interjected, "You don't object to the black children disrobing?"

"They shouldn't even be in the courtroom. It's an affront to civilized proceedings," Morgan countered.

"Gentlemen, I am getting mighty tired of this. I'm going to find you all in contempt if you don't learn to behave in a legal manner, and to address the court, not each other," The judge warned.

"Your Honor allow me to withdraw the line of questioning that I was pursuing this morning, if that would help," Sam said.

"That would be a beginning. Then I'd like to know when you're going to present your case. You haven't presented any evidence on behalf of your clients."

"I promise that will change."

###

But I now entered on my fifteenth year - a sad epoch in the life of a slave girl. My master began to whisper foul words in my ear. Young as I was, I could not remain ignorant of their import. **Harriet Ann Jacobs**

When court reconvened Stephan was sitting at the Complainant's table with Sam and Robert. Caldwell's attorneys appeared concerned, "What are you up to now, Wood?" Morgan asked.

Courtroom observers fanned themselves as the room heated with little respite despite all the windows being opened on both levels of the chambers. Judge Wilcox entered and after the formalities, he sat eyeing Sam apprehensively. A look of serene contentment graced Sam's face as he glanced at Margaret in the gallery, gave her a slight nod and smile, then continued observing the courtroom with seemingly no care in the world. But inside he was seething with indignation at the circumstances leading to this moment. It took all of his self-control not to strike out at Merle Caldwell and wipe the arrogant smirk off his face once and forever.

"Sam, the judge is speaking to you," Stephan said.

"I'm sorry, Your Honor, I didn't catch what you said."

"I asked, are you here with us or would you rather be somewhere else?'

Sam jumped up and strode around the table to the jury, "I'm anxious to get to it, Your Honor. I was just thinking of the best way to present this new evidence so as not to violate the parameters of good conduct you've set for me. And I certainly don't want to upset the genteel and refined sensibilities of my esteemed colleagues and their client. I'm prepared to proceed with all caution, because, as anyone will tell you, Sam Wood does everything in his power to avoid trouble."

Stephan looked at Robert Brumbaugh who shook his head and took a deep breath.

"Well, get to it then," the judge ordered.

"I call Merle Caldwell back to the stand."

"Merle, you're still under oath," The judge warned.

Sam took some posters from his desk and approached Caldwell. "Merle, I hold in my hand several likenesses of some people in this courtroom. I want you to identify them. Who is this?"

"That's me! What the hell you up to, Wood?"

"Just answer the questions, Merle, don't go thinking, this isn't the time to be trying something new."

Trimble leapt to his feet, "Your Honor, I must protest this belittlement of my client by Sam Wood."

"Sam, I'm starting to lose patience with you."

"I withdraw anything I've said about Merle thinking, Your Honor. Now, Mr. Caldwell, who is this?"

"That's my Nigger boy, Tom."

"He identifies, Tom, a grown man, by the way, and it is pretty clear that's who it is from the distinctive scar on his left cheek." Sam passed the photo among the jury, attorney's and finally handed it to the judge. "The next one, Merle, who is this?"

"That's the Nigger wench over there," and Caldwell

indicated Mary dismissively.

"Merle so graciously points out the lady, Mary Fedder, married to Tom and I think we all agree that it is a very good likeness down to the distinctive arrow shaped scar on the left side of Mary's eye. Your Honor, I enter all of these illustrations into evidence. Now, Merle, you may step down and I call Stephan Wood to the stand."

There was an undercurrent of excitement as if something was finally going to happen. The judge raised his gavel but hesitated as the buzz quieted when Stephan took the oath. Stephan was known throughout Ohio as a fine, honorable young man dedicated to his family, his profession and the same causes as the rest of the Wood family.

"Please state your name and occupation for the record."

"Sam, everyone here knows that I'm Stephan Wood and I'm a farmer, a carpenter, blacksmith, and preacher and about any other thing you can think of doing that needs to be done."

"Eloquently spoken, Stephan. Now, where have you been the past two weeks?"

"Philadelphia, Pennsylvania."

"And what did you find there?"

"I found Mr. and Mrs. Alphonse Aubrey."

Mary gave a gasp and put her hand to her mouth, "Praise God!" she exclaimed.

"Tell us about your visit with Mr. Aubrey, please Stephan."

"Mr. and Mrs. Aubrey are a gracious couple, well known in Pennsylvania and, in fact, direct decedents of William Penn. The Aubreys have, in their employ, Mr. Joseph Fedder and his wife Marian Fedder, who are the parents of Mary Fedder, sitting there with Tom."

Sam interrupted, "Are they employed as slaves or as freemen?"

"They are freeborn citizens and have been in the employee

of the Aubrey's for over 40 years. Mr. Aubrey identified the illustration that you just passed around as being Mary Fedder who disappeared along with her husband and two small children, thirteen years ago. They were quite relieved to hear that they are alive." Stephan looked at Mary, "Your mother and father send their love and anxious wishes to see the family soon."

"Do you have any proof of what you say, Stephan."

"Yes, I have two documents. The first is a signed affidavit from Mr. Aubrey that the picture I showed him was in fact Mary Fedder and a description of how she received that scar and that she was born free to the free black couple Joseph and Marian Fedder. The second is from the State of Pennsylvania recording office with the State Seal attesting to the signature of Mr. Aubrey."

Sam passed these documents around for all to see and entered them as evidence with the judge.

"So, there can be no doubt that Mary Fedder is a free woman."

"None!"

"And what of the claimant, Tom?"

"Mr. Aubrey only met Tom one time and he cannot attest to the fact that the illustration is the Tom who Mary Fedder married in Pennsylvania in 1837. However, I did write Fred Douglass and his response is that this man Tom is the same man Mary married, and Fred will come to Cincinnati to verify that claim, if needed."

The room was quite when Stephan finished. Sam walked to Caldwell's table where the three attorneys were conferring emphatically, then back to the jury box where he surveyed each juror, six of whom wouldn't meet his eyes.

Before Sam could say anything, Trimble rose and said, "Your honor, we concede that the woman, Mary Fedder, is a free woman but the others are not proven to be freeborn and therefore this trial should be declared over and the man and children returned to their owner, Merle Caldwell."

"Partus, your Honor," Sam shouted. "Partus Sequitur Ventrem," he continued, as the audience began murmuring.

"Why, that fools gone crazy, he's a talkin' in tongues," Caldwell said.

"No, it's a legal term, if the mother is free, the children are free," Trimble answered, shaking his head in frustration.

"What, the hell you mean? I paid good money fer them Niggers."

"It's complicated, Merle."

"Your Honor, please, I'm not finished yet. The question of Tom being freeborn is far from concluded. I still have another witness to call," Sam said.

"All right, call your witness then."

"I call Mary Fedder to the stand."

"Objection, Judge Wilcox, this is absurd. He can't call a Nigger woman to the stand. I don't care if she is free, she still isn't a citizen of this Union."

"She doesn't have to be a citizen to testify in court, she just can't be a slave," Sam countered emphatically. Your Honor, that ban was lifted in 1849 with the Free-Soil Democratic Compromise."

All eyes turned to Judge Wilcox who rubbed his face in exasperation. He looked and felt tired, worn out from a no-win trial that was sure to be his legacy no matter the result. He sighed deeply and said, "Counselor, you are the one who declared in an open court of law that she is a free woman. The laws are clear that a slave cannot testify in court but since she is no longer a slave, by your own admission, she can be sworn in and offer testimony in this trial. Call your witness, Sam."

Mary stood confidently and strode to the stand where she sat erect waiting for Sam to continue.

"Mary, you've heard the testimony here. You've been

proven correct in your quest to gain your freedom which was stolen from you thirteen years ago. Now I need you to answer some questions. Can you read?"

"Yassuh, I can read and write. Taught by Mrs. Aubrey as a young girl."

"Can your husband and children read and write?"

"Yassuh, they can. I taught them myself."

"I thought it was against the law for slaves to be educated."

"It is Mr. Wood. It is against the law in Georgia for a slave owner to educate a slave, but I don't think that it is against the law for a mother to educate her children. I tried to educate the other slaves but Massa Caldwell whipped me, so I quit that right quick and I ain't a'gona raise my shirt to show ya, but I got scars jus' like my boy." She glared at Merle Caldwell who glared right back with furrows of hatred etched in his face.

"Now, Mary, I want you to tell me when you married this man," Sam gestured for Tom to stand and face the jury.

"That's my husband, Tom that I married July 18, 1837 in Lancaster Pennsylvania."

"Is this your boy, Joseph, whose father is Tom?"

"Yassuh, freeborn, July 30, 1838."

"And is this your natural born son, Michael, whose father is also Tom?"

"Yassuh, freeborn, October 22, 1840."

"And is this your natural born daughter, Cecily, whose father is also Tom?"

"She my natural born daughter, but Tom ain't her daddy."

"Who is?"

"Massa Caldwell."

There was a gasp from the audience. Sam glanced up to see Mrs. Caldwell, a look of hatred on her face, but she wasn't looking at Sam, she was looking at her husband.

Sam continued, "How did that happen?"

"I don't likes to think about it, Mr. Sam. I don't want my children to have to bear it all again."

Sam walked into the crowd of onlookers and spoke to them, the white men in the spectator's section and the women and Blacks in the gallery sat hushed, consumed by the tension in the room.

"Mary, this is very important, not just for you but for the future of our country and the way people look at the blasphemous horror that is slavery." Sam slowly walked from the jury to the Caldwell table to the judge's podium, speaking more to the jury than to Mary. "You have the opportunity to share with these white neighbors, who don't know what's happening down there and the white people who have turned a blind eye," Sam stopped in front of Caldwell but looked up at Mrs. Caldwell who was sitting forward in her chair gripping the rail, her knuckles white and her face contorted in anger. "The people who hide the hideous truth behind the gentility and grace of the southern aristocrat, whose children grow fat and lazy off the blood and flesh of the enslaved children of God. You have to tell us what happened. We cannot allow this perversion of humanity to continue....," He stopped in front of Mary, she kept her eyes steadily on her husband, who nodded to her. "Mary, what happened to you at the hands of Mister Caldwell?"

Her voice was weak, barely audible as she shifted her gaze to the floor wringing her hands in despair at the memory, "About a week after we was sold to Massa Caldwell....,"

"Speak up Mary, let them hear you in the street, we're going to shout it to the rooftops because you did nothing wrong, you do not have to hide your face in shame...., but somebody else needs to," Sam turned and glared at the opposing attorneys. "Now, about a week after you were sold to Caldwell...., which one, Merle Caldwell?"

"No, Ole Massa Caldwell, down in Georgia," She said

clearly, but kept her eyes averted.

"Did you tell Caldwell you were free?"

"Yassuh, of course, but he already knew it, them slave traders gave him our papers. Old man Caldwell gave the papers to that Massa Caldwell," she indicated Merle. "And Merle Caldwell gave the papers to his wife, the young Missus Caldwell. I know cause' she hid them in a drawer in her bedroom and I went and found them, and she had the overseer beat me for it."

Sam looked up at Mrs. Caldwell. "Go on Mary, how did Caldwell come to be the father of Cecily?"

Mary looked at her family, the boys had their heads down, Cecily moved to stand by Tom who put his arm around her and whispered quietly trying to prepare her for what was to come.

"Put a stop to this!" Caldwell shouted at his attorneys. "Stop it, let the Nigger bastards go, I don't want em, this trial is over."

"Mr. Caldwell, you keep your mouth shut," Judge Wilcox shouted. "I will have you put in chains and gagged if you disrupt these proceedings, sir. I am disgusted enough to do it, too." Wilcox glared down from his perch in the judge's stand.

Mary continued, "Massa Caldwell come to our shack one night. We was weak from hunger and tired down to our souls from being stole' away. He brought two slaves with him and he made them chain Tom to a chair, then each of them held my boys so they couldn't do nothing, and Massa Caldwell he rape me, right in front of everyone," she sobbed. "He pull my hair, he hit me in the face cause' I clawed him, but he were too strong and he had his way…., with my own children and husband watching." Mary broke down sobbing. Cecily hid her face in Tom's chest. Merle Caldwell glared at Sam with the hatred of a man whose life is being threatened and he is helpless to stop it.

"Go on Mary," Sam said, gently.

"He said 'that's to show whose boss round' here,' then he said he would kill us if we told anyone. Tom cleaned me up and put me to bed." She looked at Tom and her family.

Sam walked to his table, retrieved his cane and strolled to Caldwell's table banging the club on the floor, then tapping it on the table in front of Merle, but this time no one said a word.

"SO," Sam shouted startling everyone, most of all Caldwell who started to stand but sank back in his chair. "So," Sam repeated, glaring down at Merle, old Mister Caldwell is Cecily's daddy?"

"Nosuh, Mister Sam, THAT Massa Caldwell is Cecily's daddy."

"I knew it," Mrs. Caldwell shouted from the gallery, standing up and pounding the rail with her fist. "You filthy animal, I knew it was you. My God, what kind of a man are you? Coming to my bed after being with a Nigger. Yes, I have the papers and here they are." She threw them and they fluttered down to the floor.

The courtroom erupted in anger. Sheriff's deputies hurried Caldwell out for his own safety as Mrs. Caldwell called down all manner of epitaphs on his head swearing to kill him if he came near her. The children were crying and trying to console her. Tom had gone to Mary and was holding her gently. Judge Wilcox sat back and waited for the deputies to restore order. Sam, Stephan and Robert were standing in a daze from the turn of events.

"It's time you quit using that line, Sam," Stephan said.

"What line," Sam asked"

"The one about always trying to avoid trouble," He said, looking at the chaos surrounding them.

Judge Wilcox motioned for Sam to approach the bench and said, just loud enough for Sam to hear, "If I was you, I'd get them out of here, right pronto," he nodded at Mary and Tom. Sam shook his head in agreement and gave orders to Stephan and Bob to lead them out. He asked a burly deputy to escort them to his wagon. The next day, Sam, Margaret and the boys, along with the

Thompsons and their children, accompanied the former slave family to the wharf where they were placed on a steamship to Philadelphia, free once more.

###

"No word of commiseration can make a burden feel one feather's weight lighter to the slave who must carry it." **Walter Scott, Rob Roy**

Margaret Wood relished her role as wife and mother. She was free to work on the issues that fueled her passion with someone she loved and knew that Sam felt the same about her. God had seen fit to bless her with all the goodness of life so that she might help those less fortunate. She didn't concern herself with why things were a certain way, why some people were poor, why black people were slaves, why some men beat their wives, why women weren't accorded the same rights as men, why some men were inflicted with a cruelty beyond human endurance; it was just the way things were. Because these things were outside her understanding, she put her trust in God; the reason 'why' was His domain, His concern and not hers. She knew that evil existed, and it was her responsibility to stop it. Margaret had an unwavering belief in God as the all-powerful creator of everything on earth and in the heavens. The evil things were created by men who failed to heed God's word, and she had to find a way to right the ship, so to speak, to eliminate the evil and restore all men to good grace. There were times that she worried for Sam's soul when he was out battling the slave-masters because he used tactics that she did not approve. Sam was a Quaker and their religion was clear about the use of force, but she also had to admit that he was successful in freeing many a runaway slave.

Her children were fast becoming the joy of her life. David, who was short and stocky like Sam; and Lloyd, who took after his mother. David had a shock of unruly, dusky brown hair and dark eyes that glistened with an intellectual fury. He wanted to understand everything and had little patience with those who didn't know or worse, wouldn't take the time to explain. His curiosity was trying at times for Sam, who was patient to a point but could become exasperated with the constant questions, especially when he was busy on a case.

"Father, I don't want to be a lawyer," David announced one evening during the Tom and Mary trial.

"Well, son, that's not something you have to decide right now. You've plenty of time to decide what you want to become."

"Caleb says I have to be a lawyer because you are," he argued, insisting that he had information from a well-respected source. "Just like he'll be a farmer like his daddy, Mr. John." Sally had married John Thompson the Underground Railroad conductor and local farmer. Caleb and David were inseparable.

"Caleb isn't the final authority in this matter, Dave." Sam was working on his closing arguments in the case and needed to finish in time to get some sleep before court the next day. He was certain to win, but he wanted to go beyond winning and make a strong condemnation against the slaveholders because the national press was in town, including Horace Greeley.

"But I don't want to be a lawyer. I want to be a farmer like Uncle Stephan," he argued not sure Sam understood the importance of what he was saying.

"Excellent choice, David. I agree that you should become a farmer. Now let me get back to work."

David looked at him with eyes that made Sam feel he was looking in a mirror. "You need to put it in writing," David insisted causing Sam to burst out laughing.

"Margaret," he yelled, she came rushing into the room fearful something had happened.

"What is it dear?"

"Margaret, are you certain that this boy is only four?"

"Five, Papa," David asserted.

"Well, I've got to get this paper written and I can't do it arguing your case while I write mine. You might not want to be an attorney, young man, but you'd make an excellent one."

Margaret had infinite patience with the children. She was patient with everyone, serving a valuable counterbalance to Sam who was quick to anger and held grudges beyond their usefulness. She was working on a theory of how to make inroads into fighting slavery in the South. It had to do with bypassing the men and working with the women. Margaret was certain that the southern women would listen to reason and she had broached the subject with her mother-in-law and many prominent women of standing in the North. For the most part they agreed with her. The men were emotionally invested in slavery and, even if they considered it an evil, they couldn't separate their masculine stubbornness from what was morally right.

Margaret and Sally spent every spare moment discussing strategy. Sally had proven a quick study and learned to read and write so fast that she was accepted at the Lutheran College. Sally and John Robinson, along with Reverend Poindexter, were quickly becoming leaders in the African American community in Columbus and beyond.

When Margaret jumped in Poindexter's carriage, he knew immediately what the problem was because he had spotted Caldwell stumbling across the street. They drove a block, stopped then crept back in the shadows to see what was happening. Mrs. Caldwell and her oldest son had come out of the mercantile, turned toward the saloon, and then stopped short when they heard Merle shouting in the street. They rushed to Caldwell's side and the boy reached for the gun only to have his father push him away and fire at Sam's office. Margaret shrieked and ran with Poindexter trying to keep up with her. Suddenly another shot rang out and Sam stepped into the street as the boy fell to the ground, his mother covering his body. Margaret stopped in horror, but Poindexter continued on and jumped on the pistol just as Caldwell reached for it. Sheriff Hunt arrived and pinned Caldwell to the ground. Sam turned back as Margaret rushed to him searching his body for gunshot wounds.

"I'm fine, darling. He shot our office and then his son. Is the boy dead?"

"I don't know Sam but let Preston and Robert handle this. I don't think you should be here." They hurried down fifth Street toward their home.

###

May 1854
Columbus, Ohio

"Be faithful, be vigilant, be untiring in your efforts to break every yoke, and let the oppressed go free. Come what may - cost what it may - inscribe on the banner which you unfurl to the breeze, as your religious and political motto - "NO COMPROMISE WITH SLAVERY! NO UNION WITH SLAVEHOLDERS" **William Lloyd Garrison**

An evening breeze blew softly, rustling the leaves of the two magnolia trees in the front yard of the Wood home on Franklin Street. The pink and purple hued coneflowers swayed delicately sheltering brilliant orange butterfly weed and the Lenten rose along the walkway. The porch swing creaked a bit as he rocked gently; conscious of silence that comes from the absence of mischievous children. Sam looked around noticing, for the first time, the brilliant colors of the well-kept yard, in which he played no part creating.

No sounds from the yard, very unusual in the Wood household where an abundance of people, whether his in-laws or his brothers and sisters, nieces and nephews, had the run of the place. Sam was often oblivious to the bustle around home because he welcomed it, he enjoyed the noise and the comradery, even though he was often lost in his own ruminations; the silence, though, disconcerted him.

Margaret appeared in the doorway.

"Where is everyone, Meg?"

"Gone to mother's house for lemonade and cookies. Kind of a going away party."

"Do you want to go over?" Sam asked. "I'll go if you want."

"No, Sam, let's just sit here and enjoy the breeze. Isn't it a fine night?"

He took Margaret's hand and held it in his lap. The breeze carried the sounds of insects and the birds singing. Sam seldom had a peaceful moment to share with his wife and he was relishing the sensation.

"Where did all of these flowers come from," he asked innocently

Margaret chuckled and with the resignation of five years of marriage to a man obsessed with his work said, "They came from Sally and John's place. He sent a crew over to plant them two summers ago, Sam. Have you forgotten when you looked out your window and thought there was a rush of runaway slaves? But they were planting flowers and grass."

Margaret sighed and added, more to herself than Sam, "Then John wouldn't let me pay for the plants or the labor."

They sat peacefully, husband and wife, lovers and parents, abolitionists and Suffragettes, but mainly friends. Margaret asked, "Do you think everyone will be there this weekend?"

"I don't know about Fred Douglass. He sent a letter expressing doubt about Brown's plans. He didn't deny the motivation, but he felt that it was too soon for any kind of armed rebellion."

"Really," Margaret said, truly surprised, "I assumed Fred would be first in line to back an armed insurrection."

"Sojourner will be there, Allan, and, of course, Poindexter, Henry Beecher. Harriet won't be a part of it. I really need to sit down with her and find out why. I don't know about the poets...."

"Poets?" Margaret asked.

"You know, Walt Whitman, Emerson and that other one...., Longfellow! He's a bit too full of himself for my taste. And Lucretia isn't sure she wants to be involved. There is a danger in having too many people in the know. John Brown is a good man but he's impulsive and while he thinks these plans of his are secret, I guarantee Washington knows exactly what he's up to. John claims to have some secret source of money in Massachusetts and men from Canada. I'm not sure what to think, Meg."

"What does Stephan say?"

"Oh, he's a hundred percent behind the plans as he understands them. I don't know that I truly understand what it is Brown is proposing. An armed insurrection, yes, but against who? Why, Franklin Pierce will bring the wrath of the Federal troops down on his head, without warning. Anyone who can get this infernal Kansas-Nebraska Act passed won't have any qualms about hunting down an anti-slavery insurrection force and Brown isn't even being discrete. I don't think we should get involved. We have to move on to Kansas. Actually, I 'm going to try and convince Brown to move to Kansas with us."

Sam was getting agitated. Margaret knew the signs and changed the subject as best she could.

"Are you having second thoughts about going to Kansas, Dear?"

"Oh, Meg, I wish I would have kept my mouth shut," he laughed kissing her knuckles and nuzzling the wedding ring that meant so much to him. I didn't really believe they would pass the Kansas-Nebraska Act, this…., affront to God and man. I blame Stephen Douglas more than the President. I honestly thought we would be able to put a stop to slavery before it spread any further. Now I know there will be war. It's inevitable, in fact, we're moving to the front. We'll be on the firing line, both figuratively and literally. Meg, it will be one bloody confrontation after another. Is there any way I can talk you and your parents into staying here until I send for you?"

Margaret pulled her hand away and Sam knew he had gone too far, "I told you that where you go, the boys and I go. Mother and Daddy can make up their own minds. Now I don't want to hear another word on that subject. Come on, Sam. We've got to get you packed and ready to leave for Philadelphia in the morning. I have a lot of things to do to get ready to leave for Kansas when you get back."

Sam put his arm around his wife's waist and strolled into the house without another word.

###

"Are right and wrong convertible terms, dependent upon popular opinion?" **William Lloyd Garrison**

May 1854

Traveling to Philadelphia, PA

"What a marvelous modern world we live in, don't you agree, sir?" The man waited for an answer, but Sam was deep in thought watching the Pennsylvania landscape race by through the train window. Undaunted, the traveling salesman continued, "Why it used to take me two weeks to make the trip from Washington to Chicago and now I can make it easy in two days."

"I know what you mean, friend," the fellow in front turned around to say. "I barely bring a hand satchel these days. I used to pack two trunks and be gone a month." He wore a derby hat atop a high collared tweed suit and appeared ready to make a sales pitch at the first sign of interest.

"I heard it from the horse's mouth, ole Commodore Vanderbilt, hisself, they's a train goes from New York to Pennsylvania, travels 60 miles an hour," the traveling salesman volunteered.

"No, it ain't possible."

"By God, I heard it from Cornelius Vanderbilt. I damn sure did."

"I believe you about the train, it's the Cornelius Vanderbilt part that I'm doubtin'." They laughed and proceeded to share the lies that men of their profession spread from one end of a sales territory to the other; never bothering to verify or question just relying on the process to sustain their energy. Sam's seatmate moved ahead to visit with his responsive new acquaintance.

Sam resumed his reverie, thinking of the coming meeting and uprooting his family to the wilds of Kansas Territory. His family and friends thought of him as a rock, solid in his decisions and unwavering in his strategy, only Margaret knew him well enough to know the fears and doubts that plagued his private thoughts. Not misgivings about his cause or the validity of his actions, but fear that he was putting others in danger, his sons and his in-laws, the runaway slaves who flocked to his door for help. Sam prayed for strength to make the right decisions for all of them. He felt no fear for his own life, he had long ago made peace with a violent death in the pursuit of justice. The inner turmoil had to do with his wavering belief in the good and just God that he had been raised to worship. At the Quaker meeting in Philadelphia the year before, he helped draft language that moved toward a more secular definition of the Quaker mission. Sam was sorely troubled about the evil that he saw all around, he had a difficult time squaring those matters with an all-knowing benevolent God. He kept these things to himself because the why of the matter was not nearly as important as what he had to do to fix it. Worrying about what God looked like wouldn't solve the issue of slavery. He would have to face the hatred of the southerners, eventually, on the battlefield. He knew it was coming.

He thought back to a recent conversation with Sally and John Thompson when Sam, for the first time since her rescue, asked Sally what had happened at the hands of the Pritkin clan.

"Mr. Sam, you don't want to hear about all that mess. You doin' the right thing for my people you don't have to share in the disgusting details."

"But I want to know Sally. Have you talked to John about it?"

John said, "We discussed it, but the truth is, I've always known what happens down there in the South. Most white people don't want to hear about it, like in that trial you just had."

"I probably couldn't have told it right when you found me Mr. Sam. But I can now since I've been educated. I doubt I could have thought of the right words to describe some of the things I've seen. What they did to me wasn't near as bad as the other women they stole, and much of the abuse was by the old Nigger men that Pritkin owned. There was one boy that they captured while I was there, a boy about 16, black as coal, they stole him from some tobacco traders that had stopped in Hagerstown on their way to Philadelphia. We never understood his name, he didn't speak a word of English just some African language. We cleaned him up after they brought him to the farm about six that night, his nose was probably busted. He was scared to death, that boy, almost broke my heart. They came for him about eight, old man Pritkin tied him over a stump in the yard and had Clarence sodomize him. He made us watch," Sally cried as John extended his handkerchief and put his arm around her.

"Clarence was a simple-minded boy; he didn't hurt anyone unless his daddy told him to. The old man said he was doing it just because he could and anyone that crossed him would die. The boy lay there when they cut him loose, then jumped up and started running for the woods. Pritkin set the dogs loose and they caught him before he got a hundred yards. By the time they called the dogs off he was most near dead and old Bean shot him in the head. We buried him among the rest of the graves out there. That poor boy." Sam sat quietly, glancing once at Margaret who had her handkerchief to her mouth, tears in her eyes.

"Mr. Sam, there is evil going on down there in the south. The black women are being raped and molested, even the little girls. I'm half white. My own daddy tried to molest me when I was a young girl. That was when my mama attacked him, almost sliced his arm off. They beat her most to death and sold her down the river. I went to live with my grandmother until Mr. Clay called me to the big house."

"No one will believe it, Sally."

"I know it, but I'm going to finish my education and I'm gonna' to write a book about it. You just watch if I don't. The white people are saying that the slaves are happy. I'm gonna' tell the truth because they're hiding all the rebellions that slaves have attempted. Nobody even knows about most of them like Denmark Vesey and Gabriel Prosser, but I do. You just wait, I'll write that book."

"I believe you will, Sally," Margaret said, "and I'll help you get it published."

The train slowed, coming to the Harrisburg depot. Sam was surprised to hear his name mentioned by the two salesmen.

"Yessir, I heard it right from the source. They're putting a $5,000 bounty on this Sam Wood's head. Gonna' make an example of him."

"By God, this country is going to hell. We had a Nigger come right to the front door of the church last Sunday, wanted to come into the service."

"No, you don't mean it."

"Just waltzed right in with his Nigger wife and three or four little pickaninnys and sat down in the back pew, Bishop Morland like to had a heart attack. We got their asses outta' there before you could shake a stick. Claimed they thought ours was the colored church."

"The abolitionists are gonna' ruin this country. They'll have the Niggers runnin' town hall and the women voting. I'm worried about it."

"That's why they put this bounty on his head. Hell, I'm thinking about stopping in Columbus on my route next month and see if I can't collect that money myself."

"He damned sure ruined the life of a mighty fine family man. Merle Caldwell was as good as they come. Wood made him out to be some kind of monster but I'm here to tell you that Merle was a fine gentleman. I know it firsthand."

"You know him?"

"Know him? Why I sold him and his wife every stitch o clothes they wear."

At Harrisburg the passengers detrained to stretch their legs and attend to personal needs. Sam strolled into town to loosen his muscles and shake the weariness from his shoulders. He spotted the two salesmen enter the Hudson Saloon on Main Street and was tempted to follow with his lemonade toast but decided against it. He was disgusted with the men, not because of the bounty, he knew about that and didn't take it seriously, plus he was a bit flattered, the true bounty was five hundred dollars not five thousand. There was a bounty on the head of every prominent abolitionist in the north. His revulsion came from the thought of a church turning away children of God because of the color of their skin. He started back for the train but did an about face after a few steps and turned into the saloon. He strode with purpose to the bar and had the lemonade drawn before the two bigots could respond.

"Gentlemen…., and ladies," Sam said spotting two waitresses, "My name is Sam Wood and I don't drink alcohol, but I would be glad to buy a lemonade for anyone who will join me in the condemnation of the worst sin in the world…., slavery and those who practice that horror of inhumanity."

The room grew silent as Sam looked directly at the loudmouth braggarts who moments ago declared their intent to do him harm. Their eyes seemed to be glued to the floor. From a table in the corner a man stood and said, "Sam Wood, by God, it is you."

Sam's old friend, Sheriff Anderson from Hagerstown, was walking toward him, "Fred, what are you doing in Harrisburg?"

"I'm the newly elected sheriff. I take office next week."

"Well, whatever the reason, it's a pleasure to see you again."

Anderson turned back to the table and motioned his friends to join them, "This is Sam Wood, gentlemen."

"Mr. Wood, we've been following your case in the paper ever since Fred told us that he knew you," one of the men said, "But we didn't really believe him."

"Fred Anderson and I share a common tragedy that will bond us forever, won't it, Fred?"

"We've heard all about it, Mr. Wood, but we'd sure enjoy hearing your version."

The two salesmen snuck through the front door, Sam's old seatmate first, hurrying away from his companion, almost as if he didn't want to be friends any more. They didn't look Sam's way and he let them go without comment. Upon boarding the train, he moved to the second passenger car.

###

"Whenever I hear anyone arguing for slavery, I feel a strong impulse to see it tried on him personally." **Abraham Lincoln**

Independence Hall, at South Sixth and Chestnut Street, was only five blocks from Sam's boarding house, so he walked. Philadelphia was an old town and some of the buildings were beginning to show their age. The brick houses were holding up well, but the wood framed homes were deteriorating in the older parts of town. Sam detoured to Market and Second to see the Great Meeting House where Benjamin Lay had created such a stir. The building was still being used by the Quakers, but no one was around and Sam didn't have time to explore. As he approached Fifth and Market his name was shouted from across the street.

"Wood…., Sam Wood," Lloyd Garrison waved to him from a restaurant on the corner. Sam dodged two buggies and joined Garrison and Henry Beecher.

"Sam, have you had breakfast?" Beecher asked.

"I have, Henry, but I will have some coffee." The waiter nodded and scurried off.

"How many people has John summoned this time?" Garrison asked. "I've been in Chicago and out of the loop."

"I really don't know," Sam answered stirring sugar into his coffee. "Margaret asked me the same thing Sunday night. Last I heard he's invited pretty much everyone, and that worries me."

"How is Mrs. Wood," Garrison asked and before Sam could answer he added, "Tell her that Helen sends her love and regrets that she won't be able to attend the suffragette meeting in Cleveland next month. We've just had our first grandchild."

After the proper congratulations, Sam said, "I guess you haven't heard, but Margaret won't be there either, we're moving to Kansas…., going to make certain she comes in as a free state."

Garrison and Beecher looked at each other, not certain that

they had heard correctly.

"You can't mean it, Sam. What about the Republican Party, have you told Abe?"

"I'll continue my involvement with the party. I plan on being at the convention in '56'. Moving to Kansas will have no bearing on that."

"Unless you're dead," Garrison protested. "Sam, we need you here. There are others who can fight that fight. We need our best people to influence the elections. We can't let Pierce or Douglas become President and there are those of us who believe you'll be the next governor of Ohio after Salmon's term is over."

"I disagree, Lloyd. I believe the fight is in Kansas. The Missouri slaveholders are pouring into the territory passing bogus laws without becoming Kansas citizens. We can't let that happen and the Federal Government is sanctioning it or at least ignoring it. We have to establish citizenship in Kansas and then elect a true and representative government. I think that's more important than what I could accomplish here. I can't unite the Whigs and Republicans...., too controversial," Sam smiled.

Garrison and Beecher did not disagree.

"You'd probably make more friends if you'd quit carrying that club around," Beecher laughed.

###

"Caution, Sir! I am eternally tired of hearing that word--caution. It is nothing but the word of cowardice!" **John Brown**

The use of Independence Hall was intended to be symbolic as John Brown attempted to drum up popular support for his plan to raise a band of guerrilla fighters and march into Virginia to free the slaves. However, only a handful of abolitionists and supporters bothered to come. Another problem was encountered upon arriving to find a large contingent of workers removing the

Liberty Bell to the ground floor because of deterioration in the brick tower. The commotion was disconcerting.

Brown did explain his tactics in more detail than usual, "The plan is pretty simple, really. I have commitments from about two thousand men, both black and white. We have 200 Sharps rifles stored in Tabor, Iowa at Stephan Wood's place."

"I didn't even know that, John, and I don't think you should broadcast that fact in a meeting. Those are tactics best kept to yourself and your council. You'll put Stephan at risk," Sam said.

Several heads nodded in agreement. Fred Douglass, Sojourner Truth, Garrison and Beecher, three of Brown's sons, John Jr., Owen and Jason, Theodore Parker and George Lucas Stearns, black businessmen. But nothing like the 50 or 60 that Brown predicted.

Brown ignored the comment and continued, "We have a large cache of pikes in Connecticut. I have money, ladies and gentlemen. I plan on marching south, into Virginia, freeing slaves as we go, those who wish to join us can do so. Those who don't will march north into Canada. We will deplete Virginia of slaves and then move further south with our reinforced army."

Sam decided not to stay for the full three days. But he did meet with Brown and his sons, the night before he left, in the same café where he had coffee with Garrison and Beecher.

"Gentlemen, I'm not opposed to the concept of what you want to do, but I firmly believe that the real action is in Kansas. I'm leaving in a few weeks and moving there with my family. I'll oppose the advancement of slavery into the territories with all of my heart and soul. That's where we have to confront the slaveholders."

Owen Brown said, "I agree, Mr. Wood. Jason and I are also leaving for Kansas next week. We'll fight those Border Ruffians side by side."

This announcement surprised Sam as much as anything he

could imagine. John looked wearily at his boys with the concern of every father whose children have outgrown his influence. John Brown was a lanky, pallid faced man with thick black hair and a creased brow that advertised the difficulty of his life. He shook his head and said, "I believe that Kansas is important, but it won't change anything that's happening in the south. We need to march now; our black brothers are suffering daily. I have a thousand former slaves in Canada who are ready to move. The longer we wait the harder it will be to keep the commitment." John took a breath and patted his son, John, Jr., on the arm. "The boys have minds of their own."

"We'll be ready when the time comes, Pa. It won't take us that long to get back here."

John turned to Sam, "Wood, I have no quarrel with you. I've never heard of you backing down from a fight. It's the rest of these two-faced do-gooders I'm disgusted with. Most of them are cowards and blowhards. They spout the gospel and preach high and mighty words but don't do anything. We can't win this battle with words. The only thing the south understands is the sword. I told Fred Douglass, last night, you can't trust the white abolitionists when the chips are down. That's why I need you here. You can talk but you can also fight. You have the ability to speak to the tenant farmers and the Senators."

Sam comforted him. "It's going to take more than words to stop the slaveholders. It will take a complete change of attitude and laws and I know the only way that will happen is war. But I still think the best thing for me to do is stop slavery before it can advance any further west. If the slaveholders are given free reign, we'll never stop them. Like Jason says, I can be back here anytime I'm needed."

"Most white abolitionists don't even like the Negro race," Owen Brown said. "They all have black friends but consider them to be exceptions to the rule."

Sam nodded his head, "You're right, Owen. People still consider the Africans to be shiftless and inferior intellectually. Then when they meet one and get to know him, they assume that they've stumbled onto one in a million. The couple that I represented in Ohio, Tom and Mary Fedder, are a prime example. Salt of the earth people, wonderful family and thriving in Boston in the shipyards, all on their own. No one has helped them, and they wouldn't accept, if offered."

"It's a result of the propaganda from the south. They have to convince people that the slaves are unable to survive on their own," Jason added.

John Brown said, "All I know is the only ones I can truly count on are my sons, the men from the League of Gileadites and the former slaves. Fred Douglass is as fine a man as I've ever met. Been through hell but can still offer respect to the white man. Sojourner Truth could be a senator if they'd let a Negro be elected."

John Jr. laughed and said, "Hell, Papa, she has a chance getting elected as a Negro. It's being a woman that's her biggest problem.

###

"The great battle between Freedom and Slavery is gradually approaching, yet the country is everywhere quiet and the public tranquility undisturbed. Not even the distant rumble of the tempest is heard. The little cloud that denotes it hovers only over a handful of people in the far West. In Kansas alone exists the speck that foreshadows the coming storm. Kansas has been invaded by slavery. It is threatened with the unending curse of that institution. A country large enough for a kingdom is there to be wrested from the possession of the free-states and blackened with African bondage." **Horace Greeley's New York Tribune, April 19, 1855**

Sam, Margaret and Lloyd boarded the packet boat, Sultana, on June 25, 1854. The steamer was a regular or 'scheduled' packet delivering mail, under contract, between Cincinnati and St. Louis. David left four weeks earlier with his grandparents, Bill and Elizabeth Lyon, accompanied by Sally and John Thompson, and their two children, Caleb and Missy. David had insisted on traveling with his best friend.

The letters from the Lyon family painted a bleak picture of the conditions on the edge of the frontier, which is what Independence, Missouri represented. Bill Lyon reported, in his straight-forward way, "We knew what we were getting into."

The Cincinnati wharf was bustling with activity as stevedores and longshoremen dashed about loading and unloading cargo. Cincinnati supplied most of the pork going south, where the slave masters fed their slaves pork instead of beef. The slaughterhouses and packing plants gobbled up workers as fast as they arrived from Pennsylvania, for the most part, but also from the southern states. A jumble of free Blacks, Germans, African slaves, Irish and even a few Indians seemed to function with no choreography, but, in spite of the chaos, the ships and boats moved in and out close to schedule. The longshoremen were constantly bickering with cries of "learn English ya filthy Hun, ya" or "Get a move on, Mick, this ain't Ireland."

The trip down the turnpike from Columbus was uneventful but the smells and noise of the busy river port startled Lloyd who had been sleeping in the back of the wagon on a pallet of clothes and soft satchels. It was a beautiful June morning as they reached the crest of the bluff on Elm Street, the vista of the wharf below. There were shouts from the longshoremen and the clank and whir of pulleys and ropes lowering freight onto the decks and into the holds of the many riverboats, flatboats, barges and steamers. Lloyd crawled onto his mother's lap then clambered over Sam's legs where he could hold the slack end of the lines while Sam drove to the Wharf Master's office.

A sea of color and smells overwhelmed them as they approached the docks. The men were constantly under time pressure to get the incoming cargo unloaded and the outgoing freight stowed. The menial jobs were parceled to the lowest classes, the slaves and the free Blacks, jobs like mucking out the stalls from the livestock on the lower deck with much of the slops going over the side into the river. New sanitation regulations had been imposed during the winter session of the Ohio State Legislature, but little was done in the way of enforcement.

Wood's wagon and team were loaded onto the main deck, their belongings lashed tight. Margaret and Sam secured a private berth on the boiler deck above the steerage passengers who sprawled where they could amongst the casks of pork, bales of cotton and general freight being hauled downriver from the upriver manufacturing plants.

The Louisville segment of the trip was uneventful. Lloyd had the run of the hurricane deck and eventually found his way to the pilot house where Captain Williamson adopted him and made him honorary co-pilot. Sam often found his son asleep in a corner while the Captain and his crew maneuvered the boat down the Ohio. The stop in Louisville gave the passengers a chance to refresh their water containers and for the steerage passengers to get food.

Winding lazily as it carved out the borders of Kentucky, Illinois and Indiana, the Ohio was tranquil and afforded opportunity to witness the beauty of the western portion of the Union at its best. The serene river was pristine, for the most part, when away from the larger cities, and while you could see from shore to shore, it was a boundless chasm between the Slave States and the northern Free States. That distinction was not lost on Sam as he watched the slaves working in the fields on the Kentucky side.

While docked in Louisville, Sam and Margaret sat on a bench on the upper deck, Sam nodding off as they waited for the boat to continue downriver. Margaret spent much of the trip from Cincinnati on the main deck tending to minor scrapes and illnesses from people being packed into small spaces in unsanitary conditions. She was glad for the chance to relax and just observe. Suddenly she witnessed something that seemed out of place. She shook Sam awake and said, "Sam, what's going on down there?"

Sam stood groggily and watched as two burly laborers accosted an elderly black man and a young girl. They were dragging the man behind stacked bales of cotton where they could not be seen from ground level.

"Hey, you there, what are you doing?" Sam shouted. The commotion was loud enough to cause the other laborers to pause and look up. "Wait right there, you men," he cautioned them, but they continued with the old man, while the young girl, about 14 or 15, begged them to stop.

Sam grabbed his cane, ran down the stairs, shoving aside those who were on the gangway. The workers resumed their business, ignoring the rich riverboat passenger whose affairs were of no consequence to them, regardless of what he was angry about. They knew better than to interfere. The two heavies were nowhere to be seen. Sam glanced up at Margaret and she yelled and pointed that they were behind the cotton bales.

"What are you men doing?" he cried.

The scene before him was reminiscent of times past, an all too familiar scene of one man holding the gentleman and the other pawing at the girl, ripping her cotton dress. They stopped abruptly and stood looking at Sam.

"Stay the hell outta' this, Bucko," the taller of the two said.

Sam said nothing, just stood his ground, blocking the exit.

"We caught this Nigger trying to sneak on the boat and we was gonna' take the fare out in trade with the bitch, if you want to know the truth. He offered her to us and we accepted."

"It doesn't look that way to me," Sam countered.

"What the hell is it to you, anyway? They just field Niggers."

Sam ignored the insult and turned to the grandfather, "Did you, in fact, attempt to sneak on board?" Sam asked.

The men were shocked that Sam spoke to the black man and didn't take their word for it. This was an affront and insult of the highest order in pro-slavery culture. They were stunned into silence at such treatment from a white man.

"No. suh, we have purchased passage. This man has our passes in his shirt pocket."

"Shut up you," he shouted and shook the elderly man back and forth causing his hat to fly off.

"Let him go...., right now...., you gob of spit," Sam said, his anger growing by the second. "You are about to cause me to do something unpleasant and that makes me mad because I was just getting ready to take a nap."

He let go of the captive and laughed at the short man with the baby face, "Are you joshing me, you little runt. Where do you come off talking to us that way? We white folk, just like you. Who the hell are you?"

"Maybe he's an abolitionist, Jeb. I been wantin' to kill one ever since I come back from Missouri. I figured we might see some of em'. Is that what you are you little rat? Hell fire, I could squash you and not even know I run over ya."

"My name is Sam Wood and I am about to bring down the wrath of the Lord God Almighty on you. Why can't you leave these people in peace, you disgusting animals? You make me sick to my stomach."

They stood at an impasse for what seemed forever to the young girl who was beginning to shake and cry from the scene before her. Her grandfather knew who Sam Wood was and, as feeble as he felt, he prepared to do battle to protect his granddaughter.

Sam finally said, "May God have mercy on your souls, because I will not."

The men stopped laughing and their eyes narrowed to dangerous slits. Their brows furrowed trying to make sense of the situation which had gone terribly wrong for them. This was typical of the luck they had encountered upon leaving the Territories. Now, when they were close to satisfying their lust and securing passage back downriver, they were confronted by an abolitionist, the lowest class of human they could imagine, lower even, than a slave.

"I heard your name somewhere," Jeb said slowly.

"Then you will know that I am serious, now, give this man his tickets. I can see them sticking out of your shirt there."

The men looked at each other, bent down to their boots and came up with ugly, long-handled knives.

"How about no, you Nigger-lovin' son-of-a-bitch? How about we kill you and the old man and take the girl for ourselves?"

"Yeah," his partner said, turning to his friend, "We'll use her up and then throw her in the river."

Sam didn't hesitate. While they looked at each other he lashed out with his cane and hit the nearest on the back of his head. He collapsed against his partner, who tried to hold him up but staggered and before he could get his knife hand free, Sam hit him across the bridge of the nose. Both men collapsed to the ground and lay there moaning. The captives gasped in amazement at what had happened so quickly. Margaret, Captain Williamson, and two crew members came charging onto the scene to find Sam reaching into the man's pocket to retrieve the tickets. He handed them to the victim as the Captain took charge.

"What in the world has happened here, Sam?"

As Sam explained the circumstances, Margaret put her arm around the young girl, "I'm going to take her on board and sew her dress. Lloyd is waiting with Mr. Stevens and probably wonders what's going on."

He nodded and turned back to the Captain. As Margaret took the girl away, the authorities arrived, led by the Agent in charge, "I should have known it was these two. We've had complaints about them for three days. Looks like they bit off a bit more than they could chew this time."

As they walked to the wharf offices, the Captain said, "Sam, I had dinner with Judge Wilcox the other night in Cincinnati. When I told him you were on the passenger manifest, you know what he said? He said, 'Freddy you'd best prepare yourself for trouble, it follows Sam Wood like a shadow.' By God, Mr. Wood, I can't wait to tell him how right he was." he laughed and allowed Sam to lead the way into the offices to file his report.

###

"Where there is so much racket, there must be something out of kilter. I think that 'twixt the Negroes of the South and the women at the North, all talking about rights, the white men will be in a fix pretty soon." **Sojourner Truth**

The Wood family and their belongings transferred from the Sultana to the Sam Cloon in St. Louis for the trip up the Missouri River. Lloyd said his tearful goodbyes to Captain Williamson, co-pilot Stevens and the rest of the pilot-house crew. Lloyd made friends easily and deeply which made parting the more difficult. Yet with boundless energy and youthful cheerfulness he scampered aboard the Sam Cloon and made straight for the upper deck before his father could collar him. When Sam reached the pilothouse, Lloyd was already in the Captain's chair with the co-pilot watching over him.

"Hello, Mr. Wood," The Captain said as Sam stood at the door. River protocol was very strict, and the captain of a riverboat was the highest office attainable even more so than a mayor or judge, he was law, both civil and judicial. He was not to be disputed in anyway.

"I apologize, Captain, he got away before I could caution him about barging in on you."

"I knew who this was the second he poked his head in the door, even before he announced, 'I'm Lloyd Wood, Captain," he said and roared a laugh that could be heard even on the docks. "I had your other son on board a few weeks ago. Fine young man he is and got to know your in-laws too. I'm Johannson, Sam. Fred Williamson sent word over that young Lloyd would be on board today. I'm proud to meet you."

"The pleasure is mine, sir, and your name is familiar to me. Have we met somewhere?"

"Not directly, but we have a common friend in Allan Pinkerton, who I see from time to time here on the river and when I am in Chicago. I understand that you're headed for Independence."

"Yes, I am Captain. My goal is to stop slavery before it advances any further West."

"You're a braver man than I, Sam. I've carried a fair number of Border Ruffians both ways, and abolitionists too. I'd have to say you're at a sharp disadvantage in numbers and weaponry. Those men are armed to the teeth and ruthless in a way that can't really be described. They'll cut your heart out and eat it before you hit the ground."

"I've heard the stories," Sam answered.

"It's no place for women and children," The Captain said pointedly, looking at Lloyd.

"Try telling that to my wife, Captain. She'll cut your heart out," Sam laughed.

"I'll be careful with my opinions when around her. Believe me Sam, I'm an old Scotsman and I know that slavery must be stopped. I see it firsthand here on the river and it breaks my heart, the cruelty and inhumanity…., I believe if the white race would take the time to get to know the Africans, they would change their thinking. These people are industrious and intelligent, if given the chance."

"You're right Captain and that is what I'm fighting for."

"You'll meet Roy Jackson here on the Sam Cloon. To my knowledge he is the first black man, on the river, to make the grade of assistant engineer. He devised a steam release valve that is being adapted to all the boats on our line. Why, I couldn't believe it when I saw it; he crafted it out of spare parts and scraps because no one took him seriously."

"That's a great story, Captain. We need to publicize it. I could get Horace Greely to write about it. It would help corroborate what we're advocating."

"I tried to Sam. You know what happened? The owner of this line doesn't think like I do. He's a staunch pro-slavery man. He stole Roy's invention and gave credit to an engineer on the 'Intrepid' who claimed to have thought of the same thing. Roy was told to keep his mouth shut or he would lose his job. I've never been so disgusted with anyone in my life."

"I've heard similar stories everywhere I go."

"I'd best get back to work. Welcome aboard, Sam. We'll watch over Lloyd and one of the men can bring him to you, if need be."

"Thank you, Captain Johannson. I'd best get back to Margaret, she was roaming the steerage, probably recruiting the women and children to her cause."

The Captain roared his friendly laugh again. "By the way Sam, there's a contingent of Mormons on board, on the way to their promised land. I think you'll like the leader, Orson Pratt. He's one of Joseph Smith's twelve apostles. Seems like a very smart man."

"That's wonderful. I don't know Pratt, but I've been wanting to discuss this new religion with someone knowledgeable.

###

Noah came before the flood. I have come before the fire.
Joseph Smith Jr., Mormon Prophet

There were times when God's Will was beyond Sam's understanding. Tragedies and natural disasters he took in stride, sickness, snake bites, disease and drought he accepted, not wishing to dwell on the reason why, any more than his wife did. Sam was a realist, steeped in the beliefs of his Quaker existence and the beliefs of his ancestors, the Moser's and Woods. Their understanding of God was that he dwelt in all men equally without prejudice.

But how some men could pervert God's love into the outrage of slavery was an unsolvable mystery. He resigned himself to the fact that it happened, but it was beyond his capacity to turn the other cheek or refuse to use violence if the need arose. He was tolerated by his fellow Quakers, even admired in some quarters, especially by those who considered themselves Hicksite or Progressive Quakers. Sam was instrumental in drafting the Exposition of Sentiments at the Pennsylvania Yearly Meeting of Progressive Friends in 1853. He proposed dedicating the meeting to Benjamin Lay but opposition to Benjamin was still fierce in parts of Philadelphia society. They did hammer out a statement:

"It has been our cherished purpose to restore the union between religion and life, and to place works of goodness and mercy far above theological speculations and scholastic subtleties of doctrine."

The mainstream Quakers and other religions labeled them

humanists or even worse, atheists. Sam was appalled. He believed in God, but he also believed that man must overcome the evil of slavery regardless from where it emanated. To Sam, God was not in the sky looking down on everyone, but inside each person, looking out. Sam was not a philosopher, he left that to others, but that didn't keep him from thinking about these things.

On the other hand, Mormonism sprang, almost stillborn, from the bowels of a Pennsylvania forest into the mind of a man, possibly deranged, possibly under the influence, or possibly a prophet. His words were transcribed from an oracle as if God was communicating through him, which is what Joseph Smith asserted. Sam's father, David Wood had known Smith, when he moved his flock to Kirtman, Ohio in the early 1830's. The Mormons were persecuted and driven from community to community much the way of the Quakers as they fled England.

David Wood said to his father-in-law, Asa Mosher, "Papa, how can you doubt that another Saint has arrived 1800 years since the last. Why is it so hard to believe that this man has been touched by God, yet you accept without question the veracity of the account of Jesus' prophecies?"

Asa replied, in his usual confrontational way, "He's a fraud, David. Use the senses God gave you. He claims to have found some golden tablets, given by an angel? Please….,"

"Moses received the Ten Commandments on tablets."

"It's a metaphor. There was no man named Moses. You know this. You're just arguing to make me angry." Asa continued, "I know Smith, he's a charlatan who abuses women, and a drunkard. He violates everything we believe in, David, he changes with the weather. When he moved to Independence, he was pro-slavery. When he moved to Nauvoo, he was anti-slavery. Use the mind God gave you, David. Don't fall for this man's lies because he can weave a spell with his words."

Time and distance often blur the memories of childhood, especially when the subject is of no interest to the child. Sam remembered bits and pieces of the conversations between his father and grandfather about the Mormons and Joseph Smith. They did not argue or raise their voices, but the men were adamant in their beliefs especially when joined by Mrs. Moser and Mrs. Wood. Both believed, as David, that Mormonism was a legitimate religion. Asa Moser considered Smith and his 'revelations', his Book of Mormon, as blasphemy and an affront to the intelligence of man.

Asa said emphatically, "I'd sooner believe that he danced a quadrille with the Devil than stumbled upon Golden Tablets. Where are they? Don't you think if you found some golden tablets, you'd be able to remember where you put them?"

"Maybe it's a metaphor," his wife said smirking.

"It's poppycock," Asa countered firmly. "You'd believe that Andrew Jackson was a paragon of virtue just because he was President. Evil is evil no matter the office of the sinner."

###

"...slavery had been the condition of all ancient culture, that Christianity approved servitude, and that the law of Moses had both assumed and positively established slavery....It is the order of nature and of God that the being of superior faculties and knowledge, and therefore of superior power, should control and dispose of those who are inferior. It is as much in the order of nature that men should enslave each other as that other animals should prey upon each other." **Southerner, Thomas Roderick Dew, 1832**

The trip was normally smooth sailing or steaming in 1854. The Sam Cloon was fast and solid, a side-wheeler with wood hull carrying 100 souls up the Missouri River that hot June day. Margaret Wood spent the first morning on the main deck looking after children who were feeling the effects of movement sickness. She was aided by a few of the Mormon wives including Sarah Pratt.

Sam Wood and Orson Pratt huddled on the hurricane deck in serious discussion about the movement to the West and what Orson had encountered on his first trip to the Salt River Valley in 1847. Orson was a tall man, fair skinned with thick brown hair and the lively, curious eyes of a scientist. His brow was smooth as was his speech. The women seemed taken with him.

"It's a different world out there, Sam. If you think you've seen a far horizon, say in the Appalachians, you're in for a shock. Multiply that vista by fifty-fold and you'll have an idea of the Great Plains or the view from the Rocky Mountains looking east. Everything is exaggerated out there."

"I understand you put your scientific training to good use," Sam said.

"I catalogued the plants and animals I'd never seen. I covered some ground that Lewis & Clark missed, so I was able to collect a few new specimens. But I spent most of my time writing essays for the church. I'm the one who nominated Brigham Young for the position of President of The Church of Jesus Christ of Latter-day Saints, after Smith's murder."

"Orson, my focus is on ending slavery. What is the position of your church? I've heard some contradictory evidence about Joseph Smith's position on the matter."

"We consider slavery an evil, but America didn't invent slavery. Slavery has been a condition of life throughout the modern and ancient worlds."

"That argument is old stuff, Orson. Just because others have done it doesn't make it right. The fact that ancient Romans had slaves isn't a valid reason to justify slavery in modern America. It's beyond reason. Wrong is wrong no matter the time or place."

The men were oblivious to anything but their conversation

as the Sam Cloon steamed up the Missouri toward Independence. Shouts from the crew and the hiss of the boilers, the clang of the pistons and camshafts did not distract the two influential men. Sam became aware that Margaret was hurrying up the gangway from steerage. He had a sixth sense about Margaret and felt her presence before he saw her. "I don't like the look of some of the passengers," she said calmly. Her eyes were focused and sparkled with an intense look of worry.

"What is it, Meg?"

"I think you'd better come see for yourself," she said turning back down the stairs.

They followed her to the lower deck and then to the stern. She had isolated two men and a woman who were suffering stomach distress and leg cramps. Their clothes were soiled with vomit and diarrhea. The smell was septic. Orson knelt down and spoke to the woman, "What is it, Sister? Are you in pain?"

"Brother Pratt, not a lot of pain but I can't keep nothing down. It just goes right through me. And my legs are cramped so I can't stand."

Sam waved Margaret back and leaned over one of the men. His face was drawn, his eyes sunken and dark. Orson, Sam and Margaret huddled back at the stairwell. Other passengers were milling about. "What is it, Brother Pratt?" one of the Mormons asked.

"We're not sure, but please see that everyone moves back until we can determine what we have here." He turned to the Wood's and whispered, "I'm afraid it's cholera."

"Yes, I agree, Orson. We need to act quickly. Margaret, get Lloyd and stay on the upper deck. Go straight to the captain and tell him what's happening. Are there any other passengers with symptoms?"

"Not that I am aware of, Sam, but you'd best check."

"Please tell my wife to do the same, Mrs. Wood. Sam and I

will tend to the sick. When you see the captain ask him if he has any laudanum or lead acetate."

Margaret hurried off to the upper decks. Sam and Orson returned to the sick.

###

"No barriers are sufficient to obstruct its progress. It crosses mountains, deserts, and oceans. Opposing winds do not check it. All classes of persons, male and female, young and old, the robust and the feeble, are exposed to its assault; and even those whom it has once visited are not always subsequently exempt; yet as a general rule it selects its victims preferably from among those already pressed down by the various miseries of life and leaves the rich and prosperous to their sunshine and their fears." **1852, Dr. George B. Wood, on Cholera.**

Cholera! Word spread quickly from the crew to the passengers. Captain Johannson locked down the upper deck and restricted the crew to their quarters and duty stations. Sam and Orson took charge of the ill. They established an infirmary forward in the bow.

Cholera is a fickle disease, a death sentence for some, while others recover fully, with no discernable reason why. Diarrhea, vomiting, cramps, all symptoms resulting from rapid dehydration through the loss of body fluids. Cholera caused panic wherever it appeared. It was just becoming apparent, in medical circles, what caused the fast spreading disease. The people still held to the miasmatic belief in bad air or even worse, a punishment by God for sinful behavior.

"Sam, we've got to have clean drinking water, and lots of it, for everyone on board. I was in London in '49' when John Snow made his discovery. We've got to flush these people with boiled water and keep the boat as clean as possible."

"I'll see to it Orson. As long as the boilers are stoked, we'll have plenty of water."

"Sam," Captain Johannson called down from the Hurricane deck. "We have none of the medical supplies you requested."

"We'll make do, Captain. Spread the word not to drink any water unless it comes from me. Can we put in anywhere to get the laudanum?"

"Not a chance. We're obligated to fly the cholera flag and the word will spread quickly along the river. No one will let us dock. There'll be armed guards at the ports."

The boiler room was hot, the men sweating from heat and exertion, but the door was barred, and the chief engineer wouldn't allow Sam inside, so he shouted through the door his instructions and backed it up with the captain's name. The water was to be boiled for 15 minutes then allowed to cool. An Irish lilt boomed through the door as it cracked open enough for Sam to see a large man with a red beard and fierce look of determination, "It na' do na' good, lad. Tis the will o' God an ye bes' let it run de course fer dem dat sinned."

"Just do as I say," Sam pounded on the door with his club. "I don't have time to argue with you."

"Will of God," Sam muttered to himself. "When will the ignorance end?" He automatically looked to the sky, then laughed at himself.

A buxom, black woman addressed Sam from the main deck as he descended the forward stairs. "Mr. Sam, I kin hep, suh."

"How so?" Sam asked.

"I survive de cholera in Cincinnati in '50'. Ya be needin' sumun tu wash dem clothes and clean de deck. Me n' ma sister kin do it."

"Bless you! Aren't you afraid?" Sam asked reaching for her hand.

She recoiled from the touch but recovered and squeezed Sam's hand, "De Lord look out fo me oncet, I imagine he member dat time. No suh, I ain't afeared."

Victims of cholera shrivel like prunes as the fluids pour from their bodies, drawing the skin taut against the structure of the bones. The face takes on a shroud of death, the color of dried leather, eyes like black holes, and air wheezing through lungs filled with mucus. The death march is as painful for the observer as the victim.

Sam sat with Jean Simmons, the sickest of the patients. He held her hand, wiped her forehead with a cool cloth and tried to force some broth, but she was too sick to eat.

"My daughter, Lisa, don't let her see me like this, Mr. Wood," she rasped.

"She comes down every day, Jean. I tell her to wait until you're stronger."

"I don't know what we would have done without you and Mr. Pratt, or the Negro women. Thank them for keeping me clean, will you Sam?"

"You can tell them yourself. Here take some of this broth, you have to keep your strength up for Lisa."

Sam and Orson had ten patients in the makeshift infirmary. The slave women, May and Violet, were a Godsend according to every crewman and passenger on board. They washed the soiled clothes and sheets that were used to cover the sick. They carried fresh water from the boiler room and swabbed the decks.

The passenger who owned the slave women was Randolph Bixby and his wife. They and their two children locked themselves in their cabin and sent for May or Violet when they needed food or to clean the room or carry out the slops from the chamber pots. The Bixby's brought 25 laying hens and two roosters along with their other belongings. Sam had confiscated the chickens in order to make soup and broth for the passengers whether ill or not. Bixby became infuriated when he discovered the 'theft'.

"You, sir, have committed a crime and I won't stand for it. Those hens are for my new farm in Kansas. I'll have the sheriff on you as soon as we land in Independence."

"If you go to Kansas, your slaves will become free souls, because Kansas will enter as a free state," Sam said calmly. He ignored the theft charge.

Bixby stuttered and stammered unable to believe what he was hearing. "I've been assured that Kansas will be a slave state. What kind of bullshit are you trying to pull on me? Who the hell are you? You don't have any say in the matter. The Kansas Legislature has already enacted slave laws."

"There is no Kansas Legislature, you fool. Kansas isn't a state. Any laws passed are bogus laws, which have no standing, enacted by Missouri Ruffians who go to Kansas and vote as Kansas citizens. I'll put a stop to that right quick, now I've got work to do so get out of my way. You might come down and be of some use instead of hiding in your room."

"I sent my Nigger women to help.

"They volunteered; you wouldn't have thought of it. I can't stand the sight of you and I'll use every one of your chickens to save these passengers and you won't do a thing about it. I'm finished with you. Go back to your room and stay out of my way, you worthless gob of spit."

He glared at the man until he retired to his cabin. When Sam turned Margaret was standing behind him with a frown, "Gob of spit, really Sam. Is it worth it to lower yourself to that man's standards?"

Sam groaned and hung his head, "I'm sorry Meg. He just rubs me the wrong way."

"I know, but we have to maintain our Christian values regardless of the circumstances. We can't sink to their level."

Sam hugged her with his forehead against hers. They gathered their composure before hurrying off to help the sick,

Sam to the patients and Margaret to the cook pots and another batch of Bixby chicken soup.

###

"The great cause of diarrhea, which has proven to be so fatal on the road, has been occasioned in most instances by drinking water from holes dug in the riverbank and long marshes. Emigrants should be very careful about this." **Abigail Scott, June 8, 1852**

The morning sun clawed itself up, throwing an ugly light on the diseased boat. Sam and Orson had been awake all night with the sick patients, three days of non-stop vigilance. They passed the dock in Jefferson City at three in the morning, but armed men waited, just as Captain Johannson predicted. Sam tried to reason with them, but they would not allow the boat to stop; nor would they bring medical supplies out in a skiff. No one was brave enough, despite the pleas of the captain. The Missouri River swung north outside of Jefferson City and the sun was starboard, Sam and Orson rigged a canvas awning to block most of the rays from the patients.

"Orson, go catch a little sleep and I'll take the morning watch."

"You don't have to mention it twice, Sam. I'm beat. I'll be down in a few hours."

"Take your time, I feel fine, right now." Sam had a strong constitution borne of good family genes and constant work as a young boy. His strength defied odds and was the envy of every crewman. Sam Wood seemed never to sleep.

The familiar boat sounds lulled the patients to sleep. Two of them had recovered enough to rejoin the healthy passengers. The eight who remained were in various stages of the illness, with Mrs. Simmons the worst. May and Violet changed the sheets under the wasted woman while Sam brought soup to the others.

"Hi, Mr. Sam. How's my mama today," Lisa called from the upper deck.

"No change, I'm afraid, Lisa. She's trying to eat something now. I'll make arrangements for you to see her later, how would that be?"

"Can I talk to you now, Mr. Sam?"

He took the stairs quickly to the main deck, "What is it, Lisa?"

"My daddy died of the cholera in St. Louis. Now I'm afraid that my mama's going to die too." She began to cry and put her arms around Sam's waist. Margaret heard the sobs and joined them, sitting with their feet dangling over the edge of the deck leaning their arms on the deck rail, Margaret put her arms around the girl and held her as she sobbed.

"Does your mother believe in God?" she asked.

"Yes," Lisa answered, drying her tears. "We do believe in God. We went to church all the time when Daddy was alive."

"Then you know that if your mama dies, she'll be in heaven with God and your daddy."

"I know but I thought when mama married Mr. Pratt, she would be safe from everything."

Margaret looked at Sam over the top of the little girl's head. "What do you mean, Lisa? Mr. Pratt is married to Sarah, not your mom."

"My mama is one of Brother Pratt's celestial wives," she said with the matter of fact innocence of the young. Margaret felt a strange feeling of discontent at what Lisa was saying. "Do you mean that all of the Mormons are 'celestial' husbands and wives of the church?"

Lisa looked puzzled, "Well, maybe, but they had a wedding and Brother Johnson married them and Brother Pratt comes to our house some nights and some nights he goes to Sarah's house."

Margaret sucked a large breath of air at this news, frowned and her mouth set with anger that would not be easily defused. "Meg now is not the time. We have more pressing problems, we can deal with this later, please take Lisa to her cabin and I'll go tend to her mother. We'll let her come down soon for a visit. Okay…., Okay, Margaret?"

The frown disappeared and she reached for Lisa. They walked off together while Sam hurried down to the makeshift infirmary.

May saw Sam coming down the forward stairs and hurried over to speak to him. She carried a bundle of clean cloth. "They gettin' better, Mr. Sam," she reported.

Try as he might, he could not get her, or any slave, for that matter, to call him just Sam. The lessons had been ingrained with whip and chain; no amount of assurance would convince them otherwise. She continued, "But I mighty worry bout' Miz Jean. She poorly, Mr. Sam. You best go to her."

"Thank you May. I need to bring Lisa down to see her. You think that's a good idea?"

"No, suh, I do not. You go judge, Mr. Sam. I fear de worse."

Only four patients, other than Jean remained of the 14 who took ill. These two men and two women were rapidly improving, eating well and drinking the clean water. Jean, however, looked and smelled of death. Her face was grey and pinched almost unrecognizable, eyes tormented, lips chapped and drawn. Sam sat beside her and bathed her forehead with a cool cloth speaking in low tones. He assured her that Lisa was well and in good hands. She reached for his wrist with a claw-like grip, her fingers thin as chicken feet. She spoke in a gasping whisper he could barely hear, "Don't let Orson have her."

"What…., what do you mean?"

No response, only a gurgle, a last gasp of breath barely audible. Her eyes stared from a lifeless face. Sam looked up to see

Orson approaching. Was this his wife? Sam looked back at the shriveled corpse of this woman who had lived life with such hopes for herself and her daughter. She had nursed her own husband through his illness into death and now she was gone to join him. Sam dealt with death and dying all his life, but Jean's passing left him empty. Maybe he was too tired to feel anything or maybe he was just becoming immune to it all. He glanced up at Orson standing over him, his blue eyes clear and blonde hair combed back, looking refreshed after his sleep, "The Lord works in mysterious ways, Sam," he said.

###

"Religion is a system of wishful illusions together with a disavowal of reality, such as we find nowhere else but in a state of blissful hallucinatory confusion. Religion's eleventh commandment is "Thou shalt not question." **Sigmund Freud, The Future of an Illusion**

Sam could not remember ever having a dream. Sometimes, he listened to his children when they awoke with what they described as 'a bad dream', but the phrase was a catch-all. Margaret asked them, when they woke suddenly in the night, "Did you have a bad dream, dear?" Then, regardless of the reason for waking, the boys would say, "I had a bad dream, mama." Sam didn't put much stock in dreams and dreaming. He was focused on action and his thoughts were always about what needed to be done next, planning and organizing occupied his thoughts morning and night. He was involved with the Republican Party, abolitionists, women's suffragettes, his attorney work, the church and his family. He had no time for dreams, they didn't fit his personality or his life. But the night after Sister Jean's death he dreamed.

The boat was slowly winding its way north and west toward

Independence, way behind schedule because of the cholera outbreak. Sam finally collapsed onto the sleeping berth about four that afternoon. Margaret let him sleep because he had been up for three days and nights tending to the patients. Lying on his back, he snored loud enough to make Lloyd laugh when he came into the room, to the point where Margaret shushed the boy back to the pilot house. The door and window were open trying to capture a bit of breeze as the boat steamed directly into the setting sun. Margaret sat outside the door knitting. She happened to glance into the room to check on him when he lurched out of bed, "Ahhh!" he screamed, reaching frantically about. Margaret rushed to his side and found him soaked in sweat, yet he claimed to be chilled.

"Sam, what is it, are you sick?"

He gathered himself and sat back, "I had a dream," he said, breathing heavily, "I was with my family in that cave in Kentucky where we used to go hunting for the crystal rocks. I was with Stephan Bishop, our guide, and crawled through a narrow opening to hide and scare him, but I got stuck and no one heard me yell. My candle went out and I couldn't go forward or pull back. There was no light and no sound. It seemed like I was there for an eternity. I tried to call to Father but no words came out of my mouth."

Margaret stood and closed the door and began removing his drenched clothes. "Let's get dry clothes on you, Sam. Did that really happen? Did you get stuck trying to hide from your brothers?"

"No, never. I loved visiting Mammoth Cave. I don't dream, you know that Margaret. I'm not going to try and analyze it, that sounds too much like Grandma Mosher, but it has something to do with the Mormon woman dying like she did. What shall we do with Lisa?"

"While you were asleep, I spoke with Sarah Pratt. She's

going to take the child and raise her. The girl has no other relatives.

Sam told Margaret about Jean Simmons strange request as she was dying, "She distinctly said, 'don't let Orson have her.'"

"Sam, did you know the Mormon men take more than one wife? Sarah says that she is disgusted by it. The men try to pass it as a revelation from God, but she thinks it's just their lustful ways; yet Sarah still loves Orson. She would never leave him and considers him almost a saint, other than this plural marriage blasphemy. Did you know about it?"

"I've heard rumors. I understand that Joseph Smith had many wives."

"Yes, and one of them is on this boat. Marinda Hyde was one of his wives. Sarah told me so."

"Listen, Margaret, Orson may not be a Saint…."

She interrupted him, "No he isn't, Sam, but you don't need to finish, I know what you're going to say. He has many faults, but he saved this boat and I'll be forever grateful, but I don't have to accept their religion and I never will."

"Fair enough, Meg. We should give thanks that we've come through this trial. Let's pray together."

They joined hands and sat quietly communing with God on the most intimate of terms. Sam contemplating a God who was within him and gave him comfort, a personal God that was guiding him to do the right thing. Margaret prayed to the all-knowing God looking over mankind from his throne on high. Whatever happened, it was His will, the one and only God, and she put her entire future into his hands.

Sam knew the real trials were still to come.

PART THREE
HOMESTEAD OF THE FREE

###

"Imagine a man standing in a pair of long boots, covered with dust and mud, drawn over his trousers, the latter made of coarse, fancy-colored cloth, well soiled, the handle of a large bowie-knife projecting from one or both boot-tops; a leathern belt buckled around his waist, on each side of which is fastened a large revolver; a red or blue shirt, with a heart, anchor, eagle, or some other favorite device braided on the breast and back, over which is swung a rifle or carbine, a sword dangling by his side; an old slouched hat; with a cockade or brass star on the front side, and a chicken, goose, or turkey feather sticking in the top; hair uncut and uncombed, covering his neck and shoulders; an unshaved face and unwashed hands. Imagine such a picture of humanity who can swear any given number of oaths in any specified time, drink any quantity of bad whiskey without getting drunk, and boast of having stolen a half dozen horses and killed one or more abolitionists, and you will have a pretty fair conception of a border ruffian, as he appears in Missouri and in Kansas." **John H. Gihon, 'Geary and Kansas' (1857)**

Independence, Missouri

Margaret and Sam were surprised by the terrain along the Missouri and Mississippi, for some reason, believing it to be flat. Nothing was further from the truth with high bluffs above the rivers and rolling hills through Independence and Westport. The bottom land was green with trees and grasses while the hills were brilliant in colorful blue verbena, pink prairie wild rose, yellow buttercup and dandelion. They were delighted by the countryside but appalled by the squalor and dust in the villages themselves.

The Wayne's Landing wharves were slowly losing trade to the Westport Landing wharves further west, but Sam and Margaret disembarked in Independence and had their wagon and team hauled up the bluffs to the village.

David and Caleb spotted the wagon as the Wood family made their way along Liberty Street toward the Mayfair Hotel where Bill and Elizabeth Lyon had taken rooms. The Thompsons lived with other black families in the eastern part of Independence, known as Niggertown. The boys charged the wagon forcing Sam to stop as they climbed aboard babbling about the sights and sounds of the western outpost of civilization. Lloyd almost fell off the wagon dancing and hugging his brother and Missy, his best friend.

"Mama," both Caleb and David shouted as they hugged Margaret exuberantly, Lloyd did the same with his grandmother and second mother, Sally Thompson.

A pair of mounted Ruffians stopped to watch the strange sight as the Lyons, Robinson and Wood families welcomed each other; the Missourians were unused to seeing black families treated so politely by their white masters. Lloyd, in turn, stared openly at the rough looking men carrying long rifles and a brace of pistols, a sword at their waist and knives in their boots. Unshaven, with hair billowing from under dirty slouch-hats, their horses festooned with bright feathers and what appeared to be human scalps, they looked disdainfully at the awestruck Lloyd.

"You eye-balling me boy?" one growled while Lloyd bolted for the shelter of his father's arms. Sam grabbed his club and was ready to advance when Bill Lyon intervened, cautioning Sam back.

"No sir, this boy is just admiring your horse. He means no harm, sir, and that's a fact." Sam looked from his father-in-law to the Border Ruffians.

"Rufus, I heard that Nigger boy call that white woman mama, did you hear that?"

"I did, Carson, heard it plain as day. Come here, boy," he shouted at Caleb. John jumped between his son and the men, "Nah, suh, nah, suh, he sed, Ma'am, Massa. Dat whut he sed…., Ma'am, cause he a respekful, Nigger boy," John said, in his best slave dialect, his head bowed not looking the men in the face. Sam dropped his cane and stood slack jawed, not believing his eyes and ears.

The Border Ruffians spit a stream of tobacco on the dirt next to John's feet and smirked at Sam as they rode by.

Sam turned to Bill, "Why, in the name of all that is holy, did you let those men speak to you that way?"

"Best to avoid bringing attention to ourselves right now. They murdered an abolitionist in Westport day before yesterday. There are a lot more Ruffians than free-state people. Pick your fights, Sam, that's what you always say."

"Sam, it's a different world here. We have to go underground, so to speak, until we can build our numbers, we need to blend in, otherwise, they'll wipe us out before we start," John said.

David and Caleb took Lloyd aside, "Don't stare at them, Lloyd."

"Who are they, Davey?"

Caleb answered, "They're Border Ruffians and they'll cut your liver out and eat it while you have to watch."

David nodded his head in agreement and added, "They're real bad men, Lloyd, don't mess with them, they kill abolitionists."

"Why? I'm an abolitionist. Why do they want to kill me?"

"Because they don't want Africans to be free?"

"But why, Caleb, aren't you an African?"

"No, dummy, I'm an American, but they call the slaves Africans and don't want them to be free because they want someone to do all their work, so they don't have to."

David clarified a point that bothered him, "But Caleb, you are black and that makes you an African."

"No it doesn't, David. I'm an American, just like you."

"But you are black," David added, to get the last word.

The men conferred next to the wagon, while the women went into the hotel seeking the shade. Bill and John explained, as best they could, the situation between the abolitionist minority and the pro-slavery majority, mostly Missouri citizens and Border Ruffians who were no more than thugs and criminals given a semblance of legitimacy by the Federal Government. On June 10, the Missourians held a meeting at Salt Creek Valley, a trading post three miles west of Fort Leavenworth, where a "Squatter Claim Association" was organized.

John reported, "They said they were gonna' make Kansas a slave state if it required half the citizens of Missouri to emigrate here. Get this part, Sam, each Missourian is supposed to kill an abolitionist, they put that in writing without so much as a by-your-leave."

"According to the Missourians, abolitionists would do well not to stop in Kansas Territory, but keep on up the Missouri River until they reach Nebraska," Bill added. "Nearly every desirable location along the river has been claimed by men from western Missouri, because of the preemption laws."

"What are the preemption laws, Sam?" John asked.

"The Law, written, about 1840 or 41, if I remember well, that gives the right to squatters to claim 160 acres of Government land before the Government offers it to the general public. Squatter's rights, basically, but they have to live on the land for it to be valid. You can't cross the river and say 'I claim 'squatter's rights' just to vote for slavery, then go back to Missouri to your wife and family. That's what we have to put a stop to."

Independence was a rough town and facilities were sparse, but the Mayfair boasted the cleanest and best bathroom in the West. An artesian well provided running water and a makeshift shower had been erected. A boiler provided hot water and a newfangled flush toilet had been installed. It was the talk of the town. Margaret confided to her mother that she was in need of the facilities and was looking forward to the promise of a hot bath. Grandmother Lyon informed Lloyd that he was due a bath and the boy was incredulous.

"Why grandmother? I had a bath on the boat, didn't I Mama?"

"Yes, you did, but that was ten days ago, before the cholera outbreak. Don't argue just get it over with." Margaret added, "Sam you need to come and take a bath. You haven't bathed since St. Louis." Sam waved Margaret away and turned back to the men.

"You do smell a bit rank, there partner," John said in agreement.

"Good Lord, I thought it was the horses," Bill laughed.

"I've got more important things to think about," Sam answered, defensively. "I had a cholera outbreak to manage plus we need to plan how to get into Kansas. I don't have time to change my shirt."

John said, "We heard about the cholera. Damned worried too. Word travels fast on the river, amazing that you only lost one patient."

"I wish you could have met Orson Pratt. He worked miracles, knew that we had to have clean water to flush out the patients and clean the clothes and boat. The Mormons sure speak high of him. Maybe we can visit with him before they go on upriver."

"Daddy," David interrupted, "Mama says come get your bath now. The tub is ready."

Bill smirked at John who said, "Yes, Sammy, best run along to your bath time."

Sam laughed, good natured, "I've learned to pick my battles."

###

Defines the boundaries of the Territory, gives it the name of Kansas, and prescribes that "when admitted as a State or States, the said Territory, or any portion of the same, shall be received into the Union with or without slavery, as their constitution may prescribe at the time of their admission." It further provides for its future division into two or more Territories, and the attaching of any portion thereof to any other State or Territory; and for the holding inviolable the rights of all Indian tribes until such time as they shall be extinguished by treaty. **Kansas-Nebraska Act Section 19**

Independence was typical of western border towns in the year 1854, full of adventurous men speculating on the advancing frontier, shopkeepers and farmers looking for a new start, even criminals looking to escape the law. Most people were flocking to Kansas for the land, 160 acres could be had by filing a claim and real estate speculation was driving the population boom. But the town was atypical because of the political and philosophical matter of Free State versus Slave State, and there were a few men, like Sam Wood, who came for ideological reasons. The issue was simple, the pro slavery men wanted the right to bring their slaves into Kansas and the Free State men were adamantly against that happening. Neither side was willing to compromise, in fact, there could be no middle ground on which to compromise, both sides espoused the democratic ideals born of the Declaration of Independence, both sides claimed the support of God.

Washington politicians had decreed, in the Kansas-Nebraska Act, that the citizens of Kansas would enact laws that reflected their will through representatives duly elected according to the Laws of the United States. This was Stephen Douglas' 'Popular Sovereignty'. The problem was that citizens of Missouri were crossing the river to vote in Kansas. Polling places were reporting 600 or 700 votes in towns with populations of 200, the bogus voting that Sam was intent on overturning. The Border Ruffians were electing their own pro-slavery candidates. Laws enacted by the Border Ruffians were a sham yet ratified by the pro-slavery faction in Washington.

With Sam's focus on the issues, was it any wonder that his shirt wasn't changed very often or that his boots weren't always shined? Margaret did her best to keep him well clothed, but he was off on his quest to save Kansas from the blight of slavery. He would no more think of changing his clothes than he would think of how he was able to breathe. Sam had important matters on his mind and cleanliness was not among them. He dressed well, but only because Margaret made or bought his clothes, just as his mother before her. Sam never bought a pair of dungarees in his life. The only matter of ablutions that interested Sam was a clean-shaven chin. He did grow a mustache, but his chin was always well groomed because whiskers scratched his wife and daughters, when they came along. Sam was conscientious of those kinds of distractions.

The bath house was all its reputation foretold. Reached

through a private entrance on the first floor of the hotel, it was staffed with female attendants who provided towels and toiletries but, most importantly, instructions on how to operate the unfamiliar bathtub with piped water and a flush toilet behind a privacy screen. This was a novelty unheard of even in the civilized regions of Illinois, Ohio and Pennsylvania, let alone the wilds of the western frontier.

"Daddy, where does it go?" Lloyd asked.

Sam was examining the ornate four-footed bathtub with warm water flowing through lead pipes.

"Sam, Lloyd is asking you where the waste goes," Margaret repeated.

"Where the waste goes...., what waste?"

"The poo and pee-pee, Daddy, where does it go? See, it's gone. The water washed it away, but where to?"

Sam studied the toilet bowl and the pipe going into the floor and a pipe leading from a water closet above. He looked at Margaret who stood smiling, then David and Lloyd who were watching him intently. Sam cocked his head to the side and put his left hand to his chin the elbow supported by the right. He studied the contraption then got down on his hands and knees and contemplated it further. David and Lloyd laughed at their daddy's antics as Sam pretended to measure and analyze the pipes and containers. Finally he jumped to his feet and said, I've got it figured out boys, it goes into the floor, then over here to this tank where it gets ground up and wooshed around and transformed and mashed up then it goes over here into this pipe and it goes round and round and comes out over here in this tub and that's where you're going to take a bath."

David and Lloyd fell to the floor laughing, "Ahhhh, ick, ick! Oh, Daddy, you did it again, you made it up. Papa Lyon already explained it's piped outside into a hole behind the hotel that is filled with sand and then it gets absorbed into the ground,"

David announced proudly.

"Absorbed," Margaret corrected him.

"Well," Sam huffed, pretending to be insulted, "Why did you ask me if you already knew?"

"Because we wanted to hear what you would make up."

Margaret hurried the boys through the bath then fostered them off to her mother. She shut the door and began running clean water into the tub. A demur glance Sam's way was all he needed to begin undressing.

"Margaret, you wicked thing, you've been planning on seducing me in this fancy tub, haven't you?"

"The thought crossed my mind. We haven't been alone since leaving Columbus. I can't think of a more romantic place right now. I've locked both doors and told the attendants to give us an hour."

Sam took her in his arms and gazed into her eyes. "Meg, I truly don't know what I would do without you." He couldn't imagine being more in love.

###

"Passed six fresh graves!... Oh, 'tis a hard thing to die far from friends and home—to be buried in a hastily dug grave without shroud or coffin—the clods filled in and then deserted, perhaps to be food for wolves..." **Esther McMillan Hanna, 1852.**

The morning dawned hot and humid with a fetid smell from the dung heaps piled east of Mill Creek. Covered wagons trailed into town billowing dust as pilgrims traveled the California, Santa Fe and Oregon Trails, many of them not knowing which path to take until they were underway. Foremost in the confusion and disorder was an undercurrent of distrust as Border Ruffians tried to distinguish the abolitionists from the true pioneers and they were none too gentle with those they suspected.

Sam was finally convinced to be careful and not confront the Ruffians, but he struggled with this unfamiliar method of dealing with the issues. He wanted to meet the menace head-on and fight it with the fury and power of God's might, but his friends and family convinced him that discretion was the watchword of the day. Sam had to bide his time, but the day of reckoning would come. Security was a problem; the walls have ears is how Bill Lyon put it. Sam was learning the hard way to keep his mouth shut. He had an altercation with a 'tough' at the post office in Westport, located about five miles west of Independence. Westport was the only post office on the frontier. Sam was posting a letter to the Cleveland Independent when a rowdy fellow elbowed his way in and accosted a young man asking for his mail; a thin faced fellow with eyeglasses and sandy hair that fell over his forehead, a scholarly looking youth with the lofty ideals of his class.

"I told you to get out of town, you miserable excuse for a man. Ain't no place for the likes a' you, by God. We gonna' kill any undesirables that ain't outta' here by tomorrow, the latest. Now we done kilt one last week and yore next in line, ya Goddamned puissant abolitionist."

The Ruffian continued his profane tirade unabated, but the man looked him in the eye without flinching, "I've got every right to be here. This is a Federal Post Office and I have as much right as you do."

The ruffian pulled a large knife, and Sam clubbed him up aside of his head. The man fell to the ground not knowing who had committed the act. Sam turned and walked silently out, mounted his horse and rode away.

Later, speaking to Bill and John, he admitted, "It was one of the hardest things I've ever done."

"What you mean, Sam? You've clubbed many an evil man," John said.

"No, I mean walking away without telling them who I am. I didn't want to bring down trouble on your heads, but I sure wanted to spread the word."

"It's best that you didn't," Bill replied. "We're going to have enough trouble as it is. Who was the fellow you saved, Sam?"

"I don't know. But he had gumption. That Ruffian would have carved him up but he stood his ground. He was a sickly looking fellow, wearing glasses and light-colored hair, with some kind of tweed suit on, like he was a newspaper man or something. I didn't waste time, I just got out as fast as I could."

"I know the man," Bill said. "I've seen him around. He preaches against slavery on the corner of Liberty and First. They call him Francis and threaten to string him up right there on the spot, but he just ignores them. I'm surprised he's made it this long."

"I hope he has the sense to get out of town. He won't last another day with that kind of behavior."

A knock at the door halted the conversation. Elizabeth announced a Felix Francis to the group and in walked the very subject of the conversation.

"Gentlemen, I apologize for the intrusion, but my name is Felix Francis and I believe we can be of mutual benefit to each other. Ah, Mr. Wood, I see you are somewhat surprised to see me. You should not have interfered this morning, I would have handled the situation and you risked giving away your identity."

The men were at a loss for words until Sam said, "Mr. Francis, that man had a knife longer than your arm. He would have carved you up before you could say, how de do."

"Maybe, maybe not. I believe that I have been chosen to lead the battle against the evil of slavery here in the Promised Land. It is my destiny."

Margaret and Sally glanced at each other, stifling laughs behind cupped hands. John voiced their thoughts, "Damn, Sam, he sounds like you."

"No he doesn't," Sam scoffed. "I've never said anything like that."

"I propose we join forces, gentlemen. We shall battle the Ruffians together," Felix said firmly.

###

"Come on, then, gentlemen of the slave states. Since there is no escaping your challenge, we accept it in the name of freedom. We will engage in competition for the virgin soil of Kansas, and God give the victory to the side which is stronger in numbers, as it is in right."

New York Senator William Seward, on the passage of the Kansas-Nebraska Act, May 1854

Felix did believe that he was chosen to put an end to slavery, an evil he attributed to the free will of man and not some supernatural force. His father, Captain Alphonse Francis, believed in God, yet his father was an exceedingly evil man, at least in Felix's mind, who had been taught that God was the source of all things good, and the devil all things bad. A medieval attitude sprung from Captain Francis' family, the Devices, living in England in the 1600's, Lancashire County, and, according to family lore, direct decedents of the Pendle witches. His mother ridiculed the idea, not the fact that Captain Francis was a Device, on his mother's side, but that there were witches, in the 17th century, or ever. But Felix wasn't so certain, witnessing the behavior of his father over the years. Something tormented the man's soul, manifesting itself in drunken fits of rage and a total disregard for his fellow humans. Having your ancestors hung as witches, after the Lancashire Witch Trials, might have had something to do with it, even if it was over 200 years ago.

Felix had no strategy for abolishing slavery other than to go where 'the action is' and do what needed to be done to root out the disgusting institution that kept men in chains. He didn't personally know any slaves. A sensitive man, Felix also hated vulgarity and all manner of rudeness and impropriety, yet he constantly sought out the roughest, vilest places to try and affect change. He was not without fear, quite the contrary, he was constantly afraid, but refused to let that fear dictate his life, he chose to confront it, just as he'd confronted his father some 15 years earlier.

He grew up in Perry, Maine along the rocky shore of Passamaquoddy Bay where his father was a seaman, skipper of a schooner, the Hermosa. Captain Francis was an abrasive man, ashamed of his effeminate son with the high ideals of changing the world. Felix's mother was a teacher and she did her best to shelter him from the raging storms that thundered into their home when Alphonse was drunk from revelry at the Maritime Public House. Captain Francis' crew joked about 'sodomites' and 'pederasts' encountered in their travels and each joke seemed to drive a spike through Felix's soul.

Although Perry, Maine was somewhat sheltered from the tempest disturbing the southern states, Felix's mother monitored the national news through the newspapers. The Missouri Compromise of 1820 admitted Missouri to the United States as a slave state with the compromise part being that Maine was admitted as a free state. Felix claimed this as a sign that he was ordained to play a part in shaping the destiny of the entire country. No one understood, except Felix, why this was true, and he didn't bother to explain it. He was born in 1830, so it wasn't because of the date itself. It had to do with a confrontation between his mother and drunken father when he was 12 years old. Captain Francis was running slaves from the Bahamas into slave markets along the southern coast and when Felix's mother found out, she confronted him about it. Captain Francis struck his wife, knocking her down and Felix, horrified at seeing his mother lying on the floor bleeding at the mouth, charged his father, fists flailing, thrashing the big man on his shoulders and arms. He was so surprised at this action by his milquetoast son that he sat down in astonishment. Felix continued to pummel his father, until the man merely swatted him away. The only comment the Captain made was, "All this fuss over a bunch of Niggers."

Felix stopped trying to punish his father, it was a useless gesture anyway, and, breathing heavily, helped his mother to her feet. The old man slowly rose from his chair, took his hat from the peg by the door and went back to the Inn.

Felix rinsed a cloth at the pump and bathed his mother's face while she tried to explain to him what the 'fuss' was, the horror of what his father was doing and how they were profiting from the misery of a whole race of people; the very bread on their table was paid for from the sale of Africans in chains. Felix was horrified and made his mind up right then and there to do something about it. That was the beginning of how he found himself on the frontier, both figuratively and literally, of the fight against slavery. A journey that had taken him to Cincinnati, Ohio during the famous Sam Wood show. When Sam struck the man in the post office, Felix knew who he was. He had observed Sam in action. Felix dedicated his entire life and small income to abolishing slavery. He was fearless in that pursuit and his new strategy was to team up with Sam Wood, the embodiment of the man he wanted to become.

###

"30 miles to water, 20 miles to wood, 10 miles to hell and I gone there for good."

Carved on a deserted shack near Chadron, Nebraska

They started into Kansas on June 25, 1854, Sam Wood, John

Thompson and Felix Francis. Bill Lyon stayed behind to recruit more like-minded Free State men and look after the women and children, something all three of the ladies protested.

"We don't need a man 'looking after' us," Margaret protested, a sentiment echoed by her mother and Sally Thompson. Bill kept a low profile, especially from Elizabeth because she was looking for a fight. Tired of dodging the Border Ruffians, she felt the time to turn the other cheek had passed, it was time to take action. Plus, she sorely missed the children who stayed behind in Ohio to continue their education. The Lyons and Thompsons had been in Independence for over a month and she was ready to make something happen.

The three men rode west following the well-worn tracks of the Santa Fe Trail. Merchants and buffalo hunters had been following the route since the 1820s, and Spanish priests and soldiers for 50 years before that. The draft horses that Sam brought from Ohio were ill-suited for the trip, so he bought a saddle horse for himself. John Thompson had already acquired a horse from a runaway slave who needed ready cash for a steam ticket up the Missouri.

They made a remarkable sight, contrasted with the savage Border Ruffians and surly teamsters, the covered wagons of the pioneers, and the occasional Indian family visiting relatives on the reservations. Sam wore a new yellow shirt, made by Margaret, John was in his coarse cotton trousers, white with a light blue cotton shirt. Felix was attired in a full tweed suit with vest and bowler hat. His mode of transportation a balky mule, large even by mule standards, who was in charge of direction and speed, a fact obvious to the most casual observer.

"Felix, why don't you get a real horse," John kidded him.

"This animal has carried me from Ohio, and I don't plan to give up on it just because others consider it to be cumbersome."

The small party of abolitionists received their fair share of attention from travelers along the trail and there were quite a few that pleasant June day. The Oregon and Santa Fe Trails routed through Independence with settlers bound for Oregon branching off in Gardner, Kansas. Sam decided to go south and west as far as Council Grove to get a view of the Tallgrass Prairie from the rolling hills above the Neosho River. The party stopped at Seth Hayes trading post. His place was billed as the last supply house before reaching Santa Fe in New Mexico Territory, 650 miles through brutal country with little water, and weather that could turn vicious in a heartbeat, not to mention the threat of hostile Indians, rattlesnakes and starvation.

They tied their mounts to a tree in the vacant lot next to the trading post because wagons, horses and other travelers clogged the immediate area around the store. Sam leaned against the building and watched the pioneers as they prepared to continue west to Colorado and then south into New Mexico, most did not know the dangers and hardships that awaited them. They were on the move for reasons as varied as the number of people, some fleeing from something, some seeking a new start, some following relatives who had gone before. Letters, passed back and forth along the trail, informed those at both ends about the news. A large oak tree in town was the depository for mail. It was a surprisingly efficient method as travelers were conscientious about seeing the letters reach whoever they were addressed to.

Shouting stayed the travelers, as a large woman clad in a long dress, once considered fashionable but now bedraggled, ragged and torn at the hem, screamed, "Damn you Hiram, you lied to me, and I won't put up with it anymore," then burst into tears. Hiram was half her size and seemed to wilt even further from the ferocious public commotion. "Six hundred and fifty miles and not a town or a trading post between here and there, are you out of your mind? I should have stayed in Altoona like mother said, like she begged me." A boy and girl, in early teens, glared angrily at their father, obviously supporting Mother's point of view.

"Now Mother," Hiram attempted to sooth her, "It won't be as bad as they say. They're trying to make people stay here. It's economics. We've fared well so far."

"We've practically starved to death," she screeched, "and I haven't had a bath in three weeks. Look at your children. They hate this worse than I do." She took a deep breath, stood up straight and announced calmly, "Either we turn around and go back together, or I will go and take the children."

"Now, Mother....," he started again before she cut him off.

"NO! I've decided. This is the last straw."

Seth Hayes came to investigate the disturbance. He was a small man with a full beard and the shrewd eyes of a horse trader who claimed to be a cousin of Kit Carson and definitely was a great-grandson of Daniel Boone. Hayes lived in a log home on the west bank of the Neosho, with a black woman, Sarah Taylor, also known in the community as Aunt Sally, a sturdy dark-skinned woman with a round face and beautiful black eyes. Considerable talk, among those who cared, attributed strong feelings between Seth and Aunt Sally; they did not affirm or deny the gossip.

Seth walked up to the family with the patience of a trained psychologist, calmed the mother and guided her to the outdoor kitchen where Aunt Sally took over the consultation. Seth strolled back to the porch, "Where you fellas headed?" he asked.

"Actually, we're scouting a place to settle down. Our wives are in Missouri waiting for us to stake a claim."

"Abolitionists?" Seth was a man of few words.

"To the core," Sam announced looking him in the eye. "Is that a problem here?"

"You a free man," he asked John, ignoring the question?

"Born free, Mr. Hayes, and I plan to help my brothers and

sisters gain their freedom."

Seth nodded and produced a pipe which the men took as a sign that he meant to visit. "My woman...., Sarah," he pronounced it 'say rah', and nodded toward the outdoor kitchen. "Most call her Aunt Sally. I've offered to give her papers but she don't want to go nowhere. She been with me many a year. I don't take sides, not good for business, but I sympathize with the colored race. No man should be in chains outside a prison. You won't find many agree with me around here."

Felix spoke for the first time, "Are there many pro-slavery bullies hereabout, sir? Do you feel that danger lurks in waiting for us?"

Seth contemplated him, tapped the pipe ashes against his boot and said, "You ain't from round' here are ya?"

Sam and John stifled a laugh. Felix took no offense and answered honestly, "No, Mr. Hayes, I'm from the State of Maine."

"You got any o' them bullies up there in Maine?"

"Just my father, sir," he said with a smile.

Seth refilled his pipe, "Come on inside and we'll see if Sarah's got anything left to eat."

###

"The road to-day was very hilly and rough. At night we encamped within one mile of Fort Hall. Mosquitoes were as thick as flakes in a snowstorm. The poor horses whinnied all night, from their bites, and in the morning the blood was streaming down their sides." **Margaret A. Frink, July 11, 1850**

Sam was taken with Seth Hayes and Council Grove, but it seemed too far from Missouri, over 100 miles to Independence. Seth explained that he had made petition for a post office, but nothing was official as yet. They ate turkey stew with other pioneers who were more interested in the dangers ahead than the politics in Kansas and Missouri. Aunt Sally advised Sam to go south to the Cottonwood River and find Pete Dawson and his wife, Guadalupe, "They good people but some thinks ole Pete daft in the haid. Don't you believe it. Seth has a ranch over that way, and I like to visit Guadalupe and her family," Aunt Sally said.

Daybreak found the three men riding into the sun on the plateau above the Neosho. This was the Tallgrass Prairie. As far as they could see the prairie grass fluttered like a school of minnows weaving in a current. The earth colors, beige and shades of brown blanketed by the blue sky caused them to pause speechless with wonder.

"I've never seen anything like this," John finally said.

"God did himself proud here," Sam agreed.

"I don't know who made it, but there stand the owners," Felix said excited for the first time since Sam and John had ridden with him. He pointed west into a draw where buffalo emerged slowly consuming the grass as they grazed unbothered by the intruders.

"Buffalo," Sam said. "I saw one once in Chicago. This is the first I've ever seen in the wild."

"Do you suppose there are savages about?" Felix asked looking very nervous indeed.

"Doubtful," John said. These Indians are from the reservation, the hostile tribes are further west.

"Doesn't mean we shouldn't be careful," Sam said squinting into the morning sun.

They turned south and rode easily with the casual conversation of men thrown together in a common cause. Felix told of his life in Maine, learning from his mother, and dodging the blows of his father. Felix Francis became an abolitionist round-about, not through religion, not through firsthand encounters, but through a chance remark by his father. Sam and John were glad to have him. He was odd, no doubt, but he had grit and they admired that in a man.

The sun was well past its zenith when they paused at the bluffs above the Cottonwood River Valley. The land sloped abruptly, then flattened to the stream; there was a rustic cabin with smoke curling from the chimney and some chickens scratching in the dirt. The crossing was easy with the river down in the summer dry season. Dogs began barking and came to investigate the strangers. A grizzled old-timer offered them tobacco and whiskey and a log to sit on outside his front porch, but none of the men used either, much to the man's amazement.

"You mean you don't chew backy nor drink whiskey?" he asked incredulously. "What the hell has this world come to? What are ya then? Preachers?"

"No sir, we're abolitionists," John answered.

"What? Hell, yore a Negro."

"Yes, I'm aware of that. Doesn't keep me from being an abolitionist."

The old man sat down, contemplating this new information. He took a long pull from the inventory and looked at his visitors. Finally, he said, "Zebulon Pike traveled through here in eighteen ought and six. Bet you didn't know that."

Sam chuckled and said, "No sir, I surely did not know that, but it is good information. My name is Sam Wood, and these are my friends, John Thompson and Felix Francis. We are scouting for a place to file a claim and build a homestead."

"Name o Pete, welcome to Pete's Place, Kansas Territory. Well sir, you won't find a finer place than this right here. You got everything you could ever need, and old Seth Hayes has a tradin post not 25-mile north o' here, plus he's got a ranch just up that bluff right there. You ain't gonna' lack fer company in this spot, and the Cottonwood River is full a fish, and there's plenty a game."

"Mr. Pete, it is a very pleasing mead and we would be most comfortable here, but I fear that we should be closer to the conflict in Missouri. It is our sworn mission to end the abominable institution of slavery," Felix said.

Pete watched Felix warily, had another pull on the jug and tried a different tack, "Well, there ain't no slaves to rescue round here. But I'd welcome the company if you was a mind to stay. The onliest Negro I know of is Aunt Sally, Seth's woman. Seth and Aunt Sally come visit from time to time. My wife, Guadalupe, sets a fine table." As if on cue the lady in question appeared from the corner of the cabin with tortillas and a container of frijoles. "Buenas tardes, señores. Bienvenido a nuestra casa. Por favor, únase a nosotros para algunos refrescos." She smiled pleasantly, her teeth straight and white against her brown skin.

"Guadalupe don't habla no English," Pete explained as two small children followed her cautiously peeking out at the strangers from behind her skirts.

"Looks like you've been busy there Pete. Them young'uns look just like you," John chided him.

Pete roared with laughter and took another swig. "Them's my grand chillum, oldest boy Romero's kids. He and his wife are off to Independence to gather some sheep and hogs. Gonna' get into the sheep bidness. Might run into em on the way to Emporia. I'll ride with ye as far as the falls at Cottonwood over Osage Hill there ahind us," Pete gestured to the east.

A mangy dog loped up with a rabbit in its mouth and dropped it on the porch where the children grabbed it up and handed it to their grandmother. She scurried off to skin it and start a rabbit stew. Felix patted his leg and called to the dog, "Here boy, here boy, come here, I'll scratch your ears."

Pete started laughing and told Felix, "Dog's name's Pedro, but he don't speak nothing but Mexican. That there's Lupe's dog, he fetches rabbits and such fer the stew pot. She don't allow us to teach him no English."

The high plains stretch from Missouri to the Rocky Mountains, and from Canada to Texas. The soil is thin and the dry winter grass prone to lightning fires which act as a cleansing of the land like a good scrub brush. Pete and those like him were hearty men who looked beyond the shortcomings in soil to the blessings in the tall grass and the abundance of game. Gardens could be coaxed from the earth and Guadalupe had a good one behind the cabin with lettuce, cabbage, carrots and corn. She surely did set a good table. When it came time to leave Sam promised to return as soon as he could and bring Margaret and the boys to visit, he meant every word, but they needed to return to Missouri and assure the others of their safety.

The four men were sitting in the shade of a large cottonwood tree while their horses watered at Prather Creek. The river flowed east but meandered a good deal in the flat land skirting the hills and vales. The prairie grass was waist high in the ravines and bottom land, shorter on the mesas. The Tallgrass portion of the Great Plains occupied the eastern portions of Kansas and Nebraska Territories. Most farmers passed by for the fertile fields farther west or north, but this area would prove popular with cattle ranchers. As they mounted and rode to the highest point above the Cottonwood River, Sam stopped to enjoy the view.

"This would be a good place to spend your life," he said.

"A most relaxing vista," Felix agreed.

They rode another three miles to the falls where they stopped to eat more frijoles and dried beef.

"I rode with him, ya know," Pete volunteered.

"Who's that Pete?" John asked.

"Zebulon Pike, back in ought and six."

"Is that the truth, Pete, you were on that expedition?"

"We come through the valley here with a full company o'

men, mules, dogs and what all. I was just a private and didn't know east from west. I wanted to come back here when we got done. I fell in love with this place. Thing is, we wasted time traipsing around the snow, following the Arkansas over to the Rockies, wasted more time tryin' to climb that damned mountain, then we trooped south along the Front Range and ended up in Mexico. We was stuck in a Mexican prison for four years; Leastways me and Josh Billings and Rafe Lafleur were. They let Pike and Lt. Wilkins and the rest of em go back to the states."

"Why'd they do that?" John asked.

"Don't rightly know, but I learned the language some and met Guadalupe and thought that she was about the purtiest gal I ever met, Mexican or no, and a hell of a lot smarter than me. I wasn't but 22 so I asked her to marry me and we came back to the Flint Hills. It wasn't anyone but us and the Indians and they let us be, helped us, in fact. We settled along Diamond Creek and been pretty content, but there's a passle a' folk about now a days. Used to be we wouldn't see anyone in a year, ceptin' the Indians, now people comin' by every month."

Pete was a pleasant companion and took a liking to Felix because they both rode mules. He pointed them north and made them promise to return, something that Sam assured, not realizing how permanent his pledge would become.

###

"Raining all day...and the boys are all soaking wet and look sad and comfortless. The little ones and myself are shut up in the wagons from the rain. Still it will find its way in and many things are wet; and take us all together we are a poor looking set, and all this for Oregon...I am thinking as I write, 'Oh Oregon, you must be a wonderful country.'"
Amelia Stewart Knight, June 1, 1853

The Neosho River ran high from the rains earlier in the week, but they found a safe place to cross and continued late into the evening, well after dark which came early because there was just a sliver of a moon. Gentle slopes and rugged arroyos and ravines marked the way along the prairie uplands, a pleasant ride during the day; they almost forgot the deadly trials awaiting them back at the Missouri border. As dusk settled, the horses grew restless and picked their way carefully until they came to what Sam thought was Elm Creek. John lit the lantern and they made camp as best they could, without wood for a fire. The hobbled horses grazed nearby, and the men lay looking into the dazzling starlit sky.

"What day is it?" Sam asked.

"I'm not precisely sure, Sam. Are you aware of the date, John?"

"Well, I'm not sure either, but I think its Sunday, maybe Monday. I hope Sunday because I prayed this morning as if it were. When I'm not near a Lutheran church, I hit my knees and pray to God to take care of my brothers and sisters back in Ohio and protect my children and Sally. I have a long list of people that I bring to the Lord's attention...., they need it, some of them."

"I never had much use for religion," Felix answered after a time. "I've studied the matter a great deal, I'm especially fond of David Hume, like him, I believe that if God does exist, he is impotent in the face of slavery, so of what value is he? How about you, Sam? Are you a devout Quaker?"

"I don't really bother about it a lot. I have a difficult time believing that the God my mother and wife pray to...., constantly," he chuckled before continuing, "They pray and believe that God is just and kind. I have a hard time believing that the God they describe to me is the same God that allows slavery."

John spoke up, "You're one of the people that I bring to the Lord's attention, Sam." Felix laughed. "No, it's true." John continued, "Because I can tell that you have doubts."

"That's why I don't think about it much one way or another. I find it easier to go ahead and do something…., the kind of thing the good and kind God would be doing if he had the time…., or if he was really up there," Sam said. Felix understood perfectly, but John resolved to pray even harder.

###

Where today are the Pequot? Where are the Narragansett, the Mohican, the Pocanet and other powerful tribes of our people? They have vanished before the avarice and oppression of the white man, as snow before the summer sun ... Sleep not longer, O Choctaws and Chickasaws... Will not the bones of our dead be plowed up, and their graves turned into plowed fields? ***Tecumseh, 1811***

They reached the Wakarusa River at the junction of the Santa Fe Trail two mornings later. Shawnee Chief, Paschal Fish, offered a place to stay for the night. Chief Fish was friendly but worried about the number of settlers who were looking to stay instead of passing through like they did for many years. He profited from the settlers who passed by on their way west. Fish was especially interested in talking with John Thompson, surprised to hear that he was a free man, "I do not understand the owning of another human being. All human beings are free just by reason of being human. Why do not your people rise up and leave the white men who mistreat them so?"

"It's not that easy, Chief. This has been going on for 250 years. The first slaves were shipped into Virginia in the early 1600's. When men are chained in a strange land, they have no recourse, they are powerless. The Cherokees over in Oklahoma Territory own slaves." Felix answered

"I know this, and I am ashamed of them. I would never let myself be chained by another human being," the Chief declared emphatically.

Felix and Sam glanced at each other knowing these words were false, he was a slave to the whims of the white man, whether he admitted it or not. Paschal Fish was a proud man with a wife and four children including a beautiful daughter by the name of Eudora. She was about 13 at the time. He was very protective of her and all the females in his village. Fish had a farm along the Kansas River and a home in the village and was considered a prosperous but fair and honest man.

"These bad white men come here and attempt to bargain for my daughter. What kind of evil men are bred in Missouri, trying to buy my daughter like she is a horse? When I refuse them, they threaten to steal the girl away. It is no life for a child to be hidden from her fellow man like a field mouse from the hawk. I ask you to petition the President in Washington to put a stop to this behavior. These men are nothing more than animals."

Sam answered, "Chief, there will be trouble whether I petition the President, or not. He supports the policies of these men, and, frankly, doesn't care about the red man or the black man. These Border Ruffians are intent on one thing, to make Kansas a place for white men to keep the Africans in chains, if you get in their way, they will cut you down."

A fire blazed along the bank of the river, children frolicked among the trees while the women cooked venison and corn cakes for the visitors. Chief Fish continued, "Many people come from the east and are making their shelters along the river bottoms, some have even built cabins. They were not a worry to me when they passed by, they bought our furs and beaver pelts, they bought our cattle and horses, our corn and vegetables. My brother, Blue Jacket, has a trading post on the turnpike where it crosses the Wakarusa, we made much money during the California Gold Rush, but the Government will drive us away from here, just as we were driven out of Ohio and Delaware before that. Soon there will be no place for us to go. Already the

Shawnee are scattered like seeds from the sunflower in the wind. The land of our ancestors is lost to us. The Agent came and said we must think of going south into Oklahoma Territory. I don't want to go to Oklahoma. This is the land that was given to us and we wish to stay here between the Wakarusa and the Kaw."

Felix spoke up, "Mr. Fish, I'm afraid there is nothing that can be done. If you resist, they will simply kill you, there is no justice for the poor. The rich people in Washington will allow the Whites to do what they want, and they want your land. They will just take it if you fight them."

"I know this to be true, I've known it for some time now," the Chief said with tears in his eyes. "I'm powerless to do anything about it. Somedays I think, I will take my sons and we will purify our bodies and paint ourselves with the symbols of war and ride against the Fort Leavenworth. Somedays I think, this way, but I know it will not happen. When they come and tell us to move, we will move. That is just the way it will be." He wore his hair braided, flannel shirt and white man's trousers; the words hit even heavier from a man who looked more like a farmer than a proud warrior. John, Sam and Felix had no words of comfort to offer him.

###

No pause, nor rest, save where the streams
That feed the Kansas run,
Save where our pilgrim gonfalcon
Shall flout the setting sun.
We'll treat the prairies as of old
Our fathers sailed the sea;
And make the West, as they the East,
The homestead of the free."

John Greenleaf Whittier, 1807-1892, from the KANSAS EXPERIENCE IN POETRY

The next day found the small party standing at the summit of Hogback Ridge looking over the Kansas River. The view was spectacular, in all directions and they knew that this is where they would settle. The Kansas River, called the Kaw by the natives, nestled on the north side of the ridge, flowing from west to east, meandering through the prairie for approximately 150 miles. The river was formed some 90 miles further west at the confluence of the Republican and Smokey Hill rivers.

Sam felt that he could see the entire length of the river valley from where he stood. It took a southerly turn and then east again at Paschal Fish's Village near the confluence of the Wakarusa and Kansas Rivers. To the west, the horizon drifted off into a hazy panorama of the endless plains stretching to the Rocky Mountains. They camped for the night making plans to return to Independence about noon the next day, but the plans changed as they prepared to leave, when four men rode into camp at eleven the next morning. One of the men rode straight up to Sam who was packing his kit preparing for the ride back. "Hello Sam Wood," the man roared.

Sam squinted, trying to recognize this burly rider who seemed to know him intimately, but all he could see was a wide brimmed hat and a large man in the shadow of the sun. John reached for his rifle, ready for any trouble; but Sam recognized Charlie Robinson, a doctor from Massachusetts he had met in Washington during the abolitionist meeting headlined by Frederick Douglass.

"Charlie," Sam said?

"I knew I'd run into you sooner than later, Sam, but damned if I can believe the luck of finding you here. This is the place to settle our roots isn't it?"

Sam was completely taken off guard. He had no idea that Robinson was in Kansas, in fact, the last he heard, Robinson was in California, elected to the California State Legislature. Felix restarted the fire and made coffee. Dr. Charles Robinson and Charley Branscomb, along with two other men, were abolitionists engaged by the Massachusetts Emigrant Aid Company to come to Kansas and scout suitable land for a settlement. The plan was to flood Kansas Territory with Free State citizens who would vote down any and all pro-slavery proposals.

The sun was up but the northwestern sky was dark with an approaching storm. The men sat on logs and rocks while their horses grazed nearby. The eastern men explained their plan to entice as many settlers as possible to fight the Border Ruffians and make Kansas a free state.

"I'm not surprised to find you out here, Sam, I expected to run into you, and this is the logical place to begin a settlement. "Fred," he indicated one of the other men, "was here last week and figured this to be the place for us," Charlie said.

"I thought you were in California, Charlie."

"I was, but I heard a speech by Eli Thayer and he motivated me to do something about slavery besides run off to California and ignore it."

"Who's Eli Thayer?" Felix asked.

"Founder of the Massachusetts Emigrant Aid Society. I guess you might say he's a politician, salesman, and abolitionist. He has a girl's school called Oread Institute in Worcester. He's organizing a large number of people to head this way," Charlie said.

"I can't say that I've heard of the Massachusetts Emigrant Aid Society," Sam said. "But we welcome anyone willing to fight, don't we John? Did you have any trouble with the Ruffians in Independence?"

"We circled up through St. Joseph and dropped down to Leavenworth and hired horses there. We didn't run into any trouble, but the word is that the Missourians are planning to stake out all the river towns and question everyone going west. They're threatening to kill abolitionists. I heard they killed a few in Westport before you stepped in and bested them. The word is that there were five or six of them, is that right, Sam?" Dr. Robinson asked with a serious look of concern.

"What?" Felix scoffed.

John explained that Sam was given credit for fights and such from Denver to Lexington, Kentucky. "Most folks think he's seven feet tall and spits fire like a dragon."

"Well, you are a mite smaller than I expected," Branscomb laughed.

"I do everything I can to avoid trouble. Walk softly but carry a big stick, that's my motto," Sam said brandishing his cane.

John whispered, "Yeah, you're a regular mediator."

"I've heard of that stick you carry. Glad I'll not have to face it in anger," Branscomb replied.

"We anticipate several hundred settlers arriving over the next few months, and this looks like the spot they'll want to build homes. You could have an influence if you would write a letter and send it to the eastern newspapers. They need to know what's happening here," Robinson said.

"I have already done so," Sam said proudly.

"Storm's approaching mighty fast gentlemen. I would suggest we find shelter pronto," John warned, looking west into the massive black clouds boiling and churning.

Lightning could be seen from horizon to horizon. The wind blasted them first, from the north, and with little shelter they could do nothing but protect their hats and hunker down. They rode hard back to Paschal Fish's farm, stripped the saddles from the horses and hustled into the barn. Though it was crowded, they managed to get the horses rubbed down and settled in to wait out the storm.

Dr. Robinson was in a talkative mood, and Sam was ready to

listen. He was curious about the men and their company, organized ostensibly to make Kansas a free state. Sam suspected ulterior motives, including land speculation.

"I heard you got married, Charlie, is your wife here in Kansas?"

"No, Sara went back east to visit family, but she'll return when I get suitable lodging. You have a wife and family, don't you, Sam?"

"Yes, Margaret and the two boys are in Independence with her mother and father, and John's wife and family. It won't be easy out here with the women and children, but they insisted on coming."

Robinson looked at John, "I didn't expect to find a free Negro working for the cause. Especially not here in Kansas Territory."

"I seem to take everyone by surprise, but someone has to protect Sam, here. He's constantly getting himself into trouble."

"It's going to be dangerous isn't it?" Robinson asked.

Felix answered, "There is much danger in this territory, Dr. Robinson, but relax, you've got the great Sam Wood to protect and defend you."

"Yeah, but who's going to protect him?" John asked seriously.

###

"If abolitionism, under its present auspices, is established in Kansas, there will be constant strife and bloodshed between Kansas and Missouri. Negro stealing will be a principle and a vocation. It will be the policy of philanthropic knaves, until they force the slaveholder to abandon Missouri; nor will it be long until it is done. You cannot watch your stables to prevent thieves from stealing your horses and mules; neither can you watch your negro quarters to prevent your neighbors from seducing away and stealing your negroes."

David R. Atchison, Pro-Slavery United States Senator

From Missouri, June 1854

After the storm, the men rode back to Westport to make preparations for provisions, tools and any building materials they could scrounge and take to Hog Back Ridge. The next day they gave their account of the trip to the rest of the family.

"We'll rename it Sam," Margaret said after hearing the narrative of their travels. "We're not living in a place called Hog Back Ridge."

"I agree, Mrs. Wood. A very unfortunate christening for the beautiful and lush land of Quivira," Felix agreed.

"What in the world is a Quivira?" Sally Thomson asked.

"Why the Spanish land of plenty, akin to the Seven Cities of Cibola, but further north, in the Kansas Territory. Don't you know your history of Coronado, Mrs. Thompson?" Felix laughed.

"Mr. Francis, you one peculiar man," Sally said shaking her head. "I don't know how you can keep from getting lost with all those strange things you got floatin' round in your head."

Felix took no offense, in fact, enjoyed the attention.

"Come on Sam, I want to go look at this beautiful place."

"Now, Margaret?" Sam questioned.

"Can you think of a better time? Daddy won't have the supplies and wagons ready for three or four more days. We might as well go have a look, so I know what we're getting into."

"You might as well go, Sam," John agreed. "I'll stay here and help Bill. Sal, you want to go with them?"

"I wouldn't miss it. Let's take the kids."

"I'm staying here to look after these two men," Elizabeth Lyon announced firmly." John laughed but Bill knew better.

The following morning, Sam, Margaret, Sally, and the four children, David and Lloyd Wood and Caleb and Missy Thompson left in a hired coach for the 30-mile trip to their new home on the Kansas frontier. It was July 3, 1854, and the territory was in turmoil with northerners flooding westward, mostly for the land, but also to stem the tide of slavery. Southerners were backing the Missouri Ruffians with money and arms to ensure that Kansas was admitted as a slave state to maintain the balance of power in the Union. The entire Nation was focused on the small area along the Missouri-Kansas border, and a collective groan was heard with every report of violence and mayhem.

The compromise that Stephen Douglas held in such high regard was quickly turning into a battleground between slaveholders and abolitionists and many were afraid it would lead to a full-scale civil war; which is precisely what Sam wanted. Not because of cruelty or revenge, but because, the brutal truth was, nothing short of war would eliminate slavery; it was too deeply imbedded in the culture and minds of the southerners. No legal argument would convince them, no moral argument was powerful enough to sway them, no religious argument commanding enough to dislodge them. The Washington lawmakers were trying to appease both sides.

The small party left before daybreak with a fine team of horses, provisions for two days and a jovial spirit. The road was still muddy from the summer squall two days earlier, but the horses and wagon were equal to the task. They reached Fish's farm on the Kansas River late in the evening. The Fish family was surprised but happy to see them and offered shelter in their comfortable cabin for that night.

The next morning, Margaret stood at the crest of the ridge and surveyed the land in all directions. The hills were bare of trees but glorious in foxtail barley and buffalo grass with the lush white aster and morning glories mingled with the yellow primrose. It was not the Garden of Eden, but it would do. The sun was hot, yet a cool breeze fanned up from the river relieving Margaret and Sally from the intense summer heat. The Indian women wore the colorful dresses of their tribe with flat brimmed hats made of fur or leather, while Margaret and Sally wore the long dresses and sun bonnets common to the pioneer women of the west.

"Chief, I see a tent down there, below the crest of that draw. Do you know who that is?"

Paschal answered quickly, "His name is Roscoe, I can't remember his last name. He has filed a claim there, but he lives in Missouri."

"Margaret, if you're still with me in this little venture, I propose we go down there and negotiate with that gentleman. It looks to me like a prime spot for our new home."

She sighed in resignation and took Sam's arm, "Come along children, let's go explore where our new home will be."

Roscoe had been watching them and a pot of coffee was ready when they stopped by his tent. He was a white-haired gentleman with a matching beard, long and pointed, he was thin, but not unhealthy, and spoke with a marked southern accent. "Welcome folks, name o' Roscoe Stream, like the river only smaller," he laughed. "I hope you plannin' to stay. I was just getting ready to start back for Westport when I seen ya arrive. Got a strong feelin' a whole passel o' folks be showin' up right smart. The Missouri Boys had a meetin' yesterday over in Atchison and they gonna' flood this country with slaves."

Sam was surprised by this account, but didn't show any emotion, instead, getting directly to the point, "Well, Mr. Stream, we would like to stay here, and this spot is precisely where I want to build a home. What will you take for your claim?"

The old timer scratched his beard and contemplated the situation glancing from Sam, to Sally, then to Margaret, and back to Sally. "Tell you what friend, I think you're one of us. Tell me if'n I'm wrong." Sam had no choice but to agree, not knowing who 'us' was, but wanting to avoid a confrontation, he nodded assent, "We are, yessir, Mr. Stream, that is a fact."

"I thought so," he laughed, "I figured that was your Nigger woman there. We gonna' fill this country with good solid Americans and keep them damned, sorry for the language, ma'am, abolitionists out of this country."

"But I'm a ab....," Lloyd began explaining to the man before Sally caught him up and said, "Now young massa, doan be intruptin' de proceedin's. When de genlmen' folk palaverin' dey bidness, young'uns n' Niggers best lay low." She carried him to the wagon while Margaret turned clear around laughing.

Mr. Stream continued shaking his head in agreement, "Since you one of us, I'll let you in on a secret, I wasn't gonna' build here no how, I just filed this claim to be able to vote in the election we callin' next month. I'll give this claim to you and go file another one some where's else. How does that sound?"

Sam made sure to pay him $50 and sign a quit claim deed on paper that he carried for his letter writing campaign. He had Paschal Fish, Sally Thompson and Margaret Wood witness the signature, not bothering to tell Mr. Stream that nary a one of the witnesses was qualified to testify in a court of law due to the shortcomings of being an Indian, an African, and his wife. The Wood and Thompson families loaded back into the wagon and surrounded by the Shawnee paraded back to Paschal's farm where they took their leave promising to remain friends forever since they were going to be neighbors. It was nigh on to five o'clock before they were back on the trail to Independence.

"Sam, I don't feel like traveling tonight. Let's stop at the trading post at Tiblow. I heard that Mr. McDaniel's wife makes a marvelous breakfast."

"How about that, Sally, kids? Shall we sleep under the stars and have a good breakfast in the morning? We could even try those mineral springs. They're supposed to cure what ails you," Sam said. A unanimous 'yes', settled the question.

David said, "But I don't have anything that ails me papa. I don't need the mineral springs."

Sam bit his tongue.

###

"There is some of the largest rattle snakes (sic) in this region I ever saw, being from 8 to 12 ft. long, and about as large as a man's leg about the knee. This is no fiction at all." **Amelia Hadley, July 19, 1851**

The settlement of Tiblow was the scene of Coronado's furthest excursion north, in 1541, in search of a city of gold known as Quivira. A stone was discovered in the vicinity with these words inscribed: 'Thus far came Francisco Coronado, General of an Expedition'. The ferry across the Kansas River had been in existence for 40 years and was considered the safest crossing before the Missouri River. Sam pulled the hired buggy into a sheltered spot near the post and the children piled out, glad to be able to stretch their legs. McDaniel allowed the use of two wagons as beds to keep the travelers off the ground. Sam was accustomed to sleeping on the ground, but the others appreciated the gesture. Sally made a pallet in the back of each wagon, giving Sam and Margaret the smaller, and arranging the four children and herself, in the larger. Margaret made an appointment for breakfast the next morning and found they would be dining with several other travelers, most from Missouri.

"Now, Sam, I want you to behave at breakfast tomorrow morning," she said as they lay in the wagon after the others had gone to sleep.

"What do you mean, Meg?"

"There are some men from Missouri here."

"It gets harder and harder to keep quiet, Meg. I'm afraid the time is coming when we won't have any choice but to confront them. I believe your mother is right about this matter. We're in

Kansas and we can't allow Missouri citizens to be involved in the legislation of our State, if they want to have a vote, let them move here."

"Just be careful what you say tomorrow, Sam."

"I will Meg. We've got a difficult journey ahead of us, don't we?"

"I'm afraid we do, Sam. I worry about how it will affect the children. I don't mind the hardships, I do wish we had a home built, I don't relish living in a tent, but I'm used to hard work and we won't be alone, with Mother and Father and John and Sally."

"And you'll like Charlie Robinson. His wife and children will be here with him. We'll make it work. I can't imagine the slavers or even the Ruffians bothering the women and children in any way."

Margaret wasn't as certain and wondered if Sam felt it truly, or if he was just comforting her. Either way, she was secure in the knowledge that they were embarking on a journey that was the right thing to do and they had God on their side. They couldn't help but succeed. He reached for her hand and held it to his lips as they gazed at the brilliant night sky and the stars that seemed to blanket them in light. The moon was in the first quarter as it moved toward its setting, so near that they could see shapes in the shadows. The night sounds faded as Mrs. McDaniel closed the building and doused the lamps. Other than the singing of the night insects, the only sound was the occasional movement by the horses, or a cough from the children. They lay quietly holding hands until sleep came. Early in the morning, just before the sun appeared, Sam awoke to find Lloyd and Missy snuggled up against his body and Margaret gazing on them fondly.

"They came over about an hour ago. I don't know how you can sleep so soundly. You didn't move a muscle."

"The sleep of the innocent, Margaret," he smiled at her.

"I hope so Sam, I worry about you. I bet that I don't hear half the ugly details of some of your encounters."

He thought it best not to remark on the veracity of that comment and optioned to give her a good morning kiss instead. The children slept soundly as he gently extracted himself and stepped behind a tree to perform his morning ablutions. Sally, Margaret and the children took advantage of a water pump and wash basin on the back porch of the establishment. The outhouse was near the river. Breakfast was ready as they made their way to the dining room about 30 minutes after daybreak, two men and their wives were already seated at the table, in addition to Mr. and Mrs. McDaniel. Sally and the children entered the front door and continued through the dining room to the kitchen where they would take their meal. The two Missouri women were visibly upset that Sally passed through the main room rather than going to the back door. Sam took notice but didn't react since nothing was said.

"How do folks, my name is Brady, my wife, Mrs. Brady, over there, Mr. and Mrs. Lynscomb. I believe you know our hosts, Mr. and Mrs. McDaniel," the man named Brady made introductions and without waiting for introductions from Sam, continued on, "We are from the great state of Missouri, just come from a constitutional organization meeting over in Atchison. We've resolved to conduct the formal meeting on November 4, and at that meeting will ensure that the Kansas Territory will be accepted into the Union as a slave state. Can you believe that a Free State man, name of Tappan, had the gall to show up and state his opinion? Well, sir, I guarantee you we set him straight, right quick, and he may still be hightailin' it east, isn't that so, Mr. Lynscomb," but didn't give Mr. Lynscomb a chance to answer, nor did it appear that the man expected to give an answer.

Sam grunted and kept his face in his plate.

Brady continued, barely stopping for a breath, "I couldn't help but observe that your Nigger and her pickaninnies was allowed in the front door. Now, I'm not one to preach to another man about how to treat his slaves, to each his own, I say, don't I say that, Mrs. Brady? But I disagree, oh yes, I disagree wholeheartedly. We cannot allow the inferior race to consort with the superior race in any way.

Now, I don't disagree with letting the white child consort with the Negro child up to a certain age. That oldest boy of yours is almost to that age now, I urge you to consider that it will be more difficult for him to maintain discipline when he becomes the owner of that grown slave. The Negro must be treated just like the oxen and the mule, they are there to work, and nothing must interfere with that relationship. Now, McDaniel uses Indian women to run the domestic side here in his establishment...."

McDaniel interrupted, "And we pay them a fair wage, don't we Mrs. McDaniel?"

"We certainly do Jim," she replied with a look of scorn at Brady.

Brady continued, not recognizing the slight, "Well, Mrs. Brady's girl wouldn't think of using the front door of an establishment, would she, Mrs. Brady? And we haven't had to raise the whip to her for more than a year. There is the right way and the wrong way to handle slaves, and the right way is don't spare the rod or the whip, or whatever is needed to knock sense into their thick skulls. Don't you agree sir?" he asked, turning to Sam.

Silence thickened the atmosphere in the room more than the smoke from Mr. Lynscomb's pipe. Margaret kept her eyes fixed on Sam and placed her hand over his arm. He had ceased eating and sat, fork and knife in hand, staring at his plate. Suddenly David and Caleb burst into the room, "Papa, can we go outside and play?" David said, crowding between Sam and Margaret. "We're done eating, aren't we, Caleb?"

Sam stood quickly, "Come on boys, I'll go with you, the

smoke is getting a little thick in here." He nodded to the ladies, went outside, and watched the boys climb a cottonwood tree next to the river. Sam was breathing heavily and took two deep breaths to calm himself. Finally, he grabbed his cane from the buggy and went back inside.

"Margaret, take the children and Sally outside..., through the front door."

"Sam...,"

He glanced at her and she did as he said, then turned to Brady and rested his club on the table, "Now, sir, what would you say is the best way to handle such a fellow as this Tappan?"

"Why, with gun and rope, what else? And we made that very clear, didn't we, Lynscomb?" But Lynscomb didn't answer because he was gawking at Sam's club.

Sam stuck the club in the blustering man's chest, "Well, sir, the fact is, I am of the same opinion as Mr. Tappan. Now draw your gun if you mean to use it." No sound was uttered. Mrs. Brady and Mrs. Lynscomb cowered behind their husbands with hands to mouth, both in tears.

"Now hold on there, friend...., I didn't mean to imply...., now, I'm a peace-loving man, ain't I, Mrs. Brady," he glared at his wife who was too frightened to answer, and unused to the request.

"You stay out of Kansas, Brady. We will come into the union as a free state. If you bring your slaves here, I will swear out a writ of Habeas Corpus and you cannot appeal to the constitution because it is silent on the matter and there are no state laws because we are not a state and you cannot utilize your Missouri Laws because they are invalid here. Your slaves will be as free as I and Mrs. Wood are."

Sam turned to the McDaniels, "Thank you for your hospitality, I believe my wife settled our account." Mrs. McDaniel nodded yes.

"Then we'll be on our way. My name is Sam Wood, you got that Brady, Sam Wood. Spread the word. Good day to all of you."

Arriving outside, Sam found the buggy hitched and loaded, Sally with the reins, and Margaret and the two smaller children in front. He found a seat in back with Caleb and David.

"Did ya have to whack him upside the head, Papa Sam?" Caleb asked with the excitement of youth, revealing that he and David had speculated about the outcome of the confrontation. They had attempted to sneak in the back door and listen from the kitchen but were thwarted by Margaret. Sam smiled and opened his mouth to answer, only to find her glaring at him from the front seat. He shook his head, no, and they drove to Independence without further comment.

###

"We have good roads comparatively. We mean good roads if the sloughs are not belly deep and the hills not right straight up and down and not rock enough to turn the wagon over." **Henry Allyn, August 11, 1852**

A well-known fact about Sam Wood, he wasn't a man of poetry, or sentimentality, he was a hard-nosed realist who dealt with the circumstances of his life face on, with action and not daydreams of what might be, not a world of make-believe and fantasy. He owned up to what he did and took credit or blame where fitting. He had no time for anything but the task at hand. Margaret Wood, however, was not above waxing poetic about the life she faced, especially given the fact that she could have been a well-respected wife of a state senator, a governor or maybe even the President of the United States, there were those who projected that lofty office for Sam, given the right circumstances. She didn't dwell on those possibilities any more than Sam did, but that didn't keep her from seeing beauty in the world and making note of it. Where Sam looked at the world as his courtroom and the slave holders as the defendants to his prosecution, Margaret saw the environment as the fulfillment of God's word to do good and be good. She was an educated woman and wasn't about to let the men take all the credit for progress against slavery. On the other hand, she was a product of her time, a mother with certain duties she had to fulfill. Margaret was the perfect wife for Sam.

Before leaving Independence for their new home on the Wakarusa, Sam wrote a letter to John Greenleaf Whittier's National ERA extolling the virtues of Kansas and urging fellow abolitionists to come running.

Bill Lyon and John Thompson had been busy gathering the tools and materials they would need to construct new homes and the ladies had laid in as many provisions as possible. The party was forced to stop in Westport for wagon repairs, and while waiting for the blacksmith to finish, several curious locals took to asking the travelers what their intentions were, "I see you and your family are passing through. Are you Free State or pro-slavery? If you're a Free State man you need to keep on going to Nebraska because Kansas is going to come into the union as a slave state." That was the tone of every conversation and there were a multitude of interested citizens that hot July day.

Margaret kept a close watch, as did John Thompson knowing that Sam was near the end of his patience with the effrontery of these Border Ruffians. A rough looking fellow strolled up to the smith's shop and said, "Rumor is you're a' abolitionist."

Sam looked at the man, and then his wife and family, turned and walked back to the anvil where the blacksmith was shaping a brake shoe. The rowdy followed him, "I was talkin' to you, you son-of-a-bitch. Don't you never walk away from me like that. Now, you need to get on that wagon and go straight north or east and get the hell out of here before we string you up with the other abolitionist scum."

Sam whirled around and stuck his cane in the man's chest, and prodded him out of the blacksmith shop, and all the way into the street, "I will, as God is my witness, do what I want to do, wherever I want to do it, and you, sir, will not get in my way, or I will bring down the wrath of the Lord upon your head. Do you understand me?"

The slaver stumbled backward and fell in the dust, dumbstruck, watching the seemingly crazed, diminutive man with the fiery voice. Finally, he got up, brushed off his pants, and walked away. Sam watched him around the corner, while Margaret pursed her lips and frowned at her husband.

"I'm sorry dear. I lost my temper," Sam said, laughing to prod Margaret out of her anger.

"At least he didn't tell him his name," John said.

###

"Starting out ahead of the team and my men folks, when I thought I had gone beyond hearing distance, I would throw myself down on the unfriendly desert and give way like a child to sobs and tears, wishing myself back home with my friends." **A young woman on the trail west.**

Honorable Horace Greeley *August 1854*
c/o New York Tribune
New York, New York

Dear Horace:

I hope this letter finds you and Mary in good health. I greatly enjoyed our last visit and long for the comforts of hearth and home such as Mary provided for Margaret and me when we were in New York City. I even enjoyed the salads and vegetables but admit I had a sizeable steak upon returning to Ohio.

We arrived in Kansas Territory in June and have been busy surviving. Unfortunately, the conditions here warrant that harsh portrayal. There are no comforts of home as yet, this is truly the frontier. Margaret's parents are with us and my sister, Sarah, and brother, Stephan, have come to help build shelter and provide food. It is hot here at this time of year but that is a blessing as the winter can be harsh.

Kansas is bleeding, Horace. The Border Ruffians are bad as advertised and the conditions couldn't be worse. You're probably aware by now of the meeting held in Weston on July 29 where General Stringfellow signed the pro-slavery resolutions that have been posted throughout the territory. Can you believe the effrontery of these hooligans to have a meeting in Missouri to determine the fate of Kansas? And those buffoons in Washington are supporting them. They sent John Whitfield to Washington to represent Kansas, but he lives in Joplin, Missouri, and owns 10-12 bedraggled slaves that are a prime testament to the cruelty of his class. I realize that he's a non-voting delegate but that begs the question. He is there representing Kansas Territory but has not a whisper of a relationship with his kingdom.

The folks here are walking on eggshells, afraid to announce themselves as abolitionists. Most padlock their lips and write, "Don't rock the boat, it isn't the time. Wait until we are stronger." But now is the time, because these Ruffians are moving heaven and earth to make Kansas a slave state. We have to stand up to them immediately. I've written to Brown and urged him to join us. I know you don't approve of his methods and I have my own doubts, but he will do something. His sons, Owen and Jason are already here. We need men of action to spread the word and quickly. We're outnumbered and out gunned, but we will man the battlements and brave the coming winter. We need reinforcements, men who will live in Kansas and vote their conscience. The time has come to organize the men into a legitimate state assembly.

Thank you for taking on young Francis as a reporter and accepting his few written lines for the Tribune. He is a fine young man, brave and committed beyond his years. I'm sending him to the next slavers' meeting over in Westport and let him file the account of the illegal proceedings. I will proof his report before sending it to you. I realize that both sides are exaggerating the happenings here, but despite the rhetoric, I will try to give you the honest details. You can discuss with Felix the financial arrangements. I attest that he will meet and exceed all of your expectations.

I remain, as always, your friend,
Samuel N. Wood

Only about 800 legitimate voters called Kansas Territory home in late July of 1854. There were a couple thousand Indians, but they had their own problems with the white man; they were not considered citizens of the United States, and couldn't vote. Ostensibly they owned the land they lived on, their reservations, but that was a sham. Of course, the women couldn't vote, nor the Black men, free or slave. The male citizens of Missouri crowded into Kansas Territory to vote, then scurried back to their homes after casting a ballot.

Sam was livid with the Indian Agents and Methodist Ministers who had slaves of their own but tried to Christianize the indigenous tribes. He wrote, in one of his early letters to the New York Tribune, "There are preachers here who drive their African slaves mercilessly, yet preach the goodness of Christ to the Indians, a people who have survived a thousand years, perfectly content in their spiritual lives. These disgusting preachers heathenize the Africans, while trying to Christianize the Indians."

Abolitionists were coming by the wagonload, summoned by his letters, and sent by the newly named New England Emigrant Aid Society, which was a merger of the Massachusetts and New York chapters of the same name. Sam was stirring the slavery pot, fanning the flames of rhetoric to a roaring blaze. The effect of the publicity was immediate and affected both sides of the issue, no one was safe; man, woman, child or beast. Whereas Sam had been well known in the east among abolitionists and suffragettes, he was not, for the most part, recognized on the frontier.

A week after moving to Hogback Ridge, Sam rode to Westport to send more articles and check for mail. As he rode up to the dentist office, which also housed the post office, he witnessed a mob of men milling about in the street and on the boardwalk. Sam rode around to the back of the store and entered through the rear door, "Dr. Earle, what's going on out there? They seem pretty riled up, looks like trouble."

"Trouble for someone," the dentist said, not looking up from his desk.

"Who?" Sam asked. He was watching the men through the window. They were becoming more agitated and drawing a crowd that included women and children.

"I don't know. I guess whoever wrote that newspaper article they're upset about. That's Sam Jones out front there, causing all the ruckus. He's the postmaster here and just got appointed to be sheriff over in the territory."

"What?" Sam asked incredulously. "Who appointed him sheriff? We didn't elect him; I know that much."

"I guess Sterling Price did, but I think he had approval from the Government or someone. I try to stay out of it."

"But Price is the Governor of Missouri," Sam protested. "What's going on here?" he demanded angrily.

"I agree with you, friend, but I'm just reporting what I heard. It might have been Senator Atchison, I don't know. I have to stay out of it, ain't good for business, you understand."

Sam posted his letters and hurried outside to find out what was going on. He watched quietly for a few minutes as Jones read from a newspaper article, stopping at the end of every sentence to make a comment. The audience was cheering and jeering with every utterance.

"Now listen up, this is how he ends the story. *'And I urge every like-minded citizen, man or woman, black or white, to make haste to Kansas and take up the fight against the agents of the devil. We are standing shoulder to shoulder against the evilest force in the history of our great country, the Slave Masters and their minions.'* "

A farmer in coveralls shouted, "What the hell's a minion?"

"Damned if I know," Jones said. "But that don't matter. The thing we got to do is find this son-of-a-bitch and string him up and leave the body for everyone to see."

"A short rope and a tall tree."

Sam turned cautiously to the farmer who had asked about minions and proceeded to confirm what the reading of the story had implied. "Say friend, what low-life scoundrel wrote that blasphemous article." He glanced around nervously as the mob grew more agitated looking for some way to vent their anger. "Don't know, I just walked up myself. Say, Jones, who wrote that?"

"Goddamned Sam Wood, the stupid son-of-a-bitch signed his name to it," he shouted brandishing the St. Louis Republican Newspaper. "Same feller that set them Niggers free up in Ohio last year. We've got to find him boys. He's a dangerous man. We've got to stop him, and I mean now. Senator Atchison, hisself, sent this paper to me. He says to do whatever we've got to do to stop this bullshit."

The crowd cheered loudly, pounded each other on the back, and fired pistols into the air. Sam joined in lustfully, raising his voice with the rest. He even shouted, "Hang the scoundrel," when Jones looked suspiciously at him. He hurried to his horse and rode to the house of his friend, J. B. Speer.

"Sam Wooood," J.B. exclaimed drawing out the name making it three syllables long. "You have stirred things up. You'd best not venture near the post office or any public gathering. Agamemnon has stormed Troy and you are the Prince they wish to lay low."

"Bill, I don't know anything about that. What I want to know is, who is this Sam Jones that was appointed sheriff of Kansas?"

"He's the local postmaster and Senator Atchison appointed him sheriff. Don't know what else to tell you. It's illegal as hell and I don't think that Reeder even knows about it."

"Who's Reeder?"

"Andy Reeder, the new Territorial Governor. Just appointed by President Pierce to the job. Hell, as far as I know, he's not even in Kansas yet. Probably still in Washington."

"My God Bill, we've got to get going. Things are happening pretty fast. We'd better get a handle on it."

Speer was a newspaper man from Illinois, and he looked the part. Though relatively young, he was bald on top with a tangled nest of black hair on each side of his head. He wore a vest over a white shirt with dark trousers, and he was a genius with the pen. "You've stirred them up with your words, Sam, the dream of every newspaper man."

"I'm not a newspaper man, I'm a lawyer and an abolitionist."

"Did you ask someone to send a printing press?"

"I did, why?"

"Because it's on its way. I'll hide it here until we can build a place in the territory to set it up. We'll need to keep it a secret, Sam. You and your family are in danger, I wouldn't be surprised if the Ruffians are riding toward the Wakarusa right now."

###

It's a matter of taking the side of the weak against the strong, something the best people have always done." **Harriet Beecher Stowe.**

John Thompson arrived at Chief Fish's home about the time

Sam was leaving Bill Speer's house in Westport. Rumors of a group of runaway slaves had reached the fast-growing community, newly named Lawrence, after Amos Adams Lawrence, a Boston merchant who was helping to finance the Emigrant Aide Society. He was also sending money to Sam. Margaret's wish of doing away with Hogback Ridge was realized. Mt. Oread was named after Ely Thayer's girls' school.

John took Caleb and David along. He figured, rightly, that Chief Fish would know everything going on within his reservation, and when they arrived, Mrs. Fish invited him in, and they shared a cup of coffee while discussing the situation.

"They came in night before last, John. They're running from someone. My people have been watching them but staying out of sight because they frighten easily, and they have guns. Sentry's are out night and day."

"How many are they?"

"Four women and four men, plus several children. They seem very poor and not knowledgeable of living off the land," Chief Fish chuckled as he remembered his youngest son bringing the news of the strangers. "Billy came riding like the wind and jumped off his pony before he stopped, 'Papa, many black-white men are camping at Silver Springs. Come see!' he was so frightened that he wanted to get a war party and ride back to confront them. I went to investigate, and they are a poor looking lot, John. They have a couple of worn-down horses. The people look to be completely exhausted. I don't know how they managed to get this far without being captured."

"Maybe they'll talk to me," John said.

"Come, I'll take you there," Paschal said. "We'll bring the boys; it might be a good experience for them to see firsthand what you abolitionists are fighting for."

John, David, Caleb, Chief Fish and two of his sons, Billy and Owen, took the well-worn game trail to Silver Springs, a beautiful natural spring hidden in the woods near the confluence of the Wakarusa and Kansas Rivers. From a bluff overlooking the spring the men could observe unnoticed. The slaves wore ragged clothing that would not protect them during the coming winter. Two women were boiling water in a tin pot but there was no sign of food. The children were listless in the heat, the youngest was naked, sitting back away from the fire.

"I'll go down and hail the camp. You wait here for me to call you," John said.

He backtracked to the horses then rode to within a hundred yards of the runaways.

"Hello the camp," he shouted. No answer ensued. "I'm a friend," he tried again.

"We got no friends here," was the reply.

"You do now, I'm riding in, my name's John Thompson and I'm unarmed."

John felt a queasiness that he hadn't experienced since the Ohio Underground Railroad days. He rode slowly and spoke calmly, calmer than he felt, in an attempt to keep them from doing anything foolish. Two men came from the trees, one pointing an old pistol that John was afraid might blow up if discharged.

"Hello, folks, I'm John Thompson. I'm here to help if I can."

A strong female voice sang out, "Why, yore a Negro."

"Yes, Maam, I'm aware of that."

"But yu talks like a white man, is yu free?"

"Born and raised in freedom, and I plan to help you gain yours. I assume you're on the run from someone. If you don't mind, I'll get down and you can tell me all about it."

"Get down, Mr. John, get down. We don't have much to offer but what we have you'll share with us."

A spindly man about 25 came forward, examined John and sidled up slowly, "Is you de same John Thompson run de undergroun' over tu Ohio?"

"I am, have we met?"

"No, suh, but I knows ya. I owes ya a debt o' gratitude. Ya save ma sister, Jinny, from ole man Wilson dese six year go."

"I remember Jinny well, is she safe?"

"Yassir, in de nort', Canada, marry a freeman up dar, got a little boy. I'm a gwin' to jin her."

"Well, praise the lord, Sam Wood will be pleased to hear the news."

"Sam Wood? He a legen'. She sang o his blessin's fightin' off dem bounties with no mo' dan de word outn' his mouth. I hope Mr. Wood still well."

"Not only well, but just a few miles from here. You'll see him soon enough. What is your name?"

"I'se Toby."

"Toby, I'm going to call some friends into camp. They'll help us decide how to get you into safe country, you're in danger here." While the men were talking, the four slave women appeared along with several boys and girls of varying ages. Before John could shout for the others, they drifted into camp having anticipated and watched the proceedings. The smaller children darted behind their mothers, eyes wide in fright at the sight of the long-haired Indians, even though they wore the clothes of a farmer rather than a warrior.

John led the group back to Chief Fish's compound, then to a meadow surrounded by a copse of cottonwoods near a spring fed creek that drained into the Wakarusa, no more than a mile from the village, the party of runaway slaves was well hidden. John was fearful about what the Border Ruffians would do should they discover the small band of slaves escaping through the territory. Indian women gathered food, blankets and clothes to share with the unfortunate travelers. They had difficulty understanding each other, the slaves speaking a southern dialect unfamiliar in Kansas, and the Indians their own language and English. Both parties benefited from a desire to learn and the native women were sincerely interested in helping these desperate people. Their shared language was the children and the hardships that frontier mothers faced, regardless of their color. John and the Chief rode to Paschal's house, leaving the boys to help with the new camp and to hunt some game for their fires.

"That's Sam's horse, Border Ruffian," John announced as they rode up to the cabin.

"Sam named his horse after the enemy?" Chief Fish asked.

"He's got a sense of humor, but it's hard to take sometimes," John laughed.

Sam came from the house as the men arrived. "I was just coming to find you. Eudora was going to guide me."

"We moved their camp," Fish announced. "They weren't safe there. I don't think they're safe anywhere in the territory, Sam. They need to go on north."

"Let's sit and talk about it. Where are the boys, John?"

"Helping with the camp. They've taken a liking to those slave kids, there are four girls and three boys. Guess who else is with them?"

Sam shrugged. "Remember Jinny, the little girl that rode with us in the wagon on the way to Bill Lyon's place, when you met Margaret?"

"How can I forget? Don't tell me she's with them?"

"No, but her brother, Toby, is. He's anxious to meet you and thank you proper, as he puts it, for saving Jinny's life. Evidently you get full credit for that, in addition to fighting off an army of bounty hunters."

"What are you talking about?" Chief Paschal asked. The men moved to the shade of the back porch.

"I was in the wagon, Pash, so I know what happened. To

hear those Negroes tell the story you'd think Sam was a mountain lion and grizzly bear combined. All he did was tell the truth and damn near got me hung. But he gets all the credit, and no one even knows we were in the bed o' that wagon dying from the heat stroke. Not to mention we couldn't see what was going on out there."

"Why, John," Sam said smugly, "You know I had everything under control. I even had a fallback plan."

"Really, and what was that plan, Mr. Wood?" John said laughing. "Run!"

"Nope, pray, cause' we would have needed Divine intervention." The sound of horses caused Paschal to reluctantly get up and go investigate.

"What do you think we should do about helping them, John?"

"Best bet would be to take them north into Nebraska. They traveled west because they were certain the slave-catchers would think they went to Illinois."

"Probably a wise thing to do," Sam agreed.

The sudden sound of dogs barking and then shouting roused them from their comfortable seats in the shade. They rounded the corner and found Sam Jones and two rough looking characters crowding Chief Fish, with their horses.

"Here now, what's going on? Back off there, you men, right pronto," Sam shouted.

"You," Jones bellowed at Sam. "I seen you at the post office, who the hell are you?"

"Who's asking?" John said.

The men stopped, open mouthed, unable to believe their ears. "What the fuck did you say, boy? Did you hear that Sheriff? Did you hear that Nigger?"

"Oh, I heard it all right, Big Bill, and we'll deal with him shortly, but right now I got a feeling that's the man we're looking for, right there."

Sam sat calmly on a stump log near the woodpile and said, "Who are you? Maybe we can help. My friend and neighbor, John Thompson, was just trying to be friendly."

"If you're friends with a Negro then you are an abolitionist and I got a feeling that you are Sam Wood. Am I right?" Jones asked.

"Yes. What do you want with me?"

"I have a warrant for your arrest. I'm taking you back to Westport."

"And I ask the same question, who are you and how can you come on my reservation and my home with such behavior?" Chief Fish said.

"I'm Sheriff Sam, by God, Jones, if it's any of your goddamned business. I got no more use for Indians than I do Niggers. All of you need to learn your manners and respect your betters."

"I don't know of a Kansas Territory sheriff by the name of Jones. I know of a postmaster in Westport, Missouri, by that name," Sam taunted him. "I guess that makes you Sam, Bogus, Jones." Everyone including his deputies laughed until Jones gave them a look.

"I have a warrant for your arrest and that's all you need to know. Now get your horse and come on with us."

Sam sat quietly watching Jones and made the decision, seeing him this second time, that he was a dangerous man, but a coward. Sam wasn't sure what he based his intuition on, but he was seldom wrong about a man. Jones seemed to be out of his league, and instead of trying to solve problems with reason he blustered and bluffed, having no other ammunition in his arsenal. "Let me see that warrant," Sam said calmly.

Jones pranced his horse around and shouted, "I don't have to show you nothing. I told you I have one, now are you resisting arrest? I'll just add that to the charges."

"What are the charges?"

"Disturbing the peace and inciting to riot. Those newspaper articles you wrote are slanderous and you are going to be tried for it in Westport."

"No, I don't think I will. First of all, Westport is in Missouri, and second, I don't recognize your authority in the territory of Kansas."

"Big Bill, arrest that man," Jones ordered.

"With pleasure boss. I hate abolitionists worse than Niggers, cause' Niggers don't know no better. These bastards stirring em' up. We'll get this one off the streets."

"Jones take your men and ride out of here, right now. If you don't, I will see that the three of you suffer the consequences. John, make sure Chief Fish and his men stay out of this," Sam said. John called to Fish to join him on the front stoop of the house, where they watched.

"Why you little shit-fer-brains," Big Bill said. "Jesus H. Christ, Sheriff, he don't know when he's outmanned."

Sam had his cane, as usual, but, since coming to the territory, he had taken to carrying a pistol under his shirt. He did not want to use it. He watched calmly. The two Ruffians dismounted. One was medium height and wide, heavy like a wrestler, wearing a brace of pistols and a short broadsword, his hat sat low on his head with hair spilling out like untended crape myrtle. His bushy beard gave him the look of a wild mountain man. The smaller man was wiry and balanced on his toes ready for battle, he had not spoken. Sam was wary of him, more so than the big man.

"I warned you," Sam said. "If you get hurt, it's your fault, not mine."

"What's the matter with this fool, Sheriff? He don't seem to understand who he's dealing with. Is he crazy?"

"It's all talk, Bill. Just go tie his hands and Lester, you cover him."

Big Bill was a simple man, but thoughtful, in fact he wasn't even certain that he was doing the right thing. His childhood in Tennessee had steeped him in the racial hatred of his family but he'd grown up with Negro children and didn't agree with their treatment by the south. As a result, Bill was overly cautious. He failed to act when Sam moved closer to the smaller man and reached out his hand in greeting, "Didn't catch your name friend."

This one was just plain stupid and he reached out to shake hands in pleasant response, "Lester...," he said as Sam grabbed his wrist and with a powerful grip held on as the man struggled to get his hand free, clawing with his left hand at Sam's right hand, but unable to budge it.

"Hey!" Bill shouted but didn't react until it was too late. Sam reached down with his left hand and pulled Lester's gun out of its holster. He pushed Lester away and pointed the gun at Bill, who put his hands up and backed off. Sam calmly took his guns.

He pointed one at Jones and said, "I have a feeling that I would save a lot of misery in this territory if I just went ahead and shot you dead."

Jones sat his horse quietly. Chief Fish and John came down from the porch along with several Indian men who stood around watching the proceedings.

Sam said, "Jones are you carrying a gun?"

"No, I didn't think I needed one with my armed escort, but I guess I overestimated them. I guarantee I'll have one next time we meet."

Sam watched the bogus sheriff as John and Paschal gathered the remaining weaponry and removed all the ammunition.

"You men get on your horses," Sam ordered.

"You can't keep our guns. That's stealing," Bill said.

Sam emptied the last of the ammunition from Bill's guns and

handed them up to him. "We'll keep the bullets and caps as a fine for impersonating law officers," he said.

"Jones, give notice to your Missouri friends that the citizens of Kansas will take care of ourselves. We don't need any Missourians to help us."

Jones turned his horse, but Sam stopped him, "And inform any Missourian who files a bogus claim on land in Kansas, his claim is invalid, and we will enforce that to the letter of the law." Jones started to speak and thought better of it. They rode off at a run.

###

"To have drunkards, idiots, horse-racing- rum-selling rowdies, ignorant foreigners, and silly boys fully recognized, while we ourselves are thrust out from all the rights that belong to citizens, it is too grossly insulting to... be longer quietly submitted to." **Elizabeth Cady Stanton 1815-1902**

Sheriff Jones didn't like it, not one bit. Riding for three hours to serve a legitimate warrant for arrest only to return empty handed; and his deputies disarmed in a humiliating manner by such an insignificant man as this Sam Wood, an abolitionist. He swore an oath right then to get revenge on Sam Wood.

"What are you going to do Sheriff? We can't let him get away with that," Lester said. "That was embarrassing."

"He ain't gonna' get away with nothing. I'll get a goddamned army and go back there to arrest him."

"Well, Sheriff, you best hurry cause the abolitionists are pourin' in here faster'n we can chase em out," Big Bill said.

"Jesus, Bill, you were worthless'er than tits on a boar hog. Why didn't you do somethin' when he grabbed me like that?" Lester whined.

Jones said, "Shut the hell up, Lester. Jesus, you were gonna' shake his hand like he was the Governor or somethin'. What the hell was you thinkin'?"

Jones was a man of average height with thick black hair and a beard that he kept trimmed to two inches. He was a family man, moved with his wife and two children to Westport from their home in Virginia. Jones didn't own any slaves himself, nor did any of his family, yet he was educated in the particular southern prejudice toward Africans which held them to be less than human. The Jones family didn't move to Missouri for any political reason like the Sam Wood family. Jones and his wife simply wanted a new start to life, on the frontier where, the rumor was, a man could make a name for himself and get ahead faster than in Virginia. He was an opportunist who had no religious beliefs beyond those of his community. He believed in whatever would help him get ahead, to get an advantage over the next guy.

Jones was staunchly proslavery as you would expect from a good southern boy. It didn't take long for him to find an opportunity to impress his fellow friends of the south. During the bogus elections of early June 1854, the Border Ruffians heard of an election in Bloomington, Kansas that had gone in favor of the abolitionists. Jones joined a party of men and they stormed into the building where the ballots were cast and destroyed the ballot box and the votes it held. They were cheered heartily by the Sons of the South and the Blue Lodge boys who were nothing more than Border Ruffians with a charter.

As a kind of political reward, Jones was appointed Postmaster of Westport by Senator David Atchison. It was a joke, even to his friends, because the man was a farmer who could barely read, but he had desire and gumption. The problem was that this political patronage and the power that went with it caused him to develop an inflated concept of who he was. He had no negotiation skills, no mediation skills and worst of all he knew nothing about compromise. He was gentle with his family, but firm in his convictions. Slavery was the only way of life he had ever known. He was cruel to those who opposed him, cruel beyond the need. He was aggressive and overbearing when he thought he had the advantage, but quick to back down when he felt outmanned.

Sam and John didn't waste any time. As soon as the report came that Jones and his men had retreated to Westport, John brought his farm wagon to the Negro camp and drove them twenty-five miles to the Pappan Brothers ferry at the community named Topeka. They crossed the Kansas and pushed north to Nebraska without any trouble. Sam sent a letter with Jinny's brother, Toby, and asked her to come visit when Negroes could travel as free as a white man, a time he assured her was coming.

Toby embraced Sam and John, claiming that they had saved his sister and now they saved him. "The Lord surely do work in mysterious ways, Mr. Sam. I don't have no way to thank ya, ceptin' to offer my hand, sir, somethin' that I have never did with a white man." Sam shook Toby's hand and said, "With pleasure." Toby turned to John and embraced him with tears in his eyes, each of the adults offered their thanks as they started their long journey to the Promised Land. They watched the small party of former slaves leave, eight adults, seven children, four horses and a couple of stray dogs. One elderly man stopped in front of John, shook his hand and said, "I never thought I would see the day I could say that I am a free man. I thank you, Mr. Thompson."

###

"I look forward to a time when each state shall be allowed to do as it pleases….I care more for the great principal of self-government, than I do for all the Negroes in Christendom." **Stephen Douglas, Speech in Alton, Illinois during the Lincoln-Douglas Senatorial Debates 1858**

Senator Stephen Douglas is of world-wide renown. All the anxious politicians of his party, or who have been of his party for years past, have been looking upon him as certainly, at no distant day, to be the President of the United States. They have seen in his round, jolly, fruitful face, post offices, land offices, marshal-ships and cabinet appointments, charge-ships and foreign missions, bursting and sprouting out in wonderful exuberance ready to be laid hold of by their greedy hands.

Abraham Lincoln, Speech in Alton, Illinois during the Lincoln-Douglas Senatorial Debates 1858

August 1854
Lawrence, Kansas Territory

Morning dawned with a blazing sun and cloudless sky that anticipated the hottest day of the year. Construction was underway on the new Wood home being built at the base of Mt. Oread. Margaret had charge of providing for basic needs, the children roamed the hills, picked dandelions and berries and searched for sandhill plums and morrel mushrooms. Stephan Wood and Bill Lyon were in charge of the construction crew using lumber milled on the river. John and Sally were organizing the free black folk living in the area, who provided most of the labor needed, including digging the basement, and Felix was busy throughout helping Indians and Negroes alike while filing regular reports to the New York Tribune.

Sam left early for Blue Jacket's house to discuss using his trading post as a meeting place for the abolitionists. Several new families had arrived from the East, enough to begin making plans for how to best confront the pro-slavery crowd. Sam had the luxury of being able to focus on the issues, to the exclusion of everything else. He was concerned with the number of Eastern families who were unable to stand the severe frontier environment and constant harassment by the Border Ruffians, many turned around and went back home after experiencing the harsh reality of the Kansas prairie.

Paschal Fish met Sam at the trading post, "Sam Wood, I'd like you to meet my brother whose name in Shawnee means Blue Jacket. Most white men call him Blue." They shook hands and sat at one of the long tables hand-crafted from cottonwood trees. The building was a long, low structure, made of wood, rock and sod; the interior framed with the same material as the tables. It was a comfortable building with Blue's home in the back. His large family ran the business. Furs and other materials were stacked around the perimeter, and vegetables and locally grown produce arranged in boxes in lean-tos outside. Sam knew that it would be a fine location for the first meeting of the Kansas Territory Free State Settlers, a name he meant to propose for the group. Arrangements were made and terms agreed upon for renting the premises with August 15, the date set. Sam proceeded to cover the circuit from Lawrence to Westport, Franklin, Osawatomie, Salina, Atchison and all areas in between to spread the word. He rode to the meeting with some neighbors who had just arrived as part of the first New England Emigrant Aid Society settlers; they included Judge John Wakefield and Major J.B Abbott, along with Felix Francis and Charlie Robinson. Their community was fast becoming the de facto center of the abolitionist movement as Sam and Dr. Robinson had predicted.

Horses and wagons of every description surrounded Blue Jacket's trading post with more men arriving by the minute. Sam expected 20 but it looked like there would be three times that number. August was hot with little relief and the prospect of being cooped up in the stuffy trading post didn't appeal to any of the men. They moved outside and congregated under the three large cottonwoods between the cabin and the Wakarusa. Sam had Blue Jacket and his boys bring tables and benches from the kitchen to the meeting area, so that he could gavel the meeting to order, but most people stood. The Indians promptly disappeared.

It started amiably enough with men introducing themselves, discovering a commonality of purpose. It didn't take long to see that there were more Free State men than Blue Lodgers at this meeting. A large man, Sam recognized as the tough he clubbed in the Post Office, pushed his way to the front and started lecturing the crowd. "My name is Roland LeCount, and, by God, I don't know who called this meeting, but these matters have already been settled by a good and honest vote in Weston three weeks ago. There ain't no need to…."

Sam banged his cane on the table, "You are out of order, sir. We will conduct this meeting in an orderly…."

"Who the hell are you," LeCount shouted?" I don't need no runty abolitionist telling me when I can talk and when I can't. Now, by God, we have settled these matters and the laws been set down on paper. I've got a copy…."

Sam banged his club on the table again and then stuck it in the man's chest, "Not another word, sir, I am a Quaker."

This set the man back on his heels. He turned to his companions who offered no help, "…., A…., A Quaker?"

"We will proceed according to the following rule," Sam continued. "Each man will be given three minutes to make his case…."

"By God, I don't give a damn…."

Sam banged the table again, but before he could strike out, the man backed away to the shelter of his friends.

Sam fairly screamed this time, pointing the club at LeCount, "I am a Quaker, sir, a Quaker! And we are non-violent. We practice pacifism and you are forcing me to lose my temper. If you cause me to strike you, you will be guilty of blasphemy. NOT ME! Now, you will speak when it is your turn and then for three minutes. DO YOU understand me? "

There was no answer, only shocked stares.

Sam continued calmly, "The rules have been established, three minutes per man, no more," he glared at the Ruffian. "I am Sam Wood. I am an abolitionist and it is my intention to bring Kansas into the Union as a free state AND to free all slaves. That meeting in Weston, Missouri, has no standing here. Now, this man is next," Sam pointed to a tall, thin man with a shock of red hair and no hat.

"I'm Fred Tappan, I am also an abolitionist and I was at that meeting in Weston, the men who spoke there were from Missouri, not Kansas. I insist that any man who votes must reside in Kansas and be able to prove it with a valid land claim and a permanent residence on that land. No land. No vote. No slaves in Kansas."

"Thank you, Mr. Tappan," Sam said, "Your name was cursed roundly by a man I met as a result of that meeting. He declared you were the devil incarnate and a scoundrel and no-account. You sound like someone I would really like." Both sides laughed but not LeCount

"Now this man," Sam said, and pointed to a man on the right.

"I don't give a damn about Niggers one way or t'other. I want to live where a man, a white man, can live like he wants and make decisions for himself and not have the Goddamned govment' telling him what he can and can't do. I come to the territory to live the way I want to. I don't own no slaves, but if a man wants and can afford em', it ain't my business or anybody elses."

Sam pointed to a man on his left.

"I came to Kansas for the land. I don't much care about Nigger's one way or the other, either, but I don't want em' here, for the simple fact that it ain't fair for a man who has em' to have free labor and I've got to pay a market wage for the same work. If we do away with slavery the labor market will be fair for every one of us."

The men on the right hissed and Sam struck his club on the table. They quit. He pointed to the next man.

"I own a few slaves and I treat em right. I should be able to bring em into Kansas Territory or anyplace I want to. Why in the hell does it make any difference to the rest of you?" He turned to the man who had just spoken. "And I paid a fair price for em'. It ain't exactly free labor."

Men on the left booed and Sam struck his club on the table for order. He pointed to the next man.

"Harold Barnet from North Carolina. I came to Kansas for the land like I think most people here are doing. But no man should own another human being. It is against all human and spiritual reason here on earth. You say you treat your slaves well. I say to you, sir, that is impossible. The simple fact of owning another human being is a disgrace. There can be no justification for it. I will not compromise on the issue."

A quiet man who claimed to be a preacher said, "Slavery has existed for centuries. There have always been masters and slaves, throughout the world. We didn't create the institution, God did."

Felix Francis spoke up, "The historical aspect of slavery has no bearing on the moral or ethical consequences of the institution. When something is wrong, it is universally wrong regardless of the number of persons who practice the immoral act. I quite doubt that a just God created such a degradation against the very beings he created. Man conceived of slavery, not God."

"Jesus Christ, would you listen to this fool?" LeCount said.

Both sides grew restless until Sam interjected, "All right, now I want all men who are against slavery over here on my left, pro-slavers on the right." A few men changed sides.

"I don't want to hear any more about which side of the slavery issue you are on because now we know. I want to know, what is the biggest problem we face in building a territorial government?"

"That's easy," Tappan said. "We have to find a way to mitigate the land-claim issue. There are people claiming land and not intending to live on it. Then others claim land that is already claimed because there isn't a fair registry of the claims."

LeCount eyed Sam nervously, then stood tall and said, "Hell, you can record any claim in Westport for 50 cents. What do you mean they ain't no place to register them?"

"Westport is in Missouri; I think I'll just send back to Ohio and register my claim. It would be just as legal, which means not at all," Sam said, causing laughter on both sides of the room.

A short stubby man with a cigar stepped forward and said, "I agree about the claims. I staked a claim in Franklin, and that man," he pointed to a burly young fellow wearing a floppy slouch hat so stained it was difficult to tell the color. "That man is trying to steal the south part of it."

The accused stammered and shuffled, unused to the spotlight. "Ah hell, Leroy, you know that little valley was part of my claim. You just want it cause' it has a spring, and your creek went dry. You tell the truth now."

"I'll show you the truth you insolent whelp. Your daddy was a thief and you're just like him." He made a menacing gesture which caused Sam to intervene, "This isn't the place to settle that issue gentlemen. If land claims are the first order of business let's deal with that, then we can look at specific legal disputes."

"Who in his right mind would want to be the registrar? You'd be taking your life in your hand. I know of two fights over claims in the last week. Someone is going to get killed," another person said, looking at the stubby claimant.

Mr. Tappan answered, "It has to be someone who isn't afraid of a confrontation."

A couple of voices answered at the same time, until J. B. Abbott said, "I nominate Sam Wood. After all, he is a Quaker."

The Border Ruffian, Roland LeCount, stormed out pointing at Sam, "By God, this proceedings is illegal. We've already had a meeting and voted on this. I'm gonna' get the sheriff and put a stop to this business." Several of the pro-slavery men followed.

Sam said, "Gentlemen, it is important for all of us to be of one mind. Those proceedings that he alludes to are illegal. Any legislation or resolutions passed by the men of Missouri must be ignored. Don't bring any proceedings against them in their courts or have any dealings with this so-called sheriff. I've already had one run in with him."

Mr. Wakefield stood for the first time and in a calm, but forceful manner, stated, "Gentlemen, Mr. Wood is an attorney and I believe that he should be the registrar. We need a name for this association to give it legitimacy. We need officers and a declaration of our intentions. I suggest the Actual Settlers Association as our name until modified at a later date."

"Hello Judge," Mr. Tappan said addressing Wakefield.

"Good to see you again, Tap. I didn't know you were coming to Kansas."

Tappan addressed the group, "Folks, Judge Wakefield is a fair and honest man. I knew him well in Illinois and I believe that he should be the President of this association."

"I second that motion," Dr. Robinson echoed and thus the first fair and honest vote was taken in Kansas Territory, August 15, 1854. The men established smaller groups to work on drafting a resolution for a general vote.

The meeting broke up with groups standing around talking, some arguing and some listening. Paschal, Blue and John Thompson came out of the shadows. They had been watching discreetly in the event that things got out of hand. Felix and Sam explained what happened to John as they rode back to Lawrence.

"That big ugly fella came storming out with a couple of his friends," John said. "What was that about?"

Felix explained the situation as best he could. "He might be even more upset if he finds out that it was Sam that punished him in Westport. He still doesn't know who it was."

"Maybe I'll tell him next time I see him," Sam said. "I don't like the looks of that guy. He's going to be trouble sooner than later."

###

"If you want to be fully convinced of the abominations of slavery, go on a southern plantation, and call yourself a Negro trader. Then there will be no concealment, and you will see and hear things that will seem to you impossible among human beings with immortal souls."

Harriet Ann Jacobs, 1813-1897

The new home on Massachusetts Avenue was the first permanent building in the village of Lawrence, as everyone was calling the settlement. The Wood family opened their doors to anyone who needed shelter and there were quite a few takers because the weather was noticeably cooler. Felix was still with them, John and Sally moved to a small house east of town. Bill and Elizabeth built a small house next to their daughter and son-in-law and Elizabeth spent most of her time looking after the children. The Sam and Margaret Wood love affair was never stronger. Such a durable feeling of contentment enabled Sam to spend his time on the affairs of the territory while Margaret took care of the needs of the family, including management of the money.

Felix found a new reservoir of meaning with the newspaper job where he could be more effective in the fight against slavery.

His words were creating havoc among the Border Ruffians who put a bounty on his head. Felix never let that discourage him, nor did he take precautions against the threats. There was no need, he felt sheltered in the shadow of the great Sam Wood, plus he was ever vigilant and never traveled alone, especially along the border with Missouri. Most of the alleged violence in the territory was bluster and drum rattling with a large number of the casualties caused by the disputes over land claims, but the problem was made worse by the slavery issue. Felix took it upon himself to define the matter, filled with excitement by this newfound weapon in the fight against slavery, one that he never expected, despite Sam's early characterization of him as looking like a newspaper man. Felix studied the matter thoroughly trying to separate fact from fiction and understand the underlying causes of the problem. He understood the economic arguments in favor of keeping the slaves, but he felt that the issue was more complex having to do with the essential hatred of the Blacks by the southerners. There was something deeper that he couldn't quite put his finger on, a fear of the Blacks by the Whites, but fear of what?

Felix had a running battle with Lawrence St. James, a French-Canadian preacher who worked on the Shawnee Reservation, which stretched from Ft. Riley to the Missouri river. He polluted the minds, according to Felix, of the Kansa Tribe who lived around Council Grove. Several times, Felix had accosted St. James for his atrocities to slaves and Indians alike, after proof had surfaced of the Preacher pocketing federal monies allocated to the tribes.

Felix accosted him in September at a town meeting in Emporia, where St. James was attempting to browbeat the mayor and alderman to allow him access to the coffers of the local Mission in accordance with his federal mandate to educate the Indians to 'the ways of the Lord'.

"You should be called Lawrence 'Satan' James, as far as I'm concerned, you pompous liar," Felix shouted from the back of the Methodist Church where they were meeting. "You've stolen thousands from these poor people who were made promises by the Government, which you have abrogated unilaterally."

"I don't even know what you're talking about, Brother Frances, I don't understand your words," St. James said in all innocence with his French accent. "I am but a humble servant of the Lord."

Felix was furious and fed up with the lies and treachery of this supposed agent of the Indians who was robbing them blind. He shouted in anger a slur which was quoted in the Emporia Gazette and widely published in the east, causing Felix some notoriety, most of it bad. "Satan James, I don't know God, never met him…., but if he has sonofabitches like you running his outfit, I don't believe I care to." Of course, Sam and John found it funny, but Felix was mortified at the editorials and opinions published in the southern press calling him immoral and worse.

When reporting the news from the meetings he did his best to report the facts as they occurred and not editorialize what he had seen, but it was difficult not to take sides. He was staunchly anti-slavery and he made no excuses for it. He soon found that accurate reporting was enough, he didn't need to editorialize; the edicts and resolutions they put out spoke for themselves, betraying the cruelty and bigotry of the slaveholders. He became a common figure attending both the Free-State meetings and the Blue Lodge meetings, reporting on both to the best of his ability, but never leaving any doubt as to his allegiance. This, of course, rubbed the Border Ruffians the wrong way and led to some close encounters but nothing more serious than intimidation and posturing. Felix didn't feel intimidated. There had been some ugly incidents and several abolitionists had been frightened into leaving but there were other circumstances, besides the bullying.

Many of the wives and some of the men just didn't like the rough living required on the frontier. The cities in the east were full of the modern conveniences of life; life on the prairie meant that each waking hour was dedicated to the basics, shelter and food. These tasks usually fell to the women.

One cold and breezy afternoon, with a bit of freezing rain falling, Sam, John Doy, Judge Wakefield, Felix, and Charlie Robinson sat comfortably at the Wood dinner table discussing plans for a constitutional convention in November. The number of anti-slavery men had grown steadily to the point that they were certain of winning the Free State agenda if the vote was fair and excluded the Missouri faction. A fire made a cheerful backdrop, the women working around the hearth placing coals in the Dutch oven and salting venison destined for the smokehouse in the backyard.

"Sam, I heard from Harold that the slavers are having a meeting in Lecompton tomorrow night. I plan on being there," Felix said.

"Judge Lecompte, is building some kind of meeting house. Supposedly he's got a roof on it and enough siding to hold a hundred people," Robinson added.

"You reckon he'll draw that many?" Sam asked.

"He might, the pro slavers are getting a lot of money from slave owners in the south and Senator Atchison is financing them and urging them on to violence. They're able to pay the Ruffians to attend, plus there'll be legitimate pro-slave voters who live on their claims. The number of pro-slave settlers is growing, just not as fast as we are. I wouldn't be surprised if he didn't have a hundred."

As it turned out, more than 200 men showed up, most of them pro-slavery. A good many of them were not residents in Kansas Territory, yet they made a lot of noise and scared a few of the abolitionists off the meeting. Felix recorded the proceedings and kept his mouth shut in the back of the room. An association was formed, and a declaration of ordinances prepared, which basically said that Kansas Territory was to be a slave state and all abolitionists were to be asked to leave and if they didn't leave, they would be forced out of the territory, with violence if needed. A long list of statutes was prepared, and speeches given espousing the horrors of the influx of abolitionists and other settlers who would not vote for slavery. The men did agree to use Sam Wood as the official Claims Registrar as they felt he was conducting the office in a fair manner regardless of the politics of the claimant.

Then the men began arguing with each other over the right to own slaves. The meeting turned ugly with emotion. Floyd Dunham, who had been at the meeting at Blue Jacket's Trading Post, pointed to Felix in the back of the room, "And Felix Francis, hiding in the back, using his pen like a knife in the side of every honest American who believes that we should be free to do as we please, which includes owning slaves, something guaranteed by the laws of our constitution. Brother Francis don't think you will go unpunished if you lie about what is happening here today, or if you paint us in an ugly way, like you've been doing lately, don't think you'll get away with it. You will be brought to justice, sir."

"I'm not your brother. But don't worry, gentlemen, I plan to report your meeting word for word, and I'll print your declarations word for word. I don't need to embellish it to get the point across. But I will say that you are wrong about the constitution because it is silent on the issue of slavery."

"You lyin' bastard, Roland LeCount screamed. "The laws of this country damn sure do gives us the right to own slaves. By God, you are an ignorant son-of-a-bitch."

"I'm not going to argue with you Roland, but the laws you speak of are state laws, not federal laws. The Constitution is silent on the issue of slavery."

The meeting broke up at dusk, Felix saddled his mule for the three-mile ride back to Lawrence."

###

"We will before six months rolls around have the devil to play in Kansas…We are organizing to meet their organization. We will be compelled to shoot, burn and hang, but the thing will soon be over."

Letter from Pro-Slavery Missouri Senator, David Atchison to US Secretary of War Jefferson Davis, September 24, 1854 describing his orders to wipe out the Kansas abolitionists.

Sam, Dr. Charlie Robinson and J.B. Abbott were chopping wood. Judge Wakefield sat on a stump and watched them work, occasionally expressing his views on whatever was being discussed, which at the moment was where the State Capital should be when they applied for statehood. Judge Wakefield was a short man with an oversized belly from 'sitting too close to the table', as his wife said. He was more inclined to thoughtful repose about the unfolding events than he was actually going out to make it happen. Sam wasn't much different than the judge, except that he did his thinking while active, whether riding throughout the territory or chopping wood.

"One thing I do know is that the State Capital can't be along the border. It needs to be more centrally located, like here in Lawrence," Wakefield said.

Sam stopped stacking wood and pulled his coat a little tighter, "Judge, this isn't exactly centrally located in the territory. We're 500 miles from the western line."

"Well, there won't be that many people living west of here on the high plains," Robinson added.

"What do you think about where they're building that new fort on the river," Abbott asked. "Fort Riley, that looks like a good location to me."

"I met the commanding officer last week, Nathanial Lyon, he's a good man, anti-slavery; although he won't admit being an abolitionist. With the new road to Leavenworth that would be a good location," Sam added.

"I haven't met General Lyon yet," Wakefield claimed.

"You need to get up on your horse and ride over there, John," Sam laughed.

"Why can't he come to me? I'm damned comfortable since we've got our home built."

"I'll bet you are. You've got the prettiest spring in the territory in your back yard." Sam removed his coat from the exertion.

"I'll tell you the best spot," Abbott said, "Council Grove."

"That's not a bad idea, J. B.," Robinson agreed. "It's a lot more central than here and pretty much everyone goes through on their way west."

"I've never been there," Wakefield said. The others shook their heads and finished the stacking.

Sam said, "I like the spot where the Pappan Brothers have their ferry across the Kansas River. Cyrus Holiday is putting a lot of time and effort into laying out a townsite, plus, the Leavenworth Road goes through there, too."

Charlie changed the subject, "What about the college that we talked about last month, Governor Reeder is in favor of it? I'll bet Amos would donate some money if we come up with the land."

"Your land on Mt. Oread would be the best location," Sam answered.

"You could donate that, Charlie," Wakefield said laughing.

The sound of horses, a wagon and shouting caused the men to turn toward the house. It was full dark. They had a lantern glowing by the wood pile. Shouts could be heard from the street and lanterns appeared across the village. "What in the world!"

Wakefield exclaimed, jumping up.

Sam grabbed his coat and started for the house when the back door flew open and David shouted, "Daddy, come quick, Mr. Francis has been hurt…., bad." His voice was choked with emotion and he broke down crying when Sam reached the porch. Harold Barnett, Mr. Branscomb, and a man Sam didn't know were laying Felix on a pallet. He appeared to be breathing erratically and his face was bloodied and battered. Dr. Robinson quickly examined him and ordered the others to move back. His wife, Sara, a nurse, began removing Felix's clothes. Margaret Wood hurried the men away and brought water from the pot boiling on the hearth.

Sam gestured Barnett outside to the front porch asking for details. "Not sure Sam, we found him on the road from Lecompton, his mule was standing over him. We were all at the Blue Lodge meeting. That asshole Dunham called Felix out in front of everyone and Sam Jones threatened him after the meeting, I heard him. Said he would be punished for what he was doing, writing false stories against the pro-slavers."

"Was LeCount there?" Sam asked.

"There were over 200 people there, ninety percent of them pro-slave," Barnett answered.

Sam walked him to his wagon and stood in the road for a while, anger building in his chest. He turned back to the house as Branscomb was leaving, "The Missus is asking for you Sam. Felix is awake now. I think it'll all turn out ok."

"Thanks, Charles, I'll probably see you tomorrow. I'm going to ride over to Franklin to deal with some land claims. I'll stop by and let you know how he's doing. Anything I need to know about the meeting tonight?"

"Nah, it was just the usual bullshit. Any abolitionist that doesn't leave when warned will be forcibly moved; Kansas will be a slave state; because it's a territory and not a state the people from Missouri can vote. All the usual crap they spout when they're together in a group. Believe me, individually they're cowards but get them in a mob and they can be dangerous."

"I know it, but I thought we were going to avoid the serious violence."

"Don't look it Sam. I think we all know who did this. I saw LeCount watching Felix as he was leaving. I stayed a few minutes and talked to some of the others and when I came out, they were both gone."

"What about Jones, you think he might have done it?"

"I just don't know, Sam."

"Did Felix have that bag he carries with his pencils and paper?"

"Didn't see it. It wasn't in his saddlebags either."

As Branscomb rode off Sam sat in the cold, on a front porch chair, and watched the few lamps that were visible so late at night. He sank into a depression as he thought of his friend laying in the next room seriously injured as a result of Sam sending him into the battle, so to speak. Felix's weapon wasn't made of iron, but words, and he wielded them well, doing more good for the abolitionist and Indian cause than all of the settlers put together. Margaret opened the door, "Sam, come in here, Felix wants to tell you something."

Felix head was bandaged and a tight wrap around his chest, his eyes were already swollen and discolored, "It was LeCount, Sam, he took my notes, all of them, not just the meeting tonight," Felix grimaced in pain and his breath was ragged. "I didn't know the other guy, but I heard them say they were going to Blue's place."

Dr. Robinson said, "That's enough Felix. You need to rest. The laudanum I gave you will help you sleep."

"Allright, Doc, but Sam get my papers, please it's my life," he lay back and closed his eyes.

"He's got broken ribs, but the worst is the blow to the back of his head. We'll have to watch him close tonight. I'm afraid he has a concussion, I don't know how bad it is and won't be able to tell until some of the swelling goes down," the doctor said.

Sam gazed down at his friend and winced each time Felix moaned, his face swollen and discolored, asleep from the medication given by Doctor Robinson. He decided that he would leave at that moment to go find LeCount. There were enough people to watch Felix since the Robinsons were guests while their house was under construction. He turned to find Margaret behind him, "Sam, could I speak to you a moment, privately."

Sam walked to the back porch and took a deep breath of the cold night air.

"I don't often interfere, Sam, but I am asking you to wait until tomorrow morning to leave."

Sam looked at her and smiled, "How did you know I was going to leave?"

"How could I not know? You're my hero, Sam, and I love you for it. But, right now, I'm asking you to wait until morning. This man LeCount will know you're coming, and he'll do something to stop you. Wait until morning light, Sam."

He pulled his wife into a bear hug and kissed her gently, "All right Margaret. I'll stay and watch Felix tonight while the rest of you get some sleep. I doubt I can even close my eyes."

"We'll take turns, Dear, I doubt I can close mine either."

The children went to bed, the adults sat around the table offering a few quiet words of encouragement to each other. Sara Robinson said, "This will not sit well with some of the least committed settlers. Many of them are looking for a reason to go on west or return to their homes in the east."

"I'm surprised there haven't been more incidents," Dr. Robinson added.

Each time Felix moaned it was like a knife to their souls.

Finally, Margaret said, "We might as well try to sleep. Sam, you're going to take the first watch?"

"Yes, someone can relieve me when you want to, but don't hurry, I can stay up all night, if need be. It can't be worse than the cholera on the Sam Cloon; I was up three nights straight there."

Sam sat listening to the sounds of the others preparing for bed. When the house was silent, he sat watching Felix until the embers were glowing in the hearth. He fed a log to the fire then struck a lamp and pulled out his papers, pen, and ink. He began drafting language for clarification of the claim process, which he would present for approval to the Settler's Association. At midnight he sensed that Felix's breathing was becoming worse and contemplated calling Robinson but thought better of it.

"Felix, can you hear me?" Sam whispered holding his hand. A slight pressure in Felix's grip assured Sam that he did. "I know you'll get better, my friend, and we'll go and find those responsible, but right now, just rest and get well. Please!" Sam felt the pressure again and let Felix sleep.

He began composing the text for a Constitution that would be presented at the Territorial Convention they were planning for November. At one in the morning, Mrs. Robinson appeared and told Sam to go to bed, she couldn't sleep and would watch Felix. They stood over him, sensing that his breathing seemed to come easier. Sam did as told and fell asleep as soon as he kissed Margaret and placed his head beside hers. Six in the morning, Sam awoke to find Lloyd and the youngest Robinson boy snuggled in bed with him. Margaret was up; Sam quickly dressed and hurried downstairs expecting to find Felix awake.

The three of them were standing over the body, they turned as he came down the stairs. Margaret put her arms around him, "He's gone, Sam."

Sam knelt and confirmed the horrible truth for himself. He tried to control his breathing as he lay his hand on the arm of his dear friend lying lifeless in his living room, a senseless death at the hands of an ignorant bully. He said a silent prayer over Felix's body, stood and reached for his cold weather travel gear. Margaret wordlessly packed a bundle of food. Little was said, the others, including David who stood with tears in his eyes knew what Sam was going to do. Sam started toward the door then stopped and turned back to his oldest son, put his arm around him and whispered in his ear. As Sam rode away, Margaret asked what his daddy had said.

"He said that Felix was one of us and we always take care of our own. What did he mean, Mama?"

"Felix is our good friend, almost like family. Daddy will find who did it and see that justice is done. I think that's what he meant, Davey."

Sam rode cautiously as he approached Blue's place, stopped and surveyed the scene; trees behind the trading post, flat prairie to the road. A hill rose gently to the east. He pulled his heavy coat tight and his hat down even lower on his face. There seemed few places for an ambush, but Sam recollected Margaret's warning from the night before. As he stood contemplating his next move, one of Blue's sons came out of the lodge and beckoned him in.

"They're gone Mr. Sam," he said. "They got tired of waiting for you and rode on to Westport."

Blue was sitting next to the stove; he stirred the embers with a black iron poker and then gently put a piece of wood inside before closing the grate. "Hello, Sam, grab a cup over there on the counter and have some coffee. We've been expecting you. They set up an ambush out along the road in a small drainage. I sent Rolo here," he indicated the boy, "to ride down and wait for you. LeCount got cold about one in the morning and rode on to Westport. I'm glad you didn't come last night."

"My wife wouldn't let me. She had a premonition."

"She is possessed of wisdom, my friend. You are a lucky

man." The men sat and drank coffee while Rolo dozed, head on his arms upon the table.

"LeCount bragged about beating Felix and taking his writing instruments. I told him Felix was a fine man and I didn't want his enemy in my house. That's when he left, pretending to ride away, but we knew he doubled back to lie in waiting. There was another man with him whose name I don't remember. LeCount is a very bad man, Sam. The boy with him is afraid. You could see it in his eyes."

Sam nodded and said, "Blue, I will take care of this matter."

"It will be difficult in Westport; Jones will protect him as he has other murderers."

The door swung open and the wind howled in, blowing snow, followed by John Thompson slapping the snow off his clothes. He went straight to the counter for a cup and poured coffee, "What took you?" Sam asked.

"Well, I didn't hear about Felix dying until eight, I was over workin' on Charlie Robinson's place, getting the windows framed. I heard last night that he was getting better. Branscomb came by on his way home and said Felix had spoken."

"He only asked about his satchel and to tell me who did it."

"LeCount?" John asked.

"That's what he said," Sam turned to Blue, "Did LeCount say anything to you?"

"Nah, he was pissed off when he left here. Mad at me, mad at the man with him because he wanted to light out for Georgia. He told LeCount, 'I don't want Wood after me for something you did'. LeCount'll just go to Westport and hide behind Jones."

Sam and John wrapped scarves around their faces for the trip to Westport. Little was said, they were both absorbed in recollection of traveling with Felix down this same road on their first visit to Kansas, plus it was too cold and windy to say much. The bleak winter prairie contained little in the way of wind break.

The few leafless trees with grey lifeless limbs seemed to be harbingers of the unbearable death of an innocent man. They arrived in Westport about three that afternoon. Sam asked, "You think he might be at the post office, John?"

"We can ride by, but I reckon a saloon's more plausible."

The snow had stopped but the wind continued out of the north, howling between the frame and brick buildings on Main Street. A few men on foot drifted by leaning into the wind or holding their hats against the elements.

Sam said, "Such a senseless death, John. Felix was a harmless man who never threatened anyone physically, in his life. It isn't fair, I go around threatening everyone and I'm still alive and he's….," Sam couldn't continue. He was talking more to comfort himself than to comment on the death. Felix had high ideals and lofty goals, yet all that was wasted. The only thing left was a letter home to his mother and a chiseled-out tomb on the rocky plains of Kansas Territory.

There were several horses and wagons at the Last Chance Bar. John noticed LeCount's horse semi-hidden in the alley along the south side of the building. Felix's valise was tied to the saddle. John retrieved it, tied it to his own horse, and they quickly stepped inside. The noise stopped as soon as the door was closed. LeCount was at the far end of the bar with another man. When LeCount spotted Sam, he stepped away and the other man backed slowly around a table.

"He's dead, Roland, you killed him."

The young man, no more than a boy, really, blurted out, "I had nothing to do with it, Mr. Wood, I tried to stop him."

"Shut up, Wayne," LeCount yelled then tried to bluff the situation. "He attacked me, Wood, I was just defendin' myself."

"Who?" Lester Jackson asked. He was a settler Sam had helped with a claim, "Who died, Sam?"

"Felix Francis," John answered.

Lester whirled on the guilty man, "Jesus Christ, LeCount, what the hell did you do? Felix Francis never raised his hand to nobody."

"He had it comin', everybody said so."

"Come on with me," Sam said. "You're going back to Kansas and stand trial."

"The hell I am. Go get Sheriff Jones," he said to Wayne. But the boy didn't budge.

LeCount pulled a knife and said, "Come on then, Wood, I guess I'll have to rid this country of you too, most around here ain't gonna' shed a tear."

Sam moved quicker than LeCount could think, grabbed the wrist of the hand holding the knife and driving with his powerful legs, pushed the bigger man into the bar. LeCount couldn't free his hand from the steel like grip. He reached over with his left hand to try and claw Sam's hold away. Sam reached up with his free hand and clutched LeCount's shirt, bent a little at the knees, lifted him and smashed his arm back against the bar breaking it. LeCount screamed in agony unable to free himself.

Sam pulled LeCount away from the bar, and pushed him into the room, where he tripped over a chair and fell. The knife plunged into his side, glanced off a rib and pierced his heart. Sam smashed his fists into LeCount's face over and over. LeCount tried to scream, but no sound escaped, only blood and an ungodly gurgling. The shaken men finally found their senses to pull Sam away and watched as the murderer gasped for air clutching at his chest, his eyes wide, blood spurting from the wound and dribbling from his mouth.

"Shall I get Doc?"

"Waste of time," the bartender, Elroy, drawled. "I say good riddance anyway. Ever man here knows it was self-defense. Onliest thing is this worthless dog owes me four-bits." He reached in LeCount's pocket for his money, then handed Sam a wet towel to wipe the blood from his hands and coat. Sam looked at the young man who was cowering in a chair, so frightened that he lost control of his bladder. Sam said in a soft voice as though he were tired, "I hear you're from Georgia, son."

"Yessir," he sobbed, "I tried, Mr. Wood, I tried to make him stop hittin' Felix, I tried real hard, sir."

Sam put his hand on the boy's shoulder, "I suggest you head toward Georgia, as soon as you can get your things together."

Wayne ran from the saloon attempting to hold back his gorge until he reached the cold air. As he flew out the door, Sam Jones came in, looked around and said, "You're under arrest for the murder of Roland LeCount, Wood. Put your hands out here in front of you. You in Missouri now boy. You n' this Nigger gonna' hang for murder."

Elroy said, "I don't think he's dead yet, Jones. You should send for the doctor."

Sam strolled to the bar and got his hat, retrieved his club from the floor and said to John, "Let's go home."

"Did you hear what I said? You're going to jail."

Sam turned and stuck the club in his chest, "You stay away from me you bogus son-of-a-bitch. You come near me or mine and I will unleash God's fury on your body and soul."

Jones stumbled back in surprise, took stock of the other men, obviously against him, and stepped aside.

On the road back to Lawrence, John said, "Never thought I'd see the day of you using a curse word."

"It's the first I've ever uttered," Sam said. He thought for a moment then added, "I don't see any need to mention it, do you?"

"Can't imagine it would do any good."

The snow began falling as they rode silently home.

###

Many are the plans in a person's heart,
but it is the Lord's purpose that prevails.
Proverbs 19:21

October 15, 1854
Lawrence, Kansas Territory

Snow fell for three days and nights. It was a week before the men could get pick and shovel into the ground to dig a hole deep enough to bury the mortal remains of Felix Francis. The body lay, that week, in the smokehouse, wrapped in the same cover that sheltered Jinny and her fellow seekers of freedom some six years earlier. David and Caleb peered in the window, fear in their eyes as if the body would rise up and begin to talk. The boys couldn't believe that this was their friend, who treated them as peers and not children, incapable of thinking for themselves. His death didn't seem real to them. If they hadn't witnessed Felix being wrapped in a sheet, by Margaret and Sally, they could just as well imagine this baggage on the table as a deer carcass or buffalo meat, the common inhabitants of the premises.

Lloyd and Missy came running when they spotted them poking around the smokehouse. "What does he look like?" Lloyd asked. Caleb looked at David, shrugged and opened the door for them to see inside.

"Where is he?" Missy asked.

"Under that cover on the table," Caleb answered.

"Can we see him?" she asked. "What does he look like, Caleb?"

"I don't know, I guess he just looks like he's asleep."

The children continued to stare into the building until Sally called them to eat. Decisions were made, with the break in the weather, the funeral would be the next day. David and Caleb ate and then rode to get Chief Fish and the representatives of his village to come for the service. They arrived in full Indian formality including headdresses and ceremonial pipes.

The preacher chosen to conduct the service was a Baptist Missionary, violently anti-slavery, who had befriended the Woods. His name, Richard Mendenhall. Margaret met him on the reservation where he tended to the sick and infirm and preached without cajoling. He was quick to participate in the meetings, becoming a force in the voice of the abolitionists. He knew Felix well and loved him for his unselfish work fighting the Border Ruffians.

The morning had dawned cold but sunny, by afternoon it was warm enough to venture to the grave site where the odd-looking group gathered to hear Reverend Mendenhall's tribute for a fallen comrade. Indian men and women, in leather and beads, bright colored blankets and ceremonial pipes, which they passed over the grave. A surprising group of Kaw Indians arrived from their villages along the Neosho River near Council Grove, along with Seth Hayes and Aunt Sally and Pete and Guadalupe. Felix was a frequent visitor to Council Grove and had made friends among the Kaw. The black members of the community turned out, twenty men, women and children. The white settlers, led by Sam and Margaret, included the Tappan's, Charlie and Sara Robinson, the Branscomb's, Harold Barnet and his family. It was a sight David Wood remembered forever, the inhabitants of Kansas Territory, Indians, Blacks, and Whites gathered together on a bluff overlooking the Kansas River Valley steamy in the October sun. Here were Quakers, Lutherans, Methodists, Spiritualists, all led by a Baptist preacher in service for an atheist, who loved them all.

Reverend Mendenhall began, "He would not want us to gather in sadness, we are here to celebrate a brave man who touched our lives in his special way, even if only for a heartbeat. Felix Francis was a friend to us all. He was an unpretentious man, but not afraid to stand up for his belief that all men are created equal…., and women," he added with a smile.

"Felix was a spiritual man, but he did not believe in the God of my church. I recall him telling me that men did not need a God to scare them into righteous behavior, and it wasn't working anyway." Some laughed, but Sam and John glanced at each other, remembering the conversation with Felix on their first trip into Kansas. Both men had tears in their eyes.

"He worshiped in his own way, not expecting us to understand, but not questioning our beliefs either. I loved Felix as a brother, having spent many evenings with him, here in Sam and Margaret's home, and on the reservations, around the fire, discussing issues that we face in our adopted land. Felix was a friend to the Indian, carrying their case to the authorities in St. Louis and even to Washington, through his letters and newspaper articles. I'm sure the powers-that-be in the Indian Bureau will sorely miss the daily letters signed, Felix Francis, Kansas Territory. His appointed goal in life was to free the slaves. He grew up in a harsh New England environment with a brutal father, but a loving mother. He educated himself about slavery and made the decision to dedicate his life to freeing his fellow man. He did not live to see that happen, but I vow to carry on that fight as my own from this day forward."

Several shouted, amen, and the Indians began to chant. Mendenhall knew enough to let them have their say. Sam and Margaret embraced, joined by their sons and prayed for themselves and their friend.

###

Oh! how shall I speak of my proud country's shame?
Of the stains on her glory, how give them their name?
How say that her banner in mockery waves—
Her "star-spangled banner"—o'er millions of slaves?
How say that the lawless may torture and chase

A woman whose crime is the hue of her face?
How the depths of forest may echo around
With the shrieks of despair, and the bay of the hound?
Eliza Harris
By Frances Ellen Watkins Harper

In Missouri, a warrant was issued for Sam's arrest, but no one ever came to serve it. The men who had witnessed the event convinced the Governor to let the matter go. Word reached Lawrence of stories being spread throughout Missouri and Kansas Territory of the superhuman strength that Sam displayed in manhandling the much larger man. His legend grew, to the amusement of his family and friends. John Thompson kidded him that they would be writing books and holding plays throughout the land. Sam wasn't amused because he again feared for those who might suffer for his actions. Stephan had gone back to his home in Iowa, Bill and Elizabeth returned to Ohio, but Sarah was living with them in Lawrence.

He did stay home for the month of November, but he wouldn't have gone to Westport anyway, he was preparing for the elections scheduled for the end of the month. He crafted the provisions of the legislative document and included a clause calling for voting rights for all males, Black, White or Indian, of Kansas Territory. This created an outpouring of anger among the Free State men that surprised even Sam and Margaret, who assumed that all anti-slavery proponents felt as they did, that equality meant all men and eventually women. This was a bit naïve on their part as the white citizens wouldn't even allow Blacks to settle in the township, instead forcing them to live east of town near the Wakarusa. John and Sally didn't mind, they were used to it, but Margaret was livid. She had a hand in the Black vote clause and insisted that it be included, even if it were voted out of the final document, which it was. Sam had made his point. He meant freedom to vote for every male residing in Kansas.

His friend and mentor Robert Brumbaugh wrote a letter admonishing his impudence and cautioned him to compromise. "This is one more example of why you aren't taken more seriously by the people who matter. You should be the first governor of Kansas, but you won't be if you don't temper your demands." Sam didn't care. He wanted what was right for all men, not just the Whites. John Brown's boys, Owen and Josh, were staunch supporters of Sam's position and he received a letter after the election from John that pledged his support if matters turned violent.

Margaret, Sally, David and Caleb drove to Westport to get supplies and the mail. This was about three weeks after the funeral. Sally and the boys went to the post office and were accosted by some Missourians who recognized David as Sam's son. One large, newly arrived, self-proclaimed Border Ruffian roughed David up and slapped him, "Tell your old man that I've been waitin' for him and he's a low down, dirty coward that's afraid to come and face me."

Sally pulled the boy away from the lunatic who was looking to make a reputation, like a bully picking a fight with the biggest man in the room. He would have assaulted her except that other citizens stepped up to escort Sally and the boys out of the building. When Sam heard about it, he immediately prepared for the trip to Westport and left even as Margaret begged him not to go. Sally ran to get John and sent him after Sam.

John caught Sam a few miles from Westport. "Who did it?"

"Don't know his name, just know that he's over six feet tall with a clean-shaven face except for a black mustache and he wears a black bowler."

"What you gonna' do?"

"Ask him to move on out of this part of the country. I think

I'll give him a choice, east or west, but he has to take one or the other."

"Well, that's mighty generous," John agreed. "I guess he can't expect any more than that...., but what if he don't want to go?"

"I'll ask him again and tell him that he doesn't have a choice."

They rode along in silence, reaching the outskirts of Westport about 5 p.m. Light was fading, and the temperature dropped as the sun set. They stopped at the Last Chance Bar. Elroy said. "He ain't here Mr. Wood. I knew you'd be looking for him eventually and I don't want my bar broke up again like last time. I suggest you look elsewhere."

"What's his name, Elroy?" Sam asked.

"They call him Moose; I don't know his real name."

In the third saloon, the Wagon Wheel, they found him. It was a relative new business although the premises had been a different bar prior to the new owner taking over. There were ten or eleven men, some playing cards at the tables, a few stood at the bar.

"Hey, asshole, we don't allow Niggers in here. What the fuck is wrong with you?" the bartender shouted at Sam.

"He's with me," Sam answered

"I don't give a shit who he's with, he ain't coming in here. Who the hell are you, anyway?"

"That's Sam Wood, Tim," one of the men at the bar said.

A howl of laughter from a table in the corner caused everyone to look; Moose reared up out of his chair. "Are you shittin' me?" he laughed, "This little bastard is the mighty Sam Wood? And he brought his Nigger to help him. I'm gonna' whore slap both of you like I did that runty boy of yours."

Sam surveyed him calmly before saying, "I want you to get on your horse and leave this country. You can go east or west, I don't care which, but you have to leave now and don't come back."

Moose laughed a big hearty laugh, actually throwing his head back and then leaning over to his knees in amusement. He took his bowler off and placed it on a hook behind the table, then started for Sam, an ugly sneer of hatred on his face.

"I warned you," Sam said. "Have you got a knife or gun? If you do, you need to pull it now."

"I don't need nothing for this job, you murderin' son-of-a-bitch. You killed Roland and now I'm gonna' kill you." When he was five feet away, Sam dropped his club and went into a crouch, charging the taller man, he grabbed him around the knees and drove him back over the table landing on top of him with his knee on his chest. Sam grabbed his hair with his left hand and smashed him four good solid blows to the face before the others could drag him off.

"Tell him to leave or the next time I see him, I'll kill him."

Sam didn't see or hear from the man again and assumed he took the advice.

###

"We hate a deceiver. And a party, like this ragged, miserly, nigger-stealing crew, who skulk behind the name Free State, we hold in meaner contempt than we do the immediate and avowed pupils of Lloyd Garrison. Their Janus-faced, double-dealing conduct must make them abhorred by God as they are despised by honorable men, and their last end will be down, like the dog, bereft of a soul to rise, but secure in earthly preservation, for no "creeping thing" of God's make will work in their accursed carcasses.

It cannot be that such wretches will triumph over all right and justice. We know the spirit of the West too well to admit to it. We will to the rescue, with lead and steel if necessary, for triumph our enemies shall not, unless God forsakes us, and this country is too new to deserve the judgment of Sodom and Gomorrah. Missourians, remember the 30th day of March, A. D. 1855, as Texans once remembered the Alamo." **Article in the Pro-Slavery 'Kansas Herald' (Leavenworth) Newspaper March 28, 1855**

Governor Reeder issued a proclamation that a Territorial election would be held on March 30. Part of his announcement was that the election would be fair and authentic allowing a vote to only those men who are citizens of Kansas, and able to swear to same. Judicial districts were defined with Chief Justice Lecompte in charge of the Leavenworth District. Voting districts were assigned, and census of those districts taken. Lawrence was in District One. Governor Reeder had every intention to conduct an authentic, impartial election consisting only of Kansas residents. What a joke, as everyone soon realized. He had an inkling the powers that be in Washington had already determined Kansas would be a slave state, but he had no idea of the extent they would go to make it happen.

Major J. B. Abbott was appointed election judge in Lawrence and asked Sam to be present at the polls because, in his own words, "Yesterday, Colonel Young informed me that he will bring 1,000 Missouri citizens to vote in Lawrence and I'd better validate their votes, or they will hang me. Sam, I'm a military man and familiar with danger, but this seems unreasonable."

There were several men sitting on the porch at Sam's home, their horses milling about in the dirt street, the sun hazed in the fall sky, and tension thick as they faced the demon they most feared, the ruthlessness of the Border Ruffians. Colonel Young's threats defied the published policies of the government and the avowed intent of Popular Sovereignty, all of which were becoming a sham.

"And how does he justify this outrage?" Judge Wakefield asked.

"He said that if someone had been in the territory for an hour, that qualified him to vote just as those people from the Emigrant Societies who had been here for a day."

Sam remained quiet, thinking of the best way to deal with the issue, and finally said, "I don't suppose the fact they haul themselves back to Missouri after voting and the legitimate voters stay at home here in the territory makes any difference to them? Regardless, we all need to be at the polls tomorrow, cast our vote and make certain that violence is not part of the equation. If there are, in fact, that many illegal voters...."

Charlie Robinson interrupted and said, "I just can't believe there will be 1,000 Border Ruffians motivated to come just to vote."

"Charlie, there will be more, the 1,000 is just in Lawrence. There'll be Missourians in all the precincts, hell, David Atchison is paying most of them," Tap protested.

"Nonetheless, we need as many witnesses as we can get, so we can protest to Governor Reeder after the fact," Sam said.

The next day, Sam rode to Lecompton where the polling would take place. He passed Collyer's Ravine and found the illegal voters gathered in wagons and around campfires waiting for the polls to open. He was hailed by Burt Blanton, the other election judge, a few minutes before 9 a.m. as he approached the Territorial Building, "Sam, those Ruffians just tried to bribe me and when I refused, they threatened to hang me. I'm not going to take a chance on getting killed. There are too many of them."

Sam tried to assure Blanton that he would be safe, the threats were false, but the man, father of eight, was not to be persuaded. He resigned his position and went home.

"Who are you people?" Sam asked a large, rowdy group of men approaching the building at about 10 a.m.

"We're here to vote."

"Voting is open only to residents of this district. I'm the Land

Registrar and I don't recognize any of you."

"By God, we'll vote or we'll burn this place down and kill every one of you abolitionist son's a bitches," a man screamed, his name was Frank Page and he continued, "I'll sign that oath and swear that I'm a resident. Whose gonna' stop me?"

"Every man here will do the same, Mr. Wood," snarled Colonel Sam Young, the leader of the Missouri mob; appointed by David Atchison to coordinate the Missouri voting fraud. "You'd best not try to stop us. We've got just the same right to vote as you do."

"No sir, you do not," Sam countered.

"Sam, I'm resigning right now," Major Abbott said, "We can't fight this many people. We'll have to leave it to Reeder to invalidate this swindle. Otherwise someone is going to get killed."

The false voting results were reported from every voting district with the illegal votes outnumbering legal residents ten to one or worse. The election judges of the Eighteenth District sent the following report to Governor Reeder:

"....On the day of election, the Missourians under Atchison, who were encamped there, came up to the polls in the Eighteenth District and voted, taking the oath that they were residents of the District. The Missourians were all armed with pistols and bowie knives and said there were sixty in their company. But (only) seventeen of the votes cast there were given by citizens of the district."

The newspapers, both Pro-Slavery and Free State, saturated the Union with their version of the events in the territorial elections. President Franklin Pierce made it clear that he accepted the votes as reported and announced that the decision had been made; Kansas would be a Slave State. When Governor Reeder invalidated the results in April, Pierce was incensed, fired the

Governor and stated, publicly, that Andy Reeder should be hung for his actions, causing a scream of outrage in the north and a cry of jubilation in the south.

The Border Ruffians took Pierce at his word and rode into Lecompton looking for ex-governor Reeder, then turned their attention to Lawrence when they found that he had fled Lecompton. Yelling and dogs barking startled David and Lloyd, who were in their yard playing with neighborhood children. Suddenly the street was full of horses stomping and rough looking men demanding to know where Governor Reeder was hiding.

He was concealed, just a few feet from the rampaging mob, in the crawl space of the Wood home, until they could figure a way to get him out of the territory. Sam stormed out of the house with his club and a pistol in hand ready to take on the whole bunch of them. Fortunately for him, Tap, John Thompson, Charlie Robinson and others confronted the men and demanded they leave.

"We ain't leavin' till we find that chicken-shit Reeder," Big Bill shouted.

"He's not here," Tap said, "Ya'll need to leave now before someone gets killed, we've got women and children here."

"Gentlemen, we don't know where the Governor is," Sam negotiated calmly, "But if you'd like to designate one representative, I'll be glad to escort him through every house so you can see for yourselves." Sam continued talking, trying to calm the mob down and he finally succeeded.

"We're going to Hickory Point, then Franklin, but we're leavin' Elroy here to make sure you ain't pullin' a fast one on us."

Most of the men rode out leaving a small group who soon grew dispirited and left, all except for the aforementioned Elroy. He took a whiskey bottle from his saddlebags, leaned against the Hay Tent, and eventually fell asleep.

Reeder was quickly brought out of hiding and disguised as a woodchopper, with a broadax over his shoulder and rucksack full of his clothes and papers on his back. A theatrical wig was placed under his hat and it was agreed that even his own wife wouldn't recognize him and a good thing it was because the Ruffians rode back at that ill-fated time when a group of Lawrence citizens were escorting him to the river and a flat bottom boat ride to Kansas City.

"Where the hell is Elroy?" Bill shouted.

Charlie directed the Ruffians to the Hay Tent and their inebriated friend.

"Where are them fools goin'?" Elroy asked, as he wobbled to his feet.

"To get wood."

"At night, bullshit, let's see who it is." They rode hard to catch up with the men who turned to face the Ruffians praying the disguise would fool them.

Tap confronted them, "You men need to get out of Lawrence or come help us gather wood for the town meeting in the morning. This charging around town, disturbing the peace, needs to stop. Come on, I've got an extra ax."

The Ruffians determined for themselves that Reeder wasn't in the group, turned and rode away.

"Jesus, let me get the hell out of here," Reeder said, as the Ruffians disappeared toward Atchison to continue their search.

They hurried down to the river where the boat was waiting.

"Keep this disguise on until you get to Illinois, and don't come back until they forget who you are," Sam laughed.

Reeder answered, as the boat pulled away, "I won't forget this, gentlemen, and I'm converted to your cause forever; God forbid we leave Kansas to that kind of scum." It was a demeaning end to a man whose sole crime was that he wanted to uphold the Union principal of fair and honest voting. The battle lines in

Kansas were defined and everyone could see that the issue would not be solved peacefully.

###

"It is important and right that all privileges of the law be ours, but it is vastly more important that we be prepared for the exercise of those privileges."

Booker T. Washington, Up From Slavery: An Autobiography

Beautiful weather on the Sabbath, April 15, 1855, found the residents of Lawrence attending an afternoon potluck picnic on Mt. Oreod, not far from the cemetery where Felix Francis was laid to rest some eleven months earlier. The hilltop was covered with spring wildflowers and John was trying to teach Sam the names of the most common, but he was a poor student, at best. The catclaw and ladies thumb were too plain for his taste, the Indian blanket he enjoyed because of its beauty; he remembered the common horse nettle, but only because he liked the name. Sam just didn't have an eye for nature, but he tried his best to please his good friend, in spite of the kidding he got from the children.

"Papa Sam, everyone knows that's sweet clover," Missy told him as they stood around a clump of the sweet smelling, bell shaped flowers.

"What do you mean, 'everyone', young lady?" Sam said with mock seriousness. "Margaret knows all these flowers, John knows them, and now I find out everyone else knows them, so why should I have to learn them?" Sam complained.

"Daddy, you're just being stubborn, you just don't want to learn the names," Lloyd said with the same tone his mother used on him when he balked at a lesson.

"Son, I don't want to use up brain space on things everyone else knows," he laughed and changed the subject as they walked back toward the food. Lloyd and Missy sprinted after a group of their friends who had found a milk snake, both wanting to hold it.

"How come we don't see the slaves anymore, John? Your home was always full. Have they stopped passing through here?"

"We're moving more of them than ever, Sam," he said. "Paschal helps hide some of them and I have a secret spot where I keep most of them until I can get them into Nebraska."

"What secret spot?"

"It wouldn't be a secret for very long if I told you," John laughed. Sam took offense at the implication, but those who know him would have to agree with the assessment.

Children dashed about, as children do, some trying to get kites in the air although the wind wasn't cooperating, unusual on the crest of a hill in Kansas, wind was a constant companion to picnics in most cases, but not today. Some children and adults played tag. A game of quoits engaged several of the couples who had set spikes in the ground not far from the tables.

All was calm and serene as the townsfolk settled down to eat their fried chicken, ham, potato salad, fresh vegetables, and, of course, the pies and cakes. David and Caleb finally gave up on getting the kite airborne and filled plates with meat until Sally made them take at least one vegetable, which they did, only to feed it to the birds when their mothers weren't looking. A serene, beautiful vista lay before those who cared to look, the river winding peacefully across the valley, the village scattered below the south and east and the majestic prairie stretching as far as they could see to the west.

Sam sat by Sally, his plate full, and asked her, "How's the book coming, Sal?"

"Pretty good, I'm working on a chapter that should interest you, It's about Anthony Burns."

"Oh yes, the Boston slave that inspired Amos Lawrence to

become an abolitionist. I don't know all the details, but I'll be anxious to read about it when you get finished."

Sally asked tentatively, "Is Mr. Lawrence still paying you to prepare the legal work for the City Charter?" Sam nodded yes. "Can I put that into my book?"

"I don't know why not, it's no secret," he agreed, as Margaret came and stood behind him with her arms around his shoulders. She leaned over to kiss him and even upside-down Sam felt that he was looking at the prettiest woman he had ever known.

Many changes had occurred in Lawrence during the past year and the small community was thriving in its own way, sprouting out of virgin ground, not on the foundation of economic growth, but the idealism of the quest to end slavery. Kansas was in turmoil and the outcome far from certain, in fact, betting men in Washington were putting their money on the slavery side. People on both sides of the issue scoured every scrap of information, which flowed from the newspapers, letters and rumors coming from the frontier. Only a few dedicated citizens stood between the slaveholders and a Free State of Kansas. Those few families lived between the Wakarusa and Kansas Rivers in Topeka and Lawrence; communities gouged from the Kansas soil like the lightning ignited wildfires that dot the high plains in spring. Lawrence grew, forged in the flames of the conflict that gripped the territory and the settlers who made the long trek west.

The Border Ruffians called Lawrence, 'Yankee Town' and hated the inhabitants with an ungodly viciousness. Had Sam and the rest of the good folks of Lawrence known what violence lay in their future, they would not have rested so easy that Sabbath day in the Year of Our Lord, 1855.

An Excerpt from

"SAM WOOD, THE WAKARUSA WAR"

"The louder she screamed, the harder he whipped; and where the blood ran fastest, there he whipped longest. He would whip her to make her scream and whip her to make her hush; and not until overcome by fatigue, would he cease to swing the blood-clotted cowskin. I remember the first time I ever witnessed this horrible exhibition. I was quite a child, but I well remember it. I never shall forget it whilst I remember anything. It was the first of a long series of outrages, of which I was doomed to be a witness and a participant. It struck me with awful force. It was the blood-stained gate, the entrance to the hell of slavery, through which I was about to pass." **Frederick Douglass**

Lawrence, Kansas Territory
May 1855

The steamboat, George Washington, passed the jetties at Lexington, Missouri on a beautiful spring day filled with the fresh scent of new blossoms. Elvira Brooks was enjoying the pleasant weather from a vantage point on the hurricane deck when she spotted her Lawrence neighbor, Sam Wood, below, on the boiler deck. She hurried down to say good morning. The pretty blue sky seemed, to Mrs. Brooks, reverent evidence of God's gift of nature with spring wildflowers bursting into color along the banks of the Missouri River as they glided toward the Kansas frontier. She assumed that Sam was enjoying the same thoughts.

"Beautiful sky today, ain't it, Mr. Wood?" she said.

Sam looked at her, confused for a moment because, truth be told, he had no idea of the condition of the day or the progress of the boat, he was thinking about the abolitionist meetings he'd attended in Rochester, New York; the Republican planning convention he chaired in Pittsburgh; and the meeting he had with President Franklin Pierce, the week before; the circumstances of the day were of no concern to him.

"Sorry, Mrs. Brooks, I hadn't noticed, but now that you mention it, it is a beautiful day and aren't those lovely Indian paintbrush flowers," he said absently, picking the only name of a flower he could vaguely remember.

Mrs. Brooks searched the near shore but failed to see the indicated blooms, yet didn't think much of it because she knew Sam and Margaret Wood very well; Sam was focused on the issue of ending slavery and had no interest in the condition of nature except to cover himself in the cold, even forgetting to do that, at times. He wore a broad brimmed hat and yellow shirt with dark suspenders. His boots were new, but un-shined, a common condition in Sam's life, when he was away from Margaret, his lovely bride.

"Is Mrs. Wood meeting you in Westport?" she asked.

"No, John Thompson will, but since we're a day late, I'm not certain. I wish Margaret were coming, I miss her terribly."

"I know you do, Sam, you two lovebirds are the cutest couple I've ever known. You're welcome to ride to Lawrence with me and Mr. Brooks. Our wagon and team are at Littlejohn's stables."

"Thank you, Elvira, but I'm going to Bill Speer's house to pick up a few things we need at the Tribune office. You and Paul go on and I'll see you in Lawrence."

"I read in the paper about your meeting with President Pierce, Sam. I guess it didn't go as well as you'd hoped," she added.

"No, Elvira, it didn't. I'm afraid that Pierce has already decided that Kansas will be a slave state. We have our work cut out for us," he lamented.

They were joined by Mr. Brooks and his younger brother, Jay, who was going to spend the summer in Lawrence waiting the first term of college at the Ohio University.

"Hello Jay...., Paul," Sam said. "Jay, how long will you be with us in Lawrence?"

"I don't need to be in Athens until October, Mr. Wood. Paul tells me you knew Manasseh Cutler."

Sam had a good laugh, much to the young man's surprise, and said, "How old do you think I am, Jay? I knew Ephraim Cutler, Manasseh's son. Ephraim passed away just a couple of years ago. Now, my dad, David, knew Manasseh quite well."

"Oh, I didn't mean to insult, I sure don't want you mad at me, I've heard all about that club you use when you get angry," Jay said, with a tone of awe in his voice.

"Don't go believing everything you hear because most of it just isn't true. I only resort to violence when I need to defend myself. I'd much rather sweet talk my way out of a tight spot than hit someone with my club," he said raising the indicated weapon to show the young man what he meant. "But I will use any means necessary to end slavery in America. I hope you're with us in that regard, Jay," he said glancing at Paul and Elvira.

"I am, Mr. Wood, I'm gonna' study the law and go into politics, maybe I'll be president someday and I'll end slavery by Executive Proclamation."

"That'll start a Civil War for sure, Brother," Paul said as they all had a good laugh over the easy solution that could never happen.

The steam whistle wailed, signifying their arrival at Westport Landing. Each return trip from the East, and there had been many lately, seemed to Sam that the wharfs had doubled in size with stevedores, longshoremen, and teamsters all shouting orders, scurrying about creating a sense of mayhem. Somehow everything got unloaded and sorted out.

He grabbed his luggage and cane, then carefully examined the docks for any suspicious characters that might be a threat. Sam had enemies everywhere, he had to be careful wherever he traveled. He said goodbye to the Brooks family, promising to get together in Lawrence so Jay could meet Margaret, Sam's sister, Sarah, and his sons, David and Lloyd.

Someone was yelling his name.

"Sam...., Sam Wood, where you headed?" John McCoy shouted.

"Are you going back to Westport, John?" Sam asked, "Can I catch a ride with you?"

"Come on, my buckboards across the street, I was just getting ready to leave."

McCoy, an early settler in Westport, owned a mercantile and the Westport Landing docks. He didn't look the part of a successful businessman, short with grey hair combed over his bald head, wearing ragged old clothes more suited to working on the docks than owning them. He was pro-slavery, yet affable and not militant about his beliefs, which wouldn't be good for his business. McCoy liked Sam because there was nothing 'false' in his personality, Sam wore his feelings on his sleeve and everyone knew where they stood with him, just the kind of man John McCoy admired, regardless of his politics, and Sam felt the same about him.

Sam walked with him to the horse and wagon in front of the Riverside Hotel, a shabby plank board building with a crudely painted sign announcing rooms by the night or week. Sam leaned over to grasp his bag and load it in the trunk.

John Thompson appeared suddenly and shouted, "Sam, get down."

Sam dove under the wagon and rolled to the other side as a shot rang out. Dust kicked up from the street where the bullet smacked into the satchel that Sam had been carrying. Thompson shouted, "upstairs window," and pointed at the third story of the hotel. Sam glanced up, staring into the barrel of a Sharps rifle pointed at him. He sprang to his feet and, along with John, sprinted for the entrance to the hotel.

"I'll go upstairs," John said, pulling a pistol. "Go around to the outside stairs."

Sam nodded, glanced up to check the window and ran toward the alley on the left side of the hotel. The Westport Landing agent's office was located in the adjacent building. Several people were standing in the street and along the jetties watching the drama. A shot fired in the middle of the morning was unusual, even in the rough and tumble town on the frontier border.

John reached the third floor, searching for the door to the room where the shot was fired. The back door to the outside stairs was open and two men dashing down, four steps at a time as John watched them. "Sam," he yelled, "Watch out, their coming down," he followed down the steps.

Sam rounded the corner of the hotel as the men reached the ground. The first swung his rifle like a club. Sam ducked, but took a glancing blow on his shoulder that sent him sprawling; he tried to trip the second man, who stumbled over the club Sam swung at his feet. The man turned and fired a wild pistol shot that splintered the corner of the hotel. Sam leapt up and gave chase running into bystanders who were trying to get out of the way.

"Stop those men," he shouted as they sprinted across the street to the docks and toward a bateau that was just pulling away, poled by three tough looking Border Ruffians who appeared to be waiting for the assassins. Sam and John charged after them, joined by Paul and Jay Brooks and a few other people who had witnessed the attempted murder.

Leaping into the boat as it swung away from the docks, the men reloaded and appeared to be searching the crowd, spotted

Sam, aimed and fired. Sam dove behind a cotton bale well before the shots rang out. "Get down," Sam yelled, "is anyone hit?"

"You stay down, Sam, they're shooting at you," Paul Brooks shouted.

McCoy came running up with a rifle. Sam took it from him and said, "Best let me do that, John, I don't want you getting in any trouble over my problems." Sam aimed the Sharps Rifle at the boatmen who quickly ducked below the stern walls. Sam lowered the rifle without firing as the boat picked up speed in the current, two men at the oars, and disappeared around the bend drifting toward Independence.

"Did anyone recognize them?" McCoy shouted.

Jay said, "It looked to me like they were waiting to ambush you, Mr. Wood."

"Yes, it did," John Thompson replied, "Welcome home, Sam," he said, shaking his head.

"Not the parade I was expecting," Sam laughed.

If you would like to be notified when "Sam Wood, The Wakarusa War" is released, please let me know at HenryEPeavler.com.

About the Author

Henry Peavler is an Author, Real Estate Developer, Professional Fund Raiser and an avid golfer. He was born in Springfield, Missouri and raised on the plains of eastern Colorado. In 1973 Henry moved to Austin, Texas, where he raised his five children. He now divides his time between family in Austin, Texas, Denver, Colorado and his residence in Mazatlan, Mexico. His first book, 'What is a Hero' chronicles his early childhood and adult battle with Lymphoma.

Henry has a BA (69) and an MA (74) from the University of Colorado at Boulder and is an avid student of history, with a special interest in the Victorian era of literature and social values.

www.ingramcontent.com/pod-product-compliance
Lightning Source LLC
Chambersburg PA
CBHW071542110726
47908CB00007B/1971

* 9 7 8 1 7 3 4 4 5 9 3 1 9 *